THE SPOON

THE SPOON

THE STORY OF TWO FAMILIES' SURVIVAL
OF THE HUNGARIAN REVOLUTION

LISA VOELKER

The Spoon:
The Story of Two Families' Survival of the Hungarian Revolution
by Lisa Voelker

This book is a work of historical fiction. To maintain the anonymity of some of the characters involved, I have changed some details. Any references to historical events, real people, or real places are used fictitiously. Other names, characters, places, and events are products of the author's imagination. Any resemblance to actual events, places, persons, living or dead, is entirely coincidental.

tintype56@gmail.com
lisavoelker.com

International Standard Book Number: 979-8986572710

Edited by Heidi Jensen

Cover/Interior design by Kent Jensen | knail.com

Author photo by Tom Owczarzak

I am nameless, for in the world
there is darkness and there is light.

Dedicated to two extraordinary people
who smiled and said "Hello"

CONTENTS

CAST OF CHARACTERS

Budapest—Hungary's capital city comprised of the ancient cities of Buda, Obuda, Pest

The Varga Family —

Katalin Varga	Great Grandmother
Béla Varga	Grandfather
Dorina Varga	Grandmother
György Varga	Father
Irén Varga	Mother
Laura Varga	Daughter
Antál Varga	Son
Maxim	György's prized Kisber stallion

The András Family —

Henri András	Laura Varga's husband
Rebeka András	Daughter
Dávid András	Son
Péter András	Son
Jani András	Son
Bella András	Daughter
Kriska	Kisber filly
Sándor	Kuvasz dog
Janga	Vizsla dog
Tomba and János	Nonius geldings

The Türea Family —

Jeno Türea	Father
Erzsébet Türea	Mother
Péter Türea	Son, student at Szeged University
Júlia Türea	Daughter, student at Budapest Technical University
Erik Hilbert	Cousin

Gizella Kovács	Maternal grandmother
József Kovács	Maternal grandfather, silversmith
Júlia Türea's Friends —	
Liliana (Lilly) Fárkas	Works at Budapest Technical University
Éva Dunay	Works at Budapest Technical University
The Fürth Family —	
Dr. Klári Fürth	Mother
Dr. Béla Fürth	Father
Mira Fürth	Daughter
Alida Damiani	Maternal aunt, opera singer
Gábor Berci	Maternal grandfather, sign painter
Ili Berci	Maternal grandmother
The Novák Family, the Fürth neighbors —	
Bence Novák	Father
Hanna Novák	Mother
Ervin Novák	Son, twin
Adrián Novák	Son, twin
The Fülöp Family —	
Elek Fülöp	Father
Zsófia Fülöp	Mother
Ágnes Fülöp	Daughter
Lukács Fülöp	Uncle
Adél Gróf	Maternal grandmother
Janka Dutka	Maternal great grandmother
The Bójtos Family of Dohány Street —	
Lászlo Bójtos	Father, friend of Péter Türea
Klára Bójtos	Mother
Barnát Bójtos	Son
Izsák Bójtos	Son

The Vadas Family of Dohány Street —	
Ilona Vadas	Mother, neighbor to the Bójtos family
Illés Kender	Ilona's father
Erzébet Kender	Ilona's mother
Tomi Vadas	Son, twin
Petra Vadas	Son, twin
The Gergő Family —	
László Gergő	Father
Etel Gergő	Mother
Penny Gergő	Daughter, Mira Fürth's friend
Karola Miska	Maternal aunt
Jakab Miska	Maternal grandfather
Tünde Gergő	Paternal grandmother

Residents of Megyer, Hungarian Countryside —

The Vizi Family —	
István Vizi	Father, Henri's childhood friend
Enikő Vizi	Mother
Henri Vizi	Son
Laura Vizi	Daughter
The Demeter Family —	
Bartal and Zita Demeter	Elderly couple
The Joost Family —	
Abel Joost	Neighboring farm
The Martal Family —	
Páli Martal	Neighboring farm

The Marton Family —	
Dávid Marton	Neighboring farm
Dominik Marton	Eldest son
The Topa Family —	
Fernec Topa	Mayor of Megyer

The Families of Castle Hill, Pest side of the Danube —

The Fárkas Family —	
Alexandra Fárkas	Mother
Charles Fárkas	Son
The Schott Family —	
Anna Schott	Mother
Bálint Schott	Father
Anikó Schott	Daughter, friend of Ágnes Fülöp
Sebestyén Schott	Son

1

GRANDFATHER

THE DOORBELL RANG, accompanied by the children's enthusiastic knocking upon the festive, wreath-adorned front door. The echoing sounds of merriment from friends and family waiting upon the doorstep were answered by the sweet laughter of children and the hearty, answering calls of the adults already arrived. Of course, the ringing of the bell and knocking upon the door was only a formality, for the door was not locked. Instead, opened by the newcomers, their greetings, laughter, joy, and warm embraces were met and matched. Christmas Eve had come, at last.

Our family looked forward to this day of gathering, reveling in each others' company as we introduced the most recent additions to our family, especially the grandchildren and great-grandchildren. All that mattered was our being together once more. How other families gather, or perhaps instead send a card, flowers, or gifts in their place, I cannot speak to. For our family, we are but a few generations here in America. We have known loss, we have known fear and chaos. We have had to make a new life in a country our grandfather chose, and having lost so much, we have learned the value of our lives in the simple existence of each other. And so we are compelled to gather.

Our grandparent's home is comfortable, airy, and light surrounded by a winters' garden of nodding, moldering flower heads. Mirrored puddles, lacy brown ferns, and falls' abundant leaves are strewn liberally across the landscape. Gathered in windblown piles against the house, in every corner, and across the welcome mat at the front door, they will soon be tracked in decorating the entry. Welcome. We are all welcome.

The house itself is a gabled, two story older building of wood and stone. A large, inviting kitchen with a raised stone fireplace is the heart of our home. Small but numerous bedrooms upstairs, and a single utilitarian bathroom on both floors, amply provide for our family. We are comfortable with each other. An oversized fieldstone fireplace in the great room flanked by large, unadorned, wood-framed paned windows is our gathering place in the evenings. A small Jotul wood stove shares the hearth and is kept stoked by the adults keeping everyone warm and comfortable. There is a back door to the garden and the surrounding forest, a mixed woods of birch and evergreen.

The Christmas tree stood unadorned in the corner nearest the entry and away from the fireplace. That night, Christmas Eve, was the beginning of the magic. The children were nestled in a pile of pillows and blankets strewn across the floor in the one room reserved for all young children. The warm fragrances of Christmas, cinnamon and spices, gingerbread and cider, cakes and cookies baking in the ovens, wood smoke and cedar, drifted upstairs tantalizing the imaginations of the children.

My father read *The Night Before Christmas* to the children while several of the parents looked on from the doorway. Meanwhile, Aunt Julia had spirited away to the back door where she slipped into her winter coat. Carefully and quietly, she lifted a length of sleigh bells from its hiding place within the closet. Cautiously, she opened the door and walked out into the brisk, starry night.

Sleigh bells are mischievous and difficult to manage if your purpose is to keep them silent. A dozen brass bells upon a narrow length of tooled leather tilt and twist at their point of attachment with the slightest of movements. The smallest degree of tilt is answered with their distinctive, happy jingle. Julia kept the bells close, pressed tightly against her under her heavy coat.

Not far from the house, Julia paused and carefully extracted the sleigh bells. Then returning to our home with exaggerated, punctuated steps, Julia let loose the bells to their jingling merriment. The sound of the bells lifted to the night sky, their song catching in the rafters and echoing there.

The children were listening raptly to the story when the imagery of Santa's reindeer prancing and pawing on the roof intermingled with the first, faint sounds of their sleigh bells. Slow realization widened already wide eyes. Each small face was mirrored in each other. Uplifted eyebrows, wide eyes, flushed cheeks, and brilliant smiles gave silent acknowledgment that yes, St. Nicholas had arrived. Shrill screams followed as the children dove under the blankets urging, pleading with father to hurry, leave, and turn off the light. St. Nicholas might pass by their home if they were not asleep. They would awake to find coal in their shoes, the certain fate for naughty children.

Downstairs, while my mother played piano, several of the younger aunts and uncles kept time on a guitar and a variety of percussion instruments mostly conjured from the kitchen and producing mostly recognizable Christmas carols. The older family members happily decorated the tree. Bright, colorful glass balls, tinsel, fairy lights, and small chocolates known in Hungary as szaloncukor, were carefully placed within view and reach of all the children.

But I am getting ahead of myself, for there is a moment that is the reason for this story. Before the decorating of the Christmas tree, before the reading of *The Night Before Christmas*, there was Christmas dinner. Grandfather would ring a little silver bell calling us to dinner. We gathered together, sitting at the long table side by each, the smallest among our company sharing chairs.

Before us, the table was laid with a bounty of traditional Hungarian and German foods, and those we'd come to savor in our new homeland, lovingly prepared by our family. The table, festooned with green boughs and red ribbon, was heavily laden. There were dishes of salmon and fish soup, sourdough bread, cabbage rolls, rice, mashed potatoes, and plates of steaming vegetables. The desserts sparkled on the buffet behind us, the sugary confections catching the lights of the candles. A Christmas Cake, pumpkin and apple pies sprinkled with coarse sugar, a poppy seed pastry roll dusted in powdered sugar and decorated with plump candied cherries, gingerbread, almond paste stollen, and cinnamon stars each lent their spicy fragrances to our joyous gathering.

Each place at the table was set with an embroidered red napkin bound with a carved, wooden napkin ring my Grandfather had made. This was laid across a brilliant white plate flanked with the silver place settings of our family from time before. Before. Before the war, before the soldiers came, before the house was burnt to embers, before the escape.

At the head of the table our Grandfather had stood, as he always had, until everyone else was seated. This was a known expectation and helped to get everyone seated amid the festive chaos. Soon after Grandfather took his place he again stood, voices quieted, and all eyes were upon him. Grandfather's eyes were blue, as blue as a crisp new morning washed with winter's white sunlight. Now they were clouded. Grandfather was remembering.

Grandfather slowly rested his fingertips upon the table to connect to the moment and steady himself. We waited quietly, respectfully, expectantly. In measured movement, one hand went to the single, bright silver teaspoon that rested on its own delicate, lacy napkin on the table above his plate. A teaspoon whose bright and mirror-like finish was unlike the others having known little wear. Wrinkled with time and experience, Grandfather's long, elegant fingers delicately raised the small spoon so that all might see. In the welling tears of remembrance and gratefulness of those gathered around the table, the light of Christmas was reflected. In that moment we all remembered the story that is our family's heritage.

2

REBEKA

IT WAS SPRINGTIME in the small Hungarian village of Megyer. The temperature was warming, and although the horses were still shaggy with their winter coats, Rebeka couldn't resist the urge to go for a ride. Her mother, Laura, had sent her into the small country village earlier in the afternoon to fetch her younger brothers and little sister from school with the promise that Rebeka could have time to herself when she returned.

Time to herself was a rarity with four siblings. Rebeka's brothers, Dávid, Péter, and Jani, although younger than she, were all quickly outgrowing her and had insatiable appetites that she, as the eldest, worked sometimes seemingly constantly to satisfy. The youngest of the András brood, little Bella, was not yet nine years old and adored her older sister, following her everywhere when not in school.

Rebeka loved her brothers but had a special relationship with Bella. When their father, Henri András, had been taken during the madness of the 1950 arrests and sent away to Kistarcsa, a prison camp for political dissidents fifteen miles northeast of Budapest, Bella had been only two. That was six years ago.

With their father gone, the farm chores fell primarily to her mother, grandfather, and brothers. Rebeka and her grandmother were given the responsibility of the house and little Bella. Rebeka loved her little sister, and little Bella adored her. Even so, Rebeka looked forward to those times when she could be alone in the stables. There, with the sweet fragrance of fresh hay and the soft light filtering through the small, open windows, the horses, pungent from the work of the day, were always glad to see the girl. Rebeka would gently work the wind knots from their manes and tails with her deft and careful fingers before combing them out. Then softly stroking their nose and face, Rebeka would massage their necks working down to their chest, withers, and legs. The horses would sometimes reach around and nuzzle her arm with a soft nicker. Watching them, it was impossible to tell who enjoyed themselves most, the horses or the girl.

The stables had been no place for a small and delicate child, but Bella had grown. Soon perhaps, Rebeka would bring her sister and teach her to groom and care for the horses. The horses were beautiful, Rebeka was deeply attached to them, but her brothers, especially Dávid, were always reprimanding her. The horses were for work, not to be fawned over. However, as much as he fussed, Rebeka knew Dávid didn't mean a word of it. Although every bit of food they were able to grow or purchase was dear, she'd seen Dávid more than once slipping a wedge of apple from his pocket to be gently worked from his fingers by each of the matched pair of black Nonius geldings, Tomba and János.

Rebeka's father had purchased the Hungarian horses as colts and broke them to the carriage himself. Although the carriage had been taken by the police long ago, Tomba and János were just as happy helping in the fields. This was, after all, better for them.

Better for them to be dirty and lathered after a hard day's labor. The AVO (military police) couldn't distinguish a good horse from bad that a little dirt and sweat couldn't hide. Of course, living in the country village of Megyer, almost 110 miles from Budapest, was also a help. Such a small village of only twenty or so homes was of little interest to the police, there just wasn't much left to take to make the travel or effort worthwhile.

The geldings shared the stable with Sándor, the András family's fiercely loyal dog. The Hungarian Kuvasz breed are known for their size, yet Sándor was not especially so; perhaps he'd been the runt, perhaps because of his tragic beginnings in this life, or perhaps both. Laura had found him shot and abandoned in a ditch along the road. Laura and her mother, Irén, had returned from yet another long and heartbreaking journey to Kistarcsa. The small puppy was barely alive, its thick white fur wet and matted with fouled dirt and blood.

Laura and her mother had been traveling since just before sunup. Both women were tired and lost in thoughts of Henri, having yet again been unable to visit him or even pass a letter. The basket of peasant food had been taken by the guard. Laura and Irén had no doubts as to what would become of it.

Although the women didn't know it, Kistarcsa held 2,800 men crowded into a small space allowing each of the men only 23 inches on the floor on which to sleep. Conditions in the prison, terrible before, were now horrific. Even from outside of the walls, the darkness of the prison was pervasive, bleak, and overwhelming.

In silence, the women returned to Megyer. Laura and Irén rode a small, dilapidated bus to the intersection just past Kossuth Road and began their long walk home. It was then, as they passed over the little stone bridge spanning the Marcal River, that Laura noticed an odd shape in the ditch. At second glance, Laura thought she discerned an almost imperceptible movement; a twitch perhaps, a shiver or spasm. Whatever it was, that one small movement saved the puppy's life. Laura knelt low to the ground at the side of the ditch, reached out and, touching the soggy, filthy mass, it whimpered. Lifting the puppy caused it a searing spasm of pain, but the puppy only gasped, his mouth open, his eyes rolling.

"Poor thing, he's so cold." Laura said, as she wrapped him in her apron.

"He looks like a Kuvasz. There must be something wrong with him that they've shot him, Laura. Shouldn't we leave him?"

"He will have a good home with us Anya, and, more importantly, we will not be returning home to only disappointment. The children will have the same news, there is no change with their father. But with this puppy they will have a distraction and a protector."

"Sándor."

Laura looked up at her mother, who answered the questioning look in her daughter's eyes, "It's an old name, defender of men."

Sándor survived the journey home to the András farm. Laura's father, György, had cleaned the bullet wound after Laura and Irén had painstakingly cleaned the thick and matted fur. The two women were careful with their ministrations. Sándor had again bravely and soundlessly gasped, working his jaws as he endured the pain. Cleaning the bullet wound proved too much for the little dog; his screams sent the children running to the barn, cowering in fright and fear for the little life they had so quickly become attached to. In the following months, under the close scrutiny and loving care of five children, Sándor had recovered and thrived. At two years, the dog weighed 95 pounds, and, fiercely loyal, Laura depended upon him as much as she did her parents.

Soon after Henri András had been taken to Kistarcsa, Laura had known she would do as her husband had asked in those horrid, rushed last moments they'd all had together. There had been no warning. Seven year old Péter had answered the knock upon the door one dark November morning and there they were. The secret police, the AVO, were standing at their door. Not a word from them as they walked in, looking about. It was Péter's protestations that brought Henri rushing into the room, only to be seized, his hands tied behind his back. Henri's hurried instructions to Laura intermingled with cries of protest, fear, and controlled anger as his family were all torn away, again, and again and again, in their futile attempts to hold on to their beloved father. With every attempt, Henri extolled them to stand back, to be quiet, to not interfere, to keep safe, to watch over each other, to remember he loved them and would one day return.

It was Henri's desire that Laura should bring her mother and father, her Anya and Apa, to live with them. "You'll need each other. The boys will need their Nagypapi to grow into fine men. You will all need the love and care of Dedi," Henri had shouted from the cart, leaning against the wooden side panel, as the officers hurried their cargo away.

Two days after Henri was taken, Laura sent for her parents, Irén and György Varga. Laura and the children had spent those two days readying the house for their arrival. Laura would share Rebeka's room, Irén and György would have the big bedroom downstairs. By the following afternoon, the horses and wagon were heard on the cobbled road leading to the András farm.

It was a slow procession, the wagon followed by a pair of Hungarian Gray cows. Laura had been working in the field when she saw her parents. Lifting the hem of her heavy skirts, Laura hurried across the field but not before the children, whose normally restrained habits and manners were forgotten as they rushed to bury their sorrow and tears in the embrace of their beloved grandparents, their Nagypapi and Dedi. When it was done, when the tears and sobbing, condolences and hugs had given way to sighs and silence, Laura and Bella walked Irén and György into the house while the brothers carried in the valises, traveling chests, and the few household items they'd brought with them. It was Rebeka who led their horse and carriage to the barn to unhitch the pretty, dark bay mare and lead her to the stable.

In the stable, Rebeka unhitched the harness, removed the bridle, then rubbed the mare down with a handful of hay. Her grandmother had named the filly Kriska. "*Kriska*," Rebeka thought to herself, "*What a perfect name for this beautiful horse with a little star just under her forelock*." As Rebeka rubbed down Kriska, she inspected every scratch, every bump, and especially the long scar on the right hindquarter. This was the last of the Kisbers her grandfather's family had raised. When the war had ended and the Soviets had taken the cattle and the horses, there were only a few left. Some horses were left for farm work to supply the state-mandated weekly quotas, some had been hidden only to be taken later. It had been a terrible time for the family, but they always felt themselves fortunate it had been the Soviets, and not the Germans, who besieged their farm.

3

THE KISBERS

THE VARGA FARM had been in the family for generations and had long been well-known throughout Hungary for their fine horses. The family home had been built near the little village of Nemesbük, in the north of Zala County, at the edge of the Transdanubian uplands, foothills to the Alps. A beech forest fringed the valley floor, bordered by a narrow country road which, crossing a little stone bridge, led to the Varga farm. It was an ideal location. Farming the rich soil was productive and provided for the family, but the Vargas, as it turned out, had a way with horses.

Farming had given way to horse breeding, the barn became a stable, and another, larger, hay barn was built. Lake Balaton, to the southeast, with its thermal baths and beautiful waters for swimming and sailing, was a day's journey by carriage. Keszthely Bay to the east was even closer to their village. Many Hungarians and tourists, especially from nearby Budapest and Vienna, visited the area. Soon the Varga horses were well known throughout the country.

Grandfather György had been riding Kisbers since he was a toddler, training them since he was a boy. As his father before him, and his grandfather before that, he'd always had an instinctive understanding of horses. The touch of his hand on a nervous, twitching flank and a few soft spoken words would quiet an unsettled horse. György loved everything about horses, including mucking out the stalls. The combined fragrances of hay, horse, and earth were deeply appealing to him. Above all, György enjoyed grooming the horses. Combing out their manes and tails, currying and brushing, watching as he worked the coat with the soft, short bristled brush slowly bring out a gleaming luster, gave Gyögry inordinate pleasure. Even picking the hooves, for it was especially then that the horse would bend its neck gently nuzzling his face and ears with velvety lips.

During April of 1918, at seventeen years of age, György was conscripted into the cavalry serving as an officer with the Hussars. Near the end of the war, he earned the Hungarian Medal of Bravery for his service in conducting reconnaissance during the Piave Offensive on the eastern front. Six months later, György returned home a hero and dedicated himself to the Kisbers.

For his twenty-second birthday, György's parents gave him a colt, Maxim, son of Hulcot, who grew into an exceptionally large Kisber stallion at 16.4 hands. Although the farm was fenced and cross fenced to separate the stallion from the other horses, Maxim was a gentle horse and put out to pasture with the broodmares. The Varga studbooks noted the many foals Maxim sired, all dark bays with good conformation, gentle natures, and a pleasure to ride.

György and Irén Varga had been married at the farm and lived there with his parents, Béla and Dorina Varga. There György and Irén had raised their two children, Laura and her brother, Antál. Both children, like their father, were introduced to the horses before they could walk. Whoever went to the stables, parents or grandparents, would bring the children with them. Working in a stall, one child was set astride a horse while the other, who had been set into a small hay wagon in the alley of the barn to wait their turn, watched. Holding on to a handful of mane while the adult groomed the horse, the child would lay their other hand on the horse feeling the heat and heaving of the horse. The children loved it and could hardly stand the anticipation waiting for their turn.

A few months after the children had been acclimated to the horses during grooming, they were riding. Set in the saddle in front of an adult, they held onto the horn with both hands, a protective arm around their waist. At first these rides were very brief but lengthened as the children grew taller and stronger. Laura, older and intuitive, instinctively knew to grip with her little legs. The adults knew whose turn it was to give the children a ride, but that didn't stop good natured attempts to claim a turn out of turn. No one tired of the children's exuberance and pure delight with the horses. The children thrilled at the chance to ride, Antál trilling and babbling, laughing and chortling, forgetting to hold onto the horn, waving his little arms in excitement. Laura beamed and laughed with pure joy.

At the age of four, Laura was given her own small saddle. By the age of seven she could saddle and bridle her small mare by herself while standing on the feed box. Laura and Antál grew up working with the horses in the barn and in the fields, helping to raise and care for them, and riding, of course, every chance they had.

The years passed. The family mourned the loss of Dorina and Béla, who died within days of each other. Laura, grown into a young woman, had met and married Henri András. The young couple lived on the farm with the family: György, Irén, brother Antál and, eventually, their own children. Rebeka, the eldest, had been born on 10 February 1940, a little over a year before Hungary became embroiled in WWII. Two years later her brothers Dávid, Péter and Jani followed in an almost annual progression.

The war had changed everything but not before taking the life of Laura's brother, Antál. Antál had been so handsome in his uniform when he left his family and the farm to join the Army, only to be returned a few days later. The creases in Antál's jacket were still crisp, the single bullet hole the only blemish. He'd been fatally shot disembarking from the troop transit.

The following years at the Varga farm had been lean and fraught with difficulties to provide for the family and the horses. No one visited the region, schools were closed, the war raged on. The family had managed to sustain themselves while also raising hay and feed for their horses. Their bountiful vegetable garden provided enough for their family to share with their neighbors. Although the nearby forests had once been fine hunting, the war and its aftermath had a devastating effect. As the effects of war plunged many into poverty and need, the creatures had all but disappeared. Still, there was fishing and an occasional rabbit that augmented the family's diet.

Throughout the war, the Varga family had managed to escape notice of the German soldiers and the ruthless Hungarian army the Germans had created. The following wave of the Red Army, and worsening conditions across Hungary, were threatening their security and safety. It was the Kisbers that saved the family.

Grandfather György had been thirteen when Archduke Franz Ferdinand of Austria and his wife were killed sparking the onset of World War I. He had seen the worst that war had to offer during his service as an officer in the Hungarian Hussars. As a grown man he had safely cared for his family and farm through the first harrowing years of World War II. György understood the horrors of war and the art of gracious acquiescence.

The terrorizing stories of the German soldiers rampaging across Hungary were fresh in memory. News of the invading Red Army had arrived long before the soldiers, but the soldiers had arrived much sooner than expected. People had been fleeing the eastern provinces heading west in front of the oncoming Soviets. Only a week before, Henri and György had wisely asked the women to prepare food for a quickly devised root cellar in the woods. Irén and Laura had left plenty in the storerooms hoping that what the family removed to storage would not be apparent. No one wanted to provide a cause for inquiry or raise tempers. The men took a circuitous route from the house through the woods, a route that would not be easily noticed nor easily traced. The family had just stocked the cellar two days prior to the arrival of Lt. Brusilov and his small detachment of soldiers.

When the Soviet soldiers had first arrived at the farm György had showed Brusilov the stables and the finest of the horses, György's prized stallion, Maxim. The soldiers knew nothing about the horses so György had given them a brief introduction of the Kisber, highlighting every prominent aspect of the breed. György noted the Kisber history bred as a military horse, then as a racing thoroughbred and then, as a riding horse. György asked Brusilov to walk with him to the tack room where he showed Brusilov the beautiful, meticulously cared for hand stitched riding bridles, reins, hand tooled breast and show collars, saddles and saddle bags. As Laura and Irén arrived with lunch, György "noticed" that the officer and he wore a similar size boot and pulled from the tack chest his pair of riding boots recently made to match Maxim's tack.

Of course, as they were both aware, lieutenant Brusilov knew the pretense being played out, as did György. It was a matter of respect playing this game. The life and well-being of every person on the farm, including the three small children, were his to decide the fate of. Technically, the Varga family were class enemies of the state. There was no reason to care one way or another, but the horses were very nice and Brusilov imagined how fine he would look astride Maxim. Who knows, he thought, after the war was over maybe he would put Maxim out to stud and have his own racehorses. Feeling magnanimous, the lieutenant nodded to György and asked him to get Maxim and the other horses ready for him and his men. The horses that didn't have tack they would line out behind privates Oblonsky and Petrova.

Irén and Laura had returned to the kitchen, quietly closing every door and window. The women admonished Rebeka, Dávid, and Péter to absolute quiet in an attempt to be unseen and unknown, forgotten by the soldiers in the courtyard. Both women struggled to radiate a sense of calm and normalcy for the children, not daring to glance at each other for fear their faces would betray the terror they felt quaking within. Each woman knew, upon a single word from their commander, the soldiers would loot and pillage the farm, burning it to the ground, terrorize the women, shoot the men, and God-knows-what would happen to the children.

Laura was the first to hear the sound of their horses being herded together into the front paddock. The mares and geldings were alternately whinnying to find each other then snorting in alarm. Above their calls was Maxim's high-pitched snorting and whinnying in response. Suddenly, the sound of hooves clattering over the cobblestones was heard by everyone gathered in the kitchen. As the horses approached the house, the clattering quickly became a thunderous cacophony, then passed and faded to the east. Simultaneously and without warning the door burst open, crashing against the wall. Laura and Irén dropped to the floor, grabbing at the screaming children to protect them, but it was Henri, only Henri, followed by György. Both men threw their arms around their family as they repeatedly assured them the soldiers had gone.

As everyone calmed, György told the family of Henri outfitting the horses, of the soldiers leaving, and then of the miracle. The last horse, Kriska, a little spring filly just a year old, had been recovering from a nasty wound to her hind leg. The officer, Brusilov, was about to shoot her when Henri asked if perhaps Brusilov and his men might also need provisions from the storerooms. They could be easily packaged and carried on the horses. Without waiting for an answer, Henri had dashed into the storerooms and brought out wheelbarrow after wheelbarrow of food. Brusilov ordered a few of his men to pack up the food while Henri, in a bold move, quietly led the filly to a nearby stall and tied her to the back wall out of sight. The soldiers had gathered in the courtyard mounted on the horses, which were proving difficult for men with too little riding experience and too much braggadocio to handle.

The stores were plenty, the horses were awkwardly packed. Brusilov seemed appeased nodding to Henri and György. As Brusilov feigned control of Maxim, the stallion fidgeted and snorted in the uncertain hands of an uncertain rider. Feeling self-important and believing himself to look quite magnificent, Brusilov was eager to be on his way. Reining Maxim toward the road, Brusilov made the mistake of many novice riders as he sharply thrust the heels of his boots into Maxim's sensitive ribs. His heels up and out for a second thrust he never had time for, Brusilov barely kept his seat as Maxim leapt forward at a gallop. The soldiers attempted to keep up without losing their seats, their hands tangled in the mane, reins, and holding onto the saddle horn. This explained the chaotic clatter of hooves that Irén, Laura, and the children had heard from the kitchen. Smiles and laughter eased the tension and calmed everyone.

Following the departure of the Red Army, the family had fearfully waited for three days before leaving the house, leaving behind almost everything they knew and owned. They knew they must. Throughout the war years they had survived because of their location and the horses. Prized by those with money, power, or both, György had carefully matched horse to rider. The satisfied customers secured a sort of neutral operational status for the family. Now it was time to go, as György had known as soon as he had seen

Brusilov and his men on the road leading to their farm. It had taken almost no time at all to devise the obvious and only plan to divert the soldier's attention.

The home and farm was a time capsule of memories and hard work for generations of the Varga family and their horses that had lived there. The house held a history of the family in the paintings, furniture, shelves of cherished books, rugs, photographs, letters, clothing, bedding, towels, and kitchenware. They left everything except the jewelry that had belonged to Györgi's mother and grandmother, Dorina and Katalin Varga.

Katalin's cherished Austro-Hungarian paneled bracelet and matching earrings, set with amethysts, small rubies, and half pearls, had been given to her for her 40th wedding anniversary. Her Holbeinesque style ruby and enameled pendant, a jeweled lorgnette, and two pair of high karat gold earrings, one set with green demantoid garnets and the other, set with small pearls, had been her aunt's. Györgi's father, Béla, had given Dorina an emerald ring when they became engaged. Although the younger women admired and prized their family keepsakes, both Irén and Laura had preferred a horse, new saddle, or tack to jewelry.

Standing by the fireplace, György had asked Laura to bring the diary he knew she kept. Laura understood what her father left unsaid. She returned with three volumes, a record of passage to womanhood, marriage, the passing of loved ones, and the lives of her children. Laura thoughtlessly fed the fire her father had morosely lit for this purpose before he had left the room. It had to be done. During the German trials individuals had been made to answer for what they'd written.

Now it was time to leave behind all that was known and familiar, all that had physically defined who they were, what they did, and those who had come before. The family had only just closed the door when Rebeka ran back into the house, her mother calling after her, reminding her to only take what could fit in her knapsack. Rebeka went directly to the living room where, amongst the photographs and awards of their horses, was the vitrine with grandfather's medal, his "hero medal" as she and her brother called it. Opening the cabinet, she delicately lifted the medal from its hook and pinned it inside her innermost layer of clothing then ran outside to her family.

Each family member had gathered only what they could easily carry. Irén and Laura had secretly and hastily tucked the jewelry deep into their skirt pockets where, easily accessible, they'd be able to quickly rid themselves of if threatened. The men, in addition to the provisions for their journey, had each taken only a small hunting knife and a single fillet knife leaving behind all of their tools. The Kisbers, with the exception of the filly, were gone. No one spoke of it, the loss was bearable only in their collective refusal to acknowledge it.

4

MEGYER

HENRI HAD FRIENDS in Megyer, a small peasant village far enough away for them to be lost to those who might look for them but close enough to walk with children. Leaving their home, no one looked back as they went to the forest to gather the stores from the root cellar. Under the cover of darkness in the quiet of night, they first walked in small groups close together eventually lining out one behind the other with György trailing.

Henri, leading Kriska, led the way. Occasionally, he would give Rebeka brief turns at leading the filly by a halter fashioned from a rope looped behind the ears and again over the nose. Laura and Irén alternately carried two year old Péter on their backs or, when he slept, in a sling fashioned from a shawl. When Rebeka tired she was set astride Kriska ahead of the improvised saddle bags and her eldest brother, Dávid, who was almost three. The nights had been chilly but the walking warmed them.

It was spring, nature was awakening. The scream, without warning, stopped everyone. Transfixed where they stood, uncertain, their hearts racing while they stood, waiting. After several moments came a long series of hoots. György chuckled softly recognizing the calls of a short-eared owl. Continuing on their journey, it seemed as if the owl soundlessly accompanied the family on their trek adding an almost comical element to the night. As soon as the family had once again settled into the silence and cadence of their journey the unnerving scream would startle them.

Several nights, as they walked through long stretches of the mixed Hungarian oak, beech, and pine forest, the ghostly hooting of a tawny owl punctuated the passing hours. The only respite while walking was to drink and collect water from any source they came upon. As dawn approached, György and Henri would scout for a safe area to sleep, eat, rest, and provide feed for the filly. Fortunately, it was spring and the temperatures were beginning to warm. It was eight days and nights before they arrived in Megyer. Most fortunate for them it hadn't rained, as it was now doing at an alarming rate, drenching them as they stood on the stone doorstep awaiting an answer to their gentle rapping.

The Varga family had arrived late at night. At first Henri thought perhaps his friends, István and Enikő Vizi, were frightened to answer their door. It soon became apparent that no one was home. There was no smoke rising from the purlin roof imperviously thatched with layers of buckwheat and rye straw, or even the scent of the fire that would certainly have been burning on a night such as this. Henri also knew that his friends raised Hungarian Pulis, the long corded-coated dogs bred as a herding dog. Yet there wasn't any barking emanating from either the house or any of the outbuildings in response to their knocking. Quietly circling around the house, courtyard, and barnyard of the small farm Henri confirmed there was no one at home, including any of the farm animals or the Pulis.

Returning to his family, it was decided they would sleep in the barn where the hayloft was fragrant with clean hay for bedding and feed for the filly. The family waited as Henri returned to the courtyard. From the well that stood at its center, Henri pulled a bucket of water. Then, when everyone had slipped into the barn, Rebeka remained behind to close and latch the door. Running around to the side of the barn she climbed in through a window with the help of her Nagypapi, Györgi. Anyone looking at the farmyard would see the barn door closed and not suspect anything was amiss. The family had the added security that, if the latch was opened, the sound of it would provide warning to all within.

In the darkness, Györgi and Henri put the filly in a stall filling the wooden manger with fresh hay. Both men inspected the filly's wound running their hands over her coat feeling for heat or proud flesh. The filly's wound was healing well, the gentle walking and long hours resting in the spring sunshine had kept the muscles of her back, and wounded hind leg, supple.

They were wet, but not soaking wet. Their coats and layers of clothes had provided some assurance of warmth and dryness. The men gave Irén and Laura their wet outer clothes. Along with the pile of their own clothes and those of the children, the women cautiously felt about in the darkness. The damp clothes were laid out on beams and rails to dry as much as they could on this wet night. Henri and Györgi positioned themselves close to the barn door while the women made a nest in the straw for the children. The children were delighted, curling up together in a tangle with their mother and grandmother on either side. The women softly whispered and sang them to sleep. Henri and Györgi alternately kept watch while the other slept.

In the morning, Henri lifted Rebeka to the window. Rebeka was excited and proud of the responsibility assigned to her. She quickly circled around to the front of the barn where she threw back the latch of the barn door. The rain had ceased. The house, although plastered and whitewashed as every other building, looked forlorn in the grey and overcast morning. The heavy clouds blowing in from the north would not be so for long. The house was empty, no one was home. Two magpies noisily perched in the sweet cherry trees at the edge of the courtyard. A small flock of hooded crows were comically meandering down the road. A gentle quiet, like a soft blanket of freshly fallen snow, seemed to shroud the little village. No one appeared to be home in Megyer.

The family ate a cold breakfast of smoked cheese and kolbász. Laura and her mother checked their food stores; sparingly they had enough to last a few more days. While the family waited in the barn, Henri went in search of any of the residents of Megyer that he might find at home.

Henri knew many of István's neighbors. Megyer was, after all, a small out of the way village with few visitors and even fewer who arrived astride a beautiful Kisber. As boys, István Vizi and Henri had been in school together. Their family farms, and the nearby Vizi mill on the Zala River in the southern region of Zala County, were close enough that the boys would help each other at harvest. When time and their fathers allowed, the boys would ride together into the countryside.

After he had married, István had moved to the small village of Megyer. Although they'd lived in Megyer only a few years, István and Enikő were well-liked in the small community. Their neighbors had no hesitancy in meeting and welcoming visitors to the Vizi farm. Henri had visited István and Enikő on those occasions when he passed through the area delivering a horse to its new home. Henri's first visit to István had been memorable. Henri had not expected all of Megyer to welcome him, but they had. All of Megyer had wanted to meet the stranger and see his fine horse.

Now, as he walked the quiet streets of Megyer, Henri found most of the houses empty. It puzzled him. The village did not bear the hallmarks of one long abandoned. The pretty white houses, courtyards, and barnyards were tidy. There were no piles of leaves or debris collected in doorways, windswept into corners, or any other telltale signs. The rock walls were neat and well-kept. Other than a small flock of scavenging wood pigeons, the church steps and courtyard were clean.

Finally, Henri found an old couple at home. Vigilant behind the lace curtains of their small framed window, the elderly couple had watched Henri approaching and recognized him. Relieved to see a familiar face, Bartal Demeter opened the door before Henri knocked. The two men embraced with a kiss on either cheek, as was the custom. The men stepped apart, laughing as each looked the other over from head to foot.

"You are much the same since I last saw you!" Henri announced as he again reached out to affectionately squeeze Bartal's shoulder with one hand while the other took Bartal's hand in his own. Bartal was easily recognizable. A tall, sinewy man with a rich brown complexion he had a shock of lively white hair in sharp contrast to the jaunty, loden green beret he was never without. A white shirt rolled to the elbows, dark jacket, slacks, and tall black boots were worn at home, in the field, or to church. The two men again laughed together before Bartal turned to his wife.

"Here is Zita! Zita, András Henri has come to visit us," Bartal said, smiling broadly, as he turned back to Henri, "Come in, come in!"

Henri learned from Bartal that word of the Soviets passing through Zala had reached the residents of Megyer. The villagers had scattered deeper into the countryside with most of their livestock and children to await the passing of the Red Army. Bartal told of István's concern when he learned that the soldiers were clumsily riding fine Kisbers. Everyone in Megyer assumed that the horses were certainly from the Varga farm. Everyone in the region had been worried for Varga György and his family but now, praise God, here they were.

Knowing his family would be watching for his return, Henri thanked the Demeters and promised to return soon. Henri hurried to the barn, but not before the morning's heavy clouds made good on their promise. Henri was thoroughly drenched by the time he made it to the barn. Laura helped him out of his wet shirt while Irén selected dry clothes for Henri to change into.

Henri recited everything he had learned from the Demeters. The family decided to wait, living in the barn, for the return of the villagers. With access to the Vizi well and fire pit they would be comfortable and dry until István and Enikő returned. The Demeters had given Henri vegetables from their root cellar, fresh bread, cheese curd, and some little pastries, pogácsa, for the children. It was more than enough with the remaining potatoes and other food stores the family had brought with them. Everyone welcomed the opportunity to rest although soon there were the day's chores to pass the time. Clothes needed to be cleaned, Kriska washed and exercised, and meals prepared. Without exception, watchful eyes and ears were alert for any approaching sound.

In the early afternoon of the third day since their arrival, Henri heard the sounds of an approaching cart. István and Enikő were returning to their farm, although it would not be to stay. István had jumped from the wagon as Henri ran to meet it. The old childhood friends were surprised, elated, and relieved to see one another. Joyful tears were welcomed as they embraced, slapping each other on the back, reluctant to pull away. The children were introduced and the adults, having previously met at Henri and Laura's wedding, were reacquainted with each other.

Amidst this happy chaos, Enikő invited everyone inside their home. The men started fires in the kitchen's cookstove and the fireplace in the main room. Enikő, Irén, and Laura happily talked together as they worked preparing a meal of vegetable soup, bread, pickled vegetables, stuffed peppers, and a small dessert of dried fruits in syrup. The children had disappeared to the barn to see the dogs István and Enikő had returned with. István had stepped out the kitchen side door to an outbuilding returning drenched, but smiling, with a small bottle of pálinka, a Hungarian fruit brandy. The house had quickly warmed. For the first time in what seemed a very long time, everyone enjoyed relief in the moment's respite, the welcoming warmth of home, the hearty meal, and the company of each other.

At last, the kettle set over the fire boiled. The table cleared, each in turn told their stories over steaming cups of root tea. When István and Enikő had evacuated the village they had fled to his parent's home. There they had left their livestock and dogs with the exception of the two puppies. The Vizi mill had been severely damaged by the German troops, as had the other mills along the Zala River. The mill's sluice gates and bridges had been dismantled and destroyed. Resources and materials for repairs were severely limited but they could make do. There was still much work to be done to restore the mill to operating function before the upcoming harvest season.

István and Enikő would be leaving, returning to the Vizi farm and mill to help István's parents, while awaiting the birth of their child. This news brought cries of delight and laughter but a curious and quiet response from Laura. Henri, of course, noticed his wife's quiet and the suggestion of a smile teasing the corners of her mouth. Henri's interested gaze in turn caught Irén's attention. Soon all eyes were on Laura. With a worried smile and laugh, Laura announced she too would be having a baby sometime in the late fall. Everyone rejoiced. The bottle of pálinka was finished.

Péter had fallen asleep in Laura's arms. Dávid was curled up against his father whose protective arm held him there. Laura helped Enikő arrange a bed of quilts on the floor near the hearth for the children. Dávid and Péter were tucked in, their sleep undisturbed.

Rebeka wearily slipped under the quilts, gratefully closing her eyes. Soon all the children were fast asleep.

Returning to the table, Laura and Enikő joined in the conversation. After a brief discussion it was decided that György and Irén would stay and take over the small, one bedroom home and farm. István would help find them a few chickens and a pair each of geese and ducks before leaving. The barn had three stalls. István knew of a neighbor that might be willing to sell a cow or two. As for Henri and his family, István knew of a little farm at the north end of town.

Located on a short side road set back into a clearing in the pinewoods, the farm had recently been abandoned by an elderly couple, Gábor Sabados and his wife. The couple had lived there for more than half a century but had recently left for Balaton to live with their son and his family. They could no longer work the farm. Gábor and his wife had grown both reticent and afraid to be alone in the countryside in this small village with all the challenges that came with war. István assured Henri that no one would question their moving in; they would speak with the village mayor in the morning.

The Sabado's farmhouse was two stories with three bedrooms. A tight squeeze for seven, comfortable for five. It made sense to have György and Irén in the Vizi home. The Sabado's farm had a central courtyard and a good well. A large, wooden, watering trough hewn from a linden tree stood nearby next to a rafter roof barn with room for a carriage and wagon. A nearby stable with six stalls would provide more than enough room for perhaps a cow or two and working horses, along with an ample hay loft above. The vegetable garden had once been very productive and the fields were in good enough condition to be plowed and planted. It was decided, the next day they would all go to the farm after first speaking with the mayor, Ferenc Topa.

Laura and Irén helped Enikő retrieve coverlets from her trunks. Enikő insisted on György and Irén having the bed for the night. Everyone else made their beds on the thick, colorful rag rugs on the floor of the main room. The fire was banked. The still somewhat weary travelers were soon asleep in warmth and comfort.

5

RESETTLEMENT

GYÖRGY AWOKE BEFORE the rest of the household. Sometime during the night the rain had stopped. As he looked out through a small-paned window, mirrored puddles glistened everywhere capturing images of blue tinted skies and rising cumulus clouds. Stepping out into the courtyard, György deeply inhaled the rich, earthy scent of the spring morning. The muted colors of dawn were giving way to crisp, golden rays arcing across the brightening sky. The birds were just beginning to awaken and call. The morning gave every promise of a brilliant spring day.

As György looked across the field, a barn owl silently emerged from the woods. In a glide, barely discernible corrections kept the owl on course. Without a single beat of his wings, the owl crossed the expanse of the recently plowed fields. György regarded the owl as it flew past, gliding through the open door of the barn's hayloft. "*A ghost bird*," György thought as he grunted, eyebrows raised, "*no mice*."

Around the courtyard, tracing across the sky, and flitting between the farm buildings, György noticed a variety of small birds.

Yellow kinglets, robins, and collared flycatchers were busily at work turning the leaf mold and bits of earth hunting caterpillars, spiders, worms, and beetles. György walked the farm inspecting the outbuildings, troughs, stones, trees, and pipes then crouched, pushing his fingers into the soil. Turning a handful of the moist earth to his nose, an exploratory sniff was followed by a satisfied, deep inhalation of the richly fragrant soil. This was good. Given time, they could make a life here.

Still set back on his heels, György's attention was taken by the sudden cacophony of a murmuration of rosy starlings over the far end of the field. Across the courtyard he hadn't heard the door to the house open behind him until the children noisily joined the adults already gathered there. Everyone's attention was fixed on the spectacle of the murmuration's undulating patterns waning and expanding across the backdrop of the brilliant morning sky.

Following breakfast, Henri and György accompanied István to the mayor's home. They found Ferenc in his barn, a small flock of chickens noisily about his feet. Ferenc was selecting his seed potatoes for a second planting from a wooden bin he'd brought up from the root cellar. The chickens, intently hunting the ground for elusive remnants of recently scattered feed, loudly protested the stranger's arrival as they scattered, wings aflutter.

After introductions, Ferenc listened to what the men had contrived. Ferenc assured the men that the arrangements were acceptable and asked them to return later in the day. There were documents to be prepared. Ferenc would have them ready to sign, giving them ownership of the properties. Despite István's congratulations, György was concerned. He turned to Henri shrugging one shoulder as he half grimaced, beetled his eyebrows, and raised one hand in a motion suggesting everyone pause.

"How is this possible?"

"Please, let me explain," Ferenc said as he looked from one to the other of the men. When Gábor Sabados had left for Balaton he had hoped that someday someone would make the house and farm a home again. He and his wife had had all they needed from the farm. They had raised their family, they had grown old. Gábor suspected the Soviets would perhaps turn farms they didn't pillage into cooperatives. This was a difficult time in Hungary, very difficult in the rural communities. Gábor had left the decision of who should have the farm, and the necessary papers, to Ferenc.

"So," Ferenc concluded, "my friends, now you understand? As far as Gábor and his wife were concerned, anyone who was acceptable to the people of Megyer was welcome to the farm with their blessing."

For a moment the men stared at each other, then back at Ferenc, before erupting in laughter and congratulations. Henri and György were filled with hope and the peace of mind in knowing they could, at least for now, provide for their family.

Enikő, Irén, and Laura had gone ahead to the Sabados farm with the children estimating that they would meet the men at the farmhouse at about the same time. The children dawdled, as they must occasionally be allowed to do. As they walked, Enikő carried Péter on her hip. Enikő had wordlessly begged Péter away from Irén. The soon-to-be mother longed to feel the weight of her own baby in her arms. The women walked slowly giving the older children time to meander and explore their new home.

Wood pigeons were in the fields, awkwardly navigating the plowed rows, scavenging new shoots and seeds. Two silvery Hungarian Gray cattle, their long, slender white horns curving up almost three feet before terminating at black points, caught Dávid's attention. He called to Rebeka and Péter to join him at the fence where they stood and stared awhile before continuing on.

Along the narrow, tree-lined road, a flock of blue tits settled into the budding trees. Busily inspecting the branches while hanging upside down, the little birds searched for insects and spiders. Stone fence posts with wooden slats neatly marked the edge of a pasture along one side of the road. On the other, neat little homes of white stucco and stone, lace curtains framing the small windows, intermittently punctuated the landscape.

Bartal and his wife, Zita, were sitting outside in front of their home enjoying the warmth of the morning sun. Along the limbs and branches of the black locust and ash trees that were only just starting to leaf in their side yard, tree sparrows were hunting. Their musical twittering rising and falling as they repeatedly congregated and dispersed, the birds moved from one yard to another. Bartal, once a shepherd, was playing a flute. The village knew him as a willing teacher for anyone who wanted to learn to play the instrument. As the family approached, Enikő greeted the elderly couple introducing Irén, Laura, and the children amidst handshakes and kisses.

The Demeters were unhappy to learn that István and Enikő would be leaving, the young couple was well-liked in the village. Enikő laughingly interrupted their protestations announcing that the Demeters would have more new friends than they were losing.

"The Varga family will be staying! Seven will replace two and soon there will be eight," Enikő said as she first clasped the hand of Zita then Laura. Bartal and Zita were both surprised, alternately laughing then congratulating and hugging Irén and Laura. Zita turned to Enikő, embracing her, Zita's lacy shawl draping their shoulders.

"Enikő. You and István will be sure to visit your old friends, won't you?"

Laura thanked the Demeters for their generosity and help. Everyone had especially enjoyed their delicious cheese curd túró and fresh bread. The children broadly smiled their enthusiastic thanks for the pogácsa pastries. Zita was just as delighted with the children. Excusing herself, Zita walked the few steps to her home and soon returned with a small, colorfully decorated plate of small, sugared, plum jam dumplings. The children squealed with delight. Rebeka looked to her mother, who nodded her approval. The children gleefully accepted the treat. Soon the powdered sugar dusted their lips, cheeks, and tips of their noses. The children's smiles and gratitude were infectious, soon everyone was smiling and laughing. In the days and weeks that followed, Zita always had pastries ready for the children as they walked home from school. Irén and Zita were soon dear friends.

The men, as it happened, having finished their business with the mayor, were certain that they were trailing far behind the women and children. Cutting across the fields and through the beech forest they approached the Sabados farmhouse. Along the way István had pointed out the neighboring farms and family names: Bartal, Joost, and Marton. The Páli Bartal family had a small flock of haired sheep and raised yellow chickens and ducks. Abel Joost and Dávid Marton both farmed vegetables and kept small flocks of chickens and grey Landes geese.

At the edge of the Sabados property György pointed out a great spotted woodpecker. The distinctive black and white bird with patches of red was feeding on a very large, old, splintering beech trunk pockmarked with years of hammering. Approaching the farmhouse, the men were surprised to see their family only just turning into the lane that led to the farm. Seeing their father and grandfather, the older children ran to them full of excitement and stories of pastries and long-horned cows. Henri put Dávid on his shoulders as György waited, arms outstretched, for toddling Péter. Together the family walked to the farmhouse.

The house had been shuttered. While Irén busied herself in the kitchen, István and György attended to the shutters. Henri followed after and, with Laura's help, moved about the rooms opening windows. The bright morning light and rain-freshened spring air only added to the serenity and charm of every room. The low ceilings were open beamed of carved pine, the white plastered walls frequently punctuated with small, many-paned windows.

At the start the boys had squirmed to be set down. Rebeka and Dávid held Péter's hands as the little group explored the home as only children can see it from their advantage. The fieldstone and tiled fireplace was a great curiosity. The fireplace cavity was so large the children marveled they could stand upright in it. Even more curious was the discovery of little alcoves in the back wall for warming food. There were cupboards and cubbyholes, a small room adjacent to the kitchen with a washstand and small enameled tub. The children climbed the stairs fingering the carved railing and banisters. Upstairs they found three bedrooms, the two end rooms each with their own gable looking out across the field.

Returning downstairs, Dávid found a narrow door that lead to a cellar. The children rummaged around the tidy cellar finding crocks of various sizes, a linden spinning wheel, one or two empty traveling chests, and odd bits of glassware.

As the family worked they found the unexpected throughout the house: trunks and furniture. Laura turned and questioningly stared at István who gave his assurance everything in the home was theirs to use as they please. The great loss the Varga family had suffered could not be measured, it had hardly been thought of for so great was the loss. This was a salve, a blessing, and they openly rejoiced.

István and Enikő left the Varga family in the company of Henri. The little group would pack István and Enikő's belongings in their wagon. István was anxious to commence their journey by the next morning having promised his father when to expect them. István did not want to worry his parents, especially at this time when there were so many very good reasons to worry. While the people of Megyer were fortunate not to have been visited by the Red Army, the same could not be said for other areas of Zala County, most notably the mills along the Zala River and around Lake Balaton. The Soviets had not been as destructive, yet, as had their predecessors, the Germans. However, the general feeling was uncertainty and anxiety as to what lay ahead for their farming community and for Hungary.

György stayed with the family, grandfather in name but yet as fit and strong as ever at 43. The women set themselves to the household chores. Irén busied herself in the kitchen organizing. Taking stock of the supplies, dishes, and kitchenware Irén thoughtfully divided the goods among the two households. Laura was seeing to the bedrooms, rifling through the trunks and the linen cupboard in the hallway. As she took inventory she also selected towels, sheets, blankets, beautifully embroidered coverlets, comforters, and other supplies to send with her parents.

The children had been exploring the bedroom Laura had designated as theirs which included a very small adjoining room consisting of four walls, a single plank shelf along the inner wall, and a line of evenly spaced wooden pegs on the outer wall. There, in the back corner, Rebeka discovered a hand painted small traveling chest. Lifting the trunk's filigree latch revealed a small artist's kit with little pots of paint and delicate paintbrushes. Two layers of tiles lined the bottom of the chest. Closing and catching the latch, Laura brought the chest to her mother.

Laura turned from her work as Rebeka entered the room. Setting the chest on the floor near Laura, Rebeka shifted the latch and raised the top. Laura stared at the contents. Kneeling, Laura carefully took each item in her hands, turning them over to inspect them. Among Laura's interests was the traditional Hungarian folk art of hand-painted tiles. Laura smiled broadly, taking Rebeka into her arms.

"Thank you, Rebeka. This is a wonderful surprise. Now go see if your brothers are getting into any mischief."

Laura returned to her work. Gathering up and moving the armfuls of bedding and towels for her parents required two trips downstairs. At the last, Laura spoke with Irén and told her of a plan. The plan required her mother's help to watch the children and prepare the evening meal without Laura's help. Irén happily agreed, bursting with pride in the kindness that lived in her daughter. Laura returned upstairs with a glass of water and sent the children down to their Dedi.

György had been in the barnyard surveying the outbuildings, trough, field, fences, well, stonework, stable, and barn as he had earlier in the day at what was soon to be his and Irén's new home. He would be able to give Henri a full accounting of the tools and supplies at hand as well as what work there was to be done. Together they would be able to fix what was necessary at both farms and get the spring planting in within the next few weeks. Both farms were in good condition.

György could hardly believe their good fortune despite the tremendous loss they had all suffered, and had yet to allow himself to acknowledge. György had always been of the opinion to submit the events of the past to the past. He was determined to be grateful they were together and alive. Another grandchild would soon bless their lives. There was much to keep his heart and mind occupied and so he would.

Everything the family needed was at hand except seed and seed potatoes. Irén and Laura had each given him the jewelry they had, unbeknownst to either György or Henri, secreted into their pockets. It would be enough, more than enough, for what they needed. As György mulled the possibilities and schedule for Henri and himself over the next weeks, his reverie was broken by a shrill call. A saker falcon flew into the woods with a ground squirrel, a suslik, in its talons.

György let his gaze sweep across the broad landscape and felt a profound sense of peace; they were home. Amid his musings, he turned in answer to the soft sounds of footsteps. It was Rebeka.

"I kept something for you, Nagypapi." Rebeka lifted her hand up as György extended his. "Here."

György stared. He didn't know how the little girl had done it or how she had kept it from him, from everyone. György looked at his precious granddaughter, full of pride and admiration for her strong spirit.

"I didn't want you not to have your hero medal, Nagypapi."

György picked the girl up, hugging her as he swung her around, their laughter filling the barn.

Early the following morning, Henri returned from the Vizi farm riding Kriska. Henri had found some tack in the stable including a riding bridle with intricately hand-braided side shallongs. The shallongs, although decorative, were an excellent fly deterrent. The bridle required only a slight adjustment, another notch in the chin strap, to fit Kriska comfortably and safely. The riding bridle was well made and suited Kriska beautifully. Rebeka was enthralled by the sight, not of her father riding, but of the filly. It hadn't occurred to her that Kriska could yet be ridden, and so a plan began to foment in her four-year-old brain. Rebeka had to find a way to spend time at her grandparents enabling her to ride Kriska. It was either that or somehow moving Kriska to their farm. Time would tell.

Henri had returned with the hope and intent that his family would see István and Enikő off to their new home. Of course the family agreed, they had worked with that same resolve long into the night after putting the children to bed. There was an excitement in the house dancing on the sunbeams streaming through the windows, a sort of frenzied happiness as everyone tidied themselves and made ready to go.

Irén lifted a bundle from the kitchen table and took Dávid's hand. In his other hand Dávid held a bouquet of spring flowers Irén had gathered and tied with a bit of colorful string. Györgi, with Péter perched on one arm folded across his chest, his hand holding onto Péter's legs, held a curious small bundle. Wrapped in a scrap of colorful fabric tied up with string, Györgi met each curious look with a smile. Laura was beaming but would not reveal what she carried in her small, wrapped bundle.

Rebeka had a plate of traditional Hungarian cookies, kiflis, which her grandmother had helped her bake. The plate was beautifully painted in a traditional Hungarian pattern familiar to Henri. Looking up at Laura his unspoken question was answered in her dancing bright brown eyes and crooked smile. Laura was so pleased he had noticed. Rebeka earnestly explained to her father there had been no sour cream for the cookies. However, she thought the nuts and fruit made up for the lack of sour cream. Rebeka explained she and her brothers had sampled them, twice, to ensure they were good enough for their friends.

As the family walked through Megyer with Henri leading Kriska, they were joined by the Demeters, Ferenc, and three other families who had recently returned to their homes. The Marton, Sindel, and Nemet families, along with their children, swelled the group to a size that they could not possibly surprise István and Enikő. The group was gay and felt hopeful as they had not been for far too long.

At the farm, István was just helping Enikő to her seat in the wagon when they both turned questioningly to the approaching sounds on the road at their backs. They were openly surprised to see their friends and neighbors. The couple had only been expecting Henri's return.

At that very moment everyone became aware of a distant but distinct and constant thrumming in the skies. Uncertain at first, everyone turned their gaze upwards, waiting, straining their necks to be the first to see the uncommon sight. As they waited the thrumming grew in intensity until, at last, the wedge of mute swans was seen by everyone breaking over the treetops at the far end of the Vizi fields. A collective gasp and cries of delight lifted from the group.

As the swans approached, every face was uplifted to the heavens, open to the rare sight rapidly closing in on Megyer. A spring migration of the large mute swans was not often witnessed. The puppies were wildly barking from the back of the wagon. Everyone there would tell the story for years to come. Everyone watched in silence, enthralled by the sight and sound, focused on every detail of this rare experience. Almost mechanically, they each pivoted simultaneously as a group watching the swans fly past. All too soon the elegant birds were out of sight, no doubt flying to Lake Balaton.

The reverie broken, the crowd erupted in laughter and delight at such a day. With fond goodbyes, embracing, and kisses the couple were repeatedly given best wishes. Everyone had a small gift, either a remembrance or a gift for the baby, or István and Enikő. At the last, the Varga family stepped forward and handed their gifts to their friends.

György's colorful fabric bundle was unwrapped revealing a wooden pull toy he had carved. Irén's gift was easily discerned, the sumptuous fragrance of two loaves of fresh bread had not gone unnoticed. Dávid blushed handing Enikő the bouquet. At her turn, to the smiling adoration of all present, Rebeka solemnly handed István the plate of kifli.

"My mother painted the plate. I made the kifli," Rebeka added, "with the help of my Dedi."

Laura then held out her gift, a slender square Enikő carefully unwrapped revealing a painted tile. A gasp escaped her lips. István looked over Enikő's shoulder to see for himself the tile that had been beautifully painted. Easily identified by all, it was Turul, wings outspread in exquisite detail. Turul, the protector spirit of babies. Enikő threw her arms around Laura whispering her thanks and appreciation.

Henri moved to the head of the wagon and held the team of black Nonius geldings while István helped Enikő up onto the wagon seat. Walking around the wagon, István climbed to his seat beside her then gathered the reins. The villagers watched as the couple left, everyone wondering when they might again see each other again.

Those thoughts returned to the present as introductions were made. Everyone in the village wanted to know what the Varga family needed and how they might be of help. György talked with the mayor and a few of the men ascertaining the best opportunity to sell the Varga jewelry. György's intention, he assured them, was to sell the jewelry then return to the village and purchase what was needed for the two farms. The degree of success György had in accomplishing this task would be of direct benefit to the entire community.

6

THE FARM

IN THE FOLLOWING days, months, and years the Varga and András families were happy and settled in their homes in Megyer. The farms provided enough for each family and, as before, to share and trade with the villagers. Laura's baby, a boy they named Jani, was born on the fifth of November. Henri and György had made another bedroom downstairs, easily sectioning off a portion of the overlarge main room. Finished, both rooms appeared as if they had always been situated just so. Henri and Laura's new bedroom had room for their bed, a chest, a cupboard, and a crib which did not leave their bedroom. No sooner was Jani moved upstairs to Dávid and Péter's room than Laura was again expecting. Little Bella was born three years after Jani, arriving on 9 November 1947. It had been a difficult birth, the umbilical had been tightly wrapped around Bella's neck. The midwife, and fervent prayers, had saved Bella.

Rebeka spent her childhood in Megyer between the farm, school, and her grandparents. As she had contrived when they first arrived at the farm, Rebeka helped at her grandparent's each afternoon after school. Rebeka never guessed that her parent's and grandparent's had known her heart's desire from the start. At ten years of age, and to her Nagypapi's delight, Rebeka had her grandfather's natural ability with horses. The girl was frequently seen riding Kriska, with their dog Janga running beside, across the fields and along the roads of Megyer. Rebeka always stayed close to home.

György and Henri had bought the matched pair of black geldings, Tomba and János, with the money György had received in trade for the Varga jewelry. The shop in Balaton, recommended by Ferenc and the men of the village, was run by an honest man everyone knew as Yitzhak.

True to his word, György had returned and their family had spent almost every forint with their neighbors. György had spared a few forints returning with a present for his grandchildren. Hidden under his coat, the present wriggled all the more as the children squealed and laughed expectantly. The Vizsla puppy, a female and the smallest of the litter, Rebeka had named Janga. The preponderance of the remaining sum was used to purchase a pair of Hungarian Gray milking cows for György and Irén which provided milk, butter, and cheese for both families. There were also a dozen broody hens, seed potatoes and seed, shoes for the children, and several needed tools. The last of the money, György had taken to István.

The Red Army never came to Megyer, at least not for six years. It was 1950 and there had been a growing unease across Hungary as the Rákosi regime targeted intellectuals, educators, and scientists. The wealthy, the perceived wealthy, and Jews were demonized as class enemies of the state. The arrested political prisoners were sent to Kaposvár, Kistarcsa, or Vác. Others were sent to labor camps.

Although Henri and György had lost the Varga farm, horses, and almost all they owned 6 years prior, Henri was identified as a class enemy of the state. Because they had once been considered wealthy, Henri was arrested. No one knew why György was spared, but everyone, especially Henri, was thankful this was so. György, along with Laura, Irén, and Rebeka, were all capable of taking care of the family in his absence. The family had looked on, Janga's furious barking muffled behind the closed door to the basement. Sándor, thankfully, was confined in the barn where he was hurling himself against the doors, furious at the unknown threat to his family. The AVO dragged Henri from the farmhouse to their wagon in the courtyard, no one knowing if they would ever see him again.

During the following years, Rákosi implemented "reforms" consolidating farms into collectives and establishing impossible production quotas. Luckily the Varga and András farms were very small. Still, the village had collective quotas to meet. Rebeka's brothers grew strong and tall; they were valuable and appreciated for all their help.

Rebeka knew her eldest brother, Dávid, held a seething hatred for the Soviet government and a growing passion for Hungary's independence. How often the family cautioned him to be careful with his thoughts and words. The younger brothers, Péter and Jani, idolized their father in his absence and lived with hope, as they all did, for Henri's return. Until that time, they were under the tutelage of their Nagypapi, György, and were growing into fine young men.

The boys and György worked diligently through each spring into early fall to meet the quotas and prepare the family and home for each coming winter. Food and firewood, repairs to the home, and hay for the animals all had to be collected and stored. Although Megyer was a small village far from Budapest, the Red Army was not far from Megyer. Everyone knew they now had to be watchful and careful.

After Henri had been arrested, two of the other villagers had also been arrested and taken away. The first had been Dávid Marton, who had the small farm to the south of the András farm. Dávid had been in the field working when the ÁVO arrived and dragged him across the field rather than letting him walk. The Marton family had three boys who now had to fill the quota for the family farm.

Next, and last, was Bartal Demeter. Bartal was arrested while the village was at church. No one understood why the AVO wanted the old man. Bartal was a simple man, he had never been wealthy. He had never been political. He and Zita had lived a quiet life on their small farm in Megyer, their field rented to Andi Sindel these last 19 years. They had taken Bartal anyway, hurrying him on unsteady feet, stumbling through the church until, with a hand under each arm, they had lifted and carried him to the wagon. Everyone was afraid yet everyone followed. Poor Zita was wailing in her despair, the church resonating with her cries. Had anyone been home anywhere in Megyer they would have heard the sound of her cries, as they all did for all of Megyer was at church that Sunday, and all bore witness to Bartal's arrest.

The village grieved. A week later, as György was taking a wagon of potatoes to the Vizi mill he found Bartal Demeter next to the road. Bartal had not made it far from Megyer, the village where he had lived all of his life. Misused and abandoned by the soldiers, his body lay sprawled and disheveled at the edge of the road. His beret lay nearby, trodden upon. György shook the dried mud from the wool, slapping the beret against his leg, before replacing it on Bartal's head. György returned Bartal to Megyer, to his Zita. The village buried him on a Wednesday. That Friday, Zita was found dead in her cottage laying on her bed in the clothes she had worn when she buried her beloved husband of sixty-one years.

Year then followed year, somewhat monotonous yet dynamic for the András family with five growing children. A subtle change began mid-summer of 1956. Most of the radios had been confiscated but news had come of Rákosi being replaced by Enrö

Gerő. Gerő was also a Stalinist and equally hated. He did nothing for the Hungarians and made no concessions; the quotas were still in place and the people were no better off than before. People began to speak as they had previously not dared to. The unrest began to build. The tension spread across Hungary, even in the little town of Megyer where everyone wondered what would happen, and it did.

Dominik Marton, the eldest son of Dávid Marton, had returned from delivering the last load of potatoes for the village quota. He had news from Budapest. University students across Hungary were calling for change, making demands of the government. Everyone was certain that there would be an uprising. Dominik announced he was going to Budapest. In two days there would be a meeting at the Technical University and he was going to be there. Although Dominik had never been to Budapest, the University, as he was told, was located along the Danube and not difficult to find.

That night, György, Irén, and Laura spoke quietly in the living room after everyone else had gone up to bed. It was a warm evening, unusual for this late in October. The news from Budapest was disquieting. They hoped Megyer would be spared the worst of the uprising should it happen.

The next morning, Irén called the children to breakfast. Rebeka and Bella, along with Janga, came running in from the stable where they had been all morning. Followed by Sándor, the girls had been brushing Kriska and the black geldings after letting the cows out to their pasture. Bella had opened the gate then squirmed between the fence rails to stand behind the fence as the massive creatures and their impressive horns leisurely plodded past. Bella lived in awe and fear of the cows and thought her sister fearless. She watched with admiration as Rebeka unhurriedly drove them from their stalls and out of the stable. Each day, with every drive, only served to intensify Bella's adoration of her sister.

Sándor had kept watch over the girls and followed them to the kitchen for his breakfast, as he did every morning. It was a pleasant routine. His was a happy and somewhat sedentary life. Although, it must be said, any threat to any of his family, four-legged or two, transformed him into a raging, fearsome beast.

Janga could not have been more different. Beguilingly sweet, enthusiastic in everything she did, walking was never an option. The agile dog preferred to run, leap, or bounce wherever she went no matter how short the distance. Her love for each member of the family was exuberant. It had taken a toll on everyone to teach her not to jump up onto people. Janga, wherever she was playing, was never late to breakfast.

"Leave Janga outside with Sándor. You are lucky your Nagypapi lets her in to sleep with you!"

"Oh, Dedi, you know he loves her as much as we all do. Just as we know you do!" Rebeka smiled at her grandmother as the sisters washed their hands at the sideboard. Her grandmother could only shake her head knowing, as they all did, that her granddaughter was right. Her eyes twinkled with delight.

"Where are your brothers? Breakfast will be cold. And your Anya, where is she?"

At that moment, Laura appeared with György. They'd been in the barn checking the stitching, then wiping down and conditioning every strap, line, rein, bridle, and saddle in preparing the horse tack for winter. They sat at the table while Irén, Rebeka, and Bella set out plates of hot fresh bread, túró cheese, and kolbász sausage on the table. There were cups of hot tea at every place.

"Where are the boys?" Irén asked again.

Laura looked up as György looked out the kitchen window. In the silence they all listened, in the silence they found their answer. György pushed back from the table and was out the door in three strides. Rebeka ran upstairs followed by Laura and Irén, Bella ran down to the cellar. Soon all four met György in the barnyard who was holding a bridled Kriska. Motioning to Rebeka, she ran up, grabbed a handful of Kriska's thick mane, then threw herself up onto Kriska's back in one deft motion.

"Go! Quickly, Rebeka. Find Mrs. Morton. Find out when Dominik left."

Rebeka and Kriska were away, Kriska's hooves noisily scattering stones from the courtyard in all directions. Janga raced alongside.

Laura spoke up, "They've gone. They've taken their coats and rucksacks."

"It looks as if they also took food from the storeroom. At least they have food," added Bella.

It didn't take long for Rebeka to return. They saw her dark hair flying in the wind behind her, Rebeka's thick braid had come undone. Galloping across the field, hardened through the long dry fall, Kriska crossed the distance between the farms effortlessly. Slipping to the ground, Rebeka repeated what Mrs. Morton had told her. Dominik had left just after sunup.

The family stood in the courtyard and talked. It was Rebeka who prevailed at the last. Bella was too young. György, as the only man, had to stay with the farm and watch over Bella and Irén. Irén certainly could not go, although she huffed at the thought that there was anything she couldn't do. When it came to a choice between Laura and Rebeka, Rebeka was insistent.

"You know how people are drawn to me, Anya. Yes, that also makes it dangerous. But it's dangerous for you as well. If I am careful, and I will be, then I also have the advantage of youth. People will help me."

György was abrupt and stern, "There's no time to waste."

Returning to the house, Irén packed and repacked a rucksack for Rebeka, while Laura placed selected notes and coins into three small cloth bags. Irén secreted the bags separately in different locations within the rucksack among Rebeka's clothes. One bag of coins was for the train to Budapest, another for the return, and the last was for whatever she and her brothers might need for food.

György and Rebeka saddled Kriska. Then, kneeling in the courtyard, György drew a rough map of Budapest and the countryside Rebeka would travel through in the event that the trains were not available. György drew a long curving line representing the Danube. The river split around Margit Island and passed the hills of Buda on the south. The urban city of Pest he indicated on the north side with rough outlines of several buildings. Hatch marks across the Danube indicated the bridges and the locations of landmarks. With an "x" György marked the location of the Technical University and Gellért Square.

The women and Bella said their goodbyes to Rebeka in the courtyard. György had tied Janga in the barn but it was of no use, the Vizsla always outwitted him. Although not yet noon, it was possible the boys had already arrived at the Budapest-Déli railway terminal. The train to Budapest was about a 4 hour ride. György, with Rebeka seated behind and Janga running alongside, rode off to the small, local train station just a short distance past the little stone bridge.

Arriving at the station, Györgi had dismounted, hooked Janga around her neck and lifted her into his arms. It took both arms to subdue Janga as Rebeka stepped onto the train disappearing into the vestibule. "Remember to change trains just before Boba, Rebeka. The train east to Budapest goes through the countryside, there should be fewer people."

Boarding the train, Rebeka found a seat near the door then called out through the open window, "I will see you soon, Nagypapi!"

"We will be watching for you, Rebeka."

7

BÉLA AND KLÁRI

FROM THE WINDOWS of their apartment on Dohány Street in Pest, opened to the fresh but still crisp air of the early spring day, Drs. Béla and Klári Fürth were having breakfast with their daughter, Mira. As it was Friday, there was work and school awaiting the family. Mira attended the local kindergarten, which was only a few blocks along the way to her parent's work at the hospital. It was time to go. The week had caught up with all of them, there was an unusual tension in the normally serene and quiet household. Added to this were the sounds rising from the street below that had grown quite agitated. Mira, ever curious, leaned onto the sill as she looked out across the street at what could only be described as mayhem.

"Apa, something is happening! The people, they are rushing about and yelling at one another."

Only slightly distracted in passing, Dr. Béla Fürth glanced out the window nearest the door as he lifted his overcoat and hat from the coat rack. It wasn't what he saw but what he indistinctly heard that stopped him, he too leaned out to better hear. Dr. Klári

Fürth was mid-sentence in admonishing her family that there was no time for such behavior, they could not be late. In answer, Mira screamed, pulling her head in and turning to her mother who was by now reservedly alarmed.

"Stalin! Stalin is dead!" Mira screamed again.

The words hardly made sense at first. Klári turned to her husband asking what it might mean for all of them and, of immediate importance, should Mira go to school.

"Yes," he answered. "By all means, it is another day. And yes, a day that might change all of our lives. It is a day worth noting. We must each attend to our work and tonight return directly home. Mira, we will be at your school to walk you home. There is no cause for concern."

Béla Fürth had been raised in Miskolc, Hungary. An intelligent and capable student, he was accepted to the University of Bologna in Italy where he intended to study and train as a medical doctor. In 1939 Béla had only recently graduated and determined to stay in Italy, but instead returned to Hungary at the behest of his mother, Erzébet. Béla's father had been killed in a car accident.

Soon after returning to Budapest, Béla was taken by the military to work in a field hospital. It was only a matter of days after he had left that the soldiers had come for Erzébet. The army had a daily quota of Jews to be delivered for transport. Béla's mother was taken from her home and shipped by train to Auschwitz, where she was murdered. During this time, Béla had only known that his letters to his mother went unanswered. Béla was only mildly concerned knowing that Hungary's infrastructure, including the post, was in tatters.

By the end of the war, there weren't many grandparents for the children of Budapest. Mira was fortunate to have her mother's parents, whom she affectionately called her Nagymama and Nagypapa.

Klári Fürth, a diminutive woman only slightly over five feet tall, had a personality and intellect adversely disproportionate to her height. Selected for what became known as the Death March from Budapest to Auschwitz in 1945, Klári had closely watched her captors. She watched as the Germans, for entertainment, threw food on the ground then watched again as their Jewish prisoners fought over the scraps. Klári knew she must escape; one day she did. While the soldiers were distracted, Klári simply walked away and returned to Budapest. Once there, Klári was hidden by her grandfather's workers to whom he had paid a significant amount of money. Any of the workers could have informed the local police of her location, but they didn't. Klári, in her quiet defiance, never wore the yellow star.

Engaged before the war, Béla returned to Klári and Budapest after his field hospital was liberated by the Soviets. Budapest, Queen of the Danube, is the capital city of Hungary. The grassy hills of Buda on one side, the shopping centers and flat expanse of Pest on the other. There is a series of five connecting bridges beginning from the south: Petöfi, Freedom, Erzsébet, Chain, and Margit Bridge, also known as the Margaret Bridge. At the north end the Danube flows around Margit Island, a place of medieval ruins, old trees, and flowering gardens.

One late summer night in September of 1946, Béla and Klári walked along the Danube, crossing the Margit Bridge to Margit Island, strolling in the moonlight. There, sitting on the grassy area at the base of the water tower, they talked of their upcoming wedding, their interest in continuing their education, their work, their hopes. Married in December, the couple lived with Klári's parents, Gábor and Ili Berci. By the time their daughter, Mira, was born in June, they had moved into their own apartment on Dohány Street.

The apartment building on Dohány Street had recently undergone many transformations. Late in the war the Nazis had arrived in Budapest sealing off the entire district around Dohány Street designating it "the Jewish Ghetto." The apartment building, designed for 80, held hundreds of Jews. During the Russian liberation that followed, the top floors were leveled during the bombing sending tenants hurrying to the basement. Not all could fit. Those who ventured outside were often killed.

The building had been haphazardly repaired and renovated in the manner dictated by the communist regime following the war, but not before the Red Army had looted and plundered every possible item. Everything of value, including kitchen sinks, were sent to Russia via freight trains. The Germans soldiers had been cruel, ugly, and ruthless but were shot if caught looting. The Russian soldiers were more disciplined and well-mannered but took everything.

For six years Béla and Klári had been working at the Central Military Hospital. During those six years Mira grew into a precocious child. It was 5 March 1953, and Stalin, the most hated man in Hungary, a brutal, murdering dictator, was dead. Béla and Klári returned home with Mira early that evening, after work and school, finally able to discuss the day's events in the relative safety of their apartment. Many people in Budapest were hopeful. The people of Budapest were hopeful the restrictions would be eased, hopeful the hated Mátyás Rákosi regime would be replaced, hopeful the prisons would be emptied of their political and Jewish prisoners.

Mátyás Rákosi, the fourth son of a Hungarian grocer, born in Serbia, was an enigma. Born a Jew, his paternal grandfather had battled alongside Lajos Kossuth in Hungary's war for independence. It was his father, Jozéf, who had changed the family name of Rosenfeld to Rákosi. It was Mátyás who rejected religion and became an atheist. Mátyás Rákosi had been leader of the

Communist Party since 1945. As such, he had been serving as the *de facto* ruler of Hungary.

Through political machinations initiated in Moscow, Rákosi was proclaimed Hungary's absolute ruler in 1949. Rákosi had already established himself as a symbol of tyranny and oppression in Hungary, he was a man to be feared. Despite his heritage, Rákosi, the terrorist puppet of the Stalinist communist regime, now oversaw the imprisonment or murder of over 350,000 Hungarians. Rákosi's quota-based policies were devastating Hungary's economy. Now, with Stalin's death, Rákosi was recalled to Moscow. They were not pleased.

Hopes were realized and soon lost when Imre Nagy replaced Rákosi only to be removed from office a year later in 1955. Ernõ Gerő, installed as Prime Minister, was yet another unpopular and hated Stalinist. Equally disturbing and threatening, the Warsaw Pact had been created as a tool to justify the Soviet troops illegally occupying Hungary in violation of the 1947 Peace Treaty. By then the people of Budapest knew the Iron Curtain was as real as any physical barrier and worse. Hungarians were not allowed to leave the country nor speak freely, and, of course, there was no political discussion. By the age of seven Mira had known that anything she said could result in her parents being sent to prison. At the hospital, Klári was often warned by her supervisor; expressing her opinions risked being arrested and sent to jail.

In 1956, when Mira was nine and in the fourth grade at General School, the family had moved to a neighborhood on Rózsa Hill. Their home was located on the Buda side of Budapest across the Danube River from Margit Island. A two-family home, Mira lived with her parents and grandparents, Gábor and Ili Berci, on the top floor above another family, the Nováks, who had twin boys. The apartment was spacious with a bathroom and another room for the toilet. Mira's grandparents occupied the bedroom next to the bathroom, Mira had her own room next to theirs. Mira's parents, Béla and Klári, slept on the living room sofa.

For the most part, the Fürth family lived a middle class life. As both of Mira's parents and her grandfather Gábor worked, grandmother Ili took care of Mira, cleaned, shopped, and did the cooking. Ili loved to cook. Whenever the market had fresh lemons, word would spread throughout the neighborhood. Ili would, quite literally, drop everything to rush to market. Freshly caught fish from the market were kept in the bathtub. In the evening, when her Nagypapa would return from his sign painting shop, he would fillet the fish for Nagymama to prepare for dinner. For some reason, perhaps it was too small, grandfather Gábor's sign painting business had been an exception to the 1947 communist takeover of privatized businesses. Whatever the reason, no one mentioned it.

8

THE TÜREA FAMILY

WITHIN A FEW months, the conditions in Budapest had grown to a general and guarded unrest. One morning at the market, Klári met Erzsébet Türea. The Türea family also lived on Rózsa Hill in an apartment that Erzsébet's grandparents and aunt had built as their home. That was before the war. After the war, the building had been appropriated, "nationalized," and turned into apartments.

Erzsébet's husband, Jeno, had been born in Transylvania, his parents were of German descent. Erzsébet's family had lived in Budapest for generations. Erzsébet's elderly father, József Kovács, had been a silversmith, as his father before him, specializing in decorative raised forms, especially teapots, water pitchers, bowls, salt cellars, and candlesticks. Erzsébet's mother, Gizella, had run the business. After the war their business had been nationalized.

By curious circumstance, the Türea family had owned the apartment building on Dohány Street where the Fürth family had so recently lived. The building had once been the Türea home, a beautiful, modern building that faced the Danube. Their son, Jeno Türea, was a chemist who had owned a cosmetic business making fine soaps and perfumes in a pretty shop also located on Dohány Street. When the Nazis arrived in 1944, the elderly Türeas had been taken by one of the first transports to Auschwitz. Jeno had been forcibly taken away to a labor camp outside of Budapest. Their home, taken by the Nazis and then nationalized by the Soviets, was converted to apartments. Erzsébet and her family shared their penthouse apartment with dozens of other people. The four story building quickly fell into disrepair and deteriorated.

When the topmost floor was bombed, Erzsébet, her parents, and her children, Péter and Júlia, had moved down to a lower floor with another displaced neighbor, Samu Kiraly. Supposedly deaf, there was no doubt of his condition after he awoke the morning of the bombing to find the front of his bedroom missing. All of the windows were shattered during the bombings, the gaping holes boarded from the inside. A peephole at the door was the only window to the outside world.

The children in the building were chronically frightened. The sound of airplanes overhead terrorized the children. The last apartment they lived in, Erzsébet and her family had shared with more than 50 people. Only the sick, elderly, and wounded were allowed to lie down, everyone else stood or leaned against a wall. At night, all of the apartment's occupants would lay down in rows. Erzsébet arranged for Júlia and Péter to sleep under the dining table, a prime location, especially during the winter. Snow would blow in through the gaping windows, the glass shattered or blown out during battles and air raids. Despite their prime location, during that winter Júlia suffered frostbite in one foot.

At the start of the war, anticipating the likely possibility of devastation and trauma, Erzsébet had taken a first aid course. The only person in the building with any medical training, Erzsébet was designated the medical officer for the building and amputated toes, set broken bones, stitched wounds, and whatever else was needed. Erzsébet also organized a collective kitchen in the central courtyard to feed everyone in the building. Metal buckets were collected and made into stoves. Furniture from the apartments was chopped providing fuel for the cook fires.

Periodically, Nazi soldiers would come to the building and order all women between the ages of 18 and 40 to come down with a bag. Erzsébet was a beautiful and fashionable woman, before the war she had made all of her clothes. When Erzsébet would appear at the door, she would be fully dressed including a hat and gloves. Taking her place at the end of the line, Erzsébet, walking gradually slower, would eventually turn around and walk home. Erzsébet did not "look" Jewish to the Nazi's and never wore the star enabling the ruse that more than once saved her life.

Her father, although elderly even then, had been collected for "work," which everyone suspected was a one-way ticket to Siberia. József, at the end of the line of prisoners, had followed his daughter's example slowing his gait. When the nearest guard averted his attention, József turned around and, seeing an old woman with a cart, took the cart in hand, pushing it for her.

Eventually, the building became too decrepit and too dangerous to live in. Erzsébet found a tiny room in an apartment on the Buda side to shelter József and Gizella while she and her children moved from building to building, hiding, using snow to help themselves keep clean.

During the Russian invasion, liberation had been won one apartment at a time. When the city was eventually liberated, Erzsébet traveled to the labor camp for Jeno. She had found her husband suffering from a bad leg as the result of a wound that wouldn't heal. Reunited, the family left Hungary, hiding in the straw of a livestock car on the first train east to Rumania, where Jeno had relatives. Upon arrival, their aunt insisted on a thorough cleaning before entering the house, including cutting Júlia's long pigtails. Júlia was stoic until she caught sight of the scissors, then cried inconsolably.

The Türea family lived an almost normal life in Rumania for about a year when Jeno preceded the family in returning to Budapest. There, he would again start a small cosmetics business. Erzsébet and their children followed when they received word from her parents, József and Gizella. József had been able to get an apartment to accommodate all of them in what had been their other apartment building on Rózsa Hill, a seven story stone building. Returning to Budapest, Erzsébet worked with Jeno; her job was to smuggle needed items over the border.

In 1946 the principle of free education as the right of all Hungarian citizens was established. The Ministry of Education was created, supplanting the Roman Catholic Church. The church had, until that time, provided the mostly secular education of Hungarian children. The new system of Marxism-Leninism stressing technical and vocational training had replaced secular education.

As young children, Péter and Júlia had spent long hours quizzing each other on geography, the elements, mathematical equations, and anything else their father chose to introduce. On rare occasions, returning from work Jeno would produce from his coat a slim volume. After dinner, the family would sit together and Jeno would provide an introduction to the author and contents of the new book. Péter and Júlia would then commit themselves to learn all they could with help as needed from their parents. Their education had been far enough advanced that the deprivations of the war years had not significantly hampered their progress once they returned to school. Now, with both children attending university, the family's evening discussions were largely centered around current events.

Péter Türea attended the University of Szeged, his sister, Júlia, attended the Technical University of Budapest. If for no other reason than to distance himself from the political rhetoric as much as possible, Péter, an exceptional student, chose to study chemical engineering. Having nearly completed that work, Péter was interested in furthering his education. His interests lay in the sciences and ranged from astrophysics to number theory. In addition to his studies, Péter belonged to a small group of twelve students who regularly met for a game of bridge, cards, discussions, and readings.

Júlia, other than being a young woman, was much like her brother. Capable and intelligent, Júlia was intent on a medical career. Well-liked and outgoing, Júlia had a talent for organizing and natural camaraderie that attracted others to her. Júlia also regularly met with a group of students, the Revolutionary Student Committee, for readings and discussions.

Both students had told their parents of the growing unrest across the country that had begun to foment during the last days of summer. Students returning to school that fall brought with them stories of a shared experience; citizens across Hungary were discontent, unfulfilled, and hungry. Returning from school in the evening, Júlia would recount to a rapt audience all that she had gleaned during the day.

Péter returned home most weekends. It took some time to discuss the events of his week. It both thrilled and terrified the Türeas listening to Péter and Júlia's revelations. Filled with a youthful sense of immortality and innocent righteousness, Péter and Júlia's enthusiasm were often met with pleadings by their parents to lower their voices. Their grandparents, József and Gizella Kovács, retired to their room by late evening and were not privy to the entirety of the conversations.

9

THE AWAKENING

JENO AND ERZSÉBET Türea were a new and valuable source of information for Klári and Béla. The Türeas and Fürths, returning from the market or passing on the street, took great care when speaking, uttering only a few brief sentences under their breath, as if in greeting. Feigning indifference, a wary watchfulness was imperative on the streets of Budapest. Informants, like the secret police, were a dark constancy in their lives.

The previous night, Jeno and Erzsébet would have worked out a division of the information gathered from Péter and Júlia. The following day they would dispense the abbreviated information whenever they might chance upon Klári and Béla, together or apart. At night, in their apartment, Klári and Béla would discuss what they had learned. It was not uncommon to require, at times, more than a day for Jeno and Erzsébet to apprise the Fürths of the entirety of the most recent news. No one considered it safe for the Fürths, or the Türeas, to meet in either of their apartments, it was simply too dangerous. Hungarians lived with the underlying threat of the secret police being ever-present, watchful, and listening.

The events of May were well known and did not require the subterfuge of Erzsébet and Jeno. Everyone in Budapest knew of the reorganization of the Petöfi Circle following the death of Stalin. Everyone also knew the Petöfi Circle had disassociated themselves from DISZ, the Union of Working Youth, the only official communist youth organization. The Petöfi Circle, chaired by Gäbor Tanczos, was comprised largely of young professionals and intellectuals, students, and recently released political prisoners. The membership of the Petöfi Circle called for the discussion and debate of critical social and cultural topics to promote freedom, humanism, and national independence. The organization, and the members, had the full support of the Hungarian Writer's Union.

Disenfranchised by Rakosi's regime, the Hungarian Writer's Union included distinguished and esteemed Hungarians. Author and poet Tibor Dery, the social democrat Arpad Szakasits, intellectual and playwright Gyula Hay, and philosopher and historian George Lukács, were among its distinguished members. In May, the discussion turned to the economic policies of Rákosi's regime. The quotas that had devastated the Hungarian economy had also eroded the quality of Hungarian products. Renowned Austrian photographer Erich Lessing documented the meeting.

The meeting of the Writer's Union in turn led to political discussion. Hungary had a rich cultural heritage and class of intellectuals who believed Hungarians should rise up. Hungarian intellectuals, regardless of their socioeconomic status, were now openly antagonistic of Rákosi and Soviet rule. In July of 1956, Rákosi had been called back to Moscow and, as rumors and speculation grew, the tension became palpable.

October, although usually cold enough for snow to have accumulated, had recently been unusually pleasant, warm, and sunny. Friday, 12 October, Klári passed Erzsébet while walking across the Margít Bridge. Erzsébet had kept her gaze lowered and passed without a glance or word. Klári returned home with a gift from a colleague for Mira, an unripened green banana. Mira was thrilled, although she had no idea what a banana was. The experience was unpleasant. Klári was equally disappointed, Béla hadn't any news from Jeno.

By Saturday, 13 October, the Fürths had learned that the group of students at Szeged University, including Péter, were meeting to discuss the creation of a student organization. Erzsébet had passed the information to Klári at work. Saturday evening, Klári was anxious to return home and discuss the day's news with Béla. Béla had learned from Jeno that Péter and his friends were distributing hundreds of handwritten and typed invitations.

By Tuesday, it was done. News quickly spread to Budapest of the organized student union in Szeged led by a small group of students, including a trio of law students, Tamás Kiss, Imre Tóth, and András Lajtényi. The students met in the Great Hall on campus, the Auditorium Maximum of the Faculty of Arts. Quickly, decisively, the students voted to resign from DISZ, the communist Union of Working Students. There would not be a reorganization of MEFSZ, the 1946 organization of the Union of Hungarian University and Academy Students. Instead, they reorganized under the title of Student Alliance. In the following days, student representatives from the three Szeged campuses would be elected, then meet on 20 October to draw up a list of demands.

The Student Alliance was short-lived expanding to the Alliance of Hungarian University and College Students. By the following day, Wednesday, 17 October, hand-typed invitations were being distributed to Hungarian campuses inviting students to join the AHUCS for the intended purpose to achieve "...freedom of thinking." Across Hungary, planned meetings were to be held in the following days. The student's meeting in Budapest was scheduled for Tuesday, 22 October.

Democratic organizations had been previously banned under the Rákosi dictatorship. The union and the upcoming meeting ignited rumors and speculation. The city throbbed with an undercurrent; like the buzz of a high tension wire, it was felt more than heard. That Tuesday morning, 13 October, the citizens of Budapest were speculative, agitated, fearful, and yet, hopeful.

Later that morning, Ili had no sooner left the apartment to walk to the bakery than she came hurrying back. Uncharacteristically bursting into the apartment as she did surprised both Béla and Klári. Ili, flushed and agitated, one hand on her pounding heart, urged Béla to hurry to Bem Square. People were openly talking, unnerving in itself, of the hundreds of university students gathered in Szeged. The meeting had been chaired by a Szeged law professor and led by a group of law students. There was talk of a list of demands of the government. Ili, shocked by her own words, was out of breath and frightened.

"And, what else did they say? What are the demands? Were any of them arrested? Was Péter arrested? Are any of the students in Budapest organizing? Were there any police on the streets?"

"Please, Klári, please," Ili begged. "I don't know. It was all a rush of words. People I don't even know; everyone was talking, telling me, asking me, yelling. There is much excitement and concern, and," Ili paused remembering how fervent some of the crowd had been, "and, anger! Please, go to the bakery for me. There are so many people! I think many are afraid of food shortages again. Mira and I will stay inside. Please, go. Be careful! Find out whatever you can. Béla, I heard that men are gathering at Bem Square. Perhaps you can learn something more there."

At that moment, Gábor returned home unexpectedly.

"What has happened?" Ili asked. A normally strong, forceful woman, she was clearly upset.

"Nothing, nothing. Nothing yet, in any case."

Klári and Béla left the apartment parting with a nod in each other's direction at the bottom of the stairs before purposefully continuing independently to their destinations. Although they would both be in the same vicinity, they chose not to draw attention to themselves. Klári, with a bag folded over her arm, turned to cross Margit Bridge. Watchful and alert, she walked to the bakery, Café Gerbeaud, along the Danube Promenade on the Pest side. Béla walked in the direction of Bem Square, located next to the bridge termination on the Buda side. It was exciting but somber business that they knew required subtlety.

Klári had been the first to return to the apartment where she found her parents, Gábor and Ili, sitting at the table, waiting. A freshly ironed embroidered tablecloth was the only brightness in the room otherwise suffused with the darkness of apprehension and worry. Mira was in her room reading but came out to greet her mother and inspect the bags of bread and pastries.

"Mira, could you please get a plate and arrange all of the fruit kifli. Put the bread into the tin for dinner tonight," Klári asked as she turned to hang up her coat, gloves, and hat. "I'll slice the torte and put on the tea kettle. When your father returns, we'll sit together."

In her daughter's absence, Ili had been keeping the teakettle warm. With Klári's return, Ili stood and went to the kitchen to arrange the cups and saucers, and measure out the tea. As she passed Klári she gave her daughter a knowing glance, who returned it with raised eyebrows and a thin smile, neither of which escaped Mira's attention.

"You needn't think to pretend, or keep me from the news. Knowing is better than not. Believe me, the other children at school have plenty to say when the teacher is busy with her work. I know you are all doing your best. I know you are trying to keep me from harm. I have lived in the shadows of war as Budapest has been rebuilt around me. That is not lost on me. I hear your discussions, you have warned me to discretion. Please, include me. Not talking is frightening. I know, everyone knows, something is about to happen."

Mira's mother and grandparents stared at her in silence, not knowing whether to laugh at her precociousness or cry. In the end, they gathered her up in their arms. Klári pulled away, holding Mira at arms length, a hand on each of her daughter's shoulders.

"Of course you do. I apologize, Mira. You are an intelligent girl. I never should've treated you otherwise. I can only say that, yes, we meant to spare you. Instead, I see we've caused you worry," Klári said as she looked into her daughter's eyes, gently cradling her chin in one hand.

They had all agreed to include Mira in discussing the events, events that were accelerating, although they could only guess as to what end. This, of course, is why they were concerned. The possibilities of what might transpire in Budapest in the coming days could make all their lives difficult. They spoke briefly of those possibilities and then resolved to set that worry aside, at least for a little while. Today they would enjoy the Dobos torte and each other's company. At that declaration the door opened. Béla stepped into the apartment hanging up his hat and coat by the door and turning with a cursory glance around their home.

"I smell something delicious!"

The family laughed, while Béla looked from one to the other in happy wonderment.

"You are right on time," Klári smiled at him. "Sit down with us."

Mira brought out the torte, forks, and plates. Ili carried out the tea.

Later that afternoon, sitting in the living room with the plate of kiflis, Klári and Béla recounted what they had learned. Klári had met a family at the bakery,

"László and Etel Gergő and their daughter, Penny, who is ten. Etel's sister and father, Karola and Jakab Miska, and László's mother, Tünde Gergő, were also there."

"Oh yes," Mira joined in, "I know Penny, she's in my class."

"That's exactly the reason I was introduced to the family. Penny recognized me and said hello."

Mira continued. "Her grandfather Janós was killed in the war, and her grandmother Júlia died. Penny has lived all over. She lived with her grandmother Tünde for awhile and then with her grandfather, Jakab. The parents and older brother were imprisoned at Kalocsa, and later, after he had been released, the Soviets wanted to put him in prison again. So, the family hid him.

"Penny and her older brother saved their father. They had returned home with groceries and saw two trucks on the street near their house, their father in one of them. Penny sent her brother on with the bags and then walked right up to her father, asking him to get off the truck and walk with her. He did! They caught up with her brother, András. He's 23 now."

"Well," said Klári, "that's enlightening. Do you know why the family was imprisoned?"

"Yes, they owned a newspaper."

Béla asked Mira if she knew what had become of the older brother.

"He had a terrible time in prison. He was only sixteen, everyone else was much older. Fortunately, he was released after nine months and returned to Budapest. He finished high school and now he's training to be an artist. He wants to be an art professor."

"How long was Penny's mother in prison?"

"Two years. Penny was able to visit twice. Just to the wall outside though. Her mother would wave from the window."

Everyone was quiet until Béla broke the silence.

"I learned some intriguing news at Bem Square today. I wouldn't be surprised at what the Türea's might tell us tomorrow. There is talk of a meeting of students at the Technical University. There is a great deal of unrest on the campus, for that matter, there is a great deal of unrest in Budapest.

"There was a man at the square, Tibor, I think was his name. He now works at the Laboratory Equipment Factory. Prior to that, he was drafted into the Hungarian Army and was one of several injured, one man was killed, during a training exercise. Following his recovery, he was sent to a forced labor camp. Of course, there were many other men gathered at Bem with a similar story.

"There were also many demands made for the camps to be closed. Everyone wonders what the student meeting tomorrow will produce."

That night, after putting Mira to bed, Klári and Béla sat in the living room with Gábor and Ili to discuss the days events and what such news might portend.

"But Béla, what of Péter? What he is undertaking is dangerous! He could be arrested," Ili asked, concerned. She admired the bright, nice young man, the son of her neighbors, an old Budapest family.

"Ili, he could be killed," the others responded in unison.

10

PÉTER

TUESDAY NIGHT, 16 October, the Türea family was sitting at the table in their apartment. Péter had only just arrived. He had taken the first train possible, returning to Budapest for a short visit. Péter had to return to Szeged and report to the AHUCS with news of student plans, if any, in Budapest. He and Júlia would go to her university and learn what they could.

Gizella set the tea and cups on the table and then sat next to Erzsébet. Everyone quietly listened as Péter told the family of the meetings held at his university. Although barely able to quell his emotions, his voice was constrained. Péter was justifiably concerned that anyone outside the apartment might overhear their discussion.

Péter recounted most of the list of 11 demands the students had compiled. He spoke of the rising support for the students at other universities and in other cities across Hungary. Péter noted the particular interest, and concern, of his family.

"Everyone is looking to Budapest, father. Across Hungary, students at other universities have organized pro-democracy student unions. People are ready for change."

Jeno nodded, arms folded, jaw set, his tea growing cold on the table in front of him. "And this is not associated with MEFSZ?"

"No father, that acronym has had too many meanings and is too confusing. Even the spelling of the acronym in adding an extra "E" simply for pronunciation presents a difficulty. The Student Alliance was approved by vote. The approved student organization, Association of the Working Youth, disapproves, of course."

Júlia was just as earnest in recounting what was being whispered among the students at the Technical University.

"What? What is being whispered?" Gizella asked, her hands tightly clasped in her lap under the table and out of view.

"They believe it is time, Nagyanya. Time to demand their freedoms. Time for the Soviet military police to leave Hungary. Time for economic policies that would restore Hungarian prosperity."

Péter continued where Júlia left off. "As I'm certain you realize, we created the list of demands based on those of the 1848 revolution. There were twelve, as you know, we had twenty and now, eleven. Hungarians have all wanted the same thing always, Apa. Freedom. Freedom and independence.

"There's been nothing on the radio. Hungarian Radio, nothing. The Radio Journal reprinted their old story, "the BBC is the citadel of lies." The BBC and Radio Vaticana has the same propaganda, as always. Radio Free Europe has said nothing of our meeting, but they know something, we're certain of it. They broadcast more of the same, propaganda to undermine the communists. However, they have recently made inferences that many believe are to influence those Hungarian citizens who are listening to take action. That Hungarians take up arms against the communist government and," his voice strained in earnestness, "that they will stand behind us, support us."

"Arms? Violence? Do you have any idea how quickly this may grow into a revolution, son? Or how quickly this could turn against you?"

"Apa, it may be tomorrow but I think not. I think we have some time although it may not be more than days."

"Will you return to university or stay with us?" Júlia asked, worried for her brother. "I am just as anxious to see change, but I'd rather we do this together. I'd rather you were home."

Erzsébet broke into the conversation sternly warning them.

"You will both need to be careful, watchful. Péter, especially you, be careful. Júlia might," Erzsébet turned to Júlia to emphasize her point before turning back to Péter, "I repeat, might, be spared that which you would not. There will be upheaval among the university students. Your father and I ask you, please, do not get mixed up in it but return directly home. You may, perhaps, find it better to walk when you arrive at the station. You will know. Be watchful. Return before there is trouble."

The next day Péter walked with Júlia to the Technical University of Budapest. They left the apartment early, it would take about an hour walking along the banks of the Danube; although there was a tram they wanted this time to talk.

"What do you think will happen, Júlia? Will the Technical University students support the demands?"

Júlia let out the breath she didn't know she was holding, then glanced behind them pretending to look at the boats on the river. No one was near although, off to the side, she could see Dr. Fürth walking in their direction.

"Péter, there is a large group of students ready to march. They have the demands, although I don't know from where. Everyone has been talking about the demands. I'm not certain what they are waiting for. I think," she paused as Dr. Fürth walked by without a word, not even glancing in their direction, obviously preoccupied, or at least pretending to be. "I think the citizens will support the students.

"My friends, Éva and Lilly, work in the university offices. Éva has said she believed something is going on, the tension is palpable. Éva lives on Váci Street and says it is the same there. Lilly agreed with Éva. She overheard something being said about the Hungarian Writer's Union being involved somehow. Lilly has only just moved to Pest a few years ago after being released from prison."

"From prison? Why was she imprisoned?"

"Actually, her name is Liliana. Liliana Fárkas. Her friends know her as Lilly." Júlia continued, "Her family published a newspaper, *Political Daily*. The entire family was labeled enemies of the state. She was held as a political prisoner for two years. Her parents were deported and have only just returned, to this no less. How Lilly ever found work at the University was a miracle. Éva, Éva Dunay, works in the same office with Lilly.

"And then there is my friend Charles. He has said there have been people talking in the cafés and shops near Dimitrov Square. Péter, I think you should come home as soon as possible. You can be of help here when the time comes."

"I will be home soon," Péter replied. "I will. I am going to see a friend first, do a quick errand, then return to school later today. I didn't want to say anything to Anya and Apa, I don't want them to expect me and then worry if I am late. Who knows what might happen. Transportation may be limited or stopped."

"When? When do you plan to return? I promise not to say anything."

"Monday. I will return Monday, that is the plan."

"The plan? Whose plan?"

"You know better than to ask. That's only your curiosity. Remember what Anya said, be careful."

Júlia and Péter arrived at the university just as it started to rain. They ran the last few steps hastily making their way indoors. There were only a few areas open. Classes were closed and would resume the next day. Everyone was watchful. It was difficult to determine who might be a threat, who might be listening. Júlia found a small group of friends and introduced Péter. They peppered him with questions and would've kept him longer but they all knew that would draw attention to each of them.

Too soon it was time for Péter to go. The tram to Blaha Juja Square was due, he had business there before returning to Szeged. A month or so ago his Nagypapa had asked for his help. There was something he had misplaced long ago, at some point nearing the end of the war, and yet hoped to find. He asked Péter to look in the basement of the apartment building the Kovács' family had lived in on Dohány Street. Péter had a friend who had recently moved into the old apartment building on Dohány Street, László Böjtös. Péter had spoken with Lászlo at a Petőfi Circle meeting and had said he would help. Last night Nagypapa reminded Péter of the request.

László was standing in front of the apartment building awaiting Péter's arrival. The two friends clasped each other's hand and kissed. László's wife, Klára, and their sons, Barnát and Izsák, were spending the afternoon with Klára's parents. László would join them later. László, eight years older than Péter, was an architect. He had met Péter at a Petőfi Circle meeting in Budapest earlier that summer. They had become fast friends. Klára and the boys liked and trusted him.

Now they were carefully descending the dimly lit stairs to the basement to look for something Péter's grandfather had lost. It seemed an improbable if not impossible task. The building had been heavily damaged when the Soviet forces liberated the area and then mostly demolished for reconstruction. The foundation and basement were original but the two men certainly could not imagine there would be anything left. They didn't even know what they were looking for. József Kovács had only told his grandson, "You will know it when you find it."

"How are your boys?" Péter asked as Lázlslo blindly searched in the darkness along the wall at the bottom of the stairs for the light switch.

"Both boys live up to their names. The young one, Izsák, is seldom serious. He makes all of us laugh. A very good-natured boy with many friends. There's another little boy and girl his age here in the apartment. Twins actually. Vadas, Tomi and Petra. They get along well at school.

"Barnát has grown since you saw him last. That was December, wasn't it? When we saw you at church?" At that moment, illustrating the point he had just made, the switch was found, the light came on. "Yes, well, Barnát is now nine and twice the size of his little brother although only two years older. I don't know where this comes from, not me!" They both laughed. László was average in height with a spare frame giving an overall appearance of being shorter than he actually was. "And strong! I tell you, that boy can do a man's work. They both have good minds and are kind. That is Klára's doing."

The two friends walked to the far end wall, each to the opposite corner, then began a series of slow passes, heads down, scrutinizing the dirt floor, meeting each other at the midpoint, adjusting their cadence as they worked to meet again at the midpoint on the next pass. By the time they had completed their search, almost an hour later, Péter was satisfied that he could assure his Nagypapa there was nothing to be found on the basement floor.

László insisted Péter follow him up to the apartment noting it would only take a few moments. Péter had told László of his plans for the morning; he would need to be at the station in half an hour to catch the train south to Szeged at 11:45. The trip to Szeged would take about three hours. László had assumed his friend had not had anything to eat since breakfast and knew from experience there would be nothing on the train.

Once inside the apartment, Péter asked, "If you don't mind my asking, how did all of you survive the war?"

László crossed the room to the small refrigerator retrieving a small paper bag as he answered, "It was Horthy," Lászlo paused then continued, "and the Jewish Council. Horthy had ordered the trains stopped. You learned of them, yes? The MAV 424 steam engines pulled a long line of German freight cars. They are outside of the city, in Taksony. The train graveyard is there. You can see them yet. Each train carried 1800 Jews from Budapest. A total of 19 trains were taken. Horthy put a stop to it on 6 July.

"However, a few days later Eichmann arranged for another train of 1,500 to be dispatched to Auschwitz. The Jewish Council informed Horthy, who had the train turned around. My parents were on that train. A few days later, Eichmann had the Jewish Council detained while he again ordered the camp to provide the same 1,500. They only found 1,200. The three hundred who managed not to be found included my parents.

"That, my friend, is how we all survived the war. "*Zachor*. Remember." László handed him the bag. "For you. You must live so that we all can live better."

Péter made it to the station on time. The black, double chimney, coal-fired, MAV engine spewed a trailing, sooty cloud across the countryside as they traveled south. The meal Klára and László had provided, although he'd gratefully accepted it, Péter hadn't thought he'd need. As usual, he'd felt the gnawing pangs of hunger only an hour into the trip.

The following morning Péter met again with the law professor and students of Szeged University to review what he had learned in Budapest. Péter recounted the meeting on Tuesday of the "official" communist student union, DISZ. The union had, as they had assumed, called for meetings at all universities on 22 October to hopefully quell the growing unrest of students on campuses across Hungary.

By early Monday afternoon Péter was on a train returning to Budapest in the company of one of the founding members of AHUCS at Szeged, Tamás Kiss. Péter had a plan, although it was not exactly what his mother had in mind. Péter was returning to Budapest. Erzsébet had specifically meant, of course, that he would return home.

It was Monday, 22 October, and the Fürths were distracted. Other than to confirm the meeting to be held the next day, Tuesday, at the university, there had been little news from either Erzsébet or Jeno Türea.

Returning home from the hospital along the cobbled streets of Budapest, Klári noted a group of young people. The four young men walking ahead of her turned off Margaret Bridge continuing on to Margaret Island. They were noticeable in their uniqueness. Each of the young men wore beautifully embroidered vests, boots, and carried knapsacks. She wondered after them, knowing it was not uncommon for people to sleep in the parks of Margaret Island.

Continuing home, Klári passed the Novák family as they crossed the bridge towards Pest. The Novák's lived in the apartment below the Fürths. Bence and Hanna, with their twin 12 year old boys, Ervin and Adrián, like most Hungarians, kept to themselves. Klári only briefly wondered what would become of them then quickly struck the thought from her mind. She would have nothing to do with premonition.

11

FLASHPOINT

ÉVA AND LILLY decided to walk to work that Tuesday morning. Approaching the tram station they had quickly ascertained it would take longer to ride the tram than walk. It was unusual, they agreed, to find the station overflowing with people. Even on a good day, it took about the same time to walk as to ride. The tram was a matter of convenience on inclement days, or respite after a long day on their feet. As many people walked as usually rode the tram. Today seemed different, there seemed to be so many more people.

The sun was shining and the weather had warmed to almost 66 degrees, very unusual for mid-October. Both women agreed it was a good day for a walk. As they passed the tram they noted most of the passengers crowded into the cars were students. Two young men jumped on just as the tram was leaving. There was barely room for them to precariously perch on the landing step and hold tight to the railings.

Although they had arrived early at the station, Péter and Tamás were almost too late. The gathering throng had filled the station and overflowed onto the streets. Almost as soon as they decided to walk, the singular "clunk" peculiar to the electrical box servicing the tram announced its departure. The electrical lines overhead hummed as the brake noisily released and the wheels ground traction with the rails. The men impulsively ran and jumped onto the last car. Although they had uncertain footing, they had a firm grasp on the handrails. Fortunately, the tram was especially slow that morning.

It was a beautiful day. An unencumbered view afforded a welcome distraction from the uncertain task imminently before them. During the brief ride Péter noted some of the points of interest and features of the city and landscape. Tamás had never had the opportunity to visit Budapest and listened with interest. Péter pointed to the imposing neo-Renaissance Opera House, its muti-tiered and spired, columned exterior prominent above the city roofline. The National Museum, the Synagogue, and the Parliament Building were easily identified, magnificent examples of Budapest's storied architectural heritage.

Ahead of them, Péter pointed across the Danube to the three hills of Buda.

"There, to the right, is Rózsa, primarily residential. Gellért is straight ahead, there," Péter indicated with his hand. "And here, to the left, is Castle. Castle was so named for Buda Castle, where Budapest was founded. Remnants of Roman baths and ancient dwellings are found among these hills."

Crossing the river, Péter named the bridges of Budapest beginning on the right. Margaret Bridge, connected Margaret Island mid-channel. Chain Bridge, the first, largest, and guarded by stone lions at either entrance, and Erzsébet. The tram they were riding started across the shortest of the bridges, the Freedom Bridge, also known as Liberty Bridge. Perhaps Budapest's most beautiful bridge, the Freedom Bridge was noted for its green color and Art Nouveau style. The last bridge, Petöfi, was to their left. As the tram crossed Freedom Bridge Péter gestured for Tamás to look up. Above them bronze statues of the Hungarian mythological falcon, Turul, surmounted both pillars at each end of the bridge.

Arrived at Gellért Station the travelers, primarily students, poured out of the tram cars onto Gellért Square. Disembarking, the crowd walked in the direction of the university. Péter and Tamás walked in apprehensive silence toward the university.

Entering the building, their attention was immediately drawn to a group of boys. Obviously from the country, the boys wore pants tucked into embroidered boots, loose shirts and vests, and each carried a rucksack. The boys were being questioned by a student union member. Tamás approached the group, listened to the conversation, and ascertained the difficulty being their student status. Interrupting the conversation, Tamás asked that the boys be allowed entry. Péter watched, impressed with the boys earnest manner. Curious about their rural clothing, Péter was about to ask the boys where they had traveled from when he heard his name called from across the entry. It was Júlia.

Júlia had been speaking with one of the organizers of the meeting, Gábor Tánczos, when Éva and Lilly entered the building. Spying Júlia amid the crowd they made their way across the crowded room. As they approached, the two women could easily overhear Júlia and Gábor in earnest conversation.

"We cannot have a confrontation here," Júlia began but was interrupted. One of the nearby students, a third year student named Márton Voros, spoke up, "Let us be clear in our purpose, we are only meeting today to determine whether to withdraw from DISZ, nothing else."

"Yes, so you've said. But look around you," Júlia motioned with her hand, "There are so many more than we anticipated much less expected. We must be informative and lead."

"This is a non-violent protest. It must be," Márton added.

Éva and Lilly were standing behind Júlia who hadn't yet realized they were there. As Éva spoke her friend's name, Júlia looked up, but before she could turn around she saw Péter just as he entered the building. Júlia, instantly relieved and exhilarated, called out to him only to immediately recoil, regretting her action. Júlia knew he'd later remind her, again, not to call attention to themselves. Turning, Júlia warmly greeted her friends relieved for the emotional support they provided simply by their presence.

Péter, momentarily distracted by a group of boys, crossed the ever-increasingly congested room with Tamás closely following. Introductions made, Éva and Lilly wordlessly noted that these were the same men they'd seen not long ago on the tram. From previous discussions with Júlia, they had known something of her brother, but had never previously met him. They had certainly not expected to see him today. Neither, it seemed, had Júlia.

The meeting was about to start, everyone had found a seat. The outside entry doors had been closed. Not long after, another tram arrived from which alighted a young woman with a long dark braid. Walking up to the front doors of the university and finding them locked, she rapped her knuckles against the doors but without response. There was such a great noise inside that she realized no one who could possibly hear her knocking. Walking back to Gellért Square, the square she had just crossed, she contented herself to wait.

The Aula, the ceremonial space of the university, had filled to overflowing. Five thousand students sat and stood wherever room allowed. Entering the space, Tamás and Péter spoke with Márton asking permission to speak to the assembly. Overheard, word quickly spread in the Aula. Soon the students were chanting, demanding that Tamás Kiss be allowed to speak.

The Party secretary, Mrs. Orbán, appeared, ascending the steps to the platform. Walking directly to the microphone she admonished the assemblage, screaming, "You have only one duty! Your duty is to study! You don't want the AHUCS of Szeged! You don't want any ideas from Szeged!"[1]

Armed members of the military marched onto the platform. The room was tense. Quite suddenly, a fifth-year architecture student, Jancsi Danner, stood. A commanding figure at over six feet tall and blond, Danner yelled, 'Let him speak!" Danner continued to stand, unmoving, red, and trembling. No one could believe what they had just witnessed. To speak out, as he had, risked imprisonment or death.

The silence gradually gave way to a growing unrest when suddenly, one of Tamás' classmates from Szeged, Laci Zsindely, started to clap. Others around her joined in and soon the Aula resonated with thunderous applause. Never before confronted with such behavior and having no experience as to how to conduct such a meeting, the attending staff and the communist party officials simply left. Tamás stood at the microphone and began, "Fellow students! Hungarians!" The resulting applause was deafening.

In the ensuing discussion there was immediate consensus in abolishing the communist youth union, DISZ, and establishing a Hungarian Student Union. Tamás then lead the discussion and debate over each of the points on the list of demands. During the debate another student, András Bálint, asked why Soviet troops were still stationed in Hungary. In answer, another student rose and yelled, "Russians go home! *Ruszkik haza!*" The Aula was soon resonating with the chant of 5,000 men and women, "*Ruszkik haza! Ruszkik haza!*"

When the assemblage quieted and discussion continued, it was announced that the Hungarian Writers Union would march to Bem Square the following day, Tuesday, 23 October. At the square they would place a crown near the statue of Polish General war hero, Jözef Bem. The march would be in support of the working people of Poland who were currently suffering in their appeals to their government for basic human rights. Tamás raised his voice to emphasize the salient points: that the striving, and the suffering, of the people in Poland were no different than that of Hungarians.

"Workers in Poland have been demonstrating, asking their government for no more than better living conditions. Access to food and to shelter, for heat, for better working conditions, and lower production quotas. For bread! There were riots. People were killed by demonstrators. The next day the police were sent to crush the uprising. A hundred were killed, more were injured. Our demands on our government must be peaceful, we must be in earnest."

By midnight the students had decided on two primary objectives: a demonstration parallel with the Writers Union in support of the Polish people, and a list of 16 demands addressing the political, social, and economic needs and concerns of the Hungarian people. The demands included personal freedoms and the immediate evacuation of all Soviet troops in conformity with the 1947 Peace Treaty. They asked for the removal of the statue of Stalin as quickly as possible and a new government constituted under the direction of Imre Nagy. They also asked for the replacement of all emblems foreign to the Hungarian people with traditional Hungarian symbols.[2] They wanted it known, and respected, that they stood in solidarity with the workers and students of Poland. Importantly, they wanted their government to know that they wanted to work with them, not against them.

The enormity and weight of both their involvement and their decisions were not lost on any one of the participants. At a time when expressing an opinion, discussing politics, or listening to an unapproved radio station resulted in certain punishment if not imprisonment or death, a protest march was incomprehensible.

It was late in the night when the assemblage left the university flowing into the streets of Budapest. They felt more enlivened, hopeful, and energized than they had ever felt before. Several small groups left together having volunteered to make stenciled copies of what many were referring to as *the manifesto*, the 16 demands. The copies would then be posted throughout Budapest on trees and lamp posts. Other groups were off into the night to secure and outfit vans with loudspeakers. In the morning the students meant to awaken the city and countryside with news of the demonstration.

As Péter turned to leave, his attention was taken by the group of country boys he'd seen earlier in the day. They emerged from the building and, seeing Péter, exchanged raised hands in salutation. The boys faces were bright and determined in the glow of the street lamps. Suddenly, surprisingly, Péter witnessed a very beautiful young woman run up to the boys, hugging each of them. The girl was wearing a head scarf and dress over which she wore a beautifully embroidered vest and apron and had a rucksack similar to those the boys carried. Distracted for the moment, he finally heard Júlia.

"Péter. Péter!" she repeated insistently, "Who are those boys? Do you know them? Who is that beautiful girl?"

Péter turned his attention to Júlia. "They're just some boys I met tonight. I'm guessing that's their sister. Let's go."

Júlia, before saying goodbye to her friends, arranged to meet Éva and Lilly the next day at Bem Square.

"Péter, you and Tamás will come back to the apartment? Yes? You can't say no. You know you can't! I'm certain our parents are anxious. I thought I'd be home long before this and had told them as much. Seeing you will take some of the attention off of me. Please? You must. I couldn't possibly keep it from them that you're in Budapest. Tamás, you'd be welcome. Besides, Bem Square is very near our home."

The three friends walked back along the Danube to the Türea apartment on Rózsa Hill. Although it was getting late, they had some confidence in the company of the many hundreds of fellow students and the absence, they thought, of any police. Along the way, looking across the river, Tamás was thoughtful.

"Is this area of the Danube, the rumored infamous site of WWII?"

Slowly nodding her head, Júlia whispered in response, "The Arrow Cross militiamen. Yes. Hungarians murdering Hungarians. 3,500 men, women, and children. Eight hundred of them Jewish. Stripped naked then shot in the back. All that was left were their clothes and shoes at the edge."

Júlia felt sickened, sickened as she always was when walking by this place. Júlia usually chose to walk on the other side of the Danube. Here, in this place, she sometimes felt more than heard the echoes of cries and gunshots. Gooseflesh would raise unbidden on her arms and, sometimes, tears. Now, with the impending demonstration and the work ahead, she felt she was doing something for all these lives lost, for what Hungary had suffered. She believed the time had arrived for the Hungarian people to reclaim Hungary. She must focus on the work that lay ahead, it would require courage. Júlia found it unnerving if she let her mind wander.

Arrived home well after midnight, the three young people were met by a solemn group. Their parents and grandparents were relieved to see Júlia and surprised to see Péter. Pleased but curious to meet Tamás, Jeno stepped forward and welcomed him to their home. The tenor of the room, only momentarily changed, reverted to serious concern. Everyone knew about the student meeting. That it went so long into the night seemed to portend trouble. That they weren't arrested was cause to celebrate. But, it was late, and now the news that there would be a demonstration in the morning. It was too much and already far too late for Gizella and József. Content that their grandchildren were safely home, they went to bed.

"Tomorrow is another day, may we all live to see it," Gizella quietly but earnestly muttered before turning to follow József to their bedroom.

12

STUDENT DEMONSTRATION

23 October 1956

THE NEXT MORNING was beautiful, sunny and dry, and very unusual for October. A flock of Bohemian waxwings had settled in the ancient black pine trees on Margit Island in the early morning. Their high pitched trills had awakened the group of boys sleeping below. The András brothers, Dávid, Péter, and Jani, and their neighbor and friend Dominik Marton crawled out from under the trees where they'd spent the night. Stretching out across the grass, they luxuriated in the warmth of the sunlight. Nearby, a flock of song thrushes had been whispering in the high branches. Disturbed by the boys, the thrushes set up their harsh alarm call, a dry chattering *krrrr*. At the sound of the alarm, other nearby birds took flight. A pair of magpies and a small flock of hooded crows were most particularly perturbed. Hopping from branch to branch they pointedly, crankily croaked their disapproval.

Yesterday, the boys had walked along the Danube and explored some of Budapest. They had marveled at the city, the cobbled streets, the Danube, and the enormous, elaborately beautiful stone buildings. Crossing the river, they were overwhelmed with the view from Castle Hill. There, the youngest, Péter and Jani, had been especially interested in the medieval ruins. The boys had heard rumors while they walked, whispers at first, then open remarks. It seemed as if the people were growing unafraid of the secret police.

By early afternoon the boys' knapsacks were empty. Descending from the hills and crossing the Danube into Pest, they found a market and purchased crackers, bread, szalámi, cheese, and fruit. While there, they overheard two young men talking about a student meeting. Péter stepped forward introducing himself to the young men before questioning them. The overheard meeting was indeed the student union meeting being held at the Technical University late that very same afternoon. Dávid had been listening and seized the opportunity at a momentary lull in the conversation to ask if the students knew the location of Kistarcsa Prison. The two young men exchanged glances and then leaned over, whispering, telling all of the boys to keep such questions to themselves when they are in public spaces. Dominik felt rebuked and a little insulted. He was, after all, 16 and Dávid was almost 15. The students weren't that much older. Besides, both he and Dávid were as tall and, apprising the students stature, definitely stronger.

The boys had left and walked to Géllert Square where they waited the remainder of the afternoon. It had been interesting watching as tram after tram disgorged a mixed multitude of students and workers. The growing assemblage was a combination of men, women, and children of about their age, some much younger and a few older. The boys had never seen so many people and never so many in one place. Sitting on benches along the outside perimeter of the square, the boys rummaged through their knapsacks for a snack. Not long after, noticing the crowd beginning to move into the university, they had followed. Crossing the threshold they were met and stopped by a subtly uniformed guard and questioned.

"One moment, please. Are you university students?"

At that moment, two men entered nearby who seemed to take an interest in their group. As the men approached, Péter and Jani judiciously stepped back in apprehension. The boys saw no malice in their open faces and looked on with interest as the two men calmly, briefly questioned the guard. The two strangers cast another glance at the boys then turned to the guard.

"Let them in. They are the future of Hungary."

The meeting had been unlike anything the boys had ever experienced. They found being in the Aula with so many people both exhilarating and overwhelming. Those feelings were soon dispelled when the assemblage began to chant and grew in intensity, "*Ruszkik haza! Ruszkik haza!*" The boys chanted, they yelled, they unabashedly shed tears, so fervent was their hatred for the government that had taken their fathers. They stood, raising their arms and waving them with each chant, "*Ruszkik haza! Ruszkik haza!*" By the end of the evening they were exhausted.

Leaving the university at midnight, the boys were happily surprised to see the men who had helped them gain entry. They held their hands up in acknowledgment only at that very moment to be nearly knocked to the ground. Rebeka, without warning and at a run, had appeared from the obscurity of the crowd and flung her arms around them. For Rebeka, it was an emotional reunion. Relief and surprise combined into giddy laughter among the boys. Péter and Jani clung to her, a closeness she welcomed.

Once the flurry of questions and answers had subsided, the boys told Rebeka where they were staying. Together, they walked back along the Danube to Margit Island. Jani and Péter, walking on either side of Rebeka, each took one of her hands into their own.

Dominik and Dávid recounted the highlights of the meeting and the particulars of the demonstration planned for the next morning. Dávid was uncharacteristically aloof towards her, which concerned Rebeka knowing this usually meant he had something on his mind. No, he told her somberly, they would not be going home. Not yet.

Tuesday morning, rising early from under the trees, scattering a flock of siskins that had settled there, the travelers awoke to an abnormally warm October day. Dominik walked with Rebeka across Margit Bridge to a pastry shop where they selected fresh bread, apples, and milk for the group. Returning across the bridge, Rebeka had paused to admire three mergansers swimming along the edge of the river. Looking up, admiring the beautiful city, she realized Dominik had continued on without her and hurried to catch up. The three brothers smiled and waved when they saw Rebeka emerge from behind a copse of sycamore trees. Rebeka was flush with happiness to be reunited with them. Together they sat on the lawn and ate, talking about all they had seen. Hooded crows had been watching from branches high above Rebeka and the boys. The birds effortlessly glided to the ground and then, like sentries, paraded back and forth awaiting their turn for any bits and crumbs that might be left. It was almost noon and the temperature had risen to a very comfortable 70 degrees when they decided to walk to Bem Square.

A short distance from Margit Bridge, the children were surprised to find other people already gathered at the square. They walked across the square, admired the statue of Józef Bem, then sat at the periphery of the square on a garden wall. Quietly they watched as more people began to arrive. Nearby sat two boys about Péter and Jani's age. Each group of children nodded acknowledgment to the other. The new boys extended their hands as they introduced themselves, "I am Novák Ervin and this is my twin, Novák Adrián. We live just there," Ervin turned, pointing in the direction of the apartment building. “Where are you from?” It was obvious to the twins that this group was not from Budapest. Their clothes, their handsome boots, their hair. They had never met anyone not from Budapest.

“Oh, you’re correct,” their new friends quickly obliged sensing the boys curiosity. “We came by train from a village near Lake Balaton where we had learned of the demonstration. Our fathers were arrested, for no known reason, they’re farmers. We are here hoping they will be released.” The Novák boys nodded knowingly, empathetically, in acknowledgment of this information. It was unnerving, really, the possibility of your father being arrested. They had heard such rumors but they had never actually met anyone who had suffered this experience.

Dávid gave them a sideways glance after looking around the square then lowered his voice and asked, “Do you happen to know where Kistarcsa Prison is located?”

The twins looked at each other and shook their heads. “Not exactly, no,” Ervin replied.

Adrián added, “It’s northwest of here at the edge of the city, it’s not too far. We’ve never been there, or even near there, but we’ve heard of it.”

Through the entirety of this discussion Rebeka had bit her lip. It was taking every effort on her part to be patient with her brothers. As soon as this demonstration was over she was going to do her best to reason that they must return home as their mother and grandparents requested.

The group of sudden friends turned to watch as more people gathered around the outlying area of the square, uncertain of what would happen. To a person, they had no experience with demonstrations. Neither did they have long to wait. From their vantage point a sort of humming could indistinctly be heard and soon began to attract their attention. Being unfamiliar with the sounds of a city, the children at first didn't realize the sound was unusual. As the humming grew in intensity it first attracted then riveted their gaze on its source.

Earlier that morning, Éva and Lilly had met Júlia, Péter, and Tamás at the Buda side of the Margit Bridge. They watched as the Novák twins from the Fürth's apartment building walked by in the direction of Bem Square. Many people were milling about on both sides of the river.

Péter spoke up, "Tamás and I are going to march with the students from Eötvös Lorand Science University. I have a friend from Petőfi I am meeting there, Böjtös László. You are welcome to join us, otherwise we'll meet up with you at the university."

The group instead decided to split up. Éva and Lilly followed Júlia to the Technical University. Júlia had promised she would help lead the march with her friend Gábor and carry the Hungarian flag. Crossing the bridge, Péter and Tamás found papers in the street and littering the sidewalk. Stooping to pick one up, Tamás exclaimed, "It's the manifesto, the 16 Points!" At that moment, a boy walked by pressing a copy of Free People, the national daily paper of the communist party, into their hands. They both stood, scanning the article, not immediately noticing the increasing number of people moving into the area and crossing the bridge to the Buda side.

"This is unbelievable," Péter remarked incredulously. "They are welcoming the "politicizing youth" of Hungary as partners in the struggle to democratize socialism. They are endorsing most of the demands! And here, look at this! They have published the Hungarian Writer's Union support of us. And here," Péter jabbed a finger into the paper, "they have published that the demonstration is to take place today at 3 p.m. This is unbelievable."

The two men hastened their footsteps continuing in the direction of the Science University. Along the way they passed the National Museum, where they met László, and then on to Szerb

Street. László spoke as they walked.

"You've seen the fliers? The newspapers refused to print the manifesto so students have been up all night plastering the city with them. The vans outfitted with loudspeakers have been broadcasting all over the city and countryside since first light. People are pouring into the city to join the march. Just wait, you'll see.

"I've also had word that Nagy has come out against the demonstration. He fears that we are jeopardizing the gains already made. He thinks that the events in Poland and Rákosi being recalled to Moscow will result in Moscow continuing the reforms of 1953." László was interrupted as he noticed the approach of two young men, one who was beckoning. "Who is that? There's a man there," László indicated with a nod of his head and one arm gesturing in the direction of Kálvin Square, "calling out to you, Péter."

Walking toward them, breathless, was a friend of Péter's from high school.

"Vari Márkó! Hello! Are you going to the demonstration? Yes? Walk with us. Please, join us!"

Márkó joined in step with the three other men as he introduced them to his friend Denes Stollar. Márkó relayed what he had just learned from his brother-in-law, László, who worked with his brother Andy at a factory in a Budapest suburb some distance from the city.

"They found the manifesto and learned of the demonstration. They were able to talk their way into a pass to come and witness the demonstration. However," he continued, repressing a laugh, "they did say their master "sternly" advised they not march and not to get into any trouble. László and Andy are certain the factory workers will join us as soon as they are off their shift at three. Have you had any word of the AVO?"

Péter told Márkó what they had learned from the morning newspaper. With the demonstration sanctioned there was hope that there wouldn't be police. As the men turned the corner approaching Szerb Street they ran into a great crowd of people. Many among the crowd either knew László or recognized Tamás and Péter from the meeting of the previous night. A cheer erupted and passed through the crowd, continued down the street, then echoed into the distance. The men's faces reflected their surprise as they looked at each other. There were already far more people than they had imagined and they weren't all university students. Among the crowd were boys, working women, and men, some aged. Until that moment, without realizing it the students were at the center of an uprising.

Márkó spoke up to be heard over the steadily increasing cacophony, "Péter, on the way here I spoke with my old classmate, Fodor Andrew. He's a cadet with the HPA. He told me that he overheard the officers talking; orders from the highest command are to remain loyal to Hungary. It's his opinion that we won't have any trouble with the army today."

Péter nodded in response. "Good. The demonstration begins at three. We arranged to meet the Technical University students after we cross the bridge to walk to Bem Square. The demonstration has already outgrown this area. I suggest we start. First to the National Museum, then to Kálvin Square, some will certainly detour to Petöfi, and then, for the bridge?" Péter offered. Everyone agreed.

13

THE MARCH

THERE HAD BEEN no appointed leader. Instead, the men worked together. Turning to walk ahead of the group of demonstrators, two men carrying Hungarian flags ran up from behind. László knew them by name, two fellow members of the Pëtofi Circle, and called to them to lead the way.

"Gergö! Rami! Let's begin. Step in behind Jónás and Ottó carrying the wreath. Lead us to the National Museum! From there to Kálvin Square and then on to Freedom Bridge!"

At the museum, Péter stepped up onto a bench above the gathered crowd and spoke. "We are here today not to defeat Communism and not in violent insurrection. No. We are here as Hungarians, representing Hungarians. We are here in peaceful demonstration for reforms representing our traditional Hungarian values, Hungarian beliefs, Hungarian ideals." Péter continued, pausing between each point, "This is what we stand for. This is our goal. This is why we are here today. This is why we march!" Péter had the crowd's unflagging support, cheering unceasingly as he spoke, raising their arms in a collective show of unanimity.

Péter went on to outline the course of the demonstration and the day's events. The assembly would walk to Kálvin Square and then continue, crossing Freedom Bridge, where they would join the students from Technical University at Gellért Square. From there they would continue to Bem Square.

Péter stood for a few minutes allowing the assembled people to vent their energy then motioned for silence as he introduced his friend Péter Veres. A communist and member of the Writer's Union, a former Defense Minister, a prosecuted politician and a writer, Péter Veres would read the manifesto to the crowd. The crowd again cheered and both men, understanding the visceral emptiness, need, and repression felt by their fellow Hungarians, stepped back and again waited for the assembly to release and revel in their emotions.

When Péter Veres alone stepped forward to the microphone it had the effect of quieting the crowd who were now ready and hungry for him to speak. Veres began, "My fellow countrymen, my fellow Hungarians..." after which he could only wait for several more minutes for the crowd to quiet before going on to read the manifesto. Again, as each point of the manifesto was read, the crowd erupted in cheers, waving flags and banners. When he had finished, Veres gave the crowd time for their enthusiasm and excitement to calm. It was soon evident that expectation was hopeless. They were ready and readying themselves as an athlete before a competition. Every action they were taking, their words, their show of support, and their assembly put them in danger of being arrested or worse. The cheering came from their heart, their soul, and to overcome their fear.

Finally, Veres spoke as loudly as he could manage. "Before we go, let us remember the words of our great poet, Sándor Petőfi.

Let us carry his words with us today. Let us have courage." The gathered throng quieted then and joined Veres in reciting in earnest the familiar and venerated words known by all present.

"Rise up, Magyar, the country calls!
It's 'now or never' what fate befalls...
Shall we live as slaves or free men?
That's the question—choose your 'Amen'!
God of Hungarians,
  we swear unto Thee,
We swear unto Thee—that slaves we shall
  no longer be!"

A roar of approval went up from the crowd. As the march restarted toward the river the students began to chant, "This we swear, this we swear, that we will no longer be slaves." The demonstration grew as they walked. The initial group of students was joined by increasing numbers of people and workers from all across Budapest. All along the way, demonstrators called out, "If you are a Hungarian, join us!"

Although not yet three in the afternoon, when the first shift would be let off for the day, people were leaving their homes and work to join the demonstration as the march continued in the direction of the Freedom Bridge. Hungarians joining the demonstration walked parallel to the students on the sidewalk until all available space was filled along the street as they walked. As the demonstration swelled so too did the shouts of approval and encouragement. People were waving flags and handkerchiefs from the windows of offices, factories, and apartment buildings. Anyone standing along the streets who didn't join the march cheered and applauded. Men tipped their hats, and both men and women dabbed at the tears on their cheeks before darting out of the way as the approaching demonstration marched by.

The demonstration crossed the inspiring Freedom Bridge in orderly rows of eight to ten abreast, arm in arm. Continuing along the Danube, their number steadily increased then swelled to tens of thousands as they briefly paused and melded with the students from the Technical University. All along the way they were continuously joined by groups of citizens. They carried pro-communist banners and demanded a more civilized society, humane treatment, and to abide by the tenants of socialism. Hungarian songs were interspersed with the crowd chanting a refrain from the censored Petöfi poem, "This we swear, this we swear, that we will no longer be slaves."

Péter, seeing Júlia join the rank of flag bearers at the front of the procession, quickened his step moving up to walk behind her, tapping her shoulder as he did so. Júlia turned her head and then called back to him over the roar of the demonstration.

"Have you seen who has joined us, there, right behind you?" she asked, her features animated, her eyes sparkling with excitement.

Péter momentarily turned to look then returned a surprised but satisfied look and momentary nod of his head at Júlia.

"The members and leadership of DISZ, yes. I spoke with them this morning when Éva, Lilly, and I first arrived. They were already at the University, waiting." Júlia paused to readjust the metal cup she had improvised on her belt to support the flagpole. She continued, "They had decided to ignore the Political Committee's ban of the demonstration, especially when they learned about the workers this morning. It seems that many of the workers and laborers support us. DISZ doesn't want to lose influence with the student body."

"Yes," Péter raised his voice to be heard, "yes! I've only just heard the same this morning. There's talk of workers joining the demonstration after the first shift."

"There's more," Júlia returned, slightly turning her head back to Péter hoping her voice would carry. "Students at the military academies have also pledged their support."

This was especially good news and supported what Márkó had said earlier. The military and officer schools were the basis of Budapest's security forces. Péter felt hopeful that violence would be avoided. From the beginning this was meant to be a peaceful demonstration. Continuing towards Bem Square, the jubilant crowd, buoyant with the heady thought of freedom, were singing old folk songs and the Hungarian national anthem, Kossuth.

All Hungarians revere Lajos Kossuth, father of the Hungarian nation and hero of the 1848 Hungarian Revolution. Béla Bartók's symphonic poem, Kossuth, spontaneously erupted from the crowd and intensified their fervor as they increasingly emphasized the phrase:

"Long live Hungarian freedom
Long live the homeland!"

"Look, Júlia, there to your right. Look!" Péter pointed in the direction of an apartment building. The motion attracted the attention of demonstrators in a rippling effect from the front to the rear of the column. There, waving as he stood on a balcony looking down upon the demonstrators, was the widely respected composer, Zoltán Kodály. A linguist, philosopher, and pedagogue, Kodály was now nearing 74 years old. Well-known and admired for his work in collecting, recording, and conserving traditional Hungarian folk songs, he was also dedicated to children's music education. As a composer, Kodály's perhaps most famous work, the Psalmus Hungaricus, was created in 1923 for the fiftieth anniversary of the union of Buda, Pest, and Óbuda forming Budapest. The performance was conducted by his lifelong friend, Béla Bartók. And now, the old gentleman was waving to the demonstrators.

All Hungarians knew of his disdain for the government. Kodály's support meant a great deal to every one of the upturned faces who now applauded him as he stood upon the balcony smiling down on them.

"Péter, I cannot believe this day!" Júlia's scalp was tingling with adrenaline. She was a little unsettled and concerned at the enormity of the crowd she led. Thoughts were racing through her mind, including her anticipated excitement in relating to her parents the appearance of Kodály, the anticipation of events at Bem Square, and wondering how they would have the crowd disperse when they finished there.

The demonstration numbered 40,000 and was still growing. The massive stone suspension bridge, Chain Bridge, the first bridge to link Buda and Pest, now lay just ahead of the march. Castle Hill and the Tunnel were on their left. Júlia called out to Péter, "We pass the lions, the guards of the bridgehead, just as the first to cross the bridge!"

Tamás, walking between Péter and László, turned inquiringly towards Péter.

"The soldiers of the Hungarian Army of Independence! They were the first to cross this bridge!" Péter loudly explained to be heard over the following crowd.

Everyone within hearing cheered.

The communist authorities, quite unexpectedly and quite quickly, found themselves in a precarious situation. Without the military schools, without the local police, with the reliability of the army even in doubt, that left only the ÁVH, the State Protection Authority, to rely upon. Their numbers were insufficient to quell much less crush the growing demonstration. This is why the defense minister, István Bata, had lifted the ban.

"Call Budapest Radio and tell them to report that the party recognizes the demonstration. Soldiers are allowed to attend, unarmed, as citizens. They are not to congregate with their units. Also ask that all party organizations take part. Do not tell them why. We must do all we can to prevent the student demands from spreading."

Bata was too late, word had already spread.

Soon the multitude, which now numbered 50,000, came into view of all who had been gathering at Bem Square. The András boys, Rebeka, Dominik Morton, and, sitting nearby, the Novák twins let out a collective gasp. Rising to their feet, they gave voice to an enthusiastic cheer as did everyone else already gathered at the square.

The demonstration filled the area before backing up along the Danube and into the side streets. People in their apartments on Rózsa Hill were at their windows looking out over the gathering. In the Türea apartment, Gizella had turned on their Grundig short wave radio. Radio Budapest was reporting the student march in solidarity with Polish students. Then to her great relief, they announced that Sándor Kopácsi, the Budapest chief of police, would not use armed force against peaceful demonstrators. The crowd had swelled to 60,000 and were singing the Hungarian National Anthem, banned for the past decade under the Communist government, which raised the fervor of the crowd

Suddenly, there was yelling across the square followed by a roar erupting from the growing multitude. There, high over the square for all to see, leaning out from a casement window, a woman waving a Hungarian flag with a hole in the center. The round medallion bearing the communist coat of arms, the hated hammer and sickle, had been raggedly cut out leaving only the tricolor red, white, and green of the traditional Hungarian flag; red for strength, white for faithfulness, and green for hope. In its newly altered state, the "hole in the flag" became the symbol of the revolution. Sixty thousand voices again began to sing the Hungarian National Anthem.

"O, my God, the Magyar bless
With thy plenty and good cheer!
With Thine aid in just cause press,
Where his foes to fight appear..."

The university students crowded around the base of the József Bem statue. As planned, a group of women stepped through the crowd and laid wreaths next to the crown that a member of the Petöfi Circle, Péter's friend László Böjtös, had just placed. Everyone's attention was then drawn to Péter Veres, who stood on top of a car, loudspeaker in hand, and read from the manifesto to the steadily growing crowd.

"We are here today in peaceful protest, not in defiance, demanding of our government that which they have promised; that which we have long asked for, patiently waited for, and have endured hardships for far too long.

"We call for the immediate evacuation of all Soviet troops, in conformity with the provisions of the Peace Treaty.

"The election by secret ballot of all Party members from top to bottom; new officers for the lower, middle and upper echelons of the Hungarian Workers Party.

"A new Government must be constituted under the direction of Imre Nagy: all criminal leaders of the Stalin-Rákosi era must be immediately dismissed.

"We demand public inquiry into the criminal activities of Mihály Fárkas and his accomplice Mátyás Rákosi.

"That general elections by universal, secret ballot are held throughout the country; the right of workers to strike be recognized.

"The revision and re-adjustment of Hungarian-Soviet and Hungarian-Yugoslav relations in the fields of politics, economics, and cultural affairs.

"The complete reorganization of Hungary's economic life.

"That foreign trade agreements and the exact total of reparations be made public; informed of the uranium deposits in our country; Hungary have the right to sell her uranium freely at world market prices.

"The revision of the norms operating in industry and an immediate and radical adjustment of salaries, a living wage.

"The system of distribution be organized on a new basis and that agricultural products be utilized in rational manner; equality of treatment for individual farms.

"Reviews by independent tribunals of all political and economic trials; release and rehabilitation of the innocent; immediate repatriation of prisoners of war and of civilian deportees.

"Complete recognition of freedom of opinion and of expression, of freedom of the press and of radio, as well as the creation of a daily newspaper for the MEFESZ.

"That the statue of Stalin, symbol of Stalinist tyranny and political oppression, be removed as quickly as possible.

"The replacement of emblems foreign to the Hungarian people by the old Hungarian arms of Kossuth; new uniforms for the Army which conform to national traditions; 15 March declared a national holiday; 6 October a day of national mourning on which schools will be closed.

"Solidarity with the workers and students of Warsaw and Poland in their movement towards national independence.

"And to organize as rapidly as possible local branches of AHUCS."[3]

As Veres read each of the 16 Points, the roar of the crowd became increasingly louder. The response to the removal of the statue of Stalin was deafening. The assembly overflowed the square and into the surrounding streets and neighborhoods. Onlookers crowded onto balconies and in the windows of homes, offices, and official buildings. The assembly and onlookers together sang the national anthem, their united voices rising to the last stanza. Rebeka, and all the boys, jumped down from the wall where they had earlier perched and proudly raised their voices in unison with all those gathered near.

> *"Pity, O Lord, the Hungarian,*
> *Who is tossed about by calamity,*
> *Extend to him a guarding arm*
> *On the sea of his suffering,*
> *To those long torn by ill fate*
> *Bring a cheerful year,*
> *This people has already paid for the sins*
> *Of the past and future!"*

14

KOSSUTH SQUARE

EMBOLDENED BY THEIR camaraderie, their unified vision for Hungary, and their sheer numbers, the demonstrators sought an outlet for their energy and passion. They sought to have their singular voice heard. From no directive in particular, the crowd turned and marched toward Parliament.

Before Rebeka could do or say anything, the boys were off with the multitude. Rebeka stood, momentarily transfixed in a numbing fog of uncertainty and disbelief. The diminishing figures of her brothers triggered a reaction, a compulsion action. Rebeka ran to catch up, squeezing through the crowd, until she was once again next to her brothers. She took Jani's hand and was grateful when he held hers and squeezed it tightly. Péter noticed and took her other hand in his saying, as he did so, "Don't worry, we'll go home after this." Rebeka, uncertain of what Péter had said, the crowd had grown larger and louder, felt confident he'd said they were going home. Rebeka, smiling at her brothers, squeezed their hands in relief.

Walking in the direction of the Margit Bridge, people continued to join the movement. They came on foot, by car, and by the truckload as office and factory workers came off shift. Lázló and Andy Fülöp, their work passes in hand, had earlier arrived downtown where they had been searching for the demonstration. Walking down Körút Road and then back to Rákóczi Avenue, they stepped onto a streetcar in the direction of Petőfi Square. From there they crossed Liberty Bridge and followed the river to Bem Square.

"Look at this, can you believe it?" Andy asked his brother as they passed trucks with DISZ painted side panels. The brothers looked on in disbelief as the young people were cheering, handing out leaflets, and flinging them haphazardly into the sky.

"Look!" Lázló excitedly pointed ahead at the column of students marching in the direction of Margit Bridge. "Let's join them!"

Andy looked at his older brother in astonishment. "Are you nuts? The master said not to march and *not*," Andy emphasized, "not, to get into any trouble! We could lose our jobs, brother. Besides, we aren't even university students, are we?" Andy noted his brother's seemingly total absorption in the events transpiring before them. "Lázló, I'm serious. We promised!"

"Listen to them, Andy! "Hungarians, march with us!" That's us! Let's go!"

Without a backward glance at his brother, Lázló was away at a run to join the march. Andy stood, momentarily shocked in a wordless struggle, deciding what he should do. The increasing distance separating him from Lázló resolved the question. Jumping from the streetcar, Andy sprinted to catch up with his brother before they both melded into the growing throng. Andy pulled on Lázló's sleeve and indicated with a crook of his thumb in the direction away from the center of the throng. Making their way to the outside margin of the column, Andy looked visibly relieved.

"That was claustrophobic, Lázló!"

A woman marching next to Lázló held out two small flags to the brothers before turning to the group of young people in front of them. To each she handed the same green, white, and red tricolor flags to wave. Everyone raised their flag as high as they could reach, triumphantly waving it. Each person marching was incredulous at where they were and what they were doing. Not one of them could have ever imagined it.

Júlia and the other flag bearers, each now carrying a revolutionary flag with a hole in the middle, were the first to cross the bridge. Dominik, the András siblings, and the Novák twins, Adrián and Ervin, had kept together moving to the outside edge of the column so as not to be hemmed in, to better keep track of each other, and to have a view.

Movement within the column was like a flooding river. In the current you were being moved along to an unknown destination, at a pace faster than what felt safe, and could easily be drawn under. Walking with her brothers at a slightly slower pace abreast of the main column, Rebeka was beginning to be caught up in the fervor of the crowd. Suddenly, a woman handed her and each of the boys a tricolor flag. At first they each stared at what had been put into their hands, they had never had such a thing before. Looking up from one to the other, a quizzical look quickly turned to triumph as they each raised their flag high and began to wave it. Rebeka turned, momentarily searching unsuccessfully for the woman who had handed them the flags. Her eyes flitted across and back the breadth and depth of the multitude who followed seemingly unendingly.

On the Pest side of the Danube, the column of demonstrators turned toward the Parliament Building just as thousands of office and factory workers were being let out for the day. Seeing the students wielding flags with the Soviet emblem removed, a roar of approval arose from those newly joining the ranks of demonstrators.

Soon there were hundreds of revolutionary flags.

The demonstration passed several military and government buildings, shouting as they went, "*Ruszkik haza*! *Ruszkik haza*!" Students climbed flagpoles, scaled walls, and descended from rooftops to remove Soviet flags and Red Stars that adorned the buildings.

Assembling in Kossuth Square, the crowd, still chanting "*Ruszkik haza!*," now numbered over 200,000. The demonstration overflowed into the side streets. Ernő Gerő, the Communist Party leader, panicked at the size and activity of the crowd. From the Parliament Building, Gerő broadcast directives across Kossuth Square for the assembled crowd to disperse. The crowd was unmoved.

Gerő realized there was little he could do. As Sándor Kopácsi had reminded him, the local government had no method for dealing with such a large crowd. János Kádár, party secretary, underscored that point. In his opinion, the students were only attempting to change the government. However, Gerő gave little consideration to the opinions of his advisors.

Standing in the square, Rebeka had been watchful as she stood behind her brothers and Dominik, Adrián, and Ervin. Their group stood on Nádor Street facing the Parliament Building, just to the left of the square. The older brothers, Dávid and Péter, stood a little apart in the crush of the crowd with Dominik and the Novák boys while Jani stood just in front of her. Rebeka constantly maneuvered their position to keep in close contact with the older boys. Still waving their flags and emboldened by the energy of the crowd, Rebeka had not been able to convince her brothers to leave. Hungry, she pulled some food from her knapsack sharing it with Jani. The other boys were uninterested, their focus on the events unfolding before them. Rebeka noticed a group of girls about her age that stood nearby. They were also waving flags and singing with the crowd. As Rebeka looked on, a young man, perhaps a university student, approached and gave each of them a tri-colored ribbon rosette. Moving from one girl to another, and then approaching Rebeka, the young man pinned a rosette on her collar.

An actor, Imre Sinkovits, stood near the front of the plaza addressing the crowd. Tall and engaging, with a loudspeaker in hand and Parliament behind, he recited Petöfi's poem, "Rise Magyar." The square resonated, with ever increasing fervor, the poem's repeating oath: "By the God of the Magyar, we do swear, we do swear, chains no longer we will wear!" The chanting was soon followed by demands for Nagy to speak and for his return to office. Slogans demanding reforms grew stronger and sharper.

To the side of the plaza, near the front, Péter stood in a group including Júlia, Tamás, László Böjtös, Péter Veres, Denes, Márkó, and Andrew. Yelling to make himself heard, Péter asked, "Did you ever imagine this?" Casting about for familiar faces, Péter saw István Bibó standing nearby with another friend from the Petőfi Circle, Árpád Göncz, along with his daughter, Kinga. Péter pointed them out to Lászlo who nudged through the crowd to greet them.

Hours passed, the sun set, and dusk turned to night as a steady stream of speeches and poems were read over loudspeakers, heard across the plaza. The presentations, mostly spontaneous, were interspersed with traditional songs, the collective voices of the now 200,000 assembled Hungarians, resounding throughout the plaza and into the night.

The square grew silent as another Petöfi poem was read:

"Liberty and love
These two I must have.
For my love I'll sacrifice
My life.
For liberty I'll sacrifice

My love."

In the momentary reverie, as the crowd stood silently introspective, the five pointed Red Star near the top of the Parliament Building was lit. A hated symbol of communist rule, the crowd immediately began to angrily roar, "Put out the Red Star!" In moments the star was dark once again.

Hoping to encourage the demonstration to disburse, the Soviets turned off all the street lights at 6:30 p.m. without warning. The demonstrators were at first unmoving, uncertain as to what the action might portend. When nothing happened, it was as if they were unaffected, carrying on as they had while making torches of newspapers. From the balcony of Parliament, poems were read and again the national anthem was sung, all interspersed with promises of Nagy's imminent appearance. A momentary hush fell over the crowd when large army trucks arrived driving slowly and carefully onto the square from opposite sides. Unarmed men jumped from the vehicles and began work to connect their electric generators to the lights of the square. A cheer rose up from the crowd, "The Army is with us! The Army is with us!"

News of Gerő soon spread through the assemblage like wildfire. Gerő had not only condemned the demonstration, he promised to undermine and destroy the peasant-worker alliance, the working class, their leadership, and the Hungarian Workers' Party. The effect of his words were volatile and produced quick results. The crowd again erupted, fervently chanting, "*Ruszkik haza*!" Russians go home!

At the other side of the square, near where Rebeka and the boys were standing, Gerő's incendiary speech had an immediate response, a call to action. One of the highly desirable, and easily achievable, points of the manifesto was the immediate removal of the statue of Stalin. No sooner did the idea erupt aloud than a large crowd assembled and hurried off towards Hero's Square. Among their number was Dominik, Rebeka's brothers, and the Novák twins, Ervin and Adrián. As she had only hours earlier, Rebeka was again transfixed in disbelief and a growing panic as she watched her brothers walk away and meld into the crowd. She heard the assembled multitude left behind in the square cheer as she ran to catch up with her brothers. Rebeka hoped it boded well, yet it did little to assuage her fears.

Standing at the north side of Kossuth Square, Tamás turned to Péter and Júlia, who yet held the revolutionary flag aloft.

"It's almost eight o'clock. Do you think Nagy will speak?"

At that moment, Márton Voros and a group of students from the Technical University approached Péter and his friends. Moved to action by Gerő's condemnation, the students' intention was to engage the people at the radio station to broadcast the manifesto.

"Budapest Radio is nearby. We are going there to read the manifesto over the radio. Will you join us?" Márton had spoken loudly to be heard above the noise of the crowd that surrounded their group. Many of those standing nearby who overheard the conversation agreed and volunteered to join. Péter and Júlia exchanged a glance and a mutual nod before Péter responded, "As organizers of the event, we must stay here but please, remember our goal. We don't want any trouble. Appeal to them as Hungarians." Márton inclined his head in understanding. Shaking Péter's hand before they walked away in the direction of the station, their number increased with every step they took.

Quite suddenly, the crowd began to cheer. All attention was averted to the Parliament Building where, standing on a balcony, overlooking the crowd, was Imre Nagy. A popular public figure, well-known and respected, Nagy was easily recognizable in his dark suit, receding hairline, bushy eyebrows, and chevron mustache with white rimmed,, round lens glasses poised at the bridge of his nose. It was 9:30 p.m.

Nagy was an unwilling participant, he did not agree with the actions taken by the students. Political associates had finally prevailed convincing Nagy to address the demonstration with specific instructions to calm down the agitators. Nagy's speech ended as soon as he began with the use of a single word. "Comrades," he began. Only those closest could hear him but word spread swiftly throughout the crowd eliciting whistles and boos in protest. Among the assembled, those closest yelled back to him, "We are not comrades!"

Nagy attempted to speak over the protestations, finally winning the attention of the assembled crowd as he began again, with more conviction in his voice, "Hungarians!"

The crowd broke out in wild applause and cheering. Nagy continued, promising reforms and a cooperative committee to address the 16 Points. He continued, expressing admiration for the demonstrators and promising that constitutional order would be restored. Throughout his speech, Nagy repeatedly urged the demonstrators to return home. Nagy concluded his speech asking that the work of reform be left to the government to address before requesting, again, that the crowd disperse and return to their homes. Somewhat disappointed but appeased, the crowd cheered. As the crowd began to disperse, a man abruptly drove into the crowd on a motorcycle, shouting as he slid to a stop, "They are shooting our boys at the radio!"

Júlia turned to Péter, grabbing his arm, "That's Sándor Victis, Péter. I saw him join the students who were walking to the radio station. I know him! Péter," Júlia paused, her hand upon his arm, "we can't." Péter hesitated, watching the crowd surge in the direction of Brody Street, their voices filling the night. "We have to leave here, Péter, and I cannot without you."

"László!" Péter called out, as he saw his friend running through the square in the opposite direction as the surging, angry crowd.

“Péter!” László raised an arm in salutation as he continued to run. “I promised my wife. I will try to return. Be careful.” With those hastily professed words, László disappeared into the night and Péter’s decision was made.

Believing the demonstration sanctioned, no one guessed that Gerő had asked his secretary to call the ÁVH and activate the Hungarian Army units to send an armed unit to Budapest Radio to quell any street demonstration.

15

HERO SQUARE

CHARLES FÁRKAS HAD agreed to meet his mother and her friends, Erzsike Sárkány and Anna Schott, for coffee and brandy at the Ruszworm Café on Castle Hill. They had been easy to find in the crowded café, all three women were tall and handsome. An intimate gathering place, the café is a Budapest favorite and not easy to find a table, inside or out, at almost any time during the day. Cherry wood and glass cabinets and countertops create an old world charm, the exquisite confections are difficult to choose from.

Everyone in the café had a copy of the manifesto and was pouring over it in discussion and debate. The tension and excitement in the room was palpable. All three women looked up as Charles approached, his mother extending a copy of the manifesto for his consideration.

"What do you think of this, Charles? I'm intrigued." Charles' mother, Alexandra, was always intrigued.

"As am I. Ladies, shall we take a walk in the direction of the National Museum?"

Sipping the last of her brandy, Erzsike immediately declined, "I'm off for home. Please be careful, both of you. You cannot be too careful. Anna?"

"I'll walk with you a ways. Anikó will be home soon if she's not already."

The group of friends split up at the front door with promises to see each other soon. Erzsike turned to Anna, smiled, and they walked away together, but separately, towards their homes.

Alexandra and Charles walked towards the city then crossed Chain Bridge just as a group of six or seven young people, intent on some purpose, went hurrying past. Charles called out after them, asking their purpose. The response was flung over their shoulders, "We're taking down the statue of Stalin! Join us!"

Charles and his mother stood with their mouths momentarily agape. Recovered, they wordlessly agreed with a mutual nod as they quickened their pace in the direction of Budapest's City Park.

Approaching Hero's Square, the main entrance to the City Park, the streets were quiet although crowded. Groups of people stood shoulder to shoulder as they looked upon the unfolding scene before them. Searchlights lit up Stalin's statue. Standing in the alley with his mother, Charles glanced at his watch. The time was a few minutes after 8:30 p.m.

Erected in 1951, what had almost immediately become a hated symbol of the nation's suppression, the 26 foot tall bronze likeness of Stalin was erected on a 13 foot tall limestone pedestal which itself stood upon a 20-foot high tribune. To topple the statue was a herculean task exaggerated by the circumstance of having only the simplest of hand tools available. Magically appearing from all directions were ladders, hammers, saws, and ropes.

Among the men and women, young and old, working to dismantle the statue were two boys who stood out from the rest. The young men were dressed in traditional Hungarian clothes and boots. At the moment, they were the center of attention as they were held aloft, ascending the statue. The young men worked at tying several ropes around the statue's neck. Once secured, the opposite end of the lines were tied to trucks. Despite repeated attempts, the effort to pull the statue down was unsuccessful. Many of the onlookers rushed to join in and lend their manpower to haul on the lines, but without effect.

Nearby, Rebeka stood with Péter and Jani. The siblings were watching in awe as Dávid and Dominik climbed the tribune, pedestal, and then up onto the shoulders of others to climb up and then stand on the shoulders of the statue. It was unsettling, to see her brother standing there, diminished in height by the staggering distance from the safety of the ground, in a setting and among people completely foreign to their experience. Rebeka was aware their clothing, unique in a crowd of thousands, made them easily identified. While helpful for her to keep track of her brothers and Dominik, Rebeka worried their clothing might perhaps make them a target. All about her a cheerless, monochromatic multitude ebbed and flowed, blending with the night. In the city, it seemed everyone wore shades of gray, black, and brown; their shoes, their knee-length overcoats, their caps, hats, and berets.

The night was growing cold. There were quite a few women, predominantly young, but a growing number of older women and a considerable number of older men. Looking up again, Rebeka watched as Dávid and Dominik descended and realized with a smile, and some pride, that she wasn't worried. Dávid was strong and capable.

The trucks revved their engines then slowly and carefully pulled the ropes taut. Leaning on the accelerators, the tires began to spin, squealing, the smell of burning rubber and billowing acrid smoke filling the air in repeated, futile attempts.

Intent on destruction, but with little effect, the situation was soon rectified. A flatbed truck arrived ferrying industrial workers with acetylene torches and oxygen cylinders. While work commenced cutting the statue at the top of Stalin's boots, others secured thick steel ropes to the statue's neck that were again held taut by eager participants below. An hour later, the 25 foot bronze statue slowly began to tilt, accelerating as the enormous weight gave in to gravity. The ground shook and the air compressed with the deafening roar of approval from the gathered crowd. Stalin's likeness, prostrate on the square, was immediately set upon, the boots alone remained upon the pedestal. Nearby stood a correspondent for the Associated Press, Endre Marton, and photographer András "Bandi" Sima. A group of boys and students climbed onto the pedestal and placed revolutionary flags into the boots. Sima's camera flashed. Marton desperately scribbled page after page. Sima's photograph was soon splashed across the front page of newspapers around the world.

Rebeka, Péter, and Jani surged forward with the crowd to see the statue. Rebeka had lost sight of Dávid, not realizing he and Dominik were in one of the trucks. She hadn't seen them when they had dropped down behind the tribune. Péter and Jani were kicking the statue, mimicking the slanders they were hearing from the men, women, and children that swarmed over the statue. Rebeka, momentarily distracted, watched her two youngest brothers. Looking up, unable to find Dávid, she reached out grabbing both brothers by the shoulder and, turning them to face her, yelling to be heard above the din, "We have to go find Dávid!"

Squeezing and wiggling through the crowd, Rebeka, Péter, and Jani eventually gained the perimeter of the square where Péter climbed a fence for a better view.

"Can you see them, Péter? Are they up by the boots?" Rebeka yelled.

"No!"

"The statue?"

"No!" Followed seconds later in surprise, "Wait, the trucks are moving! They're dragging the statue...they're leaving!"

"Do you see Dávid or Dominik?"

Péter searched the crowds still swarming over the tribune and pedestal, standing with the boots and waving Hungarian flags. His eyes darted from one group to another, searching for his brother, then to the thousands on the street, streaming in the direction that the trucks had taken. Péter had unconsciously begun to shake his head realizing he couldn't see Dávid or Dominik anywhere. Péter continued, scanning the area which had begun to clear enough that Rebeka could see across to where the statue had once stood. Watching Péter, she felt a tightness grip her throat and a ripple of gooseflesh rise on her arms.

"Get down, Péter, please. Carefully," Rebeka admonished as he jumped to the pavement. "Help me look around the square."

Charles and Alexandra had stood back against a wall, on the outer edge of the square, as more people continued to surge into the immediate area around where the statue had only moments before stood. They watched as people climbed, sat upon, and explored the tribune. Alexandra gasped. Until that moment no one, that is, no ordinary Hungarian, had ever been allowed to approach, much less to touch or enter, the tribune.

Charles and Alexandra followed the crowd as a truck, with Dávid and Dominik riding in the back helping others hold the ropes, dragged the remains of the statue along Rákóczi Street to Blaha Square. Everyone was eager for a chance to deface the statue of Stalin. Revolutionary slogans were written across the statue before being hacked at and smashed to pieces. Decapitating its head, using any tool at hand, even rocks, the work was interrupted when a line of trucks surged into the area and pulled to an abrupt stop. The driver threw open the door. Hanging on the door as he stepped out onto the running board, he raised his hand for attention and his voice for all to hear.

"The ÁVH are shooting the students at the radio station! Let's go!"

Alexandra stood, incredulous. Looking about as people swept by on all sides of her in the direction of Budapest Radio, she turned to Charles.

"Charles, I'm going home. Stay if you need to, but be careful, please."

"Yes." Charles took her hand, "Please, mother, go. You shouldn't have any trouble. It seems as if all the activity is this side of the river."

"What are you going to do?"

"I'm not certain, but," he looked at her, "I need to witness this."

All of the street lamps had been turned off. Walking in the semi-darkness of the moonlit night in the direction of Brody Street, Charles noted the great number of people in the streets. Approaching the Opera House at a hurried pace, Charles glanced at the statues of Franz Liszt and Ferenc Erke and stopped. The first beautiful strains of the Hungarian National Anthem were emanating from the elegant, softly lit, neo-Renaissance building. At the entrance, Charles took the few steps two at a time stopping at the open doors to watch the performance. He was more than surprised, at its conclusion, when the conductor appealed to the audience to join the students and the factory workers in demonstrating for human rights. The Opera House immediately began to empty. Charles hastily turned away, running into the street to continue on his way in the general direction of the radio station.

Turning onto Sándor Street, Charles found the people there were lined up, pressed against the wall. Two Russian tanks loudly maneuvered toward them via the narrow road. As the tanks drew closer and passed, Charles realized with utter astonishment that it was not soldiers but ordinary citizens, including women and children, sitting and standing on the tanks.

16

BUDAPEST

THE STUDENTS AT the Gymnasium on Isabella Street had been distracted all afternoon. Classified at the start of school into one of six categories (worker, peasant, intellectual, petty employee, other, or class enemy) the children were an amalgam of Budapest society.

Every student knew from the whispers and sideways glances of their teachers that something unusual was happening, or about to happen. They attributed the general discomfiture of the adults to the demonstration of the university students. When their teacher left the classroom after admonishing them to attend to their geography lesson, four of the students in the back row cautiously rose from their chairs. Ágnes, Ildikó, Katika, and Anikó had been friends since elementary school and now stood shoulder to shoulder peering out at the street below. Their friend Aliz stood watch near the door listening for the returning footfalls of their teacher.

"What do you see?" was whispered again and again.

"Nothing that unusual," Ildikó whispered, without turning around.

"There seem to be more people than usual on the streets though," added Katika. "Maybe not."

"Teacher!" Aliz warned. The girls scurried back to their desks, studious and innocent when the door opened.

The children of the second grade class attending the elementary school on Dohány Street could hear the ever-increasing din of voices of a very large crowd gathering nearby, although they didn't know where. For an unseasonably warm but very pleasant day, the windows had all been opened that morning. Now, to the children's restrained dismay, the windows were being abruptly closed. Their teachers were tight-faced, thin lipped, quiet, and stern. Izsák, Tomi, and Petra were all staring out the windows when their teacher sharply rapped her desk with her ruler calling their attention to the front of the classroom. It was almost three o'clock. The bell would soon ring. It would be time to go home.

Walking home from school, the young students were confused and curious. The children were ignorant of the day's events and reticent to any discussion. Every child, from the time they could talk, had been sternly and repeatedly told to never engage in any political discussion. Even so, there was a thrilling excitement felt by many of the older children who hurried home in anticipation of the news that would greet them there.

The five girls usually walked to the station together to ride the number 6 in the direction of Margit Bridge. Once arrived, they each went their separate way. This day was different. At the station they found several copies of the manifesto. Scanning the pages, the girls looked at each other wordlessly, excitedly, intrigued.

Climbing onto the streetcar, they stood together. One of the girls, Katika, pointed ahead as the streetcar approached the Nyugati Train Station. Everyone on the streetcar could see the congestion, the crowd of people swarming the area near the Danube. People were walking toward the Margit Bridge, filling the sidewalks and streets. Thousands of people were carrying Hungarian flags, marching across the bridge deck, filling it from railing to railing. The girls stopped and stood next to the Budapest Theater while they watched the oncoming demonstration move up St. Stephen Boulevard.

"Let's join them!" Katika suggested. Flushed with excitement and without another word, the girls melded into the column of demonstrators. Tens of thousands of other Hungarians joined the demonstration all along the way. From storefront windows and apartment balconies, people were waving, smiling, singing, and shouting, "Vivat!" Everyone was happy and laughing. The enthusiasm and hope for Hungary and Hungarians were exhilarating and stimulating.

At the apartment building on Dohány Street, Barnát and Izsák returned from school to their apartment on the other side of the stairs and one floor up from the twins, Tomi and Petra. The twins' grandmother, Erzsébet Kender, was waiting at the door. Their mother, Ilona Vadas, worked at an architectural firm as a draftsman during the day and attended technical classes at night. She intended to become an architect, if the party would allow it. It had been their neighbor, László, who had suggested the classes. Most nights she returned home after her children were in bed but she always came in and sat with them. Ilona would look at her children, gently run her fingers through their hair and softly sing to them as they slept.

Entering the Vadas apartment, the twins could see that their grandmother Erzsébet was worried. It was only then that the sound of voices emanated from the living room. The radio was on. Tomi and Petra were astounded to see their grandfather, Illés Kender, listening to Radio Free Europe, a station that was banned. The twins went to their room after a snack of half a sandwich and some fruit. Putting away the school books, they read and practiced their music before washing and coming to the table for dinner at six, as usual, with their grandparents.

After dinner, they sat in the living room, riveted, as they listened to the radio for hours. Grandfather turned the dial between Budapest Radio and Radio Free Europe, until Budapest Radio went silent. Both grandparents were shaking their heads over the news. Radio Free Europe was reporting violence at Budapest Radio station. Quite unexpectedly, the door to the apartment opened and slammed closed with shouted apologies from Ilona as she rushed in.

"Have you heard the news?" Ilona started. "I see, you have. Turn the radio up, please, Apa. Class was dismissed when word arrived of the demonstrations moving across the city. There were groups of demonstrators on the tram, in the square, and I came across a large group at the end of our street! They were laughing, telling me that the statue of Stalin has been taken down! Taken down and beheaded! Can you believe it? I wonder if it is true, it must be true, why else would they say such a thing?"

"Ilona, please!"

"Yes, Anya, yes, keep my voice down." Ilona, breathing deeply, settled onto a chair before she continued. "Yes, at City Park. A group of the demonstrators went there to take down the statue."

"How could they?" asked grandfather. "It's made of cast bronze. It's 25 feet tall. It weighs many thousands of tons," he said with increasing incredulity.

"Yes, exactly, Apa. They could not. But truckloads of workers came from their work to join the demonstration. Seeing the difficulty, they left and returned almost immediately with the means to disassemble the statue. They had torches and saws and hammers. Any number of demonstrators were beating on the statue."

"There were no police? How many demonstrators were there? Are there?" her mother asked.

"The demonstration originated from the universities, but Hungarians from all over Hungary have been arriving throughout the day. They are joining the demonstration, as well as the off-shift factory workers. The last I was told, there may be as many as 200,000 people!" Everyone in the room gasped, shocked. This news could never have been imagined or anticipated. Ilona squared herself in her chair, putting her shoulders back and became solemn.

"I was also told that there may have been violence at the radio building. That is not far from here. Please, everyone, let's finish our dinner. We should pack a few things for each of us to carry in case we have to leave."

"Leave?" the twins and their grandparents asked simultaneously.

"Yes, of course," grandfather answered his own question, solemnly shaking his head.

Barnát and Izsák had returned to their apartment to find their mother in a similar state of anxiety and worry. For the moment, the boys delayed asking their many questions. Almost as soon as they had put away their schoolbooks, their mother called to them to join her in the living room where she was listening to the radio. They all sat, transfixed by the news being reported. Unexpectedly, the front door opened as their father hurried in, closing the door behind him.

"László!" Klára and the boys, startled, stood up, watching László, anxiously awaiting whatever news he had. László hung his hat on a peg by the door, removed his coat then turned to stand facing his family.

"László, what is happening?" Klára asked barely able to keep the rising concern from her voice.

"It is unbelievable, Klára, boys. People are arriving, they've been arriving, all day! There are 200,000 people out on the streets. I've just come from Bem, crossing the Margit Bridge with the demonstration, to Kossuth Square. The flag has had the Soviet symbol removed. There are dozens of them, hundreds of them. I came forward for the Writer's Union and laid the crown at the foot of Bem. The students laid their wreaths next to it, and then Veres Péter was given the manifesto to read."

"You!" exclaimed Klára. "Were the police there? The AVO?"

"No, the demonstration was sanctioned, didn't you hear the news? People are arriving from across Budapest, from across Hungary! We never thought this would happen. It wasn't imagined by anyone. We may have started a revolution. I think we may have." László looked shaken, concerned, and elated as his hands fell to his sides and his shoulders momentarily slumped.

"A revolution?" Klára looked from one to the other of her sons. "But László, what are we to do? What is happening now?"

"The demonstrators marched to Parliament, to Kossuth Square. The manifesto was read, and there were many speakers. The national anthem was sung several times. There were requests for Nagy to address our assembly. At one point, the lights were turned out, but the Army arrived and used the generators for their trucks to turn them back on."

"The Army?" Klára and the boys said in unison, all equally surprised.

"Yes, the Hungarian People's Army seems to be with us. But then Gerő addressed the crowd through loudspeakers from his office. He condemned the people and threatened to destroy the working class and our leadership."

At this Klára's hand flew to her face. Immediately, her eyes narrowed intuitively knowing something had happened. László knew that look and, avoiding her gaze, continued before being asked.

"We received word that the statue of Stalin was toppled."

"We heard that on the radio, Apa!" Barnát exclaimed.

Klára took a step back, ashen. Barnát and Izsák looked at each other then back to their father.

"I came straight here to you, to all of you," László continued as he took Klára's hand and looked at his boys. "Actually, along the way I stopped to see the Gergő László family. They were walking to the station. They are thinking of leaving."

"László and Etel? Leaving?"

"Yes, considering their history they fear they will end up in prison again, even the aunts, Miska Karola and Gergő Lara."

"What about Etel's father?"

"Yes, he was there too. Miska Jakab, László's mother, Tünde. All of them. We mustn't say anything, not one word. You hear me boys?" asked László. "Not anything, to anyone. You only know the Gergő family from the neighborhood, nothing else. We will not say anything to anyone."

"László, what will you do? What will we do?" It was only then, looking at the boys, that Klára noticed something odd.

"Barnát. Where is your scarf? You know it's required."

Barnát stood facing his parents, squared his shoulders, and thrust his hand into his pocket extricating the shredded remains of his red Patriot scarf.

In the rushed chaos of the moment László had been responding to Klára's question while listening to Klára and watching Barnát's response. "I would like to return to Kossuth. If you agree, I promise to return if there is any violence."

At the sight of the red strips of cloth, both parents stopped talking, their gaze alternately shifting from their son to the shredded scarf. Izsák was staring at his brother in alternating states of disbelief and admiration.

"Barnát, what have you done?" his mother, shaken, whispered, her hand at her throat, a single finger hovering over her lips as if to prevent the words from escaping her mouth.

"We saw the demonstrators walk by the school this afternoon.

They were shouting, "Russians to go home." Our entire class cheered them before the windows were closed. It didn't matter, we could still hear them and see them. It just happened, everyone took off their scarf. But it's true mother, the Russians should go home. They are not supposed to be here, everyone knows that!"

Klára could not argue with her son, just shook her head and returned her gaze to László.

"And if there is violence, what then? Shall we stay in the apartment or should we leave Budapest? Will we be able to? What if there are no trains?"

"Wait, Klára, wait. For now, it is a peaceful demonstration sanctioned by the government. Remember, Moscow recalled Rákosi. Moscow is unhappy with the economic conditions here and wants change. We have reason to hope that they will listen. Undoubtedly, we will all compromise. Now," László bent over and threw out his arms bringing both boys into his embrace, "may I have a sandwich and return? I must be quick. The Writer's Union may read the manifesto again. In front of Parliament! It is a historic day."

Minutes later, László kissed his family and then hurried out the door. Barnát and Izsák stood quietly at the window, side by side, filled with pride as they watched their father disappear into the night.

In both apartments on Dohány Street, the voice of Communist Party chief Ernő Gerő emanated from the radios. Gerő denounced the demonstrators as fascists. Klára and Ilona, each in their own apartment, wondered what news the morning might bring. Barnát fell asleep dreaming of the heroes of Hungary, his father among them, waving the Hungarian flag.

Earlier that evening, Éva had left the demonstrators at Kossuth Square to return home. She had had enough. She had never imagined so large a crowd as gathered today at Bem Square. Walking with Júlia and Lilly, crossing Margit Bridge headed for Parliament, she had felt overwhelmed, perhaps even a sense of foreboding. Éva feared some of the talk and the earnestness in some of the people. The crowd had swelled to who knows how many. The demonstrators had started to chant,"Russians go home! *Ruszkik haza*!" Éva had found it exciting and powerful.

Along the way to Parliament, Éva had noticed a little pastry shop with its windows newly broken in. The pretty baskets had been emptied. Money had been left in each of the baskets. Éva was hungry. The moonlit night was beginning to grow cold. She decided she would have a quick dinner and change her clothes and then, perhaps, rejoin the group. Walking toward Váci Street, turning the corner, she heard her name.

"Éva!"

It was Lilly, who narrowly sidestepped a man running down the sidewalk. They both stared after him and then turned to each other.

"That was László, Péter's friend from the Writer's Union," Lilly said, watching him disappear down the street.

"He did well today. That took a lot of courage." Éva paused, considering what she had just said, then held onto her friend's arm, "I suppose we should go back, shouldn't we? Let's have something to eat and get our coats."

The two women left Éva's apartment on Váci Street walking out into the night. They had stayed overlong, uncertain about returning to the demonstration. Over dinner they had become riveted listening to the news reports on Radio Free Europe and Budapest Radio. They left when it was announced that Nagy was addressing the demonstration, encouraging them to disperse.

Not minutes away from the apartment, László again came running towards them, this time in the opposite direction, away from the Parliament Building. More concerning to the two women, he was visibly distressed. Éva and Lilly abruptly stopped in the middle of the walkway calling out to him as he passed.

"What has happened, Bójtös László? Where are you going?"

László stopped, turning to the women from only a few paces away. "A messenger came to the square from the radio station. The ÁVH has opened fire on the students who gathered there. I promised my wife I would return if there was trouble. Excuse me, I have to go."

Éva and Lilly stared momentarily at the retreating figure then turned to one another. They turned in the direction of the Parliament Building, then in the direction of Budapest Radio. Both locations were not distant from where they stood. It seemed surreal, impossible what was happening so near to them. And yet, there wasn't any indication of the turmoil, much less of what it portended, at that very moment as they stood on Váci Street.

Éva was the first to speak and then it was a stream of impulsive thoughts, "I don't know what to do. Do you think Júlia might still be at Kossuth? Yes, she might be. We should go and try to find her."

Alternately walking and running toward the Parliament Building, they were surprised to find so few people there. It was night, all of the lights in the area were out, and the moon was waning, only softly illuminating the area. They repeatedly called out for their friend as they crossed the square, never hearing her response, only random, untethered comments.

"Everyone has either returned home or left to the radio station."

"Be careful."

"Russians go home!"

"Join the demonstration at Budapest Radio!"

"Go home!"

"Revolution!"

"Free Hungary!"

Éva motioned with a twist of her head to Lilly and the two women turned in the direction of Chain Bridge. Walking there they stopped to stand by one of the stone lions on the Pest side. They stood, watching and listening as they waited, hoping to find their friend at this intersection.

"Éva, you know Júlia might walk up to Margit Bridge. We might not see her go by."

"Yes, I know. We have to make a choice, Lilly. It's also the closest bridge to the radio station on her way home. I'm just hoping we will see her. Do you want to move to Margit? We could split up," Éva said, pausing as she looked at the thousands of people streaming in every direction, "but I don't think we should."

"We shouldn't split up. It's either remain here or go to Margit. We might as well stay here and hope we see her."

As people continuously walked past the two women to cross the bridge, Éva or Lilly would occasionally ask for any news. An elegant, tall woman approached and hurriedly told them of the toppling and destruction of Stalin's statue and the arrival of trucks filled with men bearing news of shots being fired at the radio station. The woman hardly paused as she continued to walk across the bridge, calling back to them as she went, "Be careful, please."

Éva and Lilly stared in the direction of Brody Street hoping, willing, Júlia to appear.

17

THE RADIO STATION

THE DISTANCE FROM the Parliament Building to the state radio station in Central Budapest, on Brody Sándor Street, is about one and a half miles. Tamás, leading the group of demonstrators as they walked away from the demonstration at Kossuth Square, used that time to discuss what they would do on arrival and who would do it. All along the way, people were cheering and applauding from their apartments and along the streets. As they walked to the station, people of all ages were joining the procession. Several young girls ran up to Tamás, lengthening their stride to keep pace with the group.

"We want to help. We were at the demonstration. This is Ildikó and Katika, my name is Anikó. May we join?"

More than one student responded, "Join us!"

Tamás asked, "Where did you come from?"

"Váci Street. Our class watched as the demonstration walked by today demanding the Russians to go home. In solidarity, every student removed their Pioneer scarf. We used it to shine our shoes and then cut them into shreds! Russians go home!" Anikó and her friends raised their arms as they shouted and fell in step with Tamás.

The delegation continued to chant as they marched toward and arrived at the radio station. A smaller group of students, led by Tamás and including Anikó, climbed the stairs to the office door and asked to speak with the director, Valéria Benke. The assembled crowd below was demanding to read the 16 Points on the radio. Benke came to the door and introduced herself. She was quite noticeably displeased and distracted with the insisted demands being yelled from the crowd below.

Anikó stepped forward, "The radio belongs to the people." Benke took an instant disliking to the girl.

Tamás, standing next to Anikó, smiled as he gently ushered her behind him. He introduced himself to Benke as the speaker from the sanctioned meeting held the day previous at the Technical University. Tamas proceeded to present his case and negotiate for reading the 16 Points. Benke appeared to reconsider. In the silence each considered the other, eyes staring, considering, contriving.

"Alright, you may come in." Benke held up her hand to Anikó and the others on the landing as they began to step forward. "Not all of you! Here, you," Benke indicated, pointing first at Tamás and motioning with the same pointed finger into the building. Standing aside, Benke allowed ten of the protesters to pass then closed and locked the door behind them. Benke led the group to a small room where Tamás, whom the group had previously designated, would read the 16 Points. Benke motioned for Tamás.

"Sit here, please. The microphone, as you can see, is there in front of you. There's nothing for you to do, there's no switch. Just speak into it when you are given the signal," she indicated towards the producer.

"The rest of you, follow me." Benke led the rest of the delegation to the adjoining room where they could watch Tamás as he went on the air. A glass partition and a speaker would allow them to watch and listen. Along the way they passed Szepesi, the well-known sports broadcaster.

Everyone in the group inside the building was ecstatic and filled with hope.

Outside, the as yet peaceful crowd had grown apprehensive and watchful. The crowd had overflowed into the street and side streets as more and more people arrived. Anikó, Ildikó, Katika, and many others were crowded onto the landing. They were being pressed from behind as one by one the stairs filled with as many people as could manage to fit on each tread. From the street, a voice called out saying they had their radio on. The crowd grew quiet, waiting and listening.

Tamás, filled with pride, sat staring at the mike, his heart thundering in his chest. He cleared his throat, received the signal to start, then began to read from the manifesto, the 16 Points. Seconds began to tick by. Everyone was holding their breath.

"I don't hear anything," Márkó Vari remarked. He looked at the sound booth and recording area of the control room. There was a radio on a nearby table, next to the door of the room they'd been asked to wait in. Márkó crossed the distance in two strides and turned the radio on, then off, then on again. "The radio isn't on." The realization of their situation abruptly came to him, "They've turned the radio off!"

One of the station's broadcasters had joined the students in the waiting room after Benke left. Now, in a sudden, surreal outburst, he was quoting the famous Hungarian writer, István Örkény. "We lied! We lied by night, we lied by day, we lied on all wavelengths." He continued as the realization of what he was saying began to dawn on the students. "We were made to do it, I didn't want to do it. I'm Hungarian. You're right. See there? Look, look at that light.

It should be on. That plug there," he indicated a cord near the desk, "that should be plugged in. They turned it off before you came in."

Simultaneously, the crowd in the courtyard and streets below had come to the same realization. "The station isn't transmitting! They've turned the station off!"

After showing Tamás to the production booth and settling the students in the adjacent room, Valéria Benke had closed the door behind the students and walked to the back of the building. There she gently knocked and then opened the door addressing the blue uniformed ÁVH officer, who stood just within the threshold ahead of his unit of the state security police.

"They are in the building. They are in the recording studio and waiting room at the front. Young men, all students. They are unaware that anything is amiss. That may not be for long."

The officer, with an abrupt motion of his baton, led his unit swiftly to the front of the building. Tamás and the other demonstrators, looking for Benke, were visibly surprised, concerned, then angry when they saw the ÁVH. Everyone except Tamás backed toward the entrance door. Several of the ÁVH circled around the group, blocking the doorway, as Tamás spoke then argued with the officer in vain.

Attempting to detain the students, the skirmish grew loud as all of the students demanded their rights. Outside, their voices were heard; through the windows some of the crowd had glimpses of the tumult within. One of the delegation was able to break free, opening the door, yelling they'd been captured before being dragged back inside. On the landing, a cry arose and spread to the street below, "It's the ÁVH! They're inside. They've captured Tamás and our boys!"

The crowd responded forcefully, surging into the courtyard, compacting the already densely assembled masses, chanting, "Let them go! Let them go!" The sound of the crowd's protest and roar drew ever more demonstrators to the station, now overflowing into adjacent streets. The crowd began throwing stones at the building, breaking all the windows. The protest became an angry roar as those on the landing and stairs tried to force their way into the building. In response, the ÁVH threw tear gas from the windows. From the side entrance, other officers turned on fire hoses in an attempt to disperse the crowd.

Inside the building, the ÁVH officer and his men, with Tamás and the others behind urgently trying to free themselves, tried to push their way out onto the crowded landing. Waving their weapons and angrily yelling for the crowd to disperse, a single shot suddenly, instantaneously, stunned everyone. A single scream suddenly, horrifically, invisibly, but only momentarily, hung in the night air. The single scream begat a torrent of screams. Screams that flowed into the streets and out into the night.

The crowd defiantly, angrily roared as more people surged into the courtyard. The police opened fire, killing the ÁVH officer and one of the young students. In the panicked confusion, Tamás and the detained students took the chance in pushing past the police. Benke followed, slamming and locking the door behind them as they left.

Hearing the first shot, Sándor Victis, having the only motorbike, rode with a sense of grim urgency. Surging adrenaline prickled his scalp as he rushed to deliver the news to the immense crowd at Kossuth Square. Reacting to the motorcycle bearing down on them, the crowd parted. Sándor, yelling as he drove towards the center of the square, braked while simultaneously putting his left foot down to balance and pivot. As the back tire spun out, he yelled to the crowd, "They are shooting our boys at the radio!"

At that moment the demonstration became a revolution. The people erupted in fury. They ran. People filled the back of trucks, people jumped into cars or onto the running boards, clinging to the post of the open window, in their collective rush to go to the aid of their fellow Hungarians.

At the radio station, the crowd in the courtyard continued to fight the ÁVH. A group of students, women, and men worked together to roll Ildikó's body in the Hungarian flag. They held her aloft, her long hair limply hanging down, as she was passed out of the courtyard and into the street, stirring the crowd into a frenzy. As the news of the killing at the radio station rapidly spread, disorder and violence erupted throughout the capital. Police cars were set ablaze. Soviet symbols, signs, and banners were torn, hacked, hammered, or ripped down from buildings throughout Budapest as protestors raged through the streets.

The siege continued throughout the night. Despite the initial lack of weapons, the protestors were aided by the arrival of a nearly continual stream of fellow Hungarians joining the protest. As an ambulance neared, the multitude moved to allow it closer proximity to the building. Márkó and András approached and met the vehicle as the driver nervously opened his door and stepped out.

"There are injured people over here," Márkó yelled, indicating the far side of the courtyard.

"I received a call to help wounded inside the building."

"Inside the building?"

András was also puzzled and turned to Márkó. "There aren't any wounded inside the building." Turning their attention back to the driver, they both simultaneously recognized the collar of the blue ÁVH uniform beneath the driver's white coat. The collar insignia confirmed the subterfuge.

All eyes turned on the driver. A group of men had clustered around the back of the ambulance. One from among them asked of no one in particular, "What's in the ambulance?" There was no hesitation following the question, the men tore open the back doors of the ambulance.

"What is it? What's there?" Márkó called out as he heard indignant and angry remarks coming from the ambulance.

"There's a cache of weapons and munitions here! He must've intended to resupply the ÁVH!"

Márkó ran around to the back of the ambulance, leaving the driver to András and the enraged crowd gathered there.

"Open the crates and boxes, distribute everything!" Márkó yelled. The crowd needed no instruction. The weapons and ammunition were already being distributed to outstretched hands and disappearing into the fight.

Blood was spattered across the hood of the ambulance. The driver was dead. Several of the protestors, outraged at his deceit and collaboration, had fallen upon him brutally killing him. There was nothing András could have done to stop or dissuade the men. From the stairs, the now armed demonstrators shot and killed the ÁVH who had been shooting from the window of the station.

At various locations around Budapest, military arsenals were raided. Arms factory workers looted their stores transporting and distributing them to anyone who wanted a weapon.

On the streets, Hungarian Army soldiers sent to relieve the ÁVH were spotted approaching the radio station. The soldiers were led by a rather tall and imposing officer. Márkó gave a warning shout to András. In response, the lead officer held up his hands to indicate he was unarmed as he called out to the two men.

"We're here to join you." Behind the officer, the following soldiers were tearing the red stars from their caps. "I am Colonel Pál Maléter. This morning we received orders to remain loyal to Hungary. We are with you!" At this, the soldiers cheered and moved into the courtyard to join the fight.

The battle at the station continued through most of the night. Maléter returned to the army barracks to coordinate the various teams of insurgents staging around the city. The crowd, now armed with guns and pickaxes, had gained entry to the back of the radio station by climbing scaffolding. They chiseled an opening into the wall, quickly overcoming the remainder of the ÁVH unit that had barricaded themselves in the back room.

Among the ÁVH prisoners was a major in the hated ÁVO. Seized, his hands tied behind his back, the major was hustled out onto the landing and victoriously presented to the insurgents below. The identification alone, "ÁVO," was enough to galvanize the crowd into an insatiable bloodlust. The officer lost control of his bladder as the crowd carried him out to the street. A rope was thrown over a lamp post then tied around his ankles. Before stringing him up, they doused him with gasoline and then set him on fire. Mercifully, a woman standing nearby shot the major as he began to burn.

By morning, sixteen were dead and dozens injured. The protesters had won control of the radio station building. News of the events of the previous day spread throughout Hungary, inspiring similar uprisings in many cities. While victorious in the moment, the people of Budapest were unaware that during the night Gerő had contacted Moscow. Two divisions of Soviet tank units were approaching the capital. Martial law was about to be imposed.

18

THE NIGHT

CROSSING THE BRIDGE, Alexandra could not help but notice the three children sitting near the lion guarding the Buda side of the Chain Bridge. The girl, even in the shadowed darkness of the lamplit bridge, was clearly distraught. Two certainly younger boys, standing on either side of her, were not much better. All three were scanning the faces of the crowd crossing the bridge, obviously searching for a familiar face. Alexandra also noted that all three were wearing the traditional clothing of peasants, similar to the two boys she'd seen scaling Stalin's statue almost two hours ago. Alexandra assumed the children must have become separated from their family. Having crossed the bridge, Alexandra felt the greatest danger was behind her, she could certainly take the time to stop and help these children if that is what they required.

"Hello," she said, stopping to stand a few paces away. "I live there, just on the other side of Castle Hill. My name is Fárkas Alexandra."

The girl, a young woman really, introduced herself and her brothers.

"I am András Rebeka, these are my brothers, Péter and Jani."

Then, in a rush of words, Rebeka explained that her family had become separated at the demonstration in front of the Parliament Building. The older boys, there were two of them, and two friends from Budapest, had run off with the demonstrators to the radio station. One of the older boys, Dávid, was her brother, the other a friend from the same village. The boys had come to Budapest to join the demonstration. She had been sent by her mother and grandparents to find the boys and persuade them to return home. Unfortunately, to her obvious distress, she had lost two of them to this uprising and was uncertain as to what she should do.

"Were they the two who climbed the statue of Stalin this evening?"

Rebeka was uncertain if answering would be perilous.

"You have no reason to worry or fear, my dear. I was also there. We are on the same side," Alexandra cautiously smiled to encourage calm and trust among these young people. "I believe I saw your brother, and his friend, in the truck going to Blaha Square with the remains of the statue." Alexandra paused, observing the girl's reaction. "There's nothing more that any of you can do tonight that would not put you in grave danger." Alexandra did not want to cause the children to worry, so instead she invited them to accompany her to her home with as good and familiar a reason as any child should know, "It's late."

Rebeka had her mother's good sense and her father's quick intelligence to ascertain the implications of both possibilities: looking for Dávid and Dominik or accepting this kindness. Her younger brothers would be safe. They would, most probably, have the opportunity to wash and be cared for. Rebeka could hopefully have a meal, wash, and rest before going out to look for Dávid and

Dominik. She wasn't certain when that would be, but she knew she would. A quick glance to Péter then Jani, and receiving a trusting nod from each, Rebeka turned to Alexandra.

"Thank you. My brothers and I accept. This is a great kindness."

"Here, let's walk together," Alexandra said as she walked towards the tunnel. They all felt a sense of relief walking away from the growing chaos behind them. The children were surprised when Alexandra unexpectedly called out to no one they could initially discern, "Aliz!"

Rebeka then saw a girl of about her age walking toward them from the crowd. An initial twinge of uncertain familiarity was dispelled when she spied the tricolor rosette on the girls' coat. This was one of the girls she had stood next to at Kossuth Square earlier that evening. She felt Jani tense beside her and turned toward him. Jani, somewhat shy around unfamiliar girls, stepped slightly behind Rebeka. Alexandra introduced everyone and then asked Aliz if she was returning home.

"Yes, I'm a little late actually."

"I saw your mother earlier this evening, she was walking home with Anikó's mother. Don't you usually walk home with Anikó?"

"Well, yes, usually, but," Aliz hesitated.

"You were also at the demonstration?"

"You mean to say you were there as well?" Aliz asked. Alexandra laughed at the transparency of the girl's disbelief and surprise that this elegant woman would do such a thing.

"Not exactly, no. I've just come from Hero's Square where they have taken down Stalin's statue," Alexandra replied to Aliz's uninhibited amazement.

"Yes, yes, it's true. I saw it pulled down myself. Pulled down, and then dragged away by a truck with the crowd following. Now, Aliz, dear, where is Anikó. Is she still at the demonstration?"

"As far as I know." Averting her gaze to Rebeka, Aliz asked, "Weren't you there also? I think I remember you."

Rebeka quietly inclined her head and Aliz turned back to Alexandra, "We had been watching when Nagy arrived to speak," Aliz began but Alexandra, surprised by the news, interrupted.

"Nagy?"

"Yes. I was there, we were there, that is. Anikó, myself, and three others from our Gymnasium were there. We joined the march at the Margit Bridge and walked through the city to Parliament. One of my friends, Ágnes, had to go home and I knew I should too, so we left. The others stayed."

"Who is with Anikó?"

"Katika and Ildikó."

"And Ágnes?"

"We walked together to the Kossuth Bridge where she crossed and I continued on to here. She lives on Rózsa Hill and said that she knew a shortcut. I wanted to take my familiar way home."

"Please, let's walk together."

Walking home, Alexandra and the children felt comfort in each other's presence. Somewhere nearby, an eagle owl repeatedly emitted a long series of hoots. They all enjoyed the distraction as they continued on together until saying good night to Aliz near her home. Another few blocks, and they arrived at Alexandra's home. Welcoming the children inside, Alexandra showed them the kitchen, where they could wash, and where they would sleep. She handed each boy a nightshirt and a slip to Rebeka. Leaving them to settle in, Alexandra asked them to meet back in the kitchen where she would be preparing a snack and hot tea. Returning to the kitchen, Alexandra had turned on the radio and the heat beneath the kettle and was preparing a variety of cheeses when Rebeka joined her.

"My apologies, Mrs. Fárkas, but my brothers have already fallen asleep."

Alexandra gently laughed, "That's certainly understandable, considering all they've been through. And you, may I fix you some tea and a bite to eat?"

"Yes, please," Rebeka replied with an unwavering stare.

"What is it?"

"I need to find my brother."

"Rebeka. I will do this for you. If you will stay the night, get plenty of rest and eat well, you will be better able to find your brother. Do this, and I will take care of Péter and Jani until your return."

Rebeka stood, thinking, looking with an almost unnerving innocent stare at Alexandra.

"If you must, leave now and I will, of course, take care of your brothers."

Alexandra noticed a shift in Rebeka's posture and a subtle lift of her brow.

"You're very kind. I'll stay the night, thank you. I'm very anxious but," Rebeka paused, looking at Alexandra, "I trust you."

Alexandra and Rebeka sat with their cups of tea and a decorative, hand painted plate of hardboiled egg, bread, fruit, and pogácsa that Rebeka, encouraged by Alexandra, mostly consumed. They spoke only briefly. Alexandra could see how increasingly difficult it was for Rebeka to stifle yawns. Seeing her off to bed, Alexandra returned to the kitchen and wrapped some food to put in Rebeka's knapsack in the morning. Assured that everyone was asleep, she turned on the radio. Radio Free Europe was describing the mass demonstrations and violence that had erupted across Hungary. Looking at the clock and then the front door, Alexandra turned off the radio and went to bed.

Not far away, Éva and Lilly had reluctantly left their posts at the Chain Bridge and walked toward the Margit Bridge. They stood at the Pest side watching for Júlia. Just after midnight, the two women returned to Éva's nearby apartment on Váci Street. Chilled, they sat together over a steaming cup of tea. Pensive and tired, they decided Lilly should stay the night. They would call on the Türea household first thing in the morning.

Night was arriving earlier, growing longer, every day. Evening clouds were softly tinted in shades of gray and purple darkening to black. By 4:30, the enveloping darkness obscured the twin clock towers of Saint Stephen's Basilica. Many of the assorted buildings on Rózsa Hill were ablaze with lights. Every apartment had their windows open as those within looked out over their city. Excited, curious, anxious, and more than a few who were terrified.

Downstairs in the Fülöp apartment, Ágnes had returned home earlier that evening. Ágnes lived with her parents, her uncle Lukács, her grandmother Adél, and her great-grandmother Janka, her "Dédanya." They had all been listening to the radio when she had opened the door into the apartment. Her family, surprised and relieved, surrounded her, peppering her with questions. Her father, Elek, was pleased she had witnessed the demonstration at Kossuth. Janka was bursting with pride and heartfelt joy, "Thank God I will live to see freedom return to Hungary!"

Everyone returned to the front room where they resumed listening to the radio. Within moments, Gerő's ominous, threatening voice filled the room. Standing near the window, Elek, a lawyer at the Ministry of Agriculture, was furious. He turned to look out at the city where he saw the Türeas on the street below approaching the building. Crossing the apartment to the front door, Elek snatched his hat and coat from the hooks by the door.

"I'm going to the Türea apartment. I saw Péter and Júlia at the demonstration. Keep listening to the radio, I'll return quickly."

Zsófia went to the kitchen with her mother and grandmother, Adél and Janka. They cleaned the dishes and sorted the kitchen, their quiet murmuring filling in the quiet spaces as dishes clinked, doors opened and closed, water rushed, the teakettle sputtered. Ágnes and her uncle Lukács sat spellbound near the radio where Zsófia brought them each a cup of tea.

The three matriarchs momentarily stood, watching Ágnes and Lukács.

"Zsófia, we need to get food, as much as we can as soon as we can," her mother, Adél, said as she opened cupboards and drawers taking a quick survey of their contents.

"I'll go first thing in the morning. The bakery opens at 6:30."

"We'll both go, and to the grocers and the butchers. Anyu," Adél turned to her elderly, frail mother, "will you stay and listen to the radio for any important news while we're away? We'll ask Ágnes to stay," she began but was interrupted by the phone ringing. Zsófia stepped across the kitchen to answer wondering, and a little anxious at this late hour, who might be calling.

"Hallo?"

"Fülöp Zsófia? This is Schott Anna. My apologies for calling so late. Is Ágnes home?"

"Yes, about an hour ago."

"Was Anikó with her?"

"No, I'm sorry, we haven't seen her," Zsófia replied as she turned to look toward Ágnes. "Wait one moment, please, let me ask Ágnes."

Hearing her name, Ágnes sat up erect in her chair, alert, watching her mother come toward her, worry furrowing her mother's usually delicate features.

"Ágnes, it's Anikó's mother on the phone. When did you last see Anikó?"

"Perhaps I'd better speak with her, mother. She may have questions."

Ágnes picked up the phone relating a brief synopsis of the afternoon, their having joined the demonstration as it marched to Kossuth Square, and ending with Ágnes leaving just before Nagy's speech.

"Who were the other girls with you?"

"Aliz, but she left with me. We walked together partway home, only I crossed on Kossuth and she crossed on the Chain Bridge. Katika and Ildikó were there with Anikó when I left."

"Aliz? Sárkány Aliz?

"Yes, we were walking home together from the Gymnasium when we joined the march to Kossuth Square. Aliz and I left as Nagy was about to speak."

"Thank you, Ágnes. I'm very glad you are home with your family. May I speak again with your mother, please?"

Ágnes handed her mother the phone and returned to the living room to listen to the radio with her uncle.

Janka had joined them.

"Yes, how may I help," Zsófia asked, trying to keep any emotion from her voice.

"I...don't know," Anna stumbled. "If you see her, ask her to come home. I hope you are all safe. Please be careful." Anna hung up the receiver. She stood, struggling to control the emotional panic rising from her gut as if her body would purge itself. Anna turned away from her phone, a hand at her throat. Dark, ominous fears raced through her mind. The end of the war was not that long ago, how could this be happening again? How could this be happening to Hungary? To Budapest? To her family? Where was Anikó? Where was her daughter?

Zsófia momentarily stared at the receiver in her hand, then recovered, looking up at the concerned faces of her mother and grandmother. The women surmised the gist of the conversation, a daughter was missing, unaccounted for as a maelstrom was threatening to engulf them all.

"Let's not worry, it has been an exhilarating day for the young people. They are all caught up in the excitement of the day and will return home."

A piercing scream riveted their attention. Ágnes stood, hands opened then clenched, her face drawn in anguish, a sob catching in her throat, "Anya, they've shot students at the radio station!"

Inside the Fürth apartment, the Türea family sat with Klári, Béla, and Ili around their dining table. Gábor slowly turned the dial from the Budapest Radio station to Radio Free Europe. The radio crackled with static as Gábor made a minute adjustment. The announcer, mid sentence, urged the citizens to rise and take up arms against the communist leaders, support from the West would come.

Across Hungary people listened, incredulous, as the message repeated. Rise up, support would come. Suggested tactics and strategies were repeatedly broadcast throughout that evening and in the following days. The Türeas and Fürths, as did all Hungarians, believed the West was coming to aid Hungary in her struggle for independence.

What wasn't broadcast that night, what the people and parents of Budapest didn't know, was that heavily armed units of state security police, the ÁVH, had been sent to the Budapest Radio building. Mira was in the main room looking out over the city.

"Look, the lights on the Parliament Building went out!"

Everyone turned to look and in silence watched and listened. Nothing. The discussion cautiously resumed as they expectantly listened, hoping to hear any unfamiliar sounds, as if that knowledge would somehow salve their anxiety.

Mira suddenly announced, "The lights are back on!" A moment's pause followed then, "No, they're not. But there are lights on the square. That's so strange. I wonder what happened?"

"So, the West will help do you think?" Erzsébet asked of no one in particular.

The voice over the radio of Communist Party chief Ernő Gerő interrupted the group's discussion. Denouncing the protesters as fascists, Gerő condemned the demonstration. He promised to undermine and destroy the peasant-worker alliance, the working class, their leadership, and the HungarianWorkers' Party. Gerő's remarks elicited subdued, guttural grunts and gasps from everyone gathered around the table. An oppressive silence of apprehension, morbid in its possibilities, seemed to darken the room. Uncomfortable in the pressing silence, Mira asked from across the room, "What about Júlia and Péter? Where are they?"

Erzsébet and Jeno rose from the table, prompting Klára and Béla, Gábor and Ili to stand.

The adults momentarily looked from one to the other uncertain and thoughtful.

"Thank you, we should return," Erzsébet offered. "Júlia and Péter don't know we're here, why would they? If they, or anyone else comes to the apartment, we should be there."

Erzsébet hurried toward the door followed by her parents. Jeno was thanking Béla, assuring him and Klári that he and Erzsébet would get word to them as soon as they knew anything.

Walking the short block to their apartment, the disappointment of a shared unspoken hope that Júlia and Péter would be there was felt by everyone as the door opened to the quiet, hushed silence of an empty home. Gizella went to the kitchen to set the water to boil and prepare the kettle for tea. Jośef crossed the room, sat, and turned on the radio. Erzsébet and Jeno were just sitting down at their table when a single, sharp knock at the door startled everyone.

"Péter! Júlia!"

Everyone was on their feet to greet them as Péter and Júlia walked in. Having only just closed the door behind them, everyone turned in surprise to a quick succession of rapid knocks on their door. Péter cautiously opened the door.

"Fülöp Elek. Good evening, come in, please."

Jeno went forward to shake hands with his neighbor. Although Elek lived in the apartment below, he had never before been a guest of the Türea's.

"Welcome. How may we help you? Is everyone well in your family?"

"Yes, thank you. And all of you?"

Everyone nodded. Then Jeno cautiously asked, "Has something happened?"

At that moment, a loud commotion drew everyone to the Türea's windows overlooking the Danube and Pest. Looking towards Moscow Square, they could see a large truck driving through the city streets filled with people holding aloft a Hungarian flag with a hole in the center. What they couldn't hear from that distance, was the proclamations being yelled through hand-held loudspeakers. The radio broadcast bridged the distance.

"The Stalin statue was toppled! The Stalin statue has been destroyed!"

Jeno turned to Elek and József, "Can you believe what we are witnessing?"

Everyone else in the apartment turned away from the window and looked expectantly at Elek.

"When I left work at the Ministry today, I joined the demonstration at Kossuth Square," he paused, and only momentarily glanced at Péter and Júlia.

"Yes, we were there, we helped organize the demonstration. Our family is aware of where we were and our activities," Péter offered.

"I returned to my apartment when the lights of Parliament were turned off by the government," Elek continued. "My daughter, Ágnes, has only just returned a short while ago. My family and I had been listening to Nagy's speech on the radio. You have also heard the speech?" Noting their assent, Elek barely paused as he continued, "To our surprise, she and several of her friends were there. And now, have you heard Gerő's speech?" Elek was quite obviously enraged, his neck bulged and his face reddened as he squeezed his already thin lips together in a tight grimace. Elek's hands were clenched at his sides and his brows were set low over his eyes.

Without notice, so intently was everyone else listening to Elek, Gizella had walked over to the radio to hear news of Gerő's speech. She listened with growing concern then gasped, her hands flying to her face. Then a strangled cry, her voice strained, "The ÁVH has shot several students at the radio station!"

At the Fürth apartment, after he had closed the door behind the Türeas as they left, Béla went to join Mira by the window. Klári and her parents had returned to listen to the radio.

"Have you seen anything else?"

"Not yet, Apu." Mira reached out to her father laying her hand on his sleeve.

Béla looked down at his daughter, taking her hand in his. They both turned to look out into the night.

The radio crackled as Ili adjusted the control knob. Radio Free Europe was broadcasting news of the altercation at the radio station. There were several dead. Announcements followed. National councils and the worker's councils were declaring a general strike; their membership was encouraged to join the revolution.

"The revolution?" several voices within the apartment

reiterated.

An indistinct sound caught everyone's attention. Klári looked to Béla, then to Ili and Gábor, each searching the other for any sign of recognition. Mira watched as everyone shook their head, uncertain. They waited in silence, unmoving, listening. A soft tapping. Someone was at their door.

Béla traversed the front room and paused before he opened the front door.

"Hello?"

"Dr. Fürth, please," answered a voice just above a whisper.

Béla cautiously opened the door. The light from their home spilled out onto the front step revealing a young woman. Béla silently motioned for her to step inside, then cast a cursory glance out into the night as he closed the door.

The family stood watching as Klári, who obviously was acquainted with the woman, stepped towards the stranger. Béla turned to his family and introduced the young woman.

"Our family, this is Tóth Ilona. Tóth Ilona, this is Berci Gábor and Ili, my wife's parents. Our daughter, Mira." Béla continued, speaking to his family, "We work with Tóth Ilona, she is a medical student doing her internship at the hospital."

Klári looked wonderingly at Ilona, who was flushed and nervous but somber.

"What has happened?"

"Everything. I need help. We need help."

"We?"

Mira walked into the kitchen to stand with Ili. Gábor went to the door where he stood, listening.

"The students," Ilona continued. "You've heard, no doubt," she indicated with a nod of her head toward the radio that was yet broadcasting. "The demonstration at Bem and then Kossuth? The radio station?"

"Yes. We saw the lights go at the Parliament Building."

"They did. The Army came with trucks and put up other lights generated by their trucks."

"We saw that!" Mira added.

"Did you hear Gerő's announcement?" Ilona asked, looking from one to the other.

"Yes. What happened?" Klári and Béla could easily guess such inflammatory statements would have serious consequences.

"I have to hurry. People have been killed and many are injured," Ilona rushed ahead. Ili reached out to Mira, putting her hand around Mira's shoulder, drawing her closer. Ili had no idea Mira was intrigued and excited by the news, not disturbed.

"What has happened? How many?"

"After Gerő's broadcast some of the protestors went to Budapest Radio. That's where the violence began. The ÁVH fired on the crowd, two were killed. ÁVH. And a girl."

"A girl?" Mira asked, curious, stepping away from her grandmother's embrace towards Ilona. Klári glanced at her daughter, momentarily confused in concern yet intrigued by Mira's response, before repeating the question.

"A girl?"

"Yes, she was only about 14 or 15." Seeing the question written across the Fürth's faces, Ilona continued briefly, "No, I don't know her name or anything else about her."

Ilona continued, "The demonstration numbered more than 200,000 at Kossuth including workers, students, men, women, children, grandmothers, and grandfathers. Only it's no longer a demonstration or protest. The people are rising up, this is a revolution. People have been killed, many are hurt. I'm setting up a first-aid station at Kilián Barracks."

"The Kilián Barracks?" Klári and Béla both echoed in surprise.

"The Army Colonel Pál Maléter has stepped in as de facto leader of the revolution. He and the Army are dedicated to Hungary. He heard Moscow is sending tanks. The Barracks have massive stone walls. Maléter has been sending people and defectors to Kilián for protection. He has allowed me to set up a first aid station there. There is another hospital on Mária Street. It's treating the more seriously wounded that paramedics move from Kilián. We need supplies. Can you help?"

Béla had walked to the closet to retrieve their coats. Klári looked from Mira to her parents who gave her a knowing nod.

"Of course. Do you have help?"

"I have three interns helping me, you don't know them. Two girls are helping us. It was their friend who was killed at the radio station. The girls are about 15, they are courageous and helpful."

"How did you get here?"

"The ÁVH sent an ambulance with weapons but they were discovered. The driver was killed," Ilona, seeing the Fürths' horrified faces, quickly added, "No! He wasn't an ambulance driver. He was ÁVH wearing a white coat over his uniform. That's what gave him away."

"You drove the ambulance?"

"No. A student from the Technical University, Bálint András, drove. He's waiting. I really must hurry," Ilona finished as she walked to the door, one hand on the door handle.

Klári and Béla left with Ilona, hurrying down the stairs to the ambulance. Crossing Margit Bridge, Béla navigated, directing András to a street near the side entrance of the hospital. Parked, András waited there, watchful, while Béla, Klári, and Ilona went in search of supplies.

Béla had good reason for directing András to this side of the hospital. Supplies were delivered through this entrance. The storeroom was located halfway down the first corridor. The doctors found the area largely unoccupied, as they had hoped. It was late, the city was in turmoil. Many people had left their homes and their work to join the demonstration. Apparently, if the hospital was an indication, many more were now leaving to be part of the revolution.

Klári led the way to the storeroom. Béla appropriated a lone gurney stationed against a tiled wall. Falling in step behind his wife, Béla steered the gurney behind her. Ilona followed quietly behind Béla. In the storeroom, they worked quickly and quietly. Supplies of syringes, morphine, bandages, needles and sutures, anesthetic, alcohol, and iodine were placed on a stainless table in the center of the room. They found antibiotics, drapes, gauze, plaster, sheets, and blankets. Ilona found cloth bags meant for cleaning supplies and handed one to each of the Fürths. They filled the bags with the smaller items and then slung them over their shoulders. Klári and Béla stacked the remaining supplies on the gurney while Ilona covered them with a sheet.

Béla opened the storeroom door. A cursory glance down the length of the hallway in both directions revealed nothing. There was no one in sight, not a sound to indicate anyone was in their immediate area. Ilona, following Béla, pushed the gurney. Klári walked closely behind the two, holding a chart and scanning the pages as a ruse to deflect interest in their group.

In moments, they were outside the building. Ever watchful, András pulled up to the curb out of view of the doorway. The back doors to the ambulance were opened as the doctors exited the hospital. In a few swift movements, with Klári and Bèla on either side, Ilona collapsed the gurney. Together they pushed and guided it into the vehicle. Klári and Béla crouched into the back of the ambulance sitting on the bench that was there for that purpose. Ilona and András settled into the cab. With the siren blaring, András drove to the Kilián Barracks passing a bus of international tourists en route to the Austrian border. They were fleeing the city.

In the apartment building on Dohány Street, László Böjtös and his family stood at the window looking out across Pest. László had his arm around Klára's shoulders, holding her close. The boys watched, fascinated. As the family watched, they alerted each other to anything unusual. Their radio broadcast news in the background. The night was punctuated with bursts of light and sound.

László grew more uncomfortable and anxious as the evening painfully wore on. He repeatedly assured Klára he would not leave. As the moon coursed across the night sky, Klára spread a coverlet across Izsák where he had fallen asleep on the couch.

Radio Free Europe was now reporting many had been killed at the radio station including students, women, and children. ÁVH officers had been brutally killed, their bodies and charred corpses on the streets amidst piles of communist propaganda. The news transfixed Barnát's interest.

Suddenly the news was interrupted. The announcer read a poem they reported as having been widely circulated throughout Hungary:

> *"Red is the blood in the streets of Pest,*
> *The rain beats down, washing the blood,*
> *But it remains on the stones,*
> *Of the streets of Pest."*

The occasional flash of lights, searchlights, and sirens kept László, Klára, and Barnát quietly transfixed where they stood. Each pointing in the direction of a suspected fight as it occurred, the occasional intake of breath or monosyllable response to a random flurry of activity was distracted by the next. Nearing midnight they turned away from the window. They must sleep the few hours before the alarm would again call them to the day's routine, no matter its altered state. László carried Izsák to the boy's room where he covered both boys with the blanket and whispered good night. At his own bedside, he wound the round-faced, footed alarm clock and turned off the light before slipping into bed next to Klára.

Dawn came early and with it the announcement that schools were closed. Sleep deprived, László and Klára slumped back onto their bed. Izsák peeked around the corner into their room.

"Izsák? It's early, son. What is it?" László asked.

"Where's Barnát?"

19

A COMMON CAUSE

AT THE KILIÁN Barracks, Maléter had learned late last night of Gerő's request to Moscow for military intervention. Throughout the night he had been waiting. Maléter knew the Soviet reaction would come fast and hard.

Young schoolboys, anxious to be part of the revolution and fight alongside their older brothers, fathers, and grandfathers had arrived throughout the night. They clamored to be given a job, any job. They were given one as messengers and directed all over the city. It was one of these boys who had brought the news at 2:30 that morning. Long columns of Soviet tanks had arrived in the Buda Hills, fear-inspiring apparitions emerging from the dark, dense fields of fog to the south.

Maléter had been surprised by an unexpected arrival just after midnight, Lt. Colonel James Noel Cowley. As the military attaché of the British Embassy, Cowley had been attending a dinner in full dress uniform when he learned of the clash at the radio station. He had hurried home to change. Armed only with a pistol he had arrived at the Barracks in time to learn of the arrival of the Soviet T-34 tanks. He exchanged information with Maléter before secreting away into the night to gather intelligence on Soviet movement and forces.

Out on the streets, Tamás and Márton had found András and Márkó leading a large contingency to the police station. They joined the ranks. Armed and overwhelming the station, Márton asked to meet with the chief of police, Sándor Kopácsi, who made himself immediately available.

"Before you begin," Kopácsi said in earnest, "let me tell you that Gerő ordered me to fire on all of the demonstrators last night. He insists that you are all fascists. I maintained it would be a serious mistake, you are the sons and daughters of working families and peasants. We are Hungarians!" Kopácsi emphasized, standing erect and continuing, "We do not want to fight our fellow Hungarians!"

Márton responded, "All we ask is for you to display in your windows the Hungarian flag with the Communist emblem in the center cut out.[4] We will stop shooting as soon as the flags are displayed." András stood next to Márton uncertain of the officers standing behind Kopácsi.

"In March, I spoke to 1200 party members of the Police department. I criticized the Soviet model Stalinist tyranny. You and your men are welcome here. We will fight with you. Consider our headquarters a stronghold for the fight."

Kopácsi instructed four of his men to take down the flags, another searched for and found a pair of scissors. Sharpened countless times, the scissor blades were worn thin, one end broken. Three of the officers held the flag taut while the last stabbed through the material, hacking out the central Soviet hammer and sickle emblem. Standing outside, the demonstrators cheered as the flags were raised in the police station's windows.

Nearby, high above the Kilián Barracks, Anikó was suspended by a rope held by several young men and boys braced against a rooftop ledge. Anikó had been slowly lowered until she could reach the Soviet emblem that adorned the building, the outline of a red star approximately 5 feet in diameter. Pushing with her feet and legs, Anikó dislodged the star held in place by a steel bolt head within a dadoed wooden groove. The groove, already worn, gave way, splintering, sending the star crashing to the cobbled street below. The crowd below was emotional, yelling and cheering, many had tears and more than a few fearfully looked over their shoulders. Phantoms were everywhere.

Anikó watched as the star crashed to the cobbled street. Exultant, breathless, freezing, as a single laugh escaped. Anikó looked up as her companions pulled up. Grabbing at the ledge as many hands reached out pulling her over the edge, Anikó faintly heard her name. There it was again. Turning back to the ledge and looking over there, to her great surprise, was her father. Bálint Schott stood there, looking up, his hand held high. Anikó's hand flew to her mouth. Her breath caught at the back of her throat and she could feel her heart racing furiously. The girl was overcome with more concern than she'd experienced in the last 14 hours, until she realized her father was smiling. She looked again. He wasn't smiling, he was crying. She held her hand out towards him. The crowd erupted shouting and cheering.

Racing down the stairs to the front of the Barracks, Anikó found her father. Bálint had made his way to just outside the door. Hurried inside, they stood just within the threshold of a crowded room. Anikó held onto his arms as she related her story in a tangled rush of words. Describing what she had seen and experienced since leaving school the day before, Anikó was suddenly somber.

"Apa. Where is Anya? Sebestyén?"

Her father hesitated, pulling back from her embrace, furtively glancing to his right, then left.

"It's alright, Apa. Maléter is with the people. They are calling it "The Rising."

"Anikó, the situation has worsened. Moscow has sent tanks. Many of them. Your mother is terribly worried about you. She and your brother are home. You know I can't go home without you. I can't leave you here."

"Then could you stay here, Apa? She would know I was safe if you were with me. You could use the phone and call her. We're helping at the first aid station."

"We? Who is "we"?"

"My friend from school, Katika. Ágnes, Ildikó and Aliz, all of us joined the march. But Ágnes and Aliz went home from Kossuth. Apa, the ÁVH killed Ildiko! That's why I have stayed to fight, Apa. I have to. I must! I can't go home."

Bálint Schott blanched.

Several people staggered or were carried inside including an old woman who had a deep gash across her forearm. The fragmented, proximal end of her ulna was exposed. The old woman's elbow was shattered. Bálint was astonished to see his daughter unfalteringly approach the bloodied old woman.

"Who is in charge of the infirmary?" Bálint asked.

"Tóth Ilona. She's a medical student. There," Anikó indicated with a toss of her head and a glance towards Ilona before turning back to the men carrying the old woman. Anikó directed the men, pointing to a cot against the back wall where they could place the injured old woman.

"Please keep your arm unmoving as much as possible. Hold it on top of your stomach," Anikó added as they hurried past. The directive was as much for the men as it was for the old woman.

"Who are they," her father asked gesturing to a couple across the room, "that man and woman?"

"They're doctors, the Fürths. They've been helping too."

"Where's a phone I can use?"

"Through that door, there, Apa," Anikó gestured towards a door just being him.

Bálint paused before asking why Anikó hadn't called, then decided against it.

Out on the street, Barnát had left the apartment during the night when he heard the distant rumbling of the Soviet tanks. He had met a group of boys near his school. Hearing the tanks drawing close, the boys ran to nearby Kossuth Lajos Avenue where they watched an endless column of Soviet armored tanks. The massive machines passed by with a deafening roar as the grinding treads scraped across the cobbles and the monstrous V12 engines repeatedly misfired.

"Boys!"

Excited and incredulous the boys were completely absorbed. Repeated shouting drawing ever closer finally caught Barnát's attention. Turning to his right, Barnát saw a young man approaching. Tibor Arany, sprinting towards the Kilián Barracks, abruptly stopped.

"Boys! Those tanks are heading for Kálvin Square to fight against us. Would you like to help me stop them?"

The boys, without hesitation, agreed.

"My name is Arany Tibor. I served in the Army for a short period of time. I need you to find bottles, such as lemonade bottles. Find some old clothes we can tear up. We're going to make bombs and destroy the tanks."

"How?" asked Barnát.

"We'll put gasoline in the bottles and stuff a strip of fabric into the top. It's called a Molotov cocktail. Light it on fire then throw it into the gas tank."

"Where's the gas tank?"

"On the back of the tank," Tibor smiled. "They've labeled it for us. It says "petrol."

The boy's open faces revealed their mutual amazement before they all laughed derisively at Soviet ingenuity.

"Yes, just twist off the cap, drop it in, and run like the wind!"

"Where will we get the gasoline?"

"At the Kilián Barracks. I'll meet you there. You know where it is, yes? Find all the supplies you can."

At the apartment building on Dohány Street, Klára had tried to rush László out of the apartment to search for Barnát with a promise to return home as soon as they could.

"Klára, it might not be soon. And if I find our friends in immediate need of help?"

"Then you'll help. I know, I know! Just, please, please, Lázló, return to us."

"Remember the bomb shelter in the basement. Izsák, get dressed in two layers of clothes and pack your school bag. Be a help to your mother and stay with her. Do not leave her. Son?"

"Yes, sir."

Turning to Klára he continued, "Pack as much food as you can and a blanket for each of us. Take it down to the shelter. Talk to the Vadas family. You can ask them to come here, or you can both go to their apartment. If they aren't already preparing, ask them to get their things ready for the basement. I will look for you here, somewhere here."

László gave Klára a knowing glance, they had already talked privately about where they would meet if Klára and Izsák had to flee Budapest. László kissed them both, donned his cap and coat, and slipped out into the early morning.

20

DAWN

24 October 1956

EVERYONE IN THE apartment building abruptly awoke. The quiet of early morning, just before dawn, was fractured by a deep rumbling coursing through the structure of the building and echoing through the hills of Buda.

"Elek, what is that?" Zsófia asked, alarmed. She followed her husband out of their bedroom. "Ágnes! Anya!"

Seeing Ágnes bolt into the hallway, her mother took her hand saying, "Go to your grandmother. Help her with your Dédanya. I'll be there in a moment."

Zsófia hurried to the living room where Elek had turned from the window. He had only momentarily paused, looking out across the landscape. He crossed to where their radio sat on the small table near the kitchen. Rotating the Bakelite dial, the radio clicked on.

"What is it?" Zsófia asked as she stood at the window. "What is making that...Elek, look!"

Elek had already seen. His full attention was now on the radio. Zsófia turned, hurrying back down the hall to her daughter, mother, and grandmother.

"What time is it?' Ágnes asked. "What is happening out there, Anya?"

"4 o'clock. I'm not certain. Everyone, get dressed."

Ágnes glanced back at her mother, as she walked her great-grandmother, Janka, back to her room.

"Trust your mother and father, my darling," Janka said, gently squeezing the hand wrapped around her own arm.

Ágnes looked at her Dedanya, whose eyes were focused on her own careful footsteps. Ágnes looked at Dedanya's hand, her delicate fingers grown ever more slender, the skin transparent with age. She willed herself to think of nothing other taking care of Dedanya and getting dressed.

In their apartment on Castle Hill, Rebeka, Péter, and Jani had bolted straight up. Scattering the coverlets as they raced for their clothes, they ran to the kitchen where they found Alexandra standing by the radio.

"What is it?" Rebeka asked as she reached for her knapsack. Alexandra faced the children, looking at each in turn then settling on Rebeka and her knapsack.

"I'm afraid the city has just now grown more dangerous. There was no warning. You and your brothers are safer here, Rebeka. My son is also missing. Would it be alright if we wait together? Please."

Rebeka regarded her brothers. Taking a step to the window, she looked out into the darkness and was immediately repulsed, stepping into her brothers who had followed her to the window. The shadowy suggestion of enormous machines confronted and confused her. Rebeka knew she and her brothers must stay with Alexandra. Looking out across the Danube and Pest, she tried to imagine Dávid and Dominik were somewhere safe. Safe until she could find them. Standing there, transfixed, Rebeka was unaware she whispered their names. Watching Rebeka, Alexandra felt a chill pass over her arms and back.

"Péter, Jani, Rebeka. I've been listening to the news. The fighting is in Pest. I feel confident we are safe here. Please, go lie down again and rest. It could be a long day. I will stay up and promise to wake you if anything changes." Somewhat hesitant, Rebeka led her brothers back to their nest of coverlets. At their bedroom door, she turned to look back at Alexandra, questioningly.

"I promise, Rebeka."

Nearby, Anna Schott had not gone to sleep that night after speaking with Ágnes and her mother. She had not heard from Anikó. Quite concerning, Anikó's friend Ildikó also had not returned home. Her mother had called hoping the girls were together. Anna had turned the radio off following the broadcast of the students killed at the radio station. Anna's husband, Bálint, and their son, Sebestyén, had returned earlier that night after visiting Bálint's brother who lived not far from the Citadella monument. They had put Sebestyén to bed, then Bálint had gone out into the night to find their daughter. Anna waited and watched for their daughter's return. Hour followed hour, a dark and quiet abyss. Anna had felt the earth tremble and then shake before she heard the first rumbling sounds of far distant thunder. A thunder that grew until it rattled the window panes and shook the door on its hinges.

The Fürth and Türea families were also awake, as was everyone else in the hills of Buda. The massive hulks of T-34 Soviet tanks emerged from the darkness of the hill passes. They ground downhill. Illuminated as they approached the lights along the Danube, turrets opened from which silhouetted figures slowly emerged. It was a terrifying sight.

The rumbling engines and grinding tracks of the three seemingly uninterrupted columns of more than 1,100 tanks filled the night with a pervasive din and an unfaltering tremor. The acrid smell of smoke, grease, and burning rubber belts infiltrated the landscape and permeated the cool morning air rendering it sticky and oppressive. As the citizens of Buda awakened to the thunderous approach, a curious few ventured out under the cover of darkness. They retreated, repelled by the pungent stench and jarring cacophony as the tanks passed. They fled into their homes at the sight of the armed Soviet troops following behind.

The reaction was the same elsewhere in the homes of Buda. Júlia had been the first of her family to awaken to the distant sounds of what she initially perceived to be a thunderstorm. She awakened her family when she realized the vibrations, while indistinct, were constant. Crossing the apartment to the front window, Júlia looked out across the hills of Buda. József and Gizella sat at the kitchen table and turned on the radio.

The telephone rang, unanswered at first as everyone stared at the device uncertain and wary. Júlia crossed the room and reached out to lift the handset from the base. She hesitatingly answered, "...Hallo?"

"Júlia!" Éva's voice caught in her throat. She quickly composed herself. "Júlia, you are home! My apologies for calling so early. We were so concerned for you and tried to find you. We are so glad to hear your voice! Lilly is here with me. We were returning to Kossuth last night when we heard about the trouble at the radio. We watched for you at Margit Bridge then returned to my apartment and tried to call."

"I am so sorry, Éva!"

"Oh, no. Don't be. In all the confusion there was no choice in trying to find you. We are so happy you are safe! And your brother, is he with you?"

"Yes, yes."

"Have you heard the thunder? I think it might be tanks!"

"Yes, Éva, there are tanks. Long columns of them descending from Buda. So many of them, Éva."

"What will you do?"

"I am with my family, Éva. I will be going out to find food, as you should also."

"What about the tanks?"

"Stay away from Kossuth and any shooting and fighting. Stay near your apartment. Is there a bomb shelter in your building?"

"Yes."

"Then ready a bundle with food and a blanket and go there if trouble starts on your street. If you feel it's too dangerous where you are, then cross to Buda. Come to us, you'd be welcome." Júlia looked up at her grandmother, who nodded her approval.

As soon as Éva hung up the receiver she and Lilly, who had overheard the conversation, decided that Lilly would stay at the apartment rather than return to her own.

"We should go now to the bakery and delicatessen, Éva. Bread, eggs, coffee and tea, potatoes, rice, cheese. Anything that will last. We should hurry. Everyone will be looking for food."

With their berets, gloves, and coats the two friends hurried out onto Váci Street. They intended to first visit the delicatessen, then the bakery. At the corner, Éva recognized the men approaching from the side street. They were friends of Péter Türea's. She had met them at the University Aula the day before.

"Vari Márkó, Stollar Denes. We did not expect to see you," Éva cautiously greeted them as they approached.

"We are going to the Soviet Cultural Shop, we have control of the building. Would you join us?"

"What will you do there?"

"Remove all of the propaganda materials."

Éva turned to Lilly. Emboldened by the men's confidence, they nodded their mutual agreement. In step with the men, Éva and

Lilly had no other thought for the delicatessen or bakery.

Hurrying towards the shop, Váci Street became increasingly congested. The sounds of turmoil throughout Pest were quite suddenly eclipsed when enthusiastic cheering preceded their arrival. Before them, a large crowd lifted their arms in earnest supplication. Showers of propaganda literature rained down upon them from the open windows of the stone edifice before them. Home to the Soviet Cultural Shop, the office was being emptied of its propaganda materials. People, especially children, were scrambling to collect the leaflets, posters, fliers, and books littering the cobblestones. They were mounding them into propaganda haystacks. Up and down the street, the haystacks were being set ablaze to the cheering of the crowd. Soviet flags, removed from buildings, poles, and shops, were thrown upon the pyres.

Éva and Lilly looked on for a moment, reconsidering their situation. They realized their mistake. They turned to their companions.

"The work here is well taken care of, thank you. Please be careful!" Éva said and, with a nod, the two friends walked away.

Nearing an intersection they turned the corner, toward the Danube, where they came to an abrupt halt. Startled, they found themselves unexpectedly face to face with a Russian tank and a surrounding crowd.

"There's a Hungarian flag on the turret, Éva, and look there," Lilly pointed in the direction of two men. One was a Russian soldier, the other a Hungarian Army officer wearing a Freedom Fighter armband. They were standing side by side, saluting the gathering, subdued crowd who wondered at the sight before them. Lilly grabbed Éva's shoulder for stability and stepped up onto on a stone retaining wall.

"Lilly, what are you doing?"

"Get up here with me! Come on!" Lilly gave Éva her hand while bracing herself with an arm around a nearby lamppost.

"Sing with me, Éva. Sing!" Lilly urged, before beginning in her clear, strong alto voice.

"O, my God, the Magyar bless
With Thy plenty and good cheer!
With Thine aid his just cause press,
Where his foes to fight appear..."

At the first strains of the Hungarian National Anthem, the crowd riveted their attention to the two women. Inspired, with one voice they began to sing lifting their voices as if for all the world to hear. Lilly was overwhelmed with pride, gooseflesh rippling her arms. As she sang, she saw not only the students she and Éva had marched with yesterday, but also the workers that joined them at Kossuth. She saw grandmothers and grandfathers, small boys and girls. She saw members of the Hungarian Army standing at attention, and peasants from the countryside. They were all Hungarians and they were all here united in a common cause.

When they had finished, as the crowd cheered and waved their flags, Éva and Lilly edged along the outside perimeter. At the next street, they found the usual line to the delicatessen much diminished attributed to, they assumed, the spectacle they just witnessed. An old woman at the end of the line saw the two friends approach and spoke.

"Where have you come from?"

"Váci Street."

"Did you see any tanks there? Any fighting?"

"No. That one at the corner is the first we've seen. On the way we saw the Soviet Cultural Shop being emptied and the contents burned in the street."

"A column of tanks went by not long ago. You are wise to be here. They are rationing."

"Have you heard any other news?"

"The Horizon Book Shop was also attacked; they burned the books and portraits of communist leaders in the streets. The streets are littered in rubble and the dead."

The phone rang at the Fürth apartment, surprising everyone, as Gábor came through the door returning from his outing. Mira rushed to answer it. She wanted to be the first to hear whatever news was surely about to be relayed.

"Hallo?"

"Mira? This is your Nagynéni Alida. I'm so happy to hear your voice! How are you and your family?"

"We are all well, Nagynéni, thank you. Were you singing last night? Did you see the protest? Did you hear any of the fighting at the Radio?" Mira was filled with curiosity and excitement. Her aunt was elegant, mysterious, and extravagant and had always piqued her interest and inspired admiration.

Mira's aunt, her mother's younger sister, Alida Damiani, was a mezzo-soprano opera singer who sang with the Budapest Opera. She was Mira's only aunt and Mira was Alida's only niece. They adored each other.

"Yes, my dear, I was singing at the Opera House last night. I am afraid I'm in a bit of a hurry at the moment. May I speak to your Anya, please? I hope to see you very soon."

"I'm sorry, Nagynéni, but she and Apu are both out. Here, wait one moment," Mira disappointedly handed the phone to Ili who had been standing oppressively expectant beside her.

"Alida?"

In a rush of words, Alida told her mother the event of the previous night. During rehearsal, a young man had abruptly entered the building running into the great hall. Without preamble, he announced students were being shot at the radio station. Everyone in the room was stunned. Without discussion the conductor, Imre Palló, led the orchestra in the Hungarian National Anthem. Everyone, she repeated, everyone in the opera house stood and sang.

"Anya, it was unbelievable! It was the singular most moving experience I have ever had or witnessed! And that wasn't the end. No! At the conclusion, everyone left to join the students and factory workers at the radio station. Anya, I was there! Well," Alida paused and corrected, "nearby. But close enough!

"Hungarians somehow had tanks, yes, tanks! How do I know? People were riding on them, boys were sitting on them, waving guns and waving Hungarian flags," Alida continued with emphasis, "with the Soviet emblem cut out of the middle! There was shooting, but at a distance. Nonetheless, we moved away to another area where there wasn't shooting, just protesting, near the Parliament Building. Somehow the radio was being broadcast by students near the square. They played Beethoven's Egmont Overture and My Homeland repeatedly. Anya, it was such a night!"

Alida paused before continuing. "There are many dead. Anya, I saw perhaps a dozen ÁVH dead, laid in the gutters. People stand around the bodies. Women, children, grandmothers and grandfathers. Everyone looks. It was horrible. And Anya,"Alida repeated, "Anya, there are many Hungarians dead, including women and children, young and old, girls and boys, men and women."

Gábor and Mira had heard every word as Alida recounted her experience. Gábor had grown more serious at each of his daughter's revelations. Thoughtful, he held out his hand for the phone from Ili.

"Alida? Alida, where are you now, the atelier? Please come as quickly as you are able. Can you do that?" Gábor asked, although his query was more a directive.

Alida knew her father. Although a grown woman of some renown throughout Hungary and in the world of opera, she knew her father was acting in her best interest. She was solemn, understanding his sense of urgency for her safety, and acting on her behalf.

"I'll leave within half an hour, Apa."

"Walk please, I heard they're burning the streetcars. Bring only what you can fit into a small shopping bag. Do not do or say anything to draw attention to yourself."

21

THE RISING

24 October 1956

EARLY MORNING SUNLIGHT was brightening the hillsides and homes of the Buda Hills. Concerned and agitated, Júlia and Péter waited. They waited for either the return of their parents or some word from them. The siblings sat, listening thoughtfully, quietly to the radio with their grandparents.

The thread of news through the night had been alternately shocking, cause for concern, or inspired thoughtful and sometimes heated debate. They were also concerned about their friends involved with what had been a peaceful demonstration. They assumed many had joined the revolution and hoped few, if any, were hurt or worse. Through discussion they hoped to order chaos but inevitably would lapse into silence. There, flitting at the edges, they both sensed an oppressive void, it clung to the edges of their discussion, to the apartment, to the city, to the night.

"Martial law does not mean we cannot go out. It is only a curfew," Gizella paused, then added as she shook an accusatory finger towards Péter, "and no gatherings. Stay away from any crowds. Júlia, you and Péter should go to the bakery and butcher and buy what you can. And coffee if you can find it. There will be lines and shortages... just as before!"

Gizella was right, Péter knew. It was difficult to tear himself away from the radio until he reconciled himself with the thought of what he might learn on the street. Júlia and he were preparing to go when József excitedly spoke up.

"Everyone, quiet please! Listen! The Kremlin has reinstated Nagy as Prime Minister!"

Standing in stunned silence, they listened as the broadcast continued announcing 'limited concessions' to satisfy the Hungarian people.

"Péter, do you think the fighting will now stop?" Júlia asked her brother, but the question went unanswered. Everyone in the room dared to hope yet shared a sense of unease.

Júlia and Péter finished buttoning their coats. Opening the door to go in search of groceries, Júlia called out to her grandfather from the doorway, "Nagypapa, I want to know everything that happens!" Jośef and Gizella stared at the back of the door for a brief moment.

"They'll be back," Jośef assured Gizella.

As they walked down Rósza Hill to the Margit Bridge, Júlia and Péter stopped to look back at the hills of Buda. Tanks, ominous and hulking, were positioned in several locations. Their presence, unimaginable before today, seemed surreal against the backdrop of the beautiful hills and recent memories. Júlia and Péter paused only a moment, in silence, then turned to their errand.

Crossing the bridge, Júlia pointed ahead asking, "Could that queue be for the bakery?"

A passing woman nodded confirmation while displaying the single loaf of bread she had in her bag.

The siblings had been standing in line at the bakery for almost two hours when Júlia asked Péter to return and check on their parents and grandparents. The bakery had put a small radio on a display case nearest the window with the volume turned up. Budapest Radio was reporting outbreaks of fighting and rebroadcasting the Kremlin's appointment of Nagy. Weaving together overheard conversations while waiting in line, Júlia had felt a rising concern of growing violence in the city. Their grandparents were alone in the apartment.

"I'll be right here. I'll get bread and then return directly home, you have my word. Now please, Péter, go!"

Returning home, Péter met Gábor Berci walking towards him crossing the Margit Bridge.

"Türea Péter! What have you heard? I've been sent to get bread and coffee, perhaps some cheese. Klári and Béla left the apartment last night and have yet to return. Klári's sister has joined us. Alida. I believe you know her. You may not know, Nagy's speech was just broadcast."

"Oh yes, thank you. Very good. I'm certain your daughter and her husband are at a hospital and are well. And no, to answer your question, I did not hear the speech. What did Nagy say?"

"Most importantly, he promised reforms in return for an end to the violence."

"Thank you, Mr. Berci. My grandparents are home. Júlia is standing in line at the bakers, as we have for the past two hours, you may see her there."

"Yes, go. Be careful, Péter."

"And you, Mr. Berci."

Arriving at the apartment, Péter found Gizella in the kitchen preparing tea and a light meal. She and her husband both greeted Péter as he came through the door.

"What have you done with your sister?"

"We thought it best if I came home. Júlia promised to return just as soon as she can purchase some bread."

József asked Péter to join him at the table and listen to the radio.

"You've heard? There's no news from the West but continued encouragement. Nagy has asked for an end, he's meeting..." József began but was interrupted. Through a wavering current of static was the announcement that Nagy would be broadcasting again. Gizella left the tea to steep to join her family at the table. Passing the telephone, it rang, startling her just enough to wring her hands before lifting the handset. The brief conversation caused Gizella obvious concern.

"That was Schott Anna. Anikö has been found. She is with her father," she paused, "at the Kilián Barracks. She is working at a first aid clinic there. It was a school friend who was shot at the radio station last night. She was 15," Gizella looked down, holding her hands and shaking her head.

Her husband stared, his face slack. Péter started to speak. The broadcast of Nagy's speech began drawing all of their attention to the radio.

In his third speech on the radio that day, Nagy praised the students for the positive influence they had been for the benefit of all Hungarians. However, that benefit was being eroded by the 'bandits' who were fomenting turmoil. He urged the people of Budapest to give up their arms by 1:00 p.m. Nagy concluded his speech with an appeal for order.

"The "bandits?" I wonder to whom he, or they, are referring?" Péter asked with grave concern. "Nagypapa, I need to find Tamás, and my friend Lázsló. I need to know what's happened. I'm concerned for them."

"Péter, please stay. Phone our friends and relatives around the city. Find out what you can. Then you may go with my blessing.

You know your parents will not be happy with you, or," József took Péter's hand in his own, "with me."

"Yes, Nagypapa, I will. And I will not get involved in the fighting. I promise you." Looking at his grandmother, he added, "The line at the bakery is long, it may be awhile before Júlia returns. You were right to be concerned, Nagyanya."

22

THE BUNKER

24 October1956

THERE WAS A knock at the door. Péter exchanged glances with his grandfather and grandmother, then rose to cautiously answer the door. It was Elek Fülöp, holding a bag. Péter invited him in offering a chair next to his grandfather. As Elek crossed the room, he held out the bag he had been carrying to Gizella.

"For your family. My wife, Zsófia, and her mother, Adél, were at the bakery very early this morning, before they opened. They were able to get a few loaves of the first baking. When they didn't see you there, well," Elek paused with a slight shrug of his shoulders, "you know. Here, with our blessing."

"Thank you, and thank your family. This is so kind and thoughtful. Our Júlia is at the bakery now as she has been for almost three hours. Whatever she is able to buy we will share with your family. We should all be very careful," Gizella continued as she turned to the kitchen to put the bread in the tin, "remember the shortages Budapest suffered!"

"Remember? That's not easy to forget. One potato per person."

"Sometimes one potato per family," József solemnly added.

Elek sat in the proffered chair next to József as Péter took a seat across from them.

"The bomb shelter you lived in, although I don't remember for how long," Elek began.

Péter and József exchanged glances. József answered the unasked question, "Yes, it is an underground bunker on the hillside. It is still there, although unused and locked. When the bombing began we lived there for 3 months. When we emerged, the house was gone, burned to the ground... except the stones. We moved into a family home in Pest. Of course, that was nationalized after the war. A friend of Péter's lives there now, with his family, in one of the apartments."

"You saw him yesterday at Kossuth. Bójtós Lázslo. He read Petöfi," Péter added.

"Of course, yes, I remember him. Did your family build the shelter?"

"My father, grandfather, and I. A concrete cylinder with a wooden slat floor, a vent pipe, and supplies. The pipe was operated by hand. We dug a trench under the garden. It stood about 8 feet above the ground," József, raising a single brow, turned a knowing glance to Elek, "gas settles near the ground, yes? We furnished the bunker with wooden benches, shelves and containers, and the floor, of course.

"We had a green Bakelite first aid box on the wall and a wooden tool chest with the most rudimentary tools we might need, as you can imagine. A screwdriver, hammer, nails, screws, pry bar, siphon, and pliers. There were bookshelves and a box of paper, another of pens, ink, pencils and paints for the children.

"Christmas. I'm sure you remember. Christmas, when the Russians came. And so we went to the bunker. That first morning, when the bombing began, we waited, of course. The following morning we saw what was left of our home. Nothing. For some reason it was the only house in the area that had been destroyed. We were glad for our neighbors. And we were happy that we were together. There were 21 of us."

"Twenty-one!"

"Yes, including Péter's little cousin, Natalia, who was just two years old. The Russians came once. They took everything, all of our furnishings and food. Natalia would not stop crying, she was understandably very frightened. She saved us. Her crying made the soldiers nervous. They asked us to quiet her. Instead, we encouraged her; in Hungarian, of course. We made our voices sound as if we were placating her," Jözsef chuckled, "The louder she cried, the more anxious the soldiers became until they suddenly left."

"And water? The water and electricity had been shut off in most of Budapest."

"The bombing had exposed a water line on the hillside above. Every morning, before the shooting began, I would carry a pail in each hand and go for water for the day. It had to last."

"How many small children?"

"Five. Two girls. "

"Three months and with small children," Elek was intrigued. "What did the children do all day?"

"When I went for water, they were allowed outside to play for a few minutes. There was a bit of a wall that offered some protection, as a screen you understand. There was time in the morning, before the fighting began. Everyone helped to keep the children occupied. One of the mothers would sing children's songs to them. We would play, make puzzles. There was a music box that would play Christmas songs. The children were allowed to wind it up.

"Péter would make drawings for anyone who asked. One of the men made a box for his wife's birthday, and Péter drew her birthday card.

"At night, before bed, the children would assemble at one end, the adults at the other, where they would reorganize the area, placing the shelving and bedding. All this time we would sing. In turn, each child would select a song that we would all sing together as we worked."

"And you, József?"

"We read books. Many books. We prayed. Nagyanya and her sisters would sometimes sing. We survived."

"You did not have any other trouble with the Russians?"

"One other occasion. We would signal our neighbors by banging on a pot or pan that we were well, that no help was needed. The Russians thought we were signaling their enemies. That was all, until we left. Not because of the soldiers, no. We had run out of food. We had to go. When the shooting stopped that day, we took our chances and left. It was not safe. But we did. Péter here took his drawing book and reading books. That was all, except the clothes he wore. The rest of us took what we could carry." József then looked to Elek, "Where were you and your family?"

"We also lost our home. There was nothing left after the first few days of the siege. We went from the remains of one building to another. Sometimes we were fortunate and found an underground bomb shelter that had room for us. At other times, a room shared with strangers, anywhere really. We moved in search of safety, away from the fighting. And then," Elek looked at Gizella and said, with an understanding nod, "one potato."

23

STREET FIGHTING

24 October 1956

PÉTER HAD BEEN adjusting the dial on the radio, listening to the men talk, while listening for updates. He glanced at the wall clock. It was a few minutes after noon.

Elek, determined to be of assistance, had returned to his family before going to the streets of Pest. Elek passed Júlia on the stairs as he left the Türea apartment. She handed Elek a loaf of bread, barely pausing to exchange thanks. Júlia pushed open the door to the Türea apartment just as the phone rang, and as it would continue to do, almost incessantly, for most of the afternoon. No sooner would a conversation be ended than an incoming call jangled the receiver. Between incoming calls, Péter was calling friends and family around the city. In between phone calls, the family shared news of what they had learned.

József remained vigilant listening to the news. Radio Free Europe, the BBC, and Radio Vaticana continued to broadcast their support of what they now referred to as "the Freedom Fighters."

"There are many demonstrations, and fighting. Many are dead. The radio station has been taken over, they are calling it Radio Free Kossuth. Radio Free Europe expresses sympathy and admiration for the courage and spirit of the rebels and supports the demands for freedom," József paused, looking at his wife and grandchildren before continuing, "but still no news from the West. The United States Secretary of State, John Foster Dulles, has asked to convene the United Nations Security Council. There has been no resolution."

Erzsébet turned to her son, "Péter?"

"Tom Roger with the United States Legation has been seen in several locations in Budapest. His vehicle is draped with the American flag. Our cousin, Mihaly, saw him and he was seen again near the National Museum and Hero Square. There is the suggestion he is reporting the information to Washington, D.C.

"I have also learned that the protestors now have guns and," Péter paused, certain of the weight his words would have on his grandparents, "there are small schoolboys in the firefights now, and little girls. There are many dead in the streets. The bodies of ÁVH and ÁVO are being covered with lye and left in the gutters. The Hungarian dead are being taken away, I don't know where. Boxes are being left on street corners to collect money to help families with the cost of burying. There will be a service. They will all be buried together."

József held up a hand to the effect of gaining everyone's attention. "Listen. Radio Free Europe is asking Hungarians to continue in their efforts, to resist suppression."

Júlia looked across from where she was sitting at her grandfather. "Nagypapa, I fear they are a propaganda tool of the West. No help is coming."

Péter looked across at Júlia for a long moment before asking, "Why do you say this?"

"Well, where are they brother? England, France, the U.N., the U.S.? There is no response, no action. The diplomatic question of the Suez Canal may render Hungary forfeit. Eisenhower may be more concerned with the upcoming presidential election, not to mention he's ill. He's left Hungary to his minister Dulles who has done nothing.

"It is a problem not easily solved, especially now that Khrushchev has threatened Washington, D.C. with the promise to bomb every European city if everyone doesn't withdraw from Egypt at once. Eisenhower retaliated, threatening Britain and France that he would discontinue US support of the pound and franc unless they withdraw. I will continue to hope, but there are these concerns. Will Churchill's 'Iron Curtain" be lifted? We shall see."

Péter couldn't and wouldn't argue at that moment. The tension had grown too great in the apartment. Changing the subject, Júlia turned to her grandmother.

"Everyone at the bakery has said it is the same throughout Budapest, long lines for the stores that are open. Many are closed. There is talk of shortages. Péter, your friend from Petöfi, Gergő, he walked by while I was at the bakery. Bójtós Lászlo is looking for his son, Barnát."

For Gizella, it was not difficult to ascertain or understand the flash of alarm that crossed her grandson's normally controlled features, the anxiety that strained and shortened his movements.

"You must go, Péter. You must go and help your friend find his son. Here," Gizella turned from a kitchen cupboard and crossed the room pressing several forints into Péter's hand, "find a box to put this in and say a blessing." And with a measured, affectionate glance at József, added, "We will tell your mother where you have gone. Now go."

Alexandra Fárkas' son, Charles, had witnessed the events

triggering the revolution at the radio station. From there he had followed a group of Freedom Fighters into the side streets. Not far from the station, they saw two approaching tanks draped in Hungarian flags. One of the men near the front of their group called out to the men on the tank, "Why aren't you firing?"

The Freedom Fighters running the tanks responded, "We don't have any ammo!"

"Where did you get your guns?"

"The police!"

Charles turned to the sound of approaching footfall and found himself face to face with an old friend. A group of ten or twelve heavily armed men and women followed just behind. No one showed any sign of stopping in their advance.

"Januci Thierry!"

"Charles!" Thierry noticed Charles was unarmed as he ran towards the stairwell of the building opposite. "Take cover, Charles. There's going to be heavy fighting here. The ÁVH is above you."

Suddenly, shots were fired, splintering the window nearby. Shards of glass sliced through the air, cutting the faces of Charles and two men standing nearby. The three men dropped to the ground, hugging their heads with their arms to shield themselves as both sides exchanged fire. Finally, a pause lengthened to a prolonged quiet. Charles and the men stood and discovered they were standing in a jumbled array of ÁVO uniforms now littered with glass.

Charles looked up to the group of Freedom Fighters and saw among them the four or five boys, not more than 16 or 17, he knew he'd seen earlier. The boys were easily identified by their clothes and boots. One of them was a boy he hadn't previously seen. He was younger than the others and wielding a pistol. He called out, "They're shooting from the attic!" as he led the way into the stairwell of the shop across the street. Everyone followed, including Charles.

Running on adrenaline, they made their way up four flights of stairs to the attic, their number nearly filling it. In a mostly vacant room, they easily found a group of ÁVO hiding in a closet, clothed in anything they'd been able to find. They had abandoned their uniforms on the street below. Januci, and a few of his men, bound the officers and roughly took them downstairs onto the street. The throng at the edge of the multitude gathered there recognized the men. The anger grew to rage, a blinding fury of violence. Charles left the madness. He and the two other men followed the boys as they began to head back toward the radio and into the fray. At the station, everyone noticed the shooting was primarily from the studio and not being returned. One of the boys called out, "Why can't someone bring us ammunition?"

Charles was surprised to hear his own voice answer, "Let's look!"

Charles led the way searching side streets until they found a somewhat dilapidated vehicle on Mária Street. Reaching in, Charles pushed the start button, the engine responded, then stepped inside. The two men who'd been trailing Charles climbed into the cab, the other men and boys jumped into the back.

"Where to?" Charles asked as he ground the stick shift through its low gears.

The man sitting at the door called out above the noise of the engine, smiling in his certainty and feeling of imminent conquest, "The lamp factory! Everyone knows it's been stocked with guns and ammunition." He reached across the bench seat handing Charles his soiled handkerchief. Charles looked at it questioningly. "For your face." Putting a hand to his face, Charles felt a warm stickiness and drew his hand away. It was covered in blood. Charles mashed the handkerchief against the side of his face. It seemed to staunch the flow.

The lamp factory proved to be stockpiled with ammunition. In a matter of minutes they were fully loaded driving the side streets back toward Sándor Street. The man sitting in the middle turned on the radio in time to hear the last of a government broadcast demanding a ceasefire. All weapons were to be laid down. Exchanging glances, someone reached forward and turned the radio off. Nearing the station, as they slowed to a stop, the boys called out from atop the crates of ammo announcing its arrival. People left the station, swarming the truck and arranging a human chain to off-load the truck. The truck bed was emptied within minutes.

Stepping from the truck, Charles found himself increasingly cold. He stood wondering if perhaps it was the chill of the night or, perhaps, as a result of the wounds that still bled profusely. The handkerchief had proven no match for the deep gash. Gun smoke and dust hung heavy in the night air. A sudden cry went up from the assembled crowd. Looking in their direction, Charles spied a long line of trucks filled with heavily armed Hungarian infantrymen. The trucks came to a halt, parking. The troops disembarked and were ordered "at ease." The men immediately found themselves surrounded by women exhorting them to fight alongside their countrymen.

A shout permeated the awkward silence from amongst the group where Charles stood. There followed a sudden rush across the shattered glass that covered the courtyard. Boys ran up the stairwell. Off to the side, another group had found an abandoned truck loaded with ammunition crates. Inside the cab, the bodies of ÁVO officers were draped across the steering wheel and bench seat. Sándor Victis emerged from the crowd, clambered to the top of the crates, and called for assistance. Again a chain formed and the crates were quickly removed, the ammunition and firearms dispersed.

Cries of victory turned everyone's attention to the stairwell where the boys stood with the Freedom Fighters that had accessed the building from the scaffolding in the back. They stood at the top of the stairs with the station's civilian employees, including Szepesi, and an ÁVO captain. Without warning, a barrage of automatic fire rained down on the courtyard. Everyone rushed for cover under the courtyard arches and into rooms whose doors and windows had previously been forcibly broken or shattered. Charles spun on his heel and threw himself through a doorway where he found himself in the company of two students. With the windows barred, and the entrance directly in the line of fire, all they could do was wait and hope they weren't found.

When the shooting eventually stopped, the three emerged to find the wounded being carried away. Across the courtyard, ÁVO officers were surrounded by an angry, bloodthirsty mob. As Charles surveyed the scene before him he caught his breath, his heart sinking. The still, prone figure of a boy lay near the center of the blood-stained courtyard splayed across the broken glass. Crossing the courtyard, Charles knelt beside the now familiar figure clad in a vest and boots. An ever-widening pool of blood was radiating from under the boy. Charles knelt to lift the boy into his arms when one of the students, who had taken cover with Charles only moments ago, stepped forward.

"Let me carry him, you're injured. I'm Tamás. There is a first aid station at the Kilián Barracks. From there, the more seriously injured are being taken to the hospital on Maria Street."

A younger boy stepped forward, "Follow me, I know the way."

A sudden shout and mournful cry shredded the night. Charles recognized the boy's companion who lunged towards the injured boy, taking his hand in his own. He buried his face in the injured boy's chest, muffling the name he cried again and again. Charles took his arm, gently pulling him away, encouraging him to help. "Quickly, there is no time to waste, we must get him to a doctor."

As the group made their way through the streets and side streets, they passed burned out vehicles and overturned yellow street cars. Occasionally, the sound of the Red Army sent them into dark passageways until, at last, they found the Barracks where they were met by a girl.

"Anikó!"

"Tamás! Who is this?" Anikó asked, as she led them to a gurney and called for either Dr. Fürth. Klári had just finished suturing a wound and left the bandaging to Bálint.

"I don't know. We've come from the radio station."

The boy, still holding his wounded friend's hand, now spoke through clenched teeth, taking deep breaths, fighting to control the fear and panic welling up inside, "His name is András, András Dávid."

Klári was at Dávid's side, taking his pulse and listening with her stethoscope. "How long ago did this happen?"

"I'm not certain. Ten minutes, perhaps. Fifteen. We came as quickly as we were able," Charles answered.

While Klári assessed Dávid's condition, she called to Ilona for help and András to prepare to drive the ambulance. Béla had left with the last transport. There weren't many people left at the first aid station, patients or volunteers, everyone was being sent directly to other hospitals. "Traumatic pneumothorax. Ilona, find a chest tube. Let's move him, now! András!"

Anikó stood behind the group momentarily before returning to her post. The boy who had walked in was familiar to her. Standing back from the group, Anikó quietly asked, "Szabó Löci? You and I attend the same gymnasium."

Löci paused, then, with sudden recognition, "Yes. Have you been here since the beginning?"

"No, I was at the radio but came here with Máléter after Ildikó was killed."

"Ildikó? Lamos Ildikó?"

"Yes," Anikó answered, their conversation interrupted by the urgency of the moment as Ilona returned with the needed supplies.

Klári deftly inserted and secured the chest tube to Dávid's side while Ilona injected antibiotics and set up an intravenous electrolyte solution. Klári noticed with a sudden, uncharacteristic exclamation, "Thank God! I thought we didn't have any left. You're a miracle worker, Ilona. Let's get him moved, we've no time to waste. He needs a transfusion, we need to get his lung inflated, and we need an aseptic environment. We may need a vein-to-vein transfusion; I don't know what blood products we have left at the hospital."

Passing Charles, Klári noticed his pale countenance and persistent flow of blood from wounds on his head. Holding him by an arm, Klári guided Charles to a chair.

"Sit!"

Turning to the boys, Klári instructed them to carry Charles, in the chair, to the ambulance. Charles accepted the commands quite readily; he had begun to doubt his own fortitude and had begun to wonder if what he was feeling was a precursor to fainting. As Ilona passed with Dávid's gurney, Klári grabbed the siderail and together the two women guided the gurney to exit the building.

"Anikó, you and your father finish up here. The rest of the patients have sutures, they all know to leave as soon as they're able. Please box up whatever supplies are left, or don't. András may return for them, but perhaps not. You should leave as soon as possible. The fighting will come here, perhaps very soon." Little did she know, that was the last time Anikó would see either Klári or Ilona. As she hurried to her work, the young man who had arrived with the injured boy abruptly stopped Anikó and asked for directions to the hospital.

Across the river, Tibor Arany was running in the direction of the Barracks. He had enlisted more men and boys throughout the day to find materials and meet him at the Barracks. He had heard himself and these fighters being called "the Budapest Boys" and it filled him with a powerful, enabling sense of responsibility and patriotism.

Nearing the Barracks, Arany saw two of the noisy, low-profile Russian T-34 tanks slowly approaching. Standing across the street, behind the fence at the Museum of Applied Arts, Arany watched as the first tank took aim. The turret swiveled, the tank's gun sited a building on the corner. People on the street took cover behind a meter-high cobblestone barrier the Hungarian soldiers had built as a defense. A number of dead or wounded already lay scattered in the street.

Arany's experience serving in the Hungarian Army gave him a limited knowledge and understanding of tanks. He could see that the tanks would be unable to maneuver in the narrow streets. Arany ran up to the barrier and began to throw blocks at the rear treads of the tanks. One of Maléter's messenger boys ran up behind the tank and threw a Molotov cocktail into the gas tank, tripped off the back, then ran. The tank blew, its turret was blown off the chassis, the remains smoldering. The boy, perhaps 9 years old, lay dead, his blood coagulating in the street. The small, thin body was pierced and lacerated with shrapnel, the clothes burned off his back. The second tank, with one track thrown, unable to maneuver in the narrow cobbled street bordered by tall buildings, had come to an abrupt stop. The tank hatch abruptly opened with cries of, "Don't shoot!" as the 4-man crew within surrendered. Barnát, and several of the boys, climbed onto the tank helping Arany remove the machine gun from the top of the tank and take it to the Kilián Barracks.

From his home on Rózsa Hill, Péter had intended to cross Margit Bridge and walk in the direction of Dohány Street. He intended to strategically walk the streets and cross-streets in the direction of Parliament, and then Calvin Square, to search for Lászlo or Barnát. From the aspect afforded him as he approached the bridge, Péter was able to discern Red Army guards on the Pest side and altered his direction. Péter followed the Danube until he reached the unguarded Kossuth pontoon bridge, where he crossed. From there, Péter skirted the Parliament Building to the side streets leading to Dohány. The visual onslaught of destruction, debris, and corpses were repulsive. Nearing Váci Street, the area was congested with people of all ages, from all walks of life. The street was strewn with litter and smoldering piles of communist propaganda pamphlets, fliers, posters, and books. The surreal scene reminded him of a sepia snapshot of some other place and time. Somehow Péter spied Márkó and Denes in the dull, monochromatic confusion. Side stepping through the dense crowd intent on their purpose, he had almost reached his friends unnoticed when they abruptly looked up.

"Péter!" Márkó and Denes acknowledged their friend simultaneously.

"I'm glad to see you. You are well? I'm actually looking for Bójtös Lászlo, or his son, Barnát. Have you seen either of them?"

"Lászlo, several times. Barnát was working for Máléter, but Lászlo found out he's one of the Budapest Boys."

"Budapest Boys? The boys with the Molotov cocktails?"

"Yes."

"Lászlo has found him?"

"Not that we know of. Péter, we could use your help."

"I'm trying to find Barnát."

"While you are searching, there are pamphlets you could leave around the city. Encouragement, safety precautions, tactics. You don't have to pass them out, just leave them on street corners, in doorways. We've been using the press inside. It would be a big help. I was just leaving to distribute them myself. Denes will be here to print more. If you'll go east, I'll go west."

Péter nodded his assent, "Certainly. Can you get them now, please, I must continue."

Soon, Péter was off in the direction of Calvin Square, the pamphlets quickly dispersed and as quickly taken up by the eager populace.

News of the revolt in Budapest and other Hungarian cities quickly spread throughout the day to the countryside. There were many stories of heroism and courage: A mother who had walked up to a Soviet tank and stopped it. Children blowing up tanks. Children dead on the streets of Budapest. Stories of Hungarian Army soldiers tearing the Soviet insignia from their uniforms and joining rank with their Hungarian compatriots while arming them with guns and rifles. A girl, perhaps 9, laying dead in the street with a machine gun in her arms. Stories of the extraordinarily brave Hungarian colonel who had joined the Revolution, placed tanks inside and at the entrance of the Kilián Barracks, repelling all Russian attempts to capture it. Stories of Soviet tanks outside of Parliament and positioned on main roadways were ameliorated with news of young children smearing jam on the viewing slits effectively disabling the tanks. Of old men and women smearing the roads with oil and grease causing the tank tracks to spin. Of insurgents hanging saucepans, mistaken by the tank drivers as anti-tank devices, from the overhead lines. Of children, "the kids of Pest," borrowing porcelain plates from a nearby public kitchen, then laying them in the road; they were mistaken as anti-tank mines by the tank crewmen.

The Budapest Boys were taking a heavy toll effectively using Molotov cocktails against the tanks. The burned-out, abandoned hulls were evidence of their highly effective work. The narrow streets and tall buildings, combined with the lack of infantry support and the near-constant onslaught of the insurgents, were defeating the tanks. Throughout the day, there were increasing reported incidents of Soviet crewmen abandoning their tanks and handing them over in support of the Hungarians.

Larger, localized battles were being fought throughout Pest. László Iván Kovács led a resistance group in an attack at the Corvin Passage, a strategic location near the Barracks and the Radio. The radio station had finally been seized by the armed rebellion. A group of students had gained access by climbing metal shoring on the back of the building built there for repairs. Unarmed protestors were repelled at the offices of the communist newspaper, fired upon by the ÁVH, only to be driven out with the arrival of the armed rebellion.

Across Pest the hunt had begun. When ÁVH were found, the crowd was merciless. Some of the officers were lynched, some captured, and some burned. The brutalized remains lay in the streets, communist literature windblown into the cracks and crevices around their body, sticking to the blood and body fluids, an ironic, macabre collage.

'The Rising' was felt in every Hungarian household in every city, town, and village. The uprising was a common cause, an electrifying current that galvanized the populace regardless of perceived and traditional class distinctions. The Hungarian people were rising as one, an alliance against a common problem: their government's crushing economic and social policies. The communist govern-ment had not expected such widespread resistance, nor the urban guerrilla tactics being employed with overwhelming success. Hungarians everywhere were fighting back. Hungarian police were disarmed and driven from rural villages and towns. Localized battles were victorious against small detachments of the Red Army driving them from the countryside.

Throughout the country, sympathetic farmers sent carts and truckloads of food into the cities. When news of the food shortages reached Megyer late in the afternoon of the 24th, György had driven his wagon from farm to farm collecting vegetables and other food. The following day, Thursday, Abel Joost and he would drive the wagon through the countryside and collect more donations. Together they would deliver the food to the train station on Friday for the people of Budapest. György knew he would be on that train.

24

MORNING

25 October 1956

UNWILLING BUT UNDERSTANDING, Alexandra handed Rebeka her knapsack filled with food and a few forints. In the predawn, a chill indicative of the cold weather long overdue frosted their breath as they spoke on the front steps. The moon, a waning crescent, cast only a faint light. Sunrise was yet an hour away, and although the birds were starting to awaken, Rebeka's two brothers still slept. It had been a long night. Not long before Rebeka had quietly approached Alexandra in the kitchen, Charles, at last, had returned bloodied and bandaged.

The previous night, Alexandra had fallen asleep between radio broadcasts. She had been turning the dial fitfully, as she had throughout the previous day, whenever the children were sleeping. Although anxious, she had been stoic with the children. She answered their questions. As a precaution, with the added benefit to divert their attention, Alexandra found and unfurled a topographical map of Hungary. They poured over the map for hours. At Alexandra's request, the children retraced their route from Nemesbük to Megyer, locating the Zala River and Lake Balaton. As they recounted their journey, they told Alexandra of their adventures, their homes and horses, Janga and Sándor. When asked, they pointed out the route they had taken from Megyer to Budapest. Rebeka hesitated but, encouraged, asked Alexandra to show them the location of Kistarcsa.

"Here," Alexandra indicated a small spot on the map northeast of Budapest, then patiently waited.

"Our father is there, the ÁVO took him," Péter and Jani responded in unison.

Rebeka noted the compassion on Alexandra's face and continued, "I think Dávid and Dominik may have gone there. Well, at least Dávid. He thinks he can somehow free our father, or be there when he is freed, if the revolutionaries open the prisons."

Alexandra looked at them each in turn as she earnestly replied, "Let us believe this will happen. It is one of the 16 Points." Alexandra did not tell them that, in all probability, their father was not at Kistarsca but at Vác.

The children were worn out and spent the day in a repeating pattern of eating, sleeping, and questioning Alexandra. Their young, inquisitive minds questioned everything especially, of course, the tanks and activities taking place in Pest. They were all especially grateful for the delicious meals Alexandra prepared, and their clean clothes, when they awoke from an afternoon nap in the nightshirts they'd been given. Only Rebeka was unsettled. Attentive and watchful of her brothers, she would help Alexandra with the meals and clean the dishes. All the while, Rebeka cast furtive glances at the door and windows, peering into the distance yet not knowing what or where to look, dropping her eyes dejectedly when she thought no one was watching. Nothing escaped Alexandra. Her heart ached for the girl as it ached for her own son.

The near moonless night sky presented a velvet backdrop accentuating the firefights and shell explosions. The view mesmerized the children until Alexandra called them to dinner, closing the curtains while their attention was diverted. After cookies and fruit, she introduced them to the books in her library. A small room near the back of the house, its location insulated from the sounds of violence that were, thankfully, diminishing as the night wore on.

After the boys had gone to sleep, Rebeka joined Alexandra in the kitchen. They sat together listening to the news, searching the channels, gleaning all they could. Most surprising was a broadcast from Radio Budapest. The station announced the uprising had been crushed. Everyone still fighting was asked to leave their weapons in front of the nearest building.

"Do you think this is true, Alexandra? What will become of everyone who has fought?"

Alexandra could see the thought and implications of such a possibility clearly frightened the girl. In an attempt to placate her, with what she hoped was the truth, Alexandra stated firmly and simply, "No, Rebeka, I don't."

Rebeka asked more questions about the location of Kistarcsa and possible routes until, seemingly satisfied, she excused herself to go to bed.

Alexandra returned to the radio but, exhausted, had fallen asleep in the chair for what had seemed only moments. A strange sound alarmingly awoke her. Hyperfocused, Alexandra sat upright, slightly turning her head, searching for a sight or sound to disclose whatever had awakened her. The knock at her entry at first surprised her, then sent her rushing to the door, flinging it open unceremoniously, fearlessly, and, considering the circumstances, most certainly foolish.

"Charles!"

Charles was accompanied by two friends who, he explained to

his mother, had helped him. The young men had taken him to the hospital. From there, considering his condition and at the advice of the doctor who had treated his head injury, they had accompanied him home through several harrowing perils. The two young men wore long, oversized coats they'd been given to ward off the cold. Charles briefly introduced them to his mother. Alexandra, distracted by Charles return and the pressing needs at hand, quickly arranged a plate of food and seltzer water. Setting plates at the table and setting out the food, she watched as they ate.

"Please, you must stay with us. Shelter with us at least for the night. Eat, get some rest, you will be better for it, to do whatever it is you must.We would be grateful if you would allow us to do this for you after all you've done for us."

"Yes," agreed Charles. "You must stay. That is settled."

Understanding their fatigue and the near exhaustion in Charles' face, there followed a brief synopsis of the last 32 hours ending with the walk home from the hospital. Charles chose not to tell his mother about Dávid, for her sake as well as for Dominik, who sat forlorn and despondent.

"Of all the events, mother, the atrocities are almost unbearable. How they cannot see that this is what fuels the revolution! Mother, as we neared the Erzsébet Bridge, we saw two Russians lifting an injured comrade into their armored car. At that moment, an unarmed older man walked by without even a glance in their direction. Without hesitation, one of the soldiers shot him in the head."

"Shot him in the head? What was he doing?"

"He was walking. Just walking. They shot him. He fell to the ground, holding his ears, stood and ran." Seeing his mother's surprise he repeated himself, "Yes, stood and ran. It wasn't far before he fell again, head first. His arms at his side. We saw him die, his body went limp in an instant."

Soft sounds of compassionate affirmations sounded from deep within the two young men sitting across from her. Their eyes were cast downwards, their shoulders weighted with the events of the last two days. Alexandra fought back tears but was comforted in Charles' presence. Together they would find their way through this nightmare.

Charles showed his friends where they could get cleaned up and ready for sleep. Meanwhile, Alexandra gathered pillows and coverlets which she spread on the floor of Charles' room. Succinctly, given the time and fatigue, she told Charles she was sheltering three young people she'd met crossing on the Chain Bridge. They slept in the small room adjacent to his own.

"You'll meet in the morning. They are quite courageous, as you have been. I'll see you in the morning, Charles."

"Good night, mother."

Alexandra returned to the kitchen to quietly clean up. She intended to go to bed immediately afterwards. As Alexandra started to put the dishes away, she was surprised to turn and find Rebeka.

"Good morning, Alexandra. I'm sorry if I have disturbed you."

"No, no Rebeka. That is quite alright. In fact, I have good news, my son has returned."

Rebeka turned, eyes casting about the rooms within view then turning questioningly back to Alexandra.

"He returned with two friends. He was slightly injured." Noting Rebeka's concerned response she hurried on, "Not to worry, thank you! Nonetheless, considering what they've been through, they are all exhausted and have gone to sleep."

Rebeka visibly brightened and stepped forward to embrace Alexandra in an unexpected show of emotion.

"I am so happy for you!" Stepping back again, Rebeka looked solemnly at Alexandra then continued, "I must find my brother."

Alexandra, momentarily lulled into a false sense of security with the fighting seemingly curtailed and Charles' return, nodded her understanding. Without a word, Alexandra turned to ready several packages of food.

"Rebeka, could you please fetch your knapsack."

Her knapsack readied, Rebeka stood at the door facing a solemn Alexandra.

"I promise you, Rebeka, I will watch over your brothers. I will accompany them to Megyer should the need arise. However..."

Alexandra exacted a series of promises from Rebeka. Rebeka agreed to find shelter before nightfall, preferably that she would return to Alexandra, avoid all soldiers and battles, and to not, under any circumstance, travel to Kistarcsa.

As Rebeka walked into the pre-dawn darkness towards Pest, Alexandra returned to the kitchen after uncharacteristically locking the front door. There were only a few things to put away before she turned off the lights and retired to her room. As she passed the hallway alcove, Alexandra only briefly noted in the shadows the clothes the young men had left on the wall hooks, their shoes on the floor underneath. She could not see that beyond the first pair of shoes, partially eclipsed by the coat, was a pair of boots she had seen before, a pair of boots not unlike the two smaller pair in the adjacent room.

Walking down Castle Hill, the first rays of dawn began to break over the horizon. The briskness of the morning, Charles' return, and the beautiful sight of the Danube, gave Rebeka a renewed sense of optimism and hope. Looking up to the city beyond, she abruptly stopped. Rebeka's breath fell from her as her body slumped. The once beautiful city was ravaged, the landscape before her punctuated with rising columns of black, oily smoke.

The streets were torn and cratered, littered with debris, cobbles scattered, windows shattered, the beautiful facades pockmarked with bullet holes and gaping wounds. The violence exposed the wreckage within of homes, apartments, ateliers, workspaces, and businesses, some which were still occupied, the residents having nowhere else to go. Rebeka averted her eyes in shock and empathy for an older couple sitting on the edge of their bed. Exposed to the world, two of their four walls were crumpled in the street below, a pile of dust and rubble.

Rebeka crossed the Chain Bridge to Pest wondering where she should start her search for Dávid. To her left, the bakery was open, a queue forming. Rebeka walked to the bakery and stood alongside the mostly older women standing there. She couldn't help be noticed, she was a stranger wearing clothes of a country girl.

The women gradually turned their interest and gaze to the pretty young woman standing patiently nearby. She was a young, Hungarian beauty. She stirred their affections amidst the chaos and turmoil that had ruptured their lives. A slightly stooped woman, a shawl edged in delicate vines and blossoms wrapped around her neck and spilling onto her overcoat, stepped towards the girl. The girl looked lost.

"Are you alright, dear?"

Rebeka was grateful, her smile broadening, cheering all of the women.

"Thank you! Thank you, yes, I am. But, I am trying to locate my brother. We are not from Budapest."

Rebeka asked for directions to any nearby hospitals thinking she would walk in that general direction as she scouted the area. Describing her brother, no one could recall seeing him. Everyone noting, they uniformly agreed, they would remember such boots and embroidery. As she began to walk away, Rebeka thanked them. A woman at the front of the line called to Rebeka as she passed, handing her a fresh, hot roll. Everyone in line enthusiastically added their goodwill and blessings to this pretty young girl searching for her brother.

"The curfew has been lifted, be careful, take care where you go," they cautioned her.

Only steps away from the bakery, Rebeka noted the streets becoming crowded, streaming in the general direction of the Parliament Building. Standing, watching, it was hard for Rebeka to understand how this could be happening again, reminiscent of not quite two days prior. Yet it was, she assured herself. Because it was, there was a very good chance Dávid and Dominik were a part of whatever it was that was happening.

Abandoning her intended search, Rebeka joined the crowd which now seemed to be ushered in the direction of Parliament by trucks following close behind. Men standing on the truck running boards, gripping the side view mirrors, were calling for people to join the demonstration. Rebeka wondered at what she was seeing, something seemed odd to her. Passing the Ministry of Heavy Industry, a woman shouted from a window high above to the demonstrators.

"Don't go to the Parliament! Russian tanks have surrounded it!"

Rebeka looked about her but all the demonstrators looked ahead toward their goal, waving their flags, and shouting shared sentiments. No one seemed worried.

By 10:30 that morning, ten thousand unarmed people streamed onto Kossuth Square from several different directions, each "encouraged" by a following retinue of vehicles. Children, the elderly, men and women, students, and workers gathered peacefully to continue their protest. Rebeka scanned the crowd, moving through it until she gained the opposite side. There, she was surprised to find a tank with Hungarian demonstrators sitting on it, waving the flag of the revolution. Jubilant, they called out across the crowd again and again.

"The Russians are our friends!"

Looking for comfort in the reactions of those in closest proximity, Rebeka found herself questioning their seemingly oblivious response. Instead, they continued to shout slogans and sing.

Uneasy in her surroundings, Rebeka started to sidle through the crowd again. Gaining the opposite side she was surprised to find more tanks in position, guns leveled and pointed across the square. There were no Hungarians sitting on these tanks. No Hungarian flags draped across their ominous hulls, slanted armament, or held aloft. Rebeka's breathing quickened, her mind silently screaming the recent, unheeded admonishments; *avoid battles, take heed where you go, don't go to Parliament.* Fighting a rising panic, Rebeka turned, looking for any sign of Dávid or Dominik. Suddenly, the woman next to her collapsed. Dropping to her knees to help the woman, Rebeka put a hand on the woman's shoulder. Unresponsive, Rebeka gently shook the woman's shoulder and bent closer to look at the woman's turned face. Instead, an expanding pool of blood was framing the woman's head. Horrified, Rebeka recoiled, lurching upright and falling back against the crowd. Simultaneously, the square erupted in machine gun fire, hysteria, and panic.

ÁVH snipers were firing on the crowd from the rooftop of the Ministry of Agriculture and other neighboring buildings.The mass of people gathered on the square panicked, caught in a fishbowl with no where to hide. Hungarians realized too late the menacing reality of the tanks as they began to fire into the crowd; the multiple percussions at such close range were deafening, mortal. Rounds fired by a Soviet tank exploded across the square into the building where top party leaders were negotiating with Soviet comrades, including George Malenkov. The party officials fled into the cellar.

Elek Fülöp stood in the window of his office in the Ministry of Agriculture, which faced the square. He watched in disbelief and anger as the battle engaged. The pillars of the arcade underneath the Ministry provided a narrow shield from the fusillade of gunfire. As many as twenty people piled one on top of the other behind each of the pillars in an attempt to hide. Moved to action, Elek and his colleagues ran to open the first-floor windows and began pulling in men, women, and children attempting to flee the carnage. Someone was yelling, overheard through the confusion of people's desperate cries for help, the fusillade of explosives, and the calls for aid. The communist party Secretary of the Ministry demanded the windows be closed, yelling furiously at the staff to leave the people to be shot, as they deserved.

As the tanks quieted, the gunfire grew closer. Through the mottled haze of drifting smoke, Elek and his coworkers could make out the uniforms of the ÁVO. The police were hunting down every last person who may have been on the square, shooting them, and piling their bodies in the plaza. Inside the Ministry, they realized they were witnessing more than a great tragedy, this was a nightmare.

The square itself was concealed in a layer of the dead and dying, the mutilated and wounded. Rebeka had run between two tanks at the periphery of the square. She had fled to the rear, falling to the ground next to the track, folding her arms and hands to protect her head and ears. The air was saturated with a hellish fusion of fear, pain, gunfire, screaming, defiance, and anger. Rebeka fought panic, willing herself to focus on her immediate situation. Suddenly, surprisingly, the firing stopped.

Cowering, unsure of what to do, Rebeka cautiously looked from between the tanks to see who moved and where they were going. Her ears rang. Smoke lay heavily across the square, drifting unbidden into every pore, her nostrils, and causing her eyes to tear. The smoke began to lift, like a curtain drawn aside exposing a macabre scene, the grisly work of mere minutes. Nearly a thousand were dead, hundreds injured, maimed, or mutilated. As the smoke lifted into the sky so too did the cries of the wounded, the agony of the bereft, and the screams of those terrorized.

Rebeka was stunned, uncertain of what to do. Suddenly, she was being pulled to her feet, a fierce grip locked on her arm. Instinctively, Rebeka blindly fought as she screamed and raged, adrenaline coursing through her veins, stinging her scalp, the blood pounding in her ears rendering her unable to hear her name until it was screamed.

Looking up, relief was replaced with horror as two men, rushing to her aid, came up behind Dominik. The men threw Dominik to the ground, mercilessly beating him before they heard Rebeka's cries, begging them to stop.

"Dominik!" Rebeka, crying, reached out to him before looking up at the men. "I know this man, but I didn't see who he was, I was blinded by the fighting. I've been looking for him. I'm so sorry," she repeated again and again. Turning back to Dominik, "I am so sorry, Dominik! Dominik!"

Dominik, his left eye swelling, blood trickling from his left ear, grunted as he stood. He held his right side, where he'd been brutally kicked. Rebeka stood next to Dominik, worried and concerned for him, unknowing and oblivious to the immediate danger they were both in.

"Follow me, Rebeka. Stay close."

Turning away from Kossuth, Rebeka silently followed Dominik. Their pace became staggered as Dominik frequently stumbled and stopped, grimacing, catching his breath. Rebeka guardedly searched the streets and rooftops for possible assailants and unknown terrors. At length, although not far distant from the square, they reached an ambulance station. Doctors and staff, both outside and in, were working at a frantic pace to accommodate the near constant influx of both wounded and dead. The malodorous combination of blood, vomit, and fear mixed with the tumultuous din of sirens, cries, screams, orders, and commands was staggering.

Dominik continued into the hallway interrupting Rebeka's intent to find help for him, instead she rushed to catch up. Following Dominik to a corridor lined with gurneys, she saw him abruptly stop next to one. Supporting his ribcage with one hand, Dominik gently reached out with the other to hold a pale hand that had slipped from under a sheet, its owner unconscious or, perhaps, dead. Confused, Rebeka looked from Dominik to the hand he was holding. Her eyes traveled from the waxen, inert hand along the covering sheet to the face of the body lying on the gurney. The blood in her veins grew cold, her body rigid, the wind knocked out of her as surely as if she'd suffered a severe blow. Beside her, Dominik collapsed.

25

THE AFTERMATH

25 October 1956

THAT MORNING, MANY of the residents of Buda had watched the fusillade from their hillside homes and apartments, listening to the barrage of machine-gun fire and explosions. Billowing clouds of dense smoke rose from behind the Parliament Building. Anxious for news, the people of Budapest turned to their radios.

The Bójtós apartment on Dohány Street was vacant, as was every apartment in the building. The building's occupants had fled to the bomb shelter in the basement where Lászlo had found them. Lászlo carried the unconscious and bloodied body of his son, Barnát, laying him on the floor in front of Klára. Barnát would in time recover from the concussion he had suffered from a primary blast but would remain deaf in his left ear and forever bear the scars of multiple lacerations. Lászlo stepped away then crouched to the floor embracing Izsák, who buried his face in his father's coat, while Klára, Ilona, and her mother, Erzsébet, inspected and bandaged Barnát's wounds. Ilona's father sat nearby consoling his grandchildren, Tomi and Petra; their generation had never known war or its terrors.

Following the massacre, ten thousand angry and armed people, led by Tamás, Márton, András, and Márkó, returned to the headquarters of the Budapest Police, demanding weapons and the release of prisoners. Sándor Kopácsi had received orders to meet with the revolutionaries and negotiate a surrender. Instead, Kopácsi considered the probable outcomes, including the certain lynching of the police if violence broke out, as he certainly expected it would. In an amazing act of courage, Kopácsi, with two policemen, walked out into the square unarmed. Facing the crowd, Kopácsi offered to have a delegation of five people inspect conditions within the building and choose from among the prisoners all who qualified as 'Freedom Fighters.' The delegation, including Márton and András, willingly complied. After inspecting the jail, they chose fifty prisoners before leaving the building and the square encouraged, excited, and triumphant.

Across the city, another group intent on avenging the massacre at Parliament stormed the ÁVO police headquarters. Overwhelming the guards, the Freedom Fighters searched the building. The already angry mob turned violent when they found mutilated bodies of students in the basement. The Freedom Fighters threw the ÁVO guards, along with their secret files of Budapest citizens, out into the angry, mob-filled streets. The files were burned. The guards were given no quarter. Throughout Budapest, the ÁVO were beaten to death. Some were burned.

Although Nagy's government was legally in place, subversive Soviet influence was a powerful force that had yet to yield and still wielded power in the governance of Budapest. As a result of Sándor Kopácsi's negotiation with the revolutionaries, all telephone lines to Police Headquarters, including the "red phone," were disconnected. Sándor Kopácsi was declared an outlaw, an enemy of the state.

On Castle Hill, Alexandra and Charles had led Péter and Jani to a back bedroom where they had barricaded themselves. The events of the morning had taken everyone by surprise and now, how quickly every trouble and trial seemed to have escalated. Alexandra had awakened as the young András brothers were beginning to stir and went to the kitchen. Again, as she passed the room where Charles' friends had hung their clothes, she glanced in that direction. The morning light illuminated what the shadows of the previous night had hidden. Alexandra stopped, unmoving, as she stared at the familiar boots. Péter and Jani, emerging from their room, were promptly sent back to retrieve their boots. Alexandra met the boys in the hallway as they returned holding their boots, momentarily looking at her in curiosity before dropping their boots and crying out in unison, "Where did you get those?"

The door to Charles' bedroom was flung open. Dominik stood, momentarily incredulous, Péter and Jani returning his stare in disbelief, before falling to his knees catching the boys in a tumble-down embrace. Charles and Tamás stood in the background confused and dazed in their weary condition.

"You know each other?" Charles managed to ask.

"You're Rebeka's Dominik?" Alexandra was incredulous.

"Yes! We're from the same village. We're neighbors and traveled here together but became separated." To the boys Dominik continued, "Where is Rebeka?"

Péter and Jani clung to Dominik. Alexandra answered.

"Rebeka left only a short time ago. She has gone in search of her brother. Have you seen him? Rebeka assumed you were together. If you hurry you might catch her. She was walking in the direction of Chain Bridge."

Dominik gently disentangled himself from the boys then pulled his boots on and grabbed his coat from its peg. He turned to the boys. He would spare them his news of their brother hoping against hope that this day would find Dávid recovering from his wounds. Kneeling, he laid a hand on each of their shoulders as he spoke. "Please, stay here so we can find you. I will find them." And then he was gone. Soon after, Tamás followed determined to rejoin the battle.

The battle had been unexpected, no one knew with any certainty if it was confined, a singular incident, or if the city was perhaps being laid siege to. From atop the dresser, Alexandra tuned her radio to Nagy's broadcast. Across Budapest, citizens huddled around their radios in what remained of their city, their homes, and apartments. They listened as Nagy announced the beginning of negotiations for the withdrawal of Soviet troops after order was restored. They listened as he announced Sándor Racz had been elected to represent the fighting workers of Budapest. They listened as Nagy heralded the replacement of Gerő by János Kádár. But it wasn't enough. Nagy underestimated and misunderstood the will of the people and to what lengths they would go to remove the Soviet presence from Hungary.

Radio Free Europe announced elsewhere in Budapest there were calls for a general strike. Citizens rampaged through the city, searching for ÁVO and ÁVH officers. Péter Gábor, leader of the ÁVH, was arrested. Radio Budapest reported that captured ÁVO and ÁVH were being tortured, lynched at their ankles, and then burnt. The disfigured corpses were pinned with photographs of Stalin or Rakosi and spat upon. Some bodies were left in the gutters, where passersby continued to abuse the corpses of the men and women who had terrorized and brutalized their community for so many years.

Although the boys were fixated on every word, Alexandra turned the station. It was too much, too obscene. Turning the dial to the BBC, they learned protestors were in front of the US Embassy.

Citizens were calling on the United Nations for aid. There followed another announcement from Nagy declaring a general amnesty in exchange for the fighting to stop.

On Rósza Hill, Péter had returned to the Türea apartment finding it empty but locating a cryptic note left on the table that he pocketed. The note led Péter to his family in their bunker with the Fülöp, Fürth, and Novák families. Everyone had brought food and water, which was arranged on a table near the rear of the bunker. An assortment of folded coverlets was stacked nearby. Mira and Ágnes had been reading with Mira's aunt Alida when Péter walked in. Now they all looked up, expectant. Novák held his wife, Hannah, both tense with anxiety, asking if Péter had seen their twins, Ervin and Adrián. Péter had not, but mentioned finding his friend Lászlo's son, Barnát.

"I hope and pray the same will be so for your sons."

Gizella asked, "Where did you find him, Péter?"

"With Maléter and a man named Arany at the Barracks. After telling Barnát his father was searching for him, he agreed to return home, if only to reassure his mother that he was fine. I suggested he avoid the square, and I hope he did."

Barnát had not. He had seen the Hungarian students and children waving the revolution flags while riding Russian tanks in the direction of the square. Barnát believed, as so many did, the Russian soldiers had joined the revolution. Barnát had followed the tanks to the square.

North of the Kilián Barracks Lászlo had heard the barrage of gun fire and shelling. Intuition drove him to the square, arriving as the veil of acrid smoke lifted revealing horror and carnage. It hadn't taken any effort to find Barnát, he had practically stumbled over the body of his son at the periphery of the square in front of a Soviet tank.

"Péter, did you witness any of this?" his grandfather asked.

"Some, Nagypapa, some. I saw young boys taking petrol from abandoned petrol stations. These are the 'Budapest Boys' we've heard of; Barnát is one of them. The petrol is for Molotov cocktails the boys make to disable the tanks. Two hundred Soviet tanks burning on the streets of Budapest, Apa. Ordinary citizens armed with only rudimentary weapons. When I was on Váci Street, it was awash in documents and enormous piles of burning pamphlets and books from the Soviet Cultural Center. I was also told that people had broken into the ÁVO offices, where they burned files and piles of paper."

"Files? The files of the people?"

"Yes, Nagypapa. Everyone's files have been burnt."

No one spoke. Everyone stood somewhat shaken by the wonder and implications of this news. There was no longer a personal record of every citizen. No record of where they worked, no record of their associations, family, or friends. No record of their military service or prison terms. No history of where they lived or what schools they had attended. No accounting of previous transgressions, real or devised. No falsified records, no forced confessions, no catalog of what they owned, or what had been taken from them. No accusations, no arrests, no suspicions. There was no history.

Péter broke the silence, turning to Gábor Berci and asking, "Have either Dr. Fürth returned home?" Just then, a radio broadcast caught everyone's attention.

Mira's grandfather, Gábor, had brought their family's radio and set it on a bench turning the dial as requested. Now, as everyone listened, Radio Budapest reported insurgents had opened the city's prisons releasing and arming the prisoners. Rakosi's former home had been raided. The broadcaster described the luxurious and opulent rooms and furnishings the insurgents had discovered. Barricades of paving stones and burnt-out vehicles had been erected throughout the city. Seized weapons were being distributed, arming the insurgents.

"No, Péter. But we know they moved from the first aid clinic at the Barracks to the hospital on Mária Street. Klári was able to call us. It was brief. Of course they are sleeping there, the hospital is overrun with patients."

Klári and Béla Fürth had been hard at work since the moment they had arrived at the Barracks only a few days ago. Their friend Dr. Béla Orovecz, director of the National Ambulance Service, had organized the rescue operations in Budapest. Orovecz had reopened the air raid shelter of the ambulance building on Márko Street as an emergency hospital, 'Cellar Hospital,' as it came to be known.

Ambulance staff, medical students, and all area doctors including those who had retired, were hard at work. Drivers of the Budapest Bus Company volunteered and were put to work both in the rescue and transport of casualties and in delivering much needed supplies. The Ministry of Health allocated more supplies. Klári coordinated with Dr. Orovecsz the supplies needed for the first aid station at the Barracks and then, as the area was becoming more dangerous, its probable closure. When the time came, the more seriously wounded would be transferred to the Hospital in the Rock in the hills of Buda. Dr. Orovecs would make the arrangements with Dr. András Máthé, the lead surgeon at the Rock.

As predicted, as the Barracks became increasingly threatened, Orovecs had closed the first aid station in favor of the Cellar. Klári, Béla, and Ilona Tóth had removed the boy with the collapsed lung to the Central Military Hospital late last night to find the hospital overwhelmed. The hallways were lined with gurneys. There were beds in the cafeteria. Ilona anticipated Klári's request and moved ahead to the nurse's station identifying herself, the Fürths, and the condition of their patient. The nurse, her face pinched and worn from lack of sleep and grueling effort, recognized the doctors, gratefully welcoming them as they passed directly to the ICU.

"Take him upstairs, there are three or four in each room as we are able to manage. Find a space for him wherever you're able. A shipment of blood products and supplies has just arrived from the Austrian Legation. We should have what you need."

"The Austrian Legation?"

"Yes, the Austrian government has sent food, medicine, plasma, bandages, clothing, and other supplies. The Red Cross is in charge of transportation. Dr. Peinsipp at the Legation oversees the receipt and distribution. They must be very careful."

"Why is that?"

"The Soviets. That's all I know. I'm sorry, Doctors, but I have to get back to my work."

Moving Dávid upstairs the only space they found had been newly vacated in a hallway lined with gurneys. Ilona went to find the charge nurse while Klári and Béla went in search of a thoracic specialist. The morning had been long. Surgeries were back to back with more wounded pouring in. There was news of another massacre, this time at Kossuth Square. Dávid was given antibiotics, blood, and was being monitored. However, it was evident to Klári that Dávid's condition was worsening.

At last Klári found a surgeon just coming to the floor and arranged to meet in 15 minutes at the surgery. Klári returned to the unit, turning into the hallway as she called for a nurse to help her prepare Dávid for surgery. Ahead Klári saw a young couple standing beside Dávid's gurney, the woman clearly in distress. As Klári approached, the young man fell to the floor.

26

TURMOIL

26–31 October 1956

IN THE FOLLOWING days the people of Budapest emerged from what was left of their homes, shelters, and basements. In some areas schools re-opened. Fall had abruptly given way to winter. The last of October grew frigid, each day colder than the one before. Three days ago it had been sunny and 70 degrees. Overnight, the mercury had precipitously dropped to 59 degrees. The waning moon was a thin sliver, casting icy white shadows in the hollows of gathering clouds.

The uprising was spreading. Workers were striking and demonstrations demanding change were being staged in cities across Hungary. An hour and a half north of the Budapest border, guards fired on a demonstration of unarmed civilians killing 52 and wounding 86. There were other incidents of the ÁVH firing on demonstrators demanding the release of political prisoners. Demonstrators fought back with equal brutality. In Miskolc, the striking miners and workers massacred those they believed responsible for the deaths in the previous days' demonstration.

Friday morning, Charles and his mother devoted themselves to Péter and Jani, finding new ways to keep them occupied and interested. Despite the uncertainty of postal delivery, they had the boys write letters to their family in Megyer. It was a comforting endeavor, the boys felt a connection to their home and family. They enjoyed the activity so much, they asked if it would be too extravagant to have several pieces of paper that they might write individual letters to each of their parents, grandparents, and little sister. Alexandra encouraged them with suggestions of what they might include in their letters.

Nearby, the Ruszworm Café had reopened that morning, although limited baking supplies limited their offerings. Charles was able to return with a sweet roll for everyone. The boys drew a picture of the roll and described its flavor for their grandmother. Alexandra and Charles subtly took turns keeping watch at their front window, the radio nearby. Alexandra watched for Rebeka. Charles noted every disturbance, every tank, soldier, puff, or plume of smoke.

"There's an ambulance coming up Castle Hill, Anya."

In Budapest, Nagy was organizing his government and began to meet with delegations from the Writers' Union, farmers, student groups, and other councils. He repeatedly made desperate appeals to the UN for intervention.

Throughout the day, armed revolutionaries continued to gather at Corvin Passage. Corvin was the primary traffic junction near the Kilián Barracks and the Budapest Radio Station, a strategic and defensible position. László Kovács led a group of a thousand men and set up a base at the Corvin Cinema. Repeatedly, the Soviets attempted to take the position. Repeatedly they were rebuffed. The Freedom Fighters and Budapest Boys destroyed or disabled a dozen

T-34 tanks. Among the Freedom Fighters, Budapest Boys, old and young men and women fighting at Corvin, was Ericá, a girl of 15. Carrying a bag of grenades, Ericá was shot as she ran towards the tanks. Still she ran, and was shot again. And again. Finally, when she could run no further, she began to lob grenades at the tanks. Ericá succeeded in destroying one tank before she died.

On Rósza Hill, everyone had returned to their homes from the bunker leaving behind the coverlets and supplies. Klári and Béla returned early that morning, surprising their family. Mira had a litany of questions for her parents.

"What has been your most interesting case? What did you have to eat? Where did you sleep? Was it terribly difficult? How did you get here? Have many people died? Did you treat a Soviet soldier? How did you feel about that? Are you tired, would you like to go to bed? Would you like to listen to the radio, there is so much happening in Hungary all the time! Are you hungry? I missed you both so much! I'm so proud of you. I wish I could be there with you, I'm certain I could be of help."

As Mira paused for breath, Klári unhesitatingly took her daughter's shoulders in her hands and looked into Mira's earnest, eager, intelligent, beautiful face. Klári considered Mira's dark brown hair, the cosmic scattering of dainty freckles across the bridge of her pert nose and high, distinctive cheekbones, her straight, naturally delineated brow. Klári knew her daughter was strong and knew that strength was going to be tested in the coming days.

"Oh, Mira, love, yes, we missed all of you; which is why we risked coming home. It will be brief. We have eight hours, if that..." Klári paused as she looked up at her parents, Gábor and Ili Berci. Ili had walked to her daughter's side and now put her arm around Klári's shoulders, kissing her cheek, then stepping back to Gábor who clasped Ili's hand in his both of his. Alida stood at their side, utterly relieved to have her sister and brother safely home.

Klári continued, "We came by ambulance, Anya, Apa. A student, Bálint András, has been driving wherever help is needed. He was going to pick up a few patients from the hospital at the Rock. It was a safe way to travel and we were able to give safe passage to a young woman, I believe she is from the country, she wears unique, beautiful clothes and boots. She is staying with someone on Castle Hill. Her brother and their friend are both patients of ours." As Klári paused, Béla continued.

"We hoped and prayed you were all well. There was news coming in from all over the city alerting us to areas of conflict. We felt fairly certain you weren't in any immediate danger. We hope that has been the case. Apa? Anya?"

"Yes, Béla, so good of you. We were fine, weren't we, Mira?"

"It was the tanks, Anyu. At Parliament. We weren't certain if it was the beginning of a battle to take over the city!" Mira was innocently excited, unable as yet to comprehend the tragedy of war.

"I can certainly understand why you might think that. To answer your other questions, yes, we were able to eat and sleep a little and yes, I think we would both like a little refreshment," Klári paused, looking at her mother, sister, and grandmother. "Could someone put the tea kettle on, please?

"There has been a lot of trauma, Mira, many people have been wounded in all the usual ways that people suffer during times of war. We were moved from the Kilián Barracks. They've restaged the Cellar Hospital. We took a patient, a young man, to our hospital, the Military Hospital. And yes, I treated a Soviet. He was not more than a boy, Mira, perhaps 15. He was wearing the Hungarian tricolor. Had he not, I would have treated him.

"He is a human being, Mira," Klári added with gentle compassion.

Béla stood behind Klári, quiet and severe. Gábor's attention had gone back and forth between Klári and his son-in-law. There was an undercurrent between them, something unsaid laying just below the surface waiting, or needing, to be revealed.

"What has happened?"

Béla placed his hand on Klári's shoulder as everyone's attention shifted from Béla and Klári to Gábor and back again.

"What, what is it?" Ili asked. "Gábor?"

Klári squeezed Béla's hand, slightly adjusted her posture where she sat in the kitchen chair, and took a deep breath as she quietly spoke.

"We must go and visit the Nováks."

"Why?" Mira asked, wide-eyed, looking from one parent to the other until, a moment later, her innocent face became sober revealing a broader understanding. Her voice dropped as if she didn't want anyone to overhear, "Oh, are Ervin and Adrián at the hospital? Have they," she faltered, "been...hurt?"

"Mira, they are dead."

"No! No, no, no!" Mira cried and turned to the embrace of her father. Ili turned away, laying her hands on the kitchen counter as she bent over them. She stifled the sob that caught in her chest but not the tears and anguish that poured from her heart. To lose your child was a horror, but to lose two, and they your only children! Alida's hands flew to cover her face too late to muffle her cry. Watching, Gábor stood, looking momentarily at each of his beloved family, then gazed out the window. The portent of Klári's words momentarily stopped time until, with absolute clarity, the words formed then echoed in his mind, *we must leave Hungary*.

Nearby, in the Fülöp apartment, Ágnes was writing a grocery list as her mother, grandmother, and great-grandmother dictated, most often repeating what another had already said. It would be four hours until the afternoon train arrived at the Kelenföld Railway Station with food from the countryside. As everyone was aware, it was never too early to take your place in line. Ágnes must hurry.

Elek sat, watching his family, while listening to the radio. Stepping to the door, Ágnes pulled on her coat, folding and pushing the grocery list into her pocket. She glanced up, a question furrowing her brow, as her father walked over and put on his coat.

"Apa?"

"Elek?" Zsófia looked at her husband, uncertain.

Elek, putting on his coat and hat, looked from wife to daughter. "We will keep each other company. We will go together and we will return together. And together we will carry what we need." Elek turned and held out his hand to his daughter. Ágnes looked from her mother to her grandmothers, smiling in silent acquiescence.

Walking down Rózsa Hill, Ágnes was delighted to see a small flock of hawfinches fly overhead. The hills of Budapest and the Danube were usually a birders paradise. Ágnes had worried and wondered more than once if the fighting had frightened them all away.

Crossing the bridge, Elek and Ágnes walked in the direction of the grocery store. Quite suddenly, Elek abruptly stopped and grabbed Ágnes' arm. Ahead of them, a Russian tank had just completed the turn at the far corner of the street and slowly advanced in their direction. Stopping in front of the grocery, the turret rotated, lowering its gun and aiming, it seemed, at the group of mostly women and children gathered there. The effect was immediate as the people scattered, screaming, in every direction. Ágnes and Elek flattened themselves on the street where they had stood only moments ago. After several minutes, the turret again rotated. The tank advanced down the street into Pest and disappeared up a side street. Ágnes and Elek hurried the few remaining yards to the grocers. Purchasing their family ration of milk, bread, and a few groceries from the meager supplies available, they briskly returned home in subdued silence.

In the Türea apartment, the radio had been tuned to the BBC. The entire family listened raptly. News of the protest at the British Embassy, where 4,000 people had gathered demanding their freedom, elicited gasps and grunts. Later in the morning news, Budapest Radio announced that Nagy had negotiated the withdrawal of the Soviet troops. This news seemed to conflict with news that the revolution had spread to the countryside. When Júlia returned from the bakery, she brought word that the anticipated foreign correspondents had at last arrived and were reporting the horrific events. Many Hungarians yet hoped that with this news the long, longed for promise of support would arrive from the west.

Péter and Júlia were speaking with their father and mother on the other side of the room. Gizella and Gábor sat side by side at the kitchen table listening to the news. Gábor turned the dial at any hint of repetition, anxious as they were for every bit of information they could glean. They both held their breath listening to the details of a massacre Khrushchev had ordered. Fifty unarmed civilians near the Austrian border had been shot and killed by the ÁVH. Radio Free Europe reported incidents of soldiers purposefully aiming low, shooting people in the legs rather than killing them. So intent in their quiet distractions, when the telephone rang it surprised everyone with a start.

"I thought it was out of order," Gizella, nearby, said as she stood to answer the seemingly insistent ring. Gizella's hesitant greeting was the only word she spoke. When she replaced the receiver on the cradle, everyone stood expectantly waiting.

"That was Schott Anna asking how we are and the conditions here. Her daughter, Anikó, found out from her school friends that some of their teachers have been shot and killed. Also she wanted to confirm we knew of the food deliveries at the train station. We were interrupted. The line went dead again."

The family regrouped around the kitchen table.

"Anya, Apa," Erzsébet began, "Péter and Júlia are going to the University. The student group there has arranged to distribute the food and supply deliveries being transported by train to the station."

Júlia held her grandmother's hand. "The deliveries come in twice a day. A train with food from Hungarians in the countryside, another with food and supplies from Austria and the west."

Péter continued, "We will be part of the team delivering to areas near Rósza Hill. When we finish the deliveries, we will return home. If there's any trouble, we will return home."

"When? When will you do this?"

"Today, Nagyanya." Péter and Júlia crossed the room, embracing their grandmother. Standing back, she held a hand of each in hers. "I am so proud of you both. Now go! I will pray for you!"

Péter and Júlia walked along the Danube at a hurried pace toward the University. There they met with Gyula Várallyay, a fellow student Júlia knew from committee and club meetings. Two days before, the Student Revolutionary Committee had received a call from the Kelenföld Railway Station. Would the Student Union transport and deliver the aid packages being received from the West? They had accepted. Gyula had walked into the streets and stopped the first truck she found, recruited the driver, then procured gasoline from the nearby Barracks. Each day, despite widespread poverty and suffering, generous contributions of donated food was being delivered from the countryside. Additional food and emergency supplies were increasingly coming in from the West via train and airlift. Péter and Júlia had arrived in time for the delivery of donated food from the countryside.

Approaching the train, a boxcar sliding door begrudgingly raked open, the rusty door rail grating against the keepers. Gyula recognized the man standing there, inside the boxcar, from the description she'd been given. He stood, looking out, his arm raised in greeting. In the next moment, he had effortlessly jumped off onto the platform and begun offloading the precious cargo. Gyula smiled and quickened her pace to meet him and introduce herself and her friends. Péter and Júlia had already noticed the tall, handsome older man who offloaded the crates, barrels, and canvas sacks with accustomed ease.

"Varga György? Yes?

"Yes. And you? You must be Várallyay Gyula," György said, a hint of a smile in his strong, earnest face. Gyula was instantly drawn to this gentle but powerful man with hands the size of a bear's. She immediately liked him, trusted him, seeing in his blue eyes a depth of honesty and compassion.

"This is Türea Júlia, Türea Péter. They are also students." Turning to Péter and Júlia, she continued, "György helped gather and transport a shipment of food from the farms west of Balaton."

Péter bowed his head to György in acknowledgment. "Thank you, Mr. Varga. As I'm certain Guyla has informed you, the grocery stores are not always open. What little they have is severely rationed by necessity, as are the bakeries. Many people cannot get to the stores, it is either too dangerous or they are unable due to their circumstances. This generosity is an uncommon kindness. Thank you."

"Is there anything we can do for you? Will you return on this train, or would you like to stay the night? Can we offer you a meal? A place to stay?" Júlia asked.

"This food has been donated by the people of Hungary. They are proud of the bravery and courage of their fellow Hungarians here in Budapest. It is sent with their thanks." György paused, then straightened to his full height as he continued, "In answer to your questions, I have traveled here for another reason. I humbly ask for your help knowing your city is under siege, and your homes, friends, and families need you. I seek my grandchildren. There are four, three boys and a girl. The boys traveled with another boy from our area. The girl traveled alone in search of her brothers," György's pause was the interlude Péter needed to interrupt.

"It may only be a coincidence, many Hungarians traveled to Budapest to participate in the demonstration on the 23rd," Péter began.

György instantly responded, turning to Péter, his jaw set, his chest raised with a great intake of breath. "What? Tell me, please. Have you seen them?"

"I saw a group of boys, two a little older and taller, two younger, the day of the demonstration. They came to the meeting at the Aula in the University. Later that day, a young woman approached them, threw herself at them actually, which seemed to surprise them. I saw her again. They were quite noticeable, their clothes made them distinctive. They had handsome boots such as you are wearing, and the young woman had a beautifully embroidered vest. They all seemed very familiar with one another."

"I remember her, Péter! Yes, Mr. Varga, I remember her as Péter described," Júlia exclaimed.

"Have you seen any of these children since that time?"

"No, I haven't, I'm sorry, but I haven't often been outside of our home since that day. Péter?"

"I'm sorry, no, I haven't either. Mr. Varga, Pest is frequently embattled, while the Hills are currently relatively safe. We live in an area and among neighbors that have worked in various areas of the city. We have a phone and radio. May I suggest you accompany us as we make the deliveries? We can help familiarize you with some of the streets and layout of the city, and show you where they've been seen. Return with us to our home, where you would be welcome, and we will introduce you to our neighbors, and perhaps we can help you find your grandchildren."

György gripped Péter's arm in wordless thanks. The truck bed was filled, solidly packed to its maximum capacity. György followed Péter into the bed of the truck, perching precariously on bags of potatoes. With the windows down, the men were able to steady themselves by gripping the rear pillar with one hand and the top rail of the truck bed side panels with the other. Júlia climbed into the truck passenger side of the bench seat while the driver stepped up into the cab and behind the wheel. Gyula waved them off before joining other members of the student union to distribute the remaining food stores to the queue who had patiently awaited the trains' arrival for hours.

In the apartment on Castle Hill, Alexandra and Charles had moved to the kitchen to clean the dressing on Charles wound at the kitchen sink when a sudden knock sounded on the front door. Through the window, Charles was surprised to see an ambulance.

"There's an ambulance at the corner, Anya."

Alexandra opened the door to find the ambulance driver standing with his arm under Rebeka's, very obviously helping to keep the girl on her feet.

"This young woman says she knows you."

"Yes, yes, thank you. Charles! Charles, please help her!" Alexandra was startled and concerned seeing Rebeka pale, weak, and shaken. "Oh, my dear, come in. Come in!"

Although a large apartment, the boys had heard their sister's name and came running. Rebeka was briefly joyous, happy, and relieved to see her younger brothers, receiving and returning their adoration and embraces. Charles and Alexandra gently separated them, encouraging them to let their sister get some much needed sleep. Rebeka did not resist. Alexandra helped Rebeka to undress and get into bed. She gently tucked Rebeka's legs and feet under the coverlet and then covered her before closing the door. Returning to the kitchen, Alexandra met Charles's gaze.

"What has happened to her? Where is Dominik?"

"I've no idea. We didn't speak. She doesn't appear hurt in any way, but seems terribly traumatized. We'll see how she is in the morning. Until then, would you stay up for a bit with the boys while I have a rest in your room? It may be another long night. She's exhausted. Hopefully, she'll sleep through the night."

27

REVELATION

26 October 1956

AS THEY DROVE, Péter pointed out the various sites and general locations around Buda and Pest that had figured in the turmoil of the previous week. György silently noted the Technical University, Kilián Barracks, Kossuth Square, the Parliament Building, Corvin Passage, Hero Square, and Bem Square.

As they made their deliveries, skirting areas of violence, György noted the too familiar sounds of battle that resonated across the city. He was shocked to see much of the city in ruins. Budapest had been a beautiful city of elaborate architecture, much of which was now badly damaged. The rubble filled the streets, the detritus of war. Everywhere there were heaped piles and scattered quantities of pavement stones. The charred, gutted remains of trucks, trolleys, and Soviet tanks, some emblazoned with the Kossuth coat of arms, blocked streets and sidewalks. Burned, uprooted trees lent a somber and dismal blight to the carnage. And everywhere, Soviet propaganda papers, posters, and books littered the landscape.

György noted the infrastructure was also badly damaged. Trolley rails were buckled or torn up, telegraph wires sagged, and utility poles had fallen or had been splintered by detonations.

Péter pointed out the Hungarian tricolor "hole in the middle" flag, symbol of the revolution. The flag intrigued György, he nodded in agreement. Sadly, György noted that many residents were dressed as militia including old women in their aprons with nothing but a headscarf and sweater against the rain and cold. Young children carried rifles and guns while still others had what appeared to be Molotov cocktails. Accustomed as he was to the atrocities of war, György was nonetheless repulsed. Even at a distance, he felt a visceral reaction at the sight of the bodies of ÁVH men and women hung from trees, some burned, many abused. Corpses of civilians and Russian soldiers, sprinkled with lime, lay on the ground where they had fallen. György did not turn away from these horrifying sights. He acknowledged them, chronicled them, and bore witness to them.

Péter indicated several Soviet T-54 tanks that had been in place for days. Their crews were seemingly too frightened to leave their tanks. In the cramped space of each tanks' turret basket, the combined stench of gasoline and body fluids bore down on the morale of the self-imprisoned crews.

Péter suddenly fell silent. György soon saw the cause as he followed the direction of Péter's gaze. A tank was grinding down Bartók Béla Road dragging Hungarian corpses behind. Passing a bakery where a long queue awaited the next baking, the horror elicited screams, cries, and revulsion. György had seen enough. He had been patient. He turned to Péter, who wordlessly understood.

"There is one more delivery. It is near our home. I promise you, we won't be much longer."

Not long after, the driver delivered the group to the base of Rózsa Hill before turning back toward the University. Finally standing at the Türea apartment, awaiting an answer to their knocking, György was filled with anticipation. He momentarily shifted his weight from foot to foot before willing himself to quiet, as he once had quieted his beloved Kisbers.

Inside the apartment, Péter made the introductions succinctly explaining György's detained presence in Budapest. Everyone had compassion and empathized with György. Jeno invited György to sit with him while Gizella and Erzsébet applied themselves in the kitchen preparing tea. Júlia returned from the Fürth apartment, where Erzsébet had asked her to see if Klári or Béla were home and invite them to meet György. Júlia returned, but with Mira. György rose to greet the returning young woman and her friend.

"They are sleeping, Anya. They only just returned from the hospital today after leaving our apartment on Tuesday, but Mira thinks she can be of assistance."

"Varga György, this is Fürth Mira."

"Mr. Varga, sir, I'm certain my mother and father recently saw your granddaughter. When they returned home this morning they rode in an ambulance with a young woman who was going to stay at a friend's home on Castle Hill."

György was puzzled. "Rebeka doesn't know anyone in Budapest."

"Well, Mr. Varga, my mother did describe the young woman and said that she had been visiting her brother and their friend at the hospital."

"The hospital? What hospital?"

"The Central Military Hospital, where they work."

"György," Gizella broke into the conversation, "I have friends on Castle Hill. If the phone is working, perhaps they can help. Give me a moment while I phone them."

Gizella went to the phone while Mira answered questions from Mr. Varga. It wasn't long before Gizella returned.

"Mr. Varga, my friend Schott Anna is going over now to see her friend Fárkas Alexandra. She knows with absolute certainty that Alexandra has been caring for two boys and a girl that she described as being from the country. She also said the girl had been looking for her older brother."

At these words, György let out his breath, wringing his hat in his hand, while laying the other across his chest.

"Thank you, dear people, thank you. How do I find them?"

"Anna said she would have Alexandra phone. It shouldn't be too long. We have made you some tea and something to eat. We all need something to eat. Please," again indicating a chair at the table next to Jeno, "sit here with our family."

György started to protest but understood her wisdom. It had been hours since his last meal, hours filled with physical exertion and anxiety. He was hungry, and who knew how long it would be before his next meal.

György took the offered seat by Jeno. Péter joined them, sitting next to György. Júlia had walked Mira to the door who fervently implored, asking to stay, whispering, "Oh please, Júlia, let me stay and see if he finds his grandchildren. Please? Oh, please, please may I?"

"Of course, after all, it is you who has provided the key and may have found his grandchildren," Júlia whispered as she smiled at a beaming Mira. Júlia straightened and announced, "We have another joining us for dinner!"

Mira asked, then pleaded, to help. She was put in charge of setting out the plates and utensils, filling the water glasses, and placing the tea cups, sugar, and milk on the table. Júlia sliced their one loaf of bread and made the tea. Erzsébet and Gizella made a platter of curd cheese, dried fruit, sliced chicken, beans, barley cholent, and cold vegetables. Dinner preparations had emptied most of their pantry. However, with the basket of food Péter and Júlia had brought from Mr. Varga, they would need only to find bread the next day.

As they sat in friendly conversation, each felt buoyed by a pervasive, almost palpable, sense of hope. Laughter came easily and welcomed, as it hadn't for many days. Suddenly, the phone rang. Every voice quieted as Gizella rose to answer the insistent ring.

"Hallo?"

Gizella listened, then turned towards the table, extending the receiver, "For you, Mr. Varga."

György stood, unbalancing the chair then steadying it with both hands as he moved toward the phone.

"Hallo?"

A smile broadened György's face, his eyes glistened, his breathing quickened and his chest shuddered as they all heard Rebeka, Jani, and Péter's adoring exclamations, "Nagypapa!"

Overwhelming sentiment filled every heart in the Türea apartment. Mira clapped her hands accompanied by a squeal of delight. Greatly embarrassed, she soon recovered under the benevolent gaze of the older women. Gizella, who sat next to Mira, squeezed her shoulders.

György became quiet, seriously intent. Those closest to him realized he was speaking to Alexandra. As György hung up the phone he paused a moment in silence before addressing his hosts. Everyone was silent, waiting, anxious. Something ominous blanketed the room with an oppressive weight.

"Mira," György smiled at the girl, "you were correct. You have reunited our family. Thank you, my dear child. Thank you, all of you. Only hours ago I had no idea where to begin other than to arrive." He paused. Everyone waited quietly, unmoving.

"Mira was also correct in that Rebeka had been at the hospital of which you spoke, the Central Military Hospital, where her brother and our friend Marton Dominik are patients. They have both been injured. I have promised my family to return with them. I must find a way to get them out of Budapest. But first, I would like to see Rebeka and her younger brothers. Could you tell me how to get there, and if I might ask another favor, the instructions of how to get to the hospital?"

"I will take you to the Fárkas home now, if you would like," Péter said as he stood from the table. Not knowing what the night might bring, Gizella hurried slices of bread and dried fruit into napkins for their pockets.

"Yes, certainly you must go. Go now," Erzsébet urged as she ushered both men toward the door as each stuffed the food into a pocket of their coats. "Mr. Varga, Péter will go with you and bring you back to us. You must stay with us. In the morning we will discuss how to get you to the hospital and what can be done about the boys. Now go. Be very careful, both of you."

"Yes, you must return to us, Mr. Varga. We will await your return," Jeno added as he handed György his coat. The night had grown cold, a hint of ice carried on the east wind.

Péter led György through the quiet hills of Buda. Arriving at the Fárkas home, the reunion was touching. For only a brief moment, Péter let his gaze settle upon the reunited family, on the girl he had first seen in the crowd at the University, and the boys who had embraced her. That all of their lives would connect and reconnect seemed improbable but yet, they had. What some might call coincidence he felt, at that moment, was instead miraculous.

The relief that transformed Rebeka and excited the boys rendered György speechless, his cheeks glistened. He held all three to his chest in his bear-like embrace until several minutes later when the tears had turned to laughter. György asked Rebeka and the boys to sit beside him while he spoke to Alexandra and Charles.

György thanked Alexandra and Charles for their kindness and

generosity. Except for Rebeka, no one in the Fárkas apartment had known the fate of Dávid nor Dominik. György related his plan for the morning: he would return his family, and Dominik, to Megyer. He would go to the train station and check the schedule; any train headed west would do. György would visit the hospital tomorrow morning and discuss the possibility of moving the boys. Looking from Alexandra to Péter and Charles, György finished with an invitation.

"We have all lived through the war and the trials since that time. I do not think this will end well for Hungary, especially," György cast a meaningful glance at both young men, "for anyone who participated in the revolution. It would perhaps be safer for you to live in the country. My family would welcome you."

Rising, György threw open his arms welcoming his grandchildren again to his warm embrace. He hugged them tightly before leaving them with a promise to see them the next day. At the door, he overwhelmed Alexandra in a tight embrace. Parting, his hands almost painfully gripped her shoulders as raw emotion infused every sinew and muscle and his moist cheeks unashamedly glistened.

"Thank you, dear lady. Thank you."

As the two men walked, the stillness of the night was broken by the resonant, extended notes of an eagle owl. Both men found the call comforting, welcome company in a night otherwise filled with ominous possibilities. The nights were usually quiet, especially in the Hills. They were soon safely home, opening the door, and welcomed. A stranger stood there, off to the side, but not unnoticed by György.

György was introduced to their neighbor, Fürth Klári. Péter thought the introduction curious, his father hadn't addressed her as a doctor. He saw in Júlia's eyes the flash of a warning and stepped to one side inviting György to sit in the chair proffered by his father.

The women politely but earnestly peppered György with questions about his grandchildren. György happily responded oblivious, it seemed, to the marked change in the demeanor of almost every person in the room. But he was not oblivious, quite the contrary, he was intuitive and alert.

"Thank you, thank you my dear friends. Now please, what has happened?"

"Mr. Varga, I am the doctor who first attended your grandson," Klári spoke gently but clearly and with resolve.

Of all the possibilities in this time and place, this was definitely not one György had considered. He fought to maintain his composure, pressing against the chair back, forcing himself to breathe evenly. "Is he dead?"

"Yes, Mr. Varga. I'm so very sorry to tell you this."

For a brief moment, György was thoughtful. He brought both hands up just in front of his face, clasping them into a tight fist in front of his chin, his elbows supported by his knees, closing his eyes, and ever so subtly shaking his head. The room was quiet. Péter stood in stunned silence, the only other person in the room who hadn't known of the tragedy. György's head bowed and a mournful hollow cry filled the apartment, chilling everyone who heard it, unwilling witnesses to another's heartbreak. Everyone wept for Dávid, everyone wept for György. Jeno and Péter stood next to him while everyone waited. It wasn't long before he raised his head, and looked squarely at Klári patiently, wordlessly, waiting.

"Your grandson died soon after he was brought to the hospital. You would not have found him alive had you come to the hospital immediately upon your arrival in Budapest," Klári explained. She turned towards Júlia. "He had lost a significant amount of blood before he was found. He died before we had a chance to operate. We, my husband and I, and the attending surgeon, chose not to tell

Rebeka. I hope you agree. We thought it would be too traumatic for her, especially being here, alone, away from her family and so very young. She had already endured so much trauma."

"What of the other boy, Marton Dominik?" György quietly asked.

"Dominik has several broken ribs. He's stoic and brave. I believe he may have some internal injuries, perhaps bruising, but he's not complaining. The hospital ran out of film, until we get another shipment I won't know conclusively. I believe he will heal, if he will lay still."

György sat quietly a few moments before speaking.

"I don't think it will be possible to take Dávid back with us to Megyer. It will be challenging with his sister and brothers and the injured boy."

"Mr. Varga. It's a difficult time, you understand."

"Yes, there are many dead."

"Yes," Klári paused before continuing, the weight of her words difficult to lift into the light. "There is a cemetery where many Hungarians are taking their loved ones, Rákoskeresztúr. The entrance and grounds are beautiful. There is a high bell tower, and beautiful, tree-lined walkways. It is pleasant, quiet, and peaceful."

"How can we do this, and when?"

"I'll see what I can do, Mr. András."

Klári rose, leaving the apartment and hurrying away once the door closed knowing Béla and Andràs Bálint were waiting for her. She was late, very late, they were all late. András had had to drive a circuitous route to the Fürth apartment. Many roads were obstructed by either debris or blockades. He chose the same return route, delivering the doctors at the side entrance of the hospital before continuing to his next destination, he needed gasoline. Klári briefly recounted the events in the Türea apartment as she and Béla walked through the crowded corridor before stopping at the front desk. Béla continued to the surgery ward where they both had been posted. When Klári arrived she found Béla agitated. She stood, patiently waiting for whatever it was he needed to tell her.

"The boy, Dominik? He's gone. He left about four o'clock, after the shift change, but they are uncertain, there are so many volunteers and changing staff. Apparently, he found out that Dávid hadn't survived his wounds. They said he was very upset and was going to find his friends. The phones aren't working again. We can't make a call. Perhaps when Bálint András returns, we can give him a message to apprise Mr. Varga of the situation. Or, the phones will work again."

28

BALANCE—COUNTERBALANCE

27 October 1956

IMAGES OF THE Hungarian revolution dominated the world news. Images of brutality and horror, of the streets of Budapest filled with debris, ruin, and rubble flashed across television screens. The political machinations taking place in Hungary, Moscow, the United Nations, and in the seats of government of the western allies made headlines.

The UN Security Council emergency session concluded the Hungarian crisis "...did not fall into the jurisdiction of the UN." During the 11th General Assembly of the UN, the Soviets charged Austria in breach of neutrality accusing that country of supplying arms to Hungary. Austria's UN representative, Ambassador Dr. Franz Matsch, was forced to explain the Legation's humanitarian campaign in detail. Anticipating the Russian tactic, Matsch provided receipts from the Red Cross and Hungarian hospitals for the tons of food and medical supplies Austria had supplied.

Imre Nagy and his new cabinet were sworn into office on 28 October 1956. As acting Prime Minister, Nagy announced major reformations and pushed for a ceasefire. Nagy intended to broker a political solution to the ongoing conflict.

Moscow officials in Budapest finally conceded the origin of the conflict was, in fact, a revolution of a dissatisfied populace. These same officials resolved to address the protestor's demands. Noel Cowley, the British military attaché, reported, "Nothing could have been further from reality; the intervention of the Russians only seemed to make the people more angry and more determined to pursue the fight."

In the streets of Budapest, many Soviet soldiers, appalled at the sight of the suffering being endured, were moved to action. Leaving their ranks, the soldiers joined the protestors providing them with weapons and ammunition. And when the ÁVH were seen firing on civilians, there were Soviet soldiers who turned their guns on the ÁVH policemen.

The morning of Sunday, 28 October 1956, Nagy successfully prevented a massive attack on the main rebel strongholds at the Corvin Cinema and Kilián Barracks. Nagy negotiated and implemented a de facto ceasefire. The people of Hungary, and political leaders around the world, were incredulous as they listened to reports of the ceasefire.

By 12:15 the fighting was subsiding. Soviet troops were withdrawing from Budapest. Many Stalinist politicos, their families, and entourage were leaving Hungary altogether, returning to their homes in the Soviet Union. The people of Budapest lined the banks of the Danube quietly watching the families of Soviet diplomats depart.

Budapest Radio announced the release of political prisoners, including Cardinal József Mindszenty, whose civil and ecclesiastical rights were restored. The prisoners held at Vác had escaped by their own efforts but had been fired upon by the ÁVO, there were casualties.

For the first time in most people's memory, people were able to read uncensored newspapers. To the world at large, and to the people of Hungary, it appeared that ordinary citizens had defeated the Red Army.

That same afternoon, Nagy announced the dissolution of the ÁVH and the creation of a National Guard to restore order. Nagy's intention was to negotiate the full withdrawal of Soviet troops from Budapest and the restoration of the traditional Hungarian flag.

In the following days, with the Hungarian people united, the new government was sworn in. Nagy did his best to consolidate power and legitimize the revolutionary actions. Nagy declared an end to the one-party system. Together, with various factional leaders, they began to work out a renewed government structure, a democratic coalition government.

The weather had grown increasingly cold and wet. Although the temperature had dropped to 42 degrees and the rain was beating down, the citizens of Budapest were not deterred. They crowded into the streets in celebration of the Soviet exodus.

Nagy moved his office from Party Headquarters to the Parliament Building. There he continued to meet and negotiate in developing the new order for Budapest in alignment with the 16 Points doctrine. He appointed Pál Maléter as Defense Minister and tasked Sándor Kopácsi with organizing the National Guard. The Guard, composed of the combined forces of the regular police and armed rebel forces, would restore order and guard the borders of the country. Tibor Arany organized a guard duty for the Hungarian Women's Democratic Association building where the Writer's Association, headed by Péter Kucka, was located.

The effect of these events and others signaled a transformation. The ÁVO, anticipating the collapse of the Soviet doctrine and support of repression and brutality, realized they had to escape. Attempting to disguise themselves in civilian clothes proved to be an inadequate attempt. Members of the ÁVO were easily recognized on the street. Many were captured and beaten, some were killed, only a few were jailed.

The BBC, Voice of America, and Radio Free Europe continued with their own brand of propaganda. Broadcasts, insinuating support from the West, urged and encouraged the Hungarian revolutionaries to stay the fight for freedom. That insinuated support would, in fact, never materialize. Throughout the crisis all three radio stations were an important source of information and hope to the residents of Hungary. Secretary of State, John Foster Dulles, broadcast over Radio Free Europe, "To all those suffering under communist slavery, let us say, you can count on us!"

Meanwhile, Frank Wisner, head of the Directorate of Plans, an organization within the CIA accounting for the majority of the CIA budget and personnel, used Radio Free Europe to further the United States government policy. Wisners' plan was to foment a spirit of non-cooperation in the satellite countries locked behind the Iron Curtain.

The turmoil in Hungary continued despite the ceasefire and Soviet troop withdrawal. On Tuesday, 30 October 1956, one week following the demonstration that sparked a revolution, Béla Király commanded a force of the Hungarian National Guard. They attacked the headquarters of the Communist Party in Republic Square where known or suspected communists were detained, many were executed. Following a fierce battle, the ÁVH and police surrendered. Many of the captives were lynched. Widely circulated rumors of secret, underground torture chambers in the area beneath the square led the Freedom Fighters to dig deep holes in the square. Heavy equipment was brought in. Nothing was found.

Meanwhile, the Suez Crisis was intensifying, requiring the concentrated efforts of the western powers. Without discussion with other foreign powers and allies, France and Britain signed an agreement with Israel and invaded the Sinai Peninsula.

With the world in turmoil, Chairman Mao took the opportune moment to apprise the Kremlin of what they believed had been a poor decision. Did the Kremlin not anticipate that the events in Hungary could have a domino effect?

In agreeing to the ceasefire, the Kremlin had hoped that Nagy would restore communist authority. That Nagy would, in the process of balancing student demands with reasonable reforms, bring Hungary back in to the fold. While Nagy, as recently as only days prior, might have followed that course, he was instead silently supportive of the revolutionaries.

29

PRISON

FOR HENRI ANDRÁS, Vác Prison was a place to be endured. Cold and spare, its stark edifice and interior of steel and plaster were grim, unrelenting, desolate. Henri's faith was unflagging, the memories of his family sustained him with unrelenting hope.

When Henri had first arrived at Kistarcsa in 1950, he learned of Rákosi's encouragement of ÁVO policies to target wealthier Hungarians. The guards had wasted not one minute in apprising Henri of what awaited. Morally corrupt guards measured every action and word to instill fear, uncertainty, discomfort, and pain. Henri had waited, expecting an especially brutal "interrogation." Systematically, each of the men who shared his same, dank cell were taken and returned hours later bruised, bleeding, or broken. When his turn came, Henri felt fortunate to be returned to his cell relatively intact. He had mostly recovered within a week. The dark purple bruises had turned an alarming shade of orange yet to fade completely. The ringing in his left ear was only noticeable at night.

At night, Henri lay on the stone floor, side by side with his cellmates. Although it was winter, there were no blankets. Eventually, they were given saddle blankets, which provided some warmth, although they were half the size of a grown man. Days were spent standing, milling about, walking in small circles, stretching. Only occasionally were they allowed a short walk in the prison yard.

The prisoner's meals, delivered to their cell, were scant, rancid, or foul smelling. It took little experience for most of the men to quickly dispatch the meager rations. The men would gather into a circle, bowing their heads over their plates, then silently pray. Care and prudence were a necessity. Everyone was reticent to speak, never knowing who was listening, how their words might be perverted, or to be implicated in devised plots, or crimes against the state.

The one pleasure Henri found in his confinement was the prison cell's one window. Dust motes danced in ribbons of sunlight. Henri passed hours imagining the arc of the sun across the sky as he traced the narrow rectangle of light across the floor and up the wall.

Year followed year. For the most part, Henri thought himself fortunate. Although lean, with minimal and unpalatable rations, he was, in general, fairly healthy. The morning the guard called his name, Henri anticipated another interrogation, another beating. Instead, he was intrigued and watchful as he was led downstairs where he and several other prisoners were roughly chained together. They alternately stood and sat as the chains allowed, waiting, enduring, in a dimly lit, spartan room with a steel door at opposite ends. It was easy to imagine the worst and foolish to do so. Instead they quietly waited. Without preamble, a door crashed open. Two guards led the chain gang to a truck. They were being transported to Vác, a prison located about 22 miles north of Budapest on the Danube.

The next two years varied little from the last four at Kistarcsa. The differences between the two made living slightly more bearable. Although there were fewer prisoners at Vác, there weren't any criminals. Of the 1200 political prisoners, 500 were serving life sentences, including one of his cellmates, Imre Fárkas, for "anti-communist activities." Another cellmate, Jakab, had only just arrived from Recsk, a notorious work camp, where he had been questioned and tortured. Jakab was made to stand on one leg for interminable amounts of time.

The top floor of the prison was reserved for members of the clergy. Cardinal József Mindszenty had been a prisoner of Vác for years. The Cardinal, leader of the Catholic church in Hungary, had been convicted of treason in 1948. Mindszenty had denounced the oppression of Jews and lack of religious freedom.

Women prisoners were also in a separate section, in an area away from the men. The one aberration to the otherwise severe environment within the simple, spare, coldly geometric confines was the chapel. Only the chapel offered a sense of communion with the better nature of man. The walls and pillars of the Victorian era Gothic interior were lavishly painted. To simply look into the room lifted Henri's spirits.

The prison cell itself was an improvement but a great disappointment for Henri. The cell's one window, as all the windows in Vác, had been sealed shut with sheet metal. The prisoners were infrequently taken to the courtyard where they could breathe fresh air and feel the sun on their faces. In every cell, prisoners either slept on the floor on straw, or else on straw sacks laid upon iron bed frames.

Henri had spent a brief time in the solitary cell section of the prison before being moved to a narrow cell with two cellmates. Two weeks later he was moved again, to a large room shared with twenty-one prisoners. The purpose of the larger cells was to establish working teams. The teams spent their days either in the chemistry laboratory, where the inmates conducted industrial espionage, or in the "translation office", where Henri and his cellmates were assigned.

Henri persevered, remaining especially cautious of the ÁVO who were as likely to beat the guards as the prisoners. Henri found encouragement in his cellmate Imre's frequently repeated personal mantra, 'only strength of character will allow you to survive.'

Each day was relatively indistinguishable from any other with two notable exceptions. The guards would awaken the prisoners at 6 a.m., followed by breakfast, work, break, dinner, work, cell, and sleep. Occasionally they were allowed to walk in the courtyard. Indiscriminately they'd be 'interrogated.'

Henri spent his nights thinking about each of his family in turn. He imagined Rebeka, how much like her mother she was. Dávid, grown into a young man, how tall might he be? Reflecting on memories of Péter and Jani, Henri hoped they were doing well in school. Little Bella would be almost nine; would she also resemble her beautiful mother? Henri hoped his father and mother were well as he recalled each of them in their familiar places in their home, garden, and fields with their grandchildren. Laura, he always saved for last. Henri recalled her voice and laughter, her touch, and memories of her holding their babies as he finally fell to sleep looking into her eyes.

One Tuesday morning in late October, reality quite abruptly and unexpectedly shifted. Without previous notice, the guards didn't awaken the prisoners. Breakfast was late. The uneasy silence which permeated the entire prison was finally broken with the unprecedented announcement there would be no work that day. Prison cell doors remained locked throughout the day. By nightfall, rumors and suspicions were rampant among the prisoners fueled by overheard comments and whisperings of the guards.

The prisoners unease, anxiety, restlessness, and suspicions compounded with each passing day. By Thursday evening, when an ÁVO officer appeared at their cell door, the men, fearing the worst, stood at the rear of the cell, quiet, unmoving, watchful. To their disbelief, the officer raised his hand extending a carton of cigarettes, "Men, cigarettes?" As the officer moved to the next cell, Henri and his cellmates gathered to discuss the ramifications and possibilities of what had just transpired. Something had to have happened to conjure such a marked change in their tormentor. He called them "men!" Having endured years of dehumanizing, abusive treatment and brutality and now, uncharacteristically treated with kindness, was disconcerting and further cause for suspicion.

By Friday morning, the prisoners were peacefully sleeping, each rising at their own leisure. The prison atmosphere remained unchanged. The guards delivering breakfast were uneasy and unwilling to answer careful and purposefully simple questions. That afternoon, the cells were opened and everyone was allowed to walk in the prison yard. In a corner, Cardinal Mindszenty stood in the center of a group fielding questions he couldn't answer. Henri and Imre approached the group and introduced themselves to a woman standing next to them.

"András Henri. My friend and cellmate, Fárkas Imre. Political prisoners."

The woman good-naturedly smirked as she responded, "You know what they say. There are three classes of people in Hungary: those who have been in prison, those who are in prison, and those who are going to prison. Júlia Rajk, political prisoner, soon to be released."

"What?" both men responded, shocked, looking about, whispering furtively, "How do you know this?"

"My husband was also in prison here. When the ÁVO arrested us they took our son and placed him in an orphanage. I will find them both when I am free."

By the time everyone returned to their cells enough information had been gleaned from overheard bits of conversation that, pieced together between men and cell groups, they had the unfathomable answer no one had even considered, Hungary was in the midst of a revolution. Henri and many of the other prisoners spent a tense, sleepless night alternately considering the possibilities of freedom or execution, a prison lockdown or mass transport. Each wondered what their fate might be. Each wondered what would become of their families.

Saturday morning, 27 October, everyone immediately noticed the altered uniforms of the guards delivering breakfast. The red star on their caps and uniforms had been replaced with the Hungarian tricolor; a badge of red, green, and white. Henri turned his head to a sudden, unfamiliar sound in a nearby cell. Someone was singing. In the same instant of recognition at the first familiar words of the *Himnuz*, the entire prison resonated with the Hungarian national anthem raised in a reverent, communal voice.

"Oh God,
Bless the Hungarian with joy and bounty
Extend him a guarding arm,
If he strives against an enemy
Long torn by ill fate,
Bring upon him joyous times,
This people has suffered,
For sins of the past and future."

As the last refrain resounded another voice was heard. The men in Henri's cell encircled him as he stood singing in his strong baritone.

"On your feet now, Hungary calls you
Now is the moment, nothing stalls you,
Shall we be slaves or men set free
That is the question, answer me!
Slaves we have been to this hour,
Our forefathers who fell from power
Fell free and lived as free men will,
On land that was their own to till..."

Before Henri had quite finished a voice bellowed from another cell on their floor, "Let's break out!" Tossing the bedding from their bed frames, groups of four men on each side assaulted the cell doors until they gave way, crashing open. Remarkably, until that point no one had seen any guards, or any of the ÁVO officers. Meeting in the center of the cell block, everyone only briefly paused, listening for the expected armed response. When none came, they devised a plan.

Negotiating with the commander of the Security Police, the ÁVO, was promptly negated in favor of action. Henri was among the group of men who led the way as they set upon the first of the iron gates. Considering the ironmongery, Henri found the gate mechanisms not dissimilar to the heavier gates on the Varga farm in Nemesbük. Henri demonstrated how to disable the mechanism. One after the other the gates were removed until, approaching the last gate, the entrance and exit of Vác, they were met by a small group of four guards. Each man quietly considered each other. Then, without a word or constraint from his fellow guards, a single guard stepped forward and opened the gate.

The released prisoners exited the prison to the cheers of thousands of Vác residents waiting at the entrance. The prisoners had no way of knowing that Imre Nagy had announced an impending release of prisoners. The crowd before them likewise had no way of knowing that the prisoners themselves had perpetrated their own release. Family and friends had stood waiting, hopeful, nervous and anxious, for their loved ones. And now, here they were, a mass of humanity flooding toward them. Joy and happiness smudged the physical characteristics of this ragged, dirty, unshaven, motley crew angular in their diminished physical state. They were alive. They were free.

Hungarians embraced Hungarians, many were crying. As Imre Fárkas would later note, "The people, in whose name the government had sentenced the prisoners, were welcoming us." Henri saw Júlia embraced by a man who certainly must be her husband suggested by their fevered embrace. Henri stood, watchful. He felt hopeful for Julia, for them, for himself, for everyone. Imre appeared at his side and firmly took Henri's hand in his own, covering them both with his other hand.

"Good luck, my friend. May you soon find yourself surrounded by your family."

"What will you do?"

"My wife, Lilly. Her parents and her aunt live in an apartment in Budapest. I will hopefully find them there. Then I will find my Lilly."

They both turned their heads as the crowd began to sing the national anthem. The initial fusillade of automatic fire was unexpected and confusing. Time momentarily paused. Terror hit the restart button as realization, blood, ravaged and lifeless bodies altered the landscape. The Secret Police continued to spray the unsuspecting crowd with automatic fire from the roof of the prison. The people erupted in a blind, directionless panic falling over the dead or wounded.

Conspicuous in their striped prison uniforms, the prisoners were certain targets for the ÁVH. The people of Vác threw their civilian clothes to the prisoners who desperately ran through streets, alleys, and backyards. Although many Hungarians had but one overcoat, representing on average three months salary, an elderly man held out his coat to Imre as he ran past. Henri, and many of the other freed prisoners, were given jackets or sweaters. One small boy gave his comb.

30

HOPE AND DESPAIR

THE HILLS OF Buda were only just beginning to brighten with the soft, white light of a cold, winter morning when György awoke. He had not slept well, his thoughts had dwelled on Dávid and the news he would carry home to his family.

Gizella and Erzsébet had both arisen early to prepare breakfast. The family sat together, discussing what was planned for the day, as they ate their breakfast of paprika potatoes and vegetable stew. They had their breakfast thanks to the donated food György had delivered from the countryside. György was anxious to be on his way.

György had asked Péter and Júlia to visit Alexandra Fárkas and the Varga children on their way to the station for food and supply distribution. When they returned to the station, Péter and Júlia would determine the schedule of any trains headed west. György planned to go directly to the hospital and, hopefully, the cemetery. Péter and Júlia's visit was to assure the children of their grandfather's return that evening. The children needed to be ready for a quick departure. If not tonight, György planned that he and his family would return to Megyer no later than the following day.

It was time to go. György was already at the door waiting as Péter and Júlia slipped into their coats. Jeno, Erzsébet, and Gizella stood together as József closed the door behind their departing family. They held each other's hands, their concerns unspoken, biding time until they would again be reunited.

It took György some time to navigate his way through the scattered detritus, mounds of rubble, and barricades to find the hospital. Dr. Fürth made herself immediately available. Despite the chaos, she'd been expecting György. György was taken to the morgue, a gruesome sight given the conditions. Klári stood outside deterring others from entering; she had promised György a few minutes alone, at best. Standing over his eldest grandson, György found himself grateful the boy seemed peaceful, the damage to his body unseen. Laying a hand on Dávid's shoulder, György told him how proud of him he was, how much he loved him. Kneeling to the cold stone floor, György prayed for Dávid. György never took his eyes off of Dávid until, hearing Klári behind him, he kissed his boy goodbye.

There was going to be a mass burial the following day. Klári was unable to accompany György but had arranged with András to drive György and the coffin bearing Dávid to the cemetery. Nothing had been easy, but everything had been done. The coffin was crude. That was to be expected, there were far too few available. Coffins had not been thought of in the emergency supplies being delivered from other nations. At the cemetery, András would speak with the keeper and see what could be done. György made the difficult decision to bury Dávid without the children in attendance. Pest was in turmoil, one child lost was enough.

In the Fülöp apartment, Ágnes' great grandmother Janka was cheerless, her hope of a free Hungary had all but vanished. Listless and withdrawn, she grew more frail with each passing day.

The family took turns in ones or twos sitting with Janka, reading to her, telling her of any hopeful news in an attempt to brighten her spirits.

"Nagyanya," Zsöfia held her grandmother's hand as she softly spoke to her. "Nagy has ordered all the prisons to be opened tomorrow, on Sunday! Cardinal Mindszenty will be released. Here," Zsöfia pressed her grandmother's rosary into her hands. "I thought you'd like to have this to say a prayer for all those people to be reunited with their families."

Burying his grandson had been private and quiet. Dr. Fürth had been correct, the cemetery was a peaceful place to say goodbye. The rich earth had been softened by the cool rain of the last few days. The earth had willingly yielded. The caretaker, an older man, had helped György lower the coffin.

The caretaker, like György, had fought in the war. He was sympathetic and amenable although unable to bring himself to meet György's gaze. This death of someone so young, so beloved. How had they, the old warriors, not been able to protect the precious children of Hungary? György, asking for privacy, extended his hand with a few forints for the caretaker's trouble and the use of the shovels. But the old man had turned away and was gone into the labyrinth of mausoleums, angelic statuary, gray stone, and leafless bowers. A light wind carried whispered prayers and the chill of changing weather.

It wasn't yet noon as András drove György in the direction of the train station. He exclaimed with surprise the news he'd just overheard which György, lost in thought, had not.

"He's done it! Nagy is releasing all the prisoners!"

"Which prisoners?"

"All the prisoners, Mr. Varga. He has ordered all the prisons to open and release all prisoners tomorrow!"

"Tomorrow?"

"Yes, tomorrow, Sunday."

"Would that include Kistarcsa?"

"Yes, certainly. Do you know someone there?"

"Yes, I do. Dávid's father."

Sudden gunfire and responding screams caused András to swerve from the sound of the reports into a nearby street lined with tall buildings.

"This may be as close as I can get you to the train station. That was probably an ÁVH sniper. I am going to turn back and drive around the city to return to the hospital. What would you like to do?"

"I'll get out here, András. Thank you. Thank you."

György watched momentarily as András drove away. He turned and, watchful, began to cautiously walk in the direction of the station, a path that would take him in the vicinity of the shooting. Approaching the nearest cross street, an angry mob pulled a uniformed man from a heavily damaged building out onto the street. The sniper had apparently been caught. György had no interest or stomach for what was to come next and continued toward the station.

Turning down the next street György could see a crowd of people gathering at the front of what looked to be a bakery or market. There was always the possibility of some sort of trouble when there were food shortages and rationing. Finally within hearing, György realized the people gathered there, mostly women, were in distress and calling for help. Several men were running to their aid, György joining them.

As the men approached, the women moved aside only partially revealing several disheveled and bloodied bodies. Amidst their anguished cries the women choked out details of the incident. Here lay the victims of the sniper. These innocents had been standing in the queue for bread.

The other men who'd responded to the cries for help initially blocked György's view. As the men knelt to aid the victims, György saw a familiar face. Dominik lay on the ground, twisted at the waist, his arms thrown out in front of him as if attempting to deflect the fall he had momentarily anticipated. There was no need to check for a pulse. The neat wound on the side of Dominik's head belied the crater György knowingly would find on the opposite side. Dominik's face lay in a pool of already congealing blood. At first György didn't realize that the deep, mournful cries he heard rising above the crowd were his own. He also had dropped to his knees on the hard stone but in abject grief, loss, and despondency. The crowd stepped away only to return, to cry with him, to lay their hands on his back, to wait with him.

Of the four other victims, two were alive and one of those was a woman. The bullet had only nicked her shoulder, she would be fine. Another, a girl of perhaps 12, barely alive, lay in a pool of the combined blood of those around her. György, seeing her lips moving, bent down. Pressing his ear to her lips she whispered, "There is candy in my pocket, take some." Another breath followed another, then release, and she was gone.

The men moved the three bodies to the street where lime would be spread on the corpses until they could be collected. There would be a mass burial the next day. Unlike so many others, these Hungarians wouldn't lay on the street for days. Some of the men returned to György's side and stood waiting. György, kneeling beside the body of Dominik, had bowed his head and crossed himself as did everyone else. After a few minutes, György sat back on his heels. The knees of his pants were bloodied.

"What can we do to help you, sir?"

"I need to borrow a truck. Does anyone have a truck? I give you my word I will return it within an hour to anywhere you'd like."

A truck was provided. György made good on his promise.

By mid-afternoon, György had not yet been able to return to the Fárkas home. Instead, he caused quite a commotion when he returned to the Türea's where the Fürth family had joined them to listen to and discuss the news. Jeno opened the door and stopped mid-sentence in greeting. Jeno feared, incorrectly, György had been embattled and hurt.

"Oh, my friend! Come in, come in. What has happened to you?"

Everyone in the apartment stood as György entered the apartment with Jeno. Everyone admonished everyone else to give György room to breathe, time to adjust, a moment's peace. Gizella went to the kitchen, Mira at her heels to be of assistance.

"Mira, do you know the Fülöp family who lives on the level below us?"

"Not well, but I do."

"The Apa, Fülöp Elek, is a man of about György's size. Could you ask him, for me, if he has a pair of pants for György?"

"Certainly I will."

"There is a girl there," Gizella began.

"Yes, I know, Fülöp Ágnes."

"Yes, and also her Nagyanya Adél and Dédanya Janka. Her Anya is Fülöp Zsöfia. Janka is not well, so be cautious, quiet. Do you understand?"

"Yes, Mrs. Kovács, I understand. I often have to be quiet at our home as well."

Gizella smiled at the precocious girl and gave her a gentle pat on her cheek, "Get going, little imp!"

In the front room, György had begun to recount the events of the day beginning with the extraordinary help Klári had been. At any other time Gábor and Ili would have been well pleased with their daughter. At this moment they were, as was everyone else, overcome with concern for György and awaited the outcome of his story. György told of András, of the burial and then of the sniper and

András returning to the hospital. He told of witnessing the sniper's capture and then of the scene before him, the victims of the snipers' attack. Bowing his head into his hands, a few minutes passed before György spoke without raising his head. Every person in the room felt their pulse quicken, their palms grew moist. Gizella's hands flew to her face then slipped revealing her eyes and the tears welling there.

György continued, his voice a hoarse whisper of controlled, choked emotion

"One, a woman, survived. There was a girl, very young, who died moments later. There were three others, men. Dominik was one."

The women gasped, reeling backwards, crossing themselves. The men remained where they were, waiting on György.

"I was given the use of a truck. A man from a nearby factory had the use of a delivery truck. I returned to Rákoskeresztür Cemetery. I found the caretaker preparing for tomorrow's burial. He was kind. He had been so kind with Dávid. Dominik and Dávid are there, together. He was very kind. The authorities will never know. We," György shook his head, "we will know."

Everyone waited.

"I returned the vehicle but, of course, I couldn't see my grandchildren in this condition."

At this point, György willed himself to sit up and face the people who had been kind and supportive. Seeing their faces, their empathy, and their support, gave him strength. Just then, Mira returned with a bundle she handed to Gizella.

Jeno gave György a small glass of pálinka, which he unhesitatingly swallowed. Gizella gave him the clean pants and unexpected shirt that Elek Fülöp had given Mira.

"Wash, rest in the same bed as last night. Jeno will wake you in half an hour. I will have refreshment ready for you. Is there anything else we can do for you, Mr. Varga?"

"May I stay until tomorrow, possibly Monday? There has been news Nagy has ordered all prisoners to be released."

"Yes. Is there someone you know imprisoned?"

"My daughter's husband, András Henri, Dávid's father. He was arrested in 1950 as an enemy of the state. We once raised horses."

At the mention of horses, Mira had a very audible intake of breath, her eyes widening. György turned to the girl.

"Kisbers. For three generations, Vargas had raised Kisbers. Our farm was near Lake Balaton. Why they took Henri and not me was a puzzle. We were all glad they didn't take both of us. There are five," he corrected himself, "now four, children, our wives, and a small farm. Henri has been missed, as I'm certain all the prisoners have been missed by their families. If there's a chance of finding him, I'd like to stay."

"Do you know which prison?" Jeno asked.

"Kistarcsa."

"Then he is probably at Vác. They will be released tomorrow. You are welcome here."

György washed and rested, falling fast asleep for seemingly only moments. Jeno gave his shoulder a gentle jostle to rouse him. Rejoining the others in the front room, György found Péter and Júlia had returned. While György ate, Júlia recounted what she and her brother knew of the train schedules.

"Thank you for what you have done. My plans have changed. My daughter's husband will be released from prison tomorrow. I hope to find him and return with him."

"The conductor remembered you accompanying the shipment of donated food. He spoke well of you. You had given him a bag of flour, another of potatoes and other vegetables. You and your family can travel with him. He did say that timing is a problem, the trains can be sporadic. It's best to come at noon and wait."

Despite György's protestations, Péter accompanied him to the Fárkas apartment. Péter waited in the kitchen with Charles and Alexandra while the children spent two happy hours together with their grandfather.

Alexandra invited both men to stay for dinner, which gave György the unexpected time to tell the children about their brother and Dominik. He had debated whether and when to tell them, considering their experiences, living situation, and the journey ahead. Now that the situation presented itself, György believed Alexandra and Charles would provide loving support.

György somberly gathered the children around him. The children quieted, sensing the change in their grandfather. György, his voice quiet and controlled, his words practiced a thousand times, was direct.

"My dears, my beloved children. Your brother, Dávid, and Dominik, are dead. I'm so sorry."

The boys were at first unbelieving then, sobbing, fell together into the arms of their grandfather. Rebeka withdrew to the side, burying her face in her hands, her elbows posted on her knees. Rebeka's stifled but heartbreaking cries flowed with her tears between her long, delicate fingers. Alexandra quietly sat next to Rebeka, wrapping her arms around the girl. Rebeka leaned into her, sobbing. She lifted her face and buried it into Alexandra's neck putting her arms around Alexandra. Alexandra held Rebeka until her tears subsided and held her closer still as, pensive and burdened, Rebeka periodically shook her head and would weep again.

"Rebeka, it is plain to see there is worry mixed with sorrow. What troubles you?"

"So many things. If only I had been able to persuade them to go home that first day. If only I had stayed with Dávid, perhaps I could've kept him from harm, and," haltingly, "if only Dominik hadn't been injured, because of me, maybe..."

"Rebeka, look at me, please. Your brother and Dominik made their choices, as you have made yours. You can't question what they have done, or would have done. It is their life, their decisions. "If only" is unchangeable, insurmountable. All of you have been courageous, brave, and full of love for each other. The people of Hungary are in awe of the children of Hungary. There is nothing for you to castigate yourself, or them. You have all behaved remarkably. And Rebeka, this isn't over. Péter and Jani, your Nagypapi, your Apa, all need you. And your Anya and Nagyana need you to come home to them. They are waiting for you. Can you do that?"

György, who had been listening as he comforted his grandsons, nodded his thanks to Alexandra.

Rebeka, wiping a tear from her chin and cheek, straightened where she sat. Her brow was furrowed, questioning, as she looked from Alexandra to György.

"My Apa? Nagypapi, what about Apa?"

Both boys were fully alert, the sorrow for their brother a deep wound they would bear, but now another pressing concern, their Apa. They anxiously looked from Rebeka to Nagypapi.

"The radio broadcast the news that all prisoners will be released tomorrow. I will find your Apa. Together we will all return by train to Megyer. If not tomorrow, then Monday."

"Where was your son imprisoned, Mr. Varga?" Charles asked coming in from the kitchen to join everyone.

"My daughter's husband was taken in 1950 as an enemy of the state, we raised horses. He was taken to Kistarcsa."

"If that is the case then I have news for you. The political prisoners in Kistarcsa were moved to Vác prison. I heard at the café that the prisoners of Vác escaped today. There was some shooting but everyone is believed to have escaped."

31

HOME

SUNDAY. GYÖRGY, ANXIOUS to find Henri, arose early. This was the day he would shepherd his family home. More than any other day, this day he must take care, every moment precious, to exact as much from this day as needed to return to Megyer.

György wondered if Henri would look for refuge in one of the churches. There were other possibilities, perhaps Henri was already walking toward home. As it was, Henri found him.

György had accompanied Péter and Júlia to the train station anticipating the arrival of the train from the west, such as he had arrived on only a few days prior. The train was in the station, being off-loaded by students of the Revolutionary Committee. György went in search of the conductor as Péter and Júlia began to help with the produce. Hoping to find someone in the shipping office, György climbed the stairs to the crowded platform. Amid the tumultuous cacophony of the station he thought he heard his name. He stopped, gripping the rail, questioning what he had heard until, distinctly this time, he knew he heard his name.

"Varga György!"

Henri had arrived at the station late last night along with other prisoners from Vác. The men and women who had been taken from their homes in faraway towns and villages now wanted nothing more than to return to their homes. Some had started to walk, a fortunate few had found delivery trucks with sympathetic drivers. It had been a sleepless night for those who had chosen to stay at the station, hoping to find a way home by train.

Not long after daybreak, Henri was speaking to a few of the morning crew, the students who had begun to arrive for the donated food supply delivery. As another group of students approached the station, Henri had glanced in their direction. A quick second look, although the man's back was now turned towards him, elicited a joyous yelp. Henri began to run, calling again and again until he was heard. Meeting, the two men clung to each other, each unwilling to let go. Then György tightened his embrace and whispered into Henri's ear in quick succession the events of the past week. At the news of Dávid and Dominik's death, Henri would've collapsed if not for György's embrace.

The Fárkas home on Castle Hill was not far away. Péter knew the children were ready, as they had been since yesterday. It would be a quick diversion for one of the delivery trucks, provided Péter and György went alone to collect the children. Knowing their father was awaiting them at the station might serve to expedite their farewells and loading into the truck. Henri agreed and went with Júlia to arrange passage on the train with the forints György had given him.

Having done all he could, there was only time now to wait, to anxiously wait. Henri was waiting, staring in the direction Péter and György had so recently driven away. To her surprise, the delivery truck returned more quickly than Júlia had expected. Everyone at the station turned to the raucous, joyous cries of the children from the back of the approaching truck. Henri crossed the distance toward the approaching truck as the children banged on the side panels, insisting to be released. When the truck came to an abrupt stop, they jumped from the truck bed to the ground, swarming their father, overwhelmed with laughter and tears.

When thc time came to board the train, Henri turned to György dropping forints into his hand.

"The conductor would not accept it. He said to tell you thank you."

The steam locomotive MÁV class 424 deserved its nickname, Núrmi, the Buffalo. The engine steamed and hissed. Its massive bulk gave them a sense of assurance, of safety. As the train left the station, the family sat on a single bench meant for three. No one wanted to be separated from any other. Following a barrage of questions for nearly an hour, the children fell asleep. It was a peaceful sleep, charmed by the relief of their reunion, the cadence of the train rolling over the tracks, the comfort of their father's and grandfather's presence, and the knowledge they were, at last, going home.

In the quiet, his children nestled against Henri and sprawled across his lap and that of the man he loved as much as his own father. György sat shoulder to shoulder with him, his strength giving him strength. At times, Henri felt that his heart would break. Sensing his distress, György would gently lean into him. Each time, Henri would nod his thanks and then chase the demons away gazing at his children, thinking of Laura, and images of home. Knowing the man beside him kept watch, Henri gave in to sleep.

György smiled watching his family sleep peacefully. Soon they would be home. Without Dávid, without Dominik. There would be Irén and Laura to comfort, the children would grieve again. The Marton family must be told. György banished these thoughts from his mind, grateful for what he had. Grateful for what they all had. Grateful they would soon be home.

Péter and Júlia had waved goodbye to their friends. The boys waved at the windows. Rebeka solemnly placed her hand against her window, her unblinking gaze locked onto Júlia, who fought to maintain her composure. At last, Rebeka lifted her chin and, with a hint of a smile, waved. Péter had furtively watched. This country girl was an enigma to him. At the end of the day, Péter and Júlia had returned home and recited the events of the day to their family, the Fülöps, and Fürths. Everyone was concerned for the children, for György, for the family. The events of the revolution had the effect of inspiring devotion. Hungarians were committed to each other. In helping each other rise up they had found in each other their own humanity.

Péter excused himself, explaining he would like to visit Alexandra and Charles Fárkas. Their parting had been abrupt and without explanation. Péter and György's arrival had been a surprise. The departure had taken only minutes as everyone was made to understand they had a train to catch. Alexandra and Charles had been gracious and helpful without questioning or prolonging their goodbyes.

Péter's arrival at the Fárkas home could not have delighted them more. Charles and his mother had been discussing the events of the past days and their concern and worry for the country family they had so quickly come to love. Over a glass of pálinka, Péter retold the story, including the details since György's arrival.

It was late when Péter left the Fárkas home, the effects of the cold and damp masked by the events of the day. The graciousness and benevolence, the kindness of people, invigorated and warmed him. Home again, Péter found his family awaiting his return. They briefly talked and hoped surely by now György and his family were home again. Erzsébet brought out the last of their pálinka, pouring each a small glass. They all stood, smiling, looking at one another as they raised their glasses.

"Home."

32

TEMPEST

THE LAST DAYS of October were unlike any most Hungarians had ever known. Following five days of fighting, the Freedom Fighters controlled the streets.

Monday morning, the people of Budapest awoke to the news that the Russians were leaving. The rain had stopped and people were flowing into the streets. Happily sharing the news, proudly waving Hungarian flags, Hungarians gathered in groups to sing the national anthem.

The Hungarian Peoples Army, and cadets of the Artillery and Technical Artillery Officer School, were parading through the streets. Brandishing the flags of their battalion and the Hungarian Revolutionary Flag, they marched to Boráros Square to secure the area. They had orders to help direct the orderly withdrawal of Soviet troops from the city.

Márkó Vari and his brother-in-law, Lázslo Orsi, had been walking back from the bakery when Márkó saw his friend Denes Stollar. Behind Denes was the oncoming parade. The men stood, cheering the cadets as they walked by, when Márkó saw his friend Andrew Fodor march by. He threw up his arms, shouting, "Long live the People's Army!" Soon everyone had joined in. Andrew swelled with pride, tears rolling down his cheeks. As the cadets marched through the streets, here and there old men removed their hats and nodded their thanks. Women bowed their heads in prayer and people cheered and waved from blown-out windows and porticos.

As their unit approached the Petőfi Bridge, the Soviet tanks stationed there turned and withdrew. As the battalion began to march to the next location it began to rain violently. The temperature had dropped precipitously. Citizen soldiers and Freedom Fighters brought the cadets food expressing thanks and treating them as heroes of the revolution.

In Budapest, and throughout Hungary, the 8,000 prisoners Nagy had ordered released were returning to their homes. A doorbell would ring, or a knock at the door answered, revealing a usually thin, ragged but welcomed loved one. Cardinal Mindszenty returned to Budapest and prepared to speak to the Hungarian people.

Among Hungarians there was a pervasive sense of solidarity and support. Despite store windows having been broken, the merchandise inside was left untouched. People wanted to be of service, helping wherever it was needed. Ordinary citizens organized and began clearing away the worst of the rubble and debris. Bloating, lime-covered corpses were removed from the streets and taken to the local cemeteries for mass burials. The funerals were attended by hundreds, even thousands, of relatives, friends, and fellow citizens. Mourners offered prayers, multiple gun salutes, and a profusion of flowers. At the end, everyone shoveled dirt.

A natural cadence to their daily life resumed. Schools had reopened, utilities were being repaired. In the Türea apartment,

Erzsébet and Jeno, Gizella and József sat at the table, breakfast essentially untouched. Gizella spoke up, "József, please turn up the radio, I didn't hear that. What did they just say?"

"The broadcaster is quoting István Örkény, "*We lied at night, we lied at day, we lied in every wavelength.*" Radio Budapest is admitting they have been lying for years under the direction of the party." József rotated the dial prompting the family to quiet, interested to learn the latest news, yet shocked when they heard it: the ÁVH had been formally disbanded.

Later that day, Nagy announced the official declaration of the newly formed government. Nagy ensured every Hungarian freedom of speech, freedom of religion, and his pledge to re-establish free elections. These announcements elicited widespread celebration. The people of Hungary were filled with hope.

But life was not what it seemed. Nagy received intelligence that Soviet troops were massing at the borders. Nagy filed a formal protest with the Soviet Ambassador, Yuri Andropov. The reply was succinct. The new troops were there to guard the full withdrawal of troops and artillery and protect the Soviet citizens living in Hungary. Nagy was not convinced. Later that day, perhaps as a result of the massing of the troops, Nagy announced Hungary's withdrawal from the Warsaw Pact.

Despite Nagy's actions, the Kremlin made an astonishing announcement. The Kremlin was prepared to enter into negotiations with the government of the Hungarian People's Republic,[5] as well as other satellite countries of the Iron Curtain. Khrushchev invited Nagy to send a delegation to Moscow to begin negotiations. In America, Secretary of State Dulles called the Kremlin's announcement "a miracle." The people of Hungary, incredulous, celebrated their victory. The radio broadcast noted Hungarian writer Tibor Déry declaring the Hungarian Revolution "...the greatest and first victorious revolution in its history." Writer

István Örkény was also quoted stating "...the Hungarian people were the guiding star of the human race."

It was a ruse. China's Chairman Mao had contacted Khrushchev suggesting the events in Hungary, unchecked, might put the very foundation of the Eastern Bloc at risk. Kremlin leaders decided Hungary had gone too far. Without informing the Hungarian government, Khrushchev had changed his mind. Khrushchev ordered the invasion of the now peaceful Hungary by the Soviet forces.[6] Soviet troops and tanks had been ordered to the Hungarian border. Operation Whirlwind had begun.

33

NOVEMBER

THE DAYS GREW shorter, the rain incessant. The ambient temperature steadily dropped. Snow would soon blanket the city and surrounding countryside. The new moon was rising. In Budapest, Nagy continued to transform the Hungarian government abolishing the one-party rule.

In the first few days after György and his family had returned to Megyer, the family had kept to themselves as they adjusted, mourned, and recovered. György had wanted to wait but, with news of the Soviets amassing forces at the border, the time had come to speak with his family. He knew he could no longer wait.

After dinner that night, he asked everyone to gather at the fireplace. At first they had been appalled. Then they had resisted. At the last they understood. Henri must leave, as an escaped prisoner and enemy of the state, he would be hunted down and unquestionably executed. Laura, the children, and György's beloved Irén, would all accompany Henri. György would stay. A strong nationalist, he would keep the farm and bide the time until they returned. The enormity of what lay before them, blanketed with the weight of loss, was not enough to shield them from what he said next.

"Prepare tonight. We will walk to the train at first light."

On the morning of Friday, 2 November 1956, All Soul's Day, church bells rang. Hungarians lit candles. Black flags adorned doorways, homes, and marked those places where recent heroes of the revolution had lost their lives. In the afternoon, the radio broadcast Cardinal Mindszenty praising the insurgents.

"In my heart, I have no hatred against anyone. Our country is liberated, our youth deserves every praise, let us pray for the victor."

The following day, Mindszenty broadcast again in favor of recent developments of the newly formed government. Some people were euphoric, others in a state of cautious disbelief. All were rightfully proud in the unbelievable, unimaginable victory they had achieved. Ordinary citizens armed with faith, will, and the crudest of weapons had defeated the Soviet Union. For the first time in memory, Hungarians enjoyed their personal freedoms and the practice of their faith without recrimination.

Airports had reopened. International humanitarian aid was delivered by the Red Cross in the bellies of Lufthansa's D-36's. Food, medical supplies, and other aid were transferred by truck convoys to towns and the surrounding countryside. On their arrival, people swarmed the trucks. Old women in black fringed shawls raised their baskets to be filled. As relief poured in from the free world, rumors abounded that the Russians were returning. Everyone wondered if the UN would take action.

In the Fürth apartment, Gábor had been listening to the radio when Béla returned from work.

"What have you heard?"

"Radio Free Europe continues to sign off with, 'Freedom or Death!' Here, they are broadcasting the US Secretary of State, Dulles," Gábor said, as he turned the volume up.

"To all those suffering under communist slavery, let us say you can count on us."

Gábor thought a moment before looking up to Béla.

"This is an encouragement to many but perhaps foolish. Why does the West not come to our aid, as they have said?"

Nagy and the government continued to press forward with reforms at the same time as he continued to request aid from the west. The Soviet military command invited a Hungarian government delegation to attend a celebratory banquet and meeting to discuss the details in finalizing the Soviet withdrawal. The delegation, headed by Pál Maléter, agreed to attend. Maléter wanted to avoid bloodshed by pushing for a negotiated solution. Fluent in Russian, Maléter had previously negotiated with the Soviets. As Minister of Defense, Maléter had met with Russian commanders in the Parliament Building. However, the meeting wasn't just a sham, it was a trap. Upon arrival, Andropov placed Maléter and his delegation under arrest.

The following day, the United Nations Security Council met to discuss the situation in Hungary. The U.S. Representative, Ambassador Henry Cabot Lodge, introduced a draft resolution.[7] In that resolution, the US called on the Soviet Union to refrain from interfering in the internal affairs of Hungary. The Soviets responded by accusing Nagy of inciting a counterrevolution.

The Kremlin was duplicitous. As of the night of 3 November, the Kremlin had fully staged Operation Whirlwind. In an overnight session, Lodge urged the members of the Security Council to pass his resolution. Nine did, but the Soviets exercised their veto power. Later that day, a similar resolution, Resolution 120, also introduced by the United States, passed the General Assembly with only one dissident vote, the Soviets.

Late that night, Péter lay sleeping in the front room of the Türea apartment. Gentle knocking at the front door awakened him. Péter rose and walked to the apartment door without turning on any interior lights.

"Hello?"

"It's Márton."

Péter cautiously opened the door allowing Márton to furtively slip into the apartment. Gently easing the door closed behind him, Márton stood leveling Péter with one look. A whispered conference and Márton slipped away into the night, his secret whispers echoing in the darkness.

"You must leave. Now. Tonight. They've arrested the students who made the pamphlets. They have a list...and we are both on it. You must leave!"

34

BETRAYAL

4 November 1956

KLÁRI AWOKE AFTER a fitful few hours having yet again slept in her clothes on the floor of Mira's room. Everyone considered it prudent to be prepared despite yesterday's seemingly hopeful news. The radio broadcast the Soviet negotiation of their withdrawal, the establishment and status of the new provisional government, and the appointment of Imre Nagy. Everyone had gone to bed in an almost euphoric state despite the lack of anything to celebrate with. What food they had would have to last at least a day, or two, until another train or truck arrived with relief supplies. Moving cautiously, as not to awaken Mira, Klári padded out to the front room in her stocking feet. Surprisingly, the men were up and huddled around the radio wrapped in blankets. Béla and Gábor were listening, intently focused, for any news they might glean from the various broadcasts.

"Sunday, I'd almost forgotten. It gives me hope hearing the church bells," Klári said, hugging herself, as she looked out the window across the city. She was momentarily lost in thought considering the possibilities and outcomes for Budapest, for Hungarians, for her family.

"Brrrr, it's so cold and damp." Klári continued to talk as she rummaged through cupboards, "I'll make some tea, I don't think we have any coffee. I'll look. Have you been up all night? It's almost 4."

Hearing nothing, Klári turned and asked, "Anything?"

Gábor looked up, a severe and grim countenance as she had ever seen.

"What is it, Apa?"

Ili and Alida were just walking into the kitchen. Alida spoke up, "We couldn't sleep either."

"Apa?" Klári repeated, her voice echoing the clutching anxiety she felt rising, her body tensing.

"The Soviets have arrested the entire Hungarian delegation including Defense Minister Pál Maléter."

"What?" the women simultaneously asked in unison. Everyone turned their full attention to Gábor and Béla. The men exchanged a solemn nod to each other, their elbows resting on the table, hands clasped at their chin.

"The Soviets called a meeting late last night to discuss terms. The delegation was offered amnesty. It was a ruse." Gábor was quiet then, as was everyone else.

After a moment, Klári turned to the kitchen and began to set out cups that Alida took to the table, asking as she placed them, "The Soviets are in negotiation with Nagy's government, are they not?"

The still silence of night was unceremoniously shattered as Soviet tanks began to shell the city. The Kremlin, in an unprecedented reversal of its stated policy, had launched "Operation Whirlwind." 60,000 troops and 2,000 T-54 tanks had been moved into position to crush Budapest. The Kremlin had sent more troops than those present during the German occupation of Hungary during WWII. It was 4:15 in the morning. The revolutionary forces that had successfully employed guerrilla tactics with the simplest of weapons didn't stand a chance.

Nagy had been up throughout the night. The prior evening he had received disquieting intelligence: the Soviets were amassing troops around the city. Then a dispatch, Pál Maléter and the entire Hungarian delegation sent to a joint meeting with the Soviets had been arrested. After placing unanswered calls for help to western powers and neighboring countries, Nagy went to the radio.

Throughout the hills of Buda and neighborhoods of Pest panic, fear, and terror gripped the abruptly awakened, unsuspecting populace. Russian shells detonated, reverberated, and sent shock waves through the ground, their homes, and buildings. The resultant explosions were a constant onslaught, a background to the cacophony of urgent calls, screams, and cries as the citizens of Budapest frantically sought refuge wherever they could. By 5:20 a.m., although few in Budapest would hear the broadcast, Radio Free Kossuth crackled with static and began to broadcast.

"This is Imre Nagy speaking. Today at daybreak Soviet forces started an attack against our capital, obviously with the intention to overthrow the legal, Hungarian, democratic government. Our troops are still fighting; the Government is still in its place. I notify the people of our country and the entire world of this fact."

Listening, the Türea family stared at one another then vacantly into the room. Each pondered the implications as the national anthem played. While they didn't know it at the time, this was the last that anyone would hear Nagy's voice. By 8 a.m. the organized defense of the city had evaporated.

At 8:10 a.m., Radio Budapest broadcast its last appeal, a woman's plaintive exhortation: 'Help Hungary... help, help, help. Civilized people of the world! On the watch tower of 1,000-year-old Hungary, the last flames begin to go out. The Soviet army is attempting to crush our troubled hearts. Their tanks and guns are roaring over Hungarian soil. Our women—mothers and daughters—are sitting in dread. They still have terrible memories of the Russian army's entry in 1945. Save our souls. SOS—SOS—SOS . . ." before being taken off air. The radio station had been seized.

Somewhere in Pest, a newspaper journalist sent the last message to be received from Hungary: "We are quiet, not afraid. Send the news to the world and say it should condemn the Russians. The fighting is very close now and we haven't enough guns. What is the United Nations doing? Give us a little help. We will hold out to our last drop of blood. The tanks are firing now. . ."[8]

In Washington, as Soviet troops entered Budapest, Dulles received a message from the United States Ambassador Clare Boothe Luce, "Let us not ask for whom the bell tolls in Hungary today. It tolls for us if freedom's holy light is extinguished in blood and iron there."[9]

35

BLOODY SUNDAY

4 November 1956

THE CALL OF IMRE Nagy remained unanswered in Hungary's battle against the Soviet invasion, his appeal ignored. Hungary received no international assistance. Western countries, engaged in the Suez Crisis, uncertain of the weaknesses in the European balance of power, and in concern of escalating European conflict, committed Hungary to its fate. The US condemned the Soviet attack as a 'monstrous crime' but did nothing.[10]

Soviet forces invaded Budapest, seizing all vital media sources. Across Budapest, sustained gunfire and shelling was supported by air strikes that decimated the city. Much of the capital was reduced to rubble. Any hope of resistance was too late. The poet, Sándor Márai, would soon write of this day, "A nation cried out. But the only echo was silence." Nagy, to minimize damage, ordered the Hungarian Army and citizen militia, the Freedom Fighters, to not resist.

On Rósza Hill, families huddled in rooms as far as they were able from the front of their homes and windows that faced the oncoming thunderous, grinding, squealing, roar of approaching tanks. A sudden, massive, detonation violently shook every building and imploded windows. The shattered glass impaled furniture and scattered across floors.

In the Türea apartment, Erzsébet, sleepless, had heard the appalling news on the radio and alerted Jeno. Together they had awakened her parents and fled to the bunker mere minutes prior to the tank column approaching Rósza Hill.

Elek and Lukács Fülöp reeled across the floor, shaken by the blast, urging everyone to their feet, "Everyone, hurry! Hurry! To the shelter!" Lukács carried his frail grandmother Janka over his shoulder, her arm around his neck. Running from the apartment, Lukács leaned against the rail as he fled down the stairs. His calves burned, every breath a wheezing, searing pain as he hurried uphill to where Jeno stood at the entry urging them to safety in the bunker.

Ágnes Fülöp paused, transfixed by the sight as the roof of the National Archives burned; the capricious, consuming flames far reaching into the sky, glowing embers giving form to the rising, swirling plumes of hot air. The entire horizon was red. The fire was spreading. Beguiled, Ágnes at last heard Jeno's urgent calls. Inside the bunker, Lukács and Janka lay recovering on two of the wooden sleeping platforms. Zsöfia was attending her grandmother. Mira, with her aunt and grandparents, had left their apartment just as Bence and Hannah Novák had fled theirs. Together, they helped each other to the bunker.

On Dohány Street, the carnage began before first light. Commanders of the four man tank crews had instructions from Moscow to level any building being used as a stronghold. The tank crews were relentless. Students and teachers who had arrived at school that morning huddled in a corner of the basement shelter.

The building had taken a direct hit, killing a teacher and five girls. When the shelling ceased, and the rumble of the departing tanks faded into the distance, cautious refugees emerged to an unrecognizable landscape. The streets were filled with rubble. Clouds of dust shrouded the broken trees, streets, and charred remains of vehicles, buildings, the dead and the dying.

The crowded stairway in the Bójtos apartment building was treacherous. Everyone was in a state of hurried panic. Lázló leaned against the wall for support as he carried Barnát, still traumatized and suffering the effects of his wounds. Following closely behind, Ilona Vadas and her mother, Erzébet Kender, had a firm grip on Petra. Grandfather Illés Kender followed with Petra's twin, Tomi. Nearing the ground floor, Illés witnessed a young family with two small children crawling out of a billowing cloud of dust. The building next door had collapsed. Illés broke from the rank, reached out and pulled the father to his feet beseeching him to get his wife and children to the basement shelter.

The shelter filled. As the tenants and nearby residents of destroyed buildings crowded together in groups and corners, prayers were offered, cries consoled, fears and terror comforted and calmed. With each onslaught, they heard the grinding tank tracks then the squealing pivot of the turret. The explosive firing was followed by the anxious, nerve wracking moments awaiting the detonation, anticipating their demise. Quite suddenly and unexpectedly, the door to the shelter was thrown open. Two men pleaded for help as they carried an injured Russian soldier down among the refugees.

Further down the street towards the Danube, Éva and Lilly had been stoic, remaining in Éva's apartment for the past week. The two women had ventured out, only once, in the early morning to the bakery. Now, with Pest overrun with tanks, they decided to flee to Rózsa Hill, to shelter with Júlia. The women dressed in two layers of clothing each carrying a single, small bag. Exiting onto the street from Éva's apartment, people desperate for shelter ran among Freedom Fighters. The people of Budapest were seeking refuge as the ÁVO, the Red Army, and tanks terrorized the city.

Amid the chaos, a frenzied current of news thread among the fleeing populace. There was talk of renewed fighting at Corvin Passage, Széna Square, and the Army Post. Radio Free Europe had broadcast the UN calling for the withdrawal of Soviet troops. A passing old man advised against crossing either the Chain or Erzsébet Bridge. A boy, running past, said the area of Castle Hill was being bombed.

Lilly led the way, sidling through the congested areas, until Éva spied a safer route. They scrambled over the charred remains of trolley cars and buses, barriers of cobblestone, and the rubble of ruined buildings. At one juncture, as they cautiously picked their way on hands and feet over piles of stones and splintered beams, Éva's right hand fell on a smooth, pliant surface. Éva glanced to her right as she lifted her hand to find purchase ahead. Shrouded in dust, a grisly, detached arm lay across the bricks, its splayed fingers a ghostly remembrance mocking that most recent, fleeting moment of surprise. Averting her eyes Éva, retching, continued on following Lilly. Ahead they could see the Margit Bridge. Overhead, the damaged facade of the market gave way.

Across the Danube, the residents of Castle Hill had fled their homes. Alexandra and Charles had escaped to a shelter away from the city. Alexandra had been relieved to find her friends, Erzsike Sárkány and Anna Schott, with Anna's family. People huddled together quietly in groups, anxious, as the bombardment continued. Dust filtered through the cracks and floorboards settling everywhere, on everything, and everyone. Alexandra found her thoughts drifting, regretting not accepting György's invitation to accompany his family to Megyer. As the bombardment continued

Alexandra grew resolute; she would survive and she would leave. She would leave not just Budapest, she would leave Hungary. She hoped Charles would agree.

In the bunker, Gábor Berci and József Kovács fumbled with the dials of the radio while the other adults worked to organize the bedding and food supplies. Mira had fallen on the scramble up the hill, scraping her knee. The wound had continued to bleed despite the compress Mira held against it. Erzsébet easily found the bright green, Bakelite first-aid kit under the shelving shared with books and cookware and handed it to Klári. Mira nervously prattled while watching her mother, wincing and cowering with each explosion. Jeno had sat, amidst the flurry of activity that surrounded him, with a book in his hands. As the bunker gradually quieted inside, Jeno started to read aloud the words of the beloved Hungarian poet, Endre Ady.

"...I know I believed that on that night
Some neglected God would soon alight
To take me and deliver me to death
But I am still alive, though different
Transfigured by that shattering event
And as I am waiting for a God
I remember that terror-haunted
Devastating, world burying night;
It was a curious,
Curious summer night."

Closing the book, Jeno looked to each of the familiar and well loved faces whose attention was intently focused on him. The sounds of their world being torn apart dully echoed through the pipe.

"Do not worry, dear ones. We have lived through this before and we will again. Let us all give thanks that we are here together."

Although already a small space, they crowded together, heads bowed, and prayed.

The army cadets had been startled awake by an alarm at dawn with the news that the Russians were returning in force. All of the cadets, including Andrew Fodor, were eager to fight. The young men organized their kits and dressed quickly to assemble on the grounds with the 27th Division. Their orders were to organize the defense of the southern section of Budapest. The commander of the division disagreed with the defense of the school under the overwhelming odds they faced. The head of the Revolutionary Council insisted on protocol, the orders were to be carried out. The alarm sounded, and the cadets moved into firing position.

The first column of Soviet tanks appeared, sweeping away the anti-tank weapons the cadets had installed. A Russian officer and two soldiers approached the building on foot and demanded a meeting with the school commander. The Russian officer offered terms: surrender within the hour or suffer the bombardment by the tanks now assembled at People's Park until the building was demolished. The commander, in his experience, understood the futility of resistance. The cadets rallied to fight, vowing suicide before laying down their arms. In the ensuing confusion, several armed cadets, including Andrew and his friend István escaped out the back of the building. Everyone who stayed, some crying in frustration, surrendered.

Running through the streets, Andrew and István found refuge in the basement of an abandoned building ravaged by the fighting of the last two weeks. Shattered and broken weapons, rubble, crumbled mortar, and dust were spread across floors littered with body parts and the dead. There were others, mortally wounded, including a boy of no more than sixteen, who stood in the corners or slumped against the walls.

For many Hungarians, there was no place to hide. War, as always, manages to target the innocent and vulnerable. A small church opened its doors to a group of women who'd arrived seeking shelter and safety from Russian soldiers, but to no avail. The bishop had stood on the stone steps, his arms thrown wide in supplication, entreating the group of drunken soldiers to honor the sanctity of the church and those who sought refuge therein. The bishop's last words caught in his throat as he sank to his knees. A single bullet had torn through his vestments, his life ebbing, helpless, as the soldiers walked around and over him to enter the church.

Although isolated pockets of resistance would continue for several days, the battle was over by Friday, 9 November. The revolution had been crushed. Widespread resistance was no longer possible. Isolated incidences of resistance were summarily defeated. Snipers, and the buildings they fired from, were reduced to rubble. Budapest lay in ruin. In the end, more than 25,000 Hungarians had been killed, approximately 20,000 wounded and, in the weeks following Bloody Sunday, 22,000 were imprisoned. Of that number dozens would be executed.

Around the world, agencies were mobilizing. Humanitarian aid and methods of delivery and disbursement were being organized. Robert Quinlan orchestrated the volunteers and aid being provided by the National Catholic Welfare Conference. The Conference was one of many religious organizations to provide aid and support to the refugees. The Austrian Minister, Oskar Helmer, sent an appeal to the United Nations and an urgent cable to the League of Red Cross for help. Cardinal Mindszenty, so recently released from prison, arrived at the US Embassy seeking asylum.

The Soviet High Command offered Nagy an ultimatum, surrender by noon or Budapest would be bombed. Nagy, with Gábor Tánczos and many of his other followers, sought asylum at the Yugoslavian Embassy next to Hero Square. The siege began. Unlike 23 October and the days following, this time the Soviet tanks were not only greater in number but were accompanied by tens of thousands of ground troops and air support. All commands were given directives to put down the rebellion, fire at will, and destroy any bastion of resistance.

36

IRON FIST

4 November 1956

THE PEOPLE OF Budapest emerged from their bunkers, basements, and hiding places to find their city destroyed. The streets were reduced to rubble and the elegant facades of multi-storied buildings lay in ruins on the streets exposing the damaged contents of the apartments within. Dust-laden furniture, paintings hanging askew on crumbling walls, multicolored odds and ends of clothing and draperies caught on corners, pipes, wires, and broken bits of masonry were exposed to the elements. The mountains of rubble and remains of lifetimes lay in a jumble on the streets. The families who once called the area home huddled together in abject loss.

Everyone who was able stayed in what was left of their home in the evenings. The remains of streets and sidewalks were mostly impassable by the massive amount of rubble, abandoned vehicles, and the charred remains of tanks, buses, and streetcars. School had resumed, but the ominous absence of certain teachers, and the accounts of their circumstances or demise, cast a pall over every classroom. Every day saw fewer and fewer children in attendance, always an excuse of illness or death in the family, but those that remained knew better.

No one talked of the revolution for fear of reprisal. Every man, woman, and child was afraid of the Soviets, afraid of the unseen, afraid of the ÁVO. People were leaving. No one dared even mention any form of the words "leave" or "escape." However, escape is exactly what many had on their minds. Across Hungary a quiet, urgent reckoning was taking place in almost every home in almost every city and village.

Nagys' government had been replaced by János Kádár, most recently a member of Nagy's government. Kádár, under Nagy, had pledged his support of the new, liberal reforms. Instead, he formed a repressive government in the immediacy of the aftermath of the revolution.

In their cheerless apartments and homes, the windows sheeted in plywood and scraps as could be found, every family considered and discussed one topic, survival. There was no fresh food, no electricity, no water, and no deliveries. The United Nations High Commissioner for Refugees, founded in 1951 and established with a five-year mandate set to expire, was a pariah, unwelcome in both Hungary and Russia. Instead, emergency aid, in additional to its transportation and delivery, was funneled through the Red Cross. That too came to a stop when János Kádár's regime insisted on control of all aid. Those in need were left wanting.

For many Hungarians survival meant escape, to leave Hungary. The Iron Curtain would once again be drawn across the Hungarian border. To leave before the route was sealed off required hasty decisions. Into this forbidding darkness came a ray of hope. From town to town, neighborhood to neighborhood, and home to home word spread quickly. All Hungarian refugees would be granted political asylum in Austria.

Following the Soviet re-occupation of Budapest, Tamás Kiss returned to Szeged with other members of the University of Szeged. His parents had been watchful, waiting for their son's return. Upon his arrival, his parents had furtively hurried him inside with news that the police were already looking for Tamás. The police had arrested one of the students Tamás had been working with distributing "illegal" pamphlets. Believing that the students involved with the demonstration in Budapest were also being hunted, Tamás devised a method to warn them. A young student, Péter Mansfeld, was returning to Budapest, and would advise the student union.

Tamás hurried to collect all of the MEFESZ and AHUCS documents, letters, and pamphlets in his possession, burning and stirring the ashes. His parents packed a small knapsack and gave him what money they had. The family stoically embraced, saying what they all knew was most probably their last goodbye. Tamás would have to leave the country as soon, and as quickly, as he was able. What he would do was left unsaid for the protection of his parents.

Radio Free Europe reported the United Nations declaration. The declaration stated the Soviet Union had violated Article 4 of the Warsaw Pact. Further, the Soviet Union was not acting in accordance with international law or agreements currently in force. Regardless, Soviet reoccupation of Hungary continued undeterred. Pockets of resistance fought bravely, desperately defending the hard-fought victories of the revolution. That resistance ended on Saturday, 10 November, when the last confrontation was silenced in a bloodied blanket of snow. In less than a week, Operation Whirlwind had claimed the lives of over 3,500 Hungarians and 700 Soviet troops. In the smaller villages that dotted the countryside, unarmed resistance and protest was met with a fusillade.

The Fürths had returned to their apartment to find the windows shattered, the floor and some of the apartment rain-soaked. Cold and damp, without electricity or heat, they bundled in blankets in the back rooms. Through connections at the hospital, Klári had been able to get word to her brother in Sweden. The coming days were spent waiting for a response, keeping warm, and venturing out to find food for their family of six. They didn't have long to wait. A postcard from Mira's uncle arrived. On the back, a single sentence in his elegant handwriting: *It's sunny in Vienna*. This was the clue they had been waiting for. The arrangements had already been made, it was time for their family to escape Hungary.

In the apartment below the Türea's, the Fülöp family were in mourning. Janka had died. Erzsébet had helped with the preparations and arranged for burial. The ground had grown cold and was difficult to shovel, snow had begun to fall, but they had managed. Now they sat in their windowless apartment planning their escape by day and grieving at night. The flickering light and shadow of candles illuminated Janka's photograph as they knelt and prayed for her. They knew, as did everyone else, that the border would be closing. This would be their only chance to escape.

The Türeas sat in earnest discussion. Gizella and József would stay; they were old, what hadn't they endured? They knew cousin Jakab had left as soon as he had escaped Vác, determined to find his way to Switzerland. Júlia must escape the country. Her involvement with the student unions and the demonstration would mean certain arrest as soon as the Soviets had reestablished their government and operatives in Budapest. Júlia would go to England. A friend of the family had offered Júlia a position there which would allow her to resume her studies.

Jeno knew that when the time came to send Júlia he would also send Erzsébet. For now, that discussion could wait. Péter had left with the hope of making his way to Switzerland, or perhaps

America, where he could continue his studies. No one spoke of Péter. They all shared the same anxiety, the same hope, the same fear as they all waited. Péter had promised he would somehow contact them once he had crossed the border.

Cautious and uncertain, few ventured outside as the temperature dropped. A heavy, wet snow continued to fall. Such a snow meant accumulations of ice. Tomorrow. Tomorrow Júlia and Erzsébet will leave. Tomorrow they will hear from Péter. Tomorrow he, Jeno, will begin a life without his wife, without his daughter, without his son.

37

FLIGHT

THE EXODUS BEGAN on 23 October 1956 and inexorably grew until 4 November when the veritable floodgates opened. More than 5,000 refugees crossed the Hungarian border into Austria by noon of that bitterly cold November day. Most escaped on foot.

In the weeks following Operation Whirlwind, 113,810 refugees had escaped across the border primarily into Yugoslavia and Austria, many through the Austrian border towns of Eisenstadt and Traiskirchen. They escaped before the bridge at Andau was destroyed, before the highways were blockaded, before the minefields were laid, before the so recently removed Iron Curtain was rebuilt effectively closing the border to Austria.

The desperation of the refugees' circumstances were compounded by the certain knowledge that their window of opportunity would soon slam shut. These circumstances compelled the refugees into a veiled and frozen wintry landscape of unseen and lethal hazards. Even so, they left. They fled their homeland by truck and train but primarily on foot. In total, more than 200,000 left their native homeland. They left family, friends, homes, possessions, and all they had ever known in the balance of living behind the Iron Curtain and certain reprisal.

Of the 200,000 refugees, ten percent of the refugees were unaccompanied minors. These 20,000 children were representative of the "wartime generation," born between the years 1939 and 1944. This group was comprised of escapees from state orphanages, industrial apprentices, peasant children, and other children from Budapest. Two thirds of the refugees were men. Of that number, more than half were under the age of twenty-five. Another third of the refugees were between the ages of twenty-five and thirty-nine. The high educational level and vocational training of the refugees would prove to help ease the normal constraints of immigration.

Despite, or perhaps because, the Soviets had regained military and political control of the countryside, Hungary and its people were in a state of siege. Russia interrupted the delivery of supplies to Budapest. What food supplies there were sold out by early morning. Food was rationed. Bread, a staple in Hungarian households, was limited to 10 ounces per person when it was available.

For many Hungarians, their future seemed without hope. Instead, they faced want, deprivation, religious persecution, and abuse. And for anyone having any association in the least with the activities of the last two weeks, they faced deportation to Moscow or execution. Hungarians could only suspect what was to come. History records that by December the Soviets would establish their control of Hungary and institute a more rigorous patrol on both sides of the border. Three months later, the border would be closed completely. In the aftermath of the revolution, for any Hungarian who would seek refuge, the time to go was now.

Most Hungarians fled in fear. Many fled knowing the price to be paid for their involvement in the demonstration or revolution of the previous two weeks: 229 civilians were executed during the first days following 4 November.

Many of the refugees fled to avoid Soviet reoccupation. Hungarians were all too familiar with certainties of imprisonment, horrors, persecutions, and reprisals that would unquestionably ensue. Others fled weary of the near-constant turmoil, privations, and insecurities they'd endured living under a brutal regime. Some fled to a hoped-for life of possibilities, while others fled to give the next generation those possibilities. 18,000 Jews fled, certain of religious persecution under the reinstated communist government. Previously, by decree, only a select few of their children had been able to receive an education. Many Hungarians fled in hope of the one word that served as a beacon of light and hope: freedom.

People from the country, "peasants," were the first to seek refuge in the days following the 23 October revolution. Initially, this group represented the largest percentage of people fleeing Hungary. Following Bloody Sunday, the vast majority of refugees were from urban areas and of those, more than half were from Budapest.

Everyone knew the circumstances were not only dynamic, they were volatile. The border, the politics, the Kremlin, the status of the various police, and security personnel; each represented a challenge that, combined, would be insurmountable in exponentially increasing increments with every passing day. Panic-driven in front of the oncoming Red Army, people from eastern provinces were fleeing west. They fled with their children in hand. They fled by cart, truck, train, or any other means with little else than what they wore.

All roads led to Budapest but all roads were patrolled. Travelers were not only required to show their identification but reason for travel and destination. Refugees who fled by rail traveled from Southern Railway Station. Trains would ferry refugees to Sopron, the largest Hungarian city closest to the Austrian border. However, passengers were again required to show their identification, the reason for travel, and their destination.

For many refugees, the greater portion of their journey was completed on foot, a challenge in itself. Hungarian shoes were mostly mismatched and barely functional due to extreme production quotas and mismanagement by the one and only Hungarian manufacturer, the Danube Shoe Company.

Hand carts, trucks, wagons, and other vehicles provided other clandestine means of escape. Cart paths were seldom patrolled. Having gained the distance crossing the expanse of Hungary, refugees could ride city trolleys to the end of the line. There, passing through a mile of woods, fields, and across an unmonitored wooden bridge, lay the border to Austria.

As refugees flooded into the landscape nearing the Hungarian border, Hungarians from all walks of life helped their countrymen. Hungarians provided shelter, food, and guidance despite the recent Soviet edict announcing anyone giving aid or shelter to refugees would be imprisoned or executed.

38

THE REFUGEES

GYÖRGY LED HIS family to the station early the next morning. From there, they had all traveled north to Sopron. The country train line, far west of Budapest, was quiet. The temperature had dropped. November had turned cold, very cold. The Soviets were massing at the eastern border preparing for Operation Whirlwind. The Varga family, while alert and traveling with little else than the layers of clothes on their backs, a single valise, and one small bag, encountered little hardship.

North of Sopron the line came to an end. György led his family walking across the frozen ground. They walked through the night crossing into Klingenbach, Austria. Exhausted but exhilarated, the family was somber. György was surrounded by his family and fiercely embraced. Tears welled and silently spilled. In turn, György cupped each precious head in his large hands, first kissing then laying his cheek upon theirs. To each he whispered words of enduring love, encouragement, and that glad day when they would one day be together again.

György took Henri aside for one last consultation, one last embrace. Henri was reluctant to release his grasp as György stepped away and turned, silently walking in the direction from which they had only just arrived.

Rebeka, certain she could feel her heart breaking, stood at the front of the family. She had followed several footsteps behind her beloved Nagypapa after he had turned to leave. Laura stood shaking, not from the biting cold, watching her father. Laura held her mother, who held her daughter, both uncertain of the nightmare they were living. Henri had stooped to lift Bella into his arms and now stood watching György. Henri could feel his heart straining within his chest, aching for this man he had grown to love so dearly. Henri understood with certainty the task at hand that György had charged him with. Péter and Jani, forlorn, stood behind and to the side of their father, making every effort to be brave as their Nagypapa had just asked of them.

Suddenly, György stopped and turned. For just a moment, elation supplanted anguish, hopes rose, and smiles lit up every face. György raised his hand high, gently bowed, and rose again. No one dared to move, at that moment each of their lives had never before felt so fragile. Suddenly, György turned and was gone. Henri's voice, just as suddenly, brought them back to their present situation.

"This way. Rebeka, Laura, boys. Irén. It is time. György is certain there will be many who will follow in the days and weeks ahead. Eisenstadt is about another three hours journey. We will find something to eat along the way. Laura, please, lead the way. Boys, Rebeka, follow your mother. Irén, please go ahead, Bella and I will follow."

In the forest north of the village of Megyer, István helped Enikő into the cart and then put their small bundle of food, wrapped in a bit of cloth, under her feet. He lifted their little boy, Henri, to the seat beside Enikő. Their 11-month-old baby girl, Laura, slept quietly in her arms. They had begun their journey in Megyer with the help of György, who had only just returned from the border crossing with his own family. The cart, small and lightweight, had belonged to Bartal and Zita Demeter. It was perfectly suited for the small horse they had brought with them from what was left of the Vizi farm. They would make good time over the frozen cart path. Time was of the essence. It had been three days since Operation Whirlwind.

When news of the Soviet reprisals had come from Lake Balaton, István had secreted Enikő and the children to the forest. István's parents had not survived the carnage. Now, with a last embrace, György and István parted. István led the horse as the small family began their journey traveling the narrow cart roads to the border. Soviet troops had not yet moved into the western region. Walking together, their children asleep in the cart, István and Enikő crossed into Austria under the cover of darkness in relative safety.

Across the border, István found lodging with a farmer and registered with the Red Cross at the local mission. Their visa application at the US Embassy was granted when the Hungarian Church sponsored their family. Two days after their arrival in Austria, István and Enikő were at the mission with their children for a health and welfare checkup.

"Vizi? Vizi István and Enikő?"

"Yes, these are our two children, Henri and Laura."

"Yes, beautiful children," the nun seated behind the desk smiled. "Your family has been scheduled on tomorrow's transport to Bremerton, Germany. There, you and your family will board a ship bound to your new home in America."

Hearing this news, Enikő reached into their small cloth bundle extracting from among its meager contents the tile of Turul she had been given, what now seemed like, a lifetime ago. Enikő wondered where Laura and her family might be. Would she ever see them again? István saw the tile and smiled. He hadn't known Enikő had carried it with them. Putting his hand on Enikő's shoulder, he was reminded of the many memories of his friends. He softly spoke.

"Protector."

Enikő let her fingers lightly trace the beautiful painting before wrapping and placing the tile back into their bundle.

The Gergő family had left at the first intimation of Soviet backlash following the demonstration. The terrible food shortages had put a thin soup on their table three meals a day. Once a week they had a small ration of meat. They were fortunate to have a cousin who lived on a small piece of land densely planted with fruit trees. In the past, the family would gather to pick and can the harvest each summer. Those efforts had supplemented their otherwise meager fare in the days following the revolution. During that time, a plan began to foment and then take shape in Etel's mind.

Among the first to leave, the Gergő family fled to a small village where a traditional annual three day festival, the fall pig slaughter, was about to take place. Etel Gergő had arranged for a small group of refugees to travel together to attend the festival. Such a group of holiday travelers was widely expected and accepted. Etel had paid a farmer to send them an invitation. When Etel received the invitation, she gave it to her mother, Tünde, who had chosen to stay behind. The invitation would act as a paper trail when the authorities would, unquestionably, come looking for them.

The following day, arriving by train, the small group of "holiday" travelers were met by a farm family who made great pretense of familiarity. Each traveler carried only one small bag as a three day journey would reasonably justify. The farmer loaded the bags into the wagon as the group climbed in amid much talking and laughing, as attending a festival would usually instill such a joyful banter. As was the custom, each family was dropped off at a farm. The Gergő family stayed with the family that had picked them up at the station.

The days were spent in repetition, a big breakfast followed by the killing of pigs and chickens. At ten years old, Penny had never seen so much food on a table and had never had so much to eat. On the third and last day, a large, burly man named Zoltán arrived in the late afternoon driving a team of horses hitched to a hay wagon. The visiting celebrants were being treated to a hay ride.

The refugees who had traveled north with the Gergös were already in the box, bundled against the cold, making a great pretense of camaraderie and celebration. The few possessions they had carried with them were stored under the hay. Climbing into the box, Penny clung to the heavy, three quarter length deerskin coat her mother had insisted she wear. Penny had been disgruntled at the start of the trip but now appreciated her mother's foresight. Penny still had a grip on the side of the box, steadying her, as Zoltán laid the reins along the backs of the pair of Hungarian Muraközi draft horses. Jerking the wagon into motion, the horses set off at an even cadence easily pulling their freight.

It wasn't long before the driver extracted a bottle of pálinka from under the seat and began to pass it around. The night was bitingly cold, ice shrouded the landscape. A sip of pálinka was just what was needed. However, before they were halfway along their journey to the border, Zoltán was drunk. Wavering on the seat, he jovially called out to anyone they passed, "We're going to the border, come with us!" Finally, one in the group sternly cautioned him to a reserved silence. Good-naturedly, Zoltán instead began to loudly sing traditional Hungarian folk songs. Penny broadly smiled and began to sing along. Soon everyone was singing.

As night shrouded the landscape, the driver pulled the horses to the side of the road adjacent to a field bordered by trees. Climbing down from the wagon, Zoltán turned as lights from an oncoming jeep lit up the road. Coming to a stop directly in front of Zoltán, the lights focused on their group. Blinded, they held up their arms and squinted into the night. Four uniformed Soviet soldiers emerged from the glare and stood before them. One soldier addressed Zoltán.

"Where are you traveling?"

"Nowhere, officers. We're having a hayride!" Zoltán responded, a little too enthusiastically, with a flowery flourish of both hands.

Two of the soldiers approached the box and asked for everyone's papers. Penny's mother, Etel, knew a little Russian and noted their slurred speech. She signaled for the bottle of pálinka, offering it to the soldiers as part of the fall festivities. Having their attention, Etel managed to bargain with money and jewelry she quickly gathered from the group of travelers. A deal struck, the soldiers left and the group lost no time in setting off across the field. The receding strains of Zoltán singing to his horses carried away into the night unheard by the travelers now focused on the last, perilous segment of their journey.

One of the men in the group, Bartalan, knew the way; his farm host had familiarized him with the terrain. Bartalan guided the refugees across the frozen fields, a small river, and a fence. The group walked in silence, tense and terrified in the frigid cold. When at last they approached Austria, Penny was alarmed to see soldiers.

"Are these good soldiers or bad soldiers?"

They were, to everyone's relief, Austrian border guards. One of the guards, following the established protocol, escorted the group of refugees to the Austrian army barracks. The Gergös, and those they'd traveled with, were given steaming cups of hot chocolate to warm themselves. As they sat, laughing at the miraculous wonder of having made it to Austria, they welcomed other refugees brought to the barracks. Most were exhausted after the harrowing journey. Every refugee was given a bed with special care to keep the families together.

In the following days, the Red Cross helped Etel contact her sister in the US. Her sister arranged to sponsor the Gergő family enabling them to quickly and easily apply for and receive their visas to travel to America.

Klára and Lászlo Bójtos had known they had to leave Hungary as they sat huddled in the bomb shelter with Budapest literally falling apart all around them. When the shelling had ceased, and the sounds of the tanks receded, they had emerged from the shelter. The family had dressed in multiple layers of salvaged clothing and hurried away ahead of the oncoming Red Army. Friends of Lászlo had arranged the family's escape. They knew both Lászlo and Barnát would undoubtedly face arrest, and probable execution, for their part in the revolution.

Klára and Lászlo had hidden with their sons, Barnát and Izsák, in the back of a truck under a tarpaulin that was being driven to Zalaegerszeg. A bone chilling hour had passed when Lászlo felt the vehicle slow. Ahead, at the side of the road, a solitary Hungarian soldier was flagging the driver to stop. The family had been perilously close to being discovered and turned back, or worse. The Hungarian soldier, sympathetic to the plight of his fellow countrymen, pretended not to see them under the tarpaulin and let them pass.

From Zalaegerszeg, the Bójtos family rode a train to Sopron. From there, at nightfall, they embarked on the perilous journey crossing on foot into Austria. Lászlo carried Barnát, his Budapest Boy, on his back over the rough and frozen, furrowed fields. Barnát, still suffering from his wounds, found it impossible to hold on. Lászlo pulled the belt from his trousers and Klára buckled it in a loop diagonally across Lászlo's shoulder to his waist creating a sort of sling. A lithe man, László was surprised at the relative ease with which he carried his remarkably sturdy man-child. Barnát showed every inclination to living up to the meaning of his name, bear.

Despite the dipping temperatures and frozen crust on the fields, sweat began to weigh down the first layer of clothing now chaffing his skin. Lászlo laughed under his breath.

"What is it, Apa?" Barnát asked, his mother and brother curious to hear the answer.

"It must be adrenaline that makes me feel as if I am carrying a feather."

Izsák was holding his mother's hand while walking beside his father and brother. He frequently glanced protectively at his brother. When his father had first returned to the bomb shelter cradling Barnát's broken body, Izsák had been horrified, transfixed by the sight. He had been certain his brother was dead. When Barnát, bleeding but breathing, was laid before Klára, the relief had been overwhelming. Izsák had buried his face in his father's coat, crying inconsolably. Now, although his parents had advised him of the cautions they must take on this journey, it seemed all of their lives were in jeopardy. Walking across this open, plowed field that turned and cut at his ankles seemed foolish. His shoes were proving no match for the frozen fields. He only hoped they would hold together until they crossed.

Lifting his eyes from the treacherous ground and glancing again at Barnát, Izsák was suddenly blinded. "Down!" his father called. Lázslo threw out an arm grabbing at Klára's sleeve before collapsing prone upon the field. Both Lászlo and Barnát grunted at the sudden impact. A search light scanned the field beyond them and then passed on, illuminating the darkness in an uninterrupted sweep. The family didn't know, couldn't know, the border guards were both uninterested and reluctant to intercept any refugees. Instead, they were terrified. Even so, Lázló stood.

"It's alright, Klára, boys. Up we go. Come on now. We are nearly there. Can you see the lights of Austria? Barnát? Can you see them? Point the way, son, we are almost there."

Dr. Klári Fürth had kept in contact with her brother in Sweden. She had remained hopeful that one day she would be able to send Mira to him despite the government's past repeated refusals. The events which had transpired over the past two weeks had set Klári's resolve. Together, Béla and she would take Mira and escape the much-hated communist regime.

Klári's mother, Ili, had urged her daughter to escape, she would stay with her husband. Alida would stay with her parents. Everyone was confident that Alida's status with the Russians would protect both her and her parents. When Klári learned the landmines along the Austrian border had been removed she knew the time to escape was at hand, the clock was winding down. She had made arrangements through a contact with a farmer who lived at the border. For a fee of 10,000 forints the Fürth's would make their way to freedom. There was no time to waste, they would leave the following morning.

"Mira, sit by the window and eat your breakfast. Watch for the morning patrol. Béla, your coat?"

"Yes, I have it. Here is yours and Mira's. Napa Ili, here, this is for you," Béla pressed forints and papers into her hand and then, wordlessly, held her close. Mira had spirited to his side.

"The guard has just passed our building, Apa."

"Klári, it is time."

Klári walked from the back room snapping her bag closed and then lifting its strap over her shoulder.

"Ready. Anya," she spoke softly as she lowered her head and lifted her mother's hands in her own. "Anya," she said again looking into her mother's eyes.

"It is time to go, daughter. I will tell your Apa. Together we will pray for you," Ili said as she continued with a loving smile. "I had a dream about you, all of you. You will be well. You will have a happy life. I will live with this knowledge, it will be my joy. Now go."

Walking to the east train station of Keleti, they found a cab and were about to get in when a passerby called out, first to Klári then, seeing Béla, again.

"Dr. Fürth? Dr. Fürth?" as he looked from one to the other.

Klári and Béla turned to face a colleague from the hospital. The doctor stood, momentarily wondering, then smiled and only briefly chatted. Klári and Béla stepped into the waiting cab. Their colleague had quite obviously surmised the situation. Despite their lack of traveling clothes or suitcases he had instead played along with the ruse. With a knowing look and a nod of his head he touched the brim of his hat and said goodbye.

From the cab to the station, the Fürths boarded the westbound train for the Austrian border. Mira followed her parent's example and said nothing, which was not to say she hadn't a thousand questions. Mile after mile, Mira thoughtfully analyzed questions and both possible and probable answers. What had her mother put in her purse? What would they do for food? For clothing? Who would they live with? What would they do for money? And, most importantly, just where were they going once they arrived in Austria? Mira did know that they lacked the special permits allowing travel to the border towns. She rightly surmised she would walk across the border with her parents.

For Mira, absorbed in her thoughts, time passed quickly. Her mother touched her knee as the train slowed and stopped. The passengers disembarked and quickly dispersed. Klári and Béla walked, with Mira between them, toward the locomotive. Mira glanced about, then at her parents expectantly. Would they start their journey? Were they going to follow the tracks? Instead, Mira was delightfully surprised to find themselves among a small group of people that re-boarded the train riding in the locomotive. Standing as they rode the last leg, the engine compartment was hot. The floor of the compartment was somewhat unstable reacting to every track, tie, and switch. Béla removed his wool hat, laying it on what turned out to be the engine housing. His only hat was immediately, regrettably, singed.

It was dusk as the train pulled to a stop at the border town of Sopron. Béla, the first to exit, stood at the bottom of the treacherously steep, metal grate steps. He offered his hand to each of his fellow passengers as they disembarked. The group reassembled, awaiting the train engineer to lead them to where they would await their guide to Austria. Béla stood between his wife and daughter, holding them close to his side, waiting.

Anxiety and stress were taking a toll. Mira stood, her mind wandering, wondering if the engineer might turn them in. Béla, feeling his child's hand in his turn warm and sweaty, bent down to her ear and whispered, assuring her that they were safe. Mira turned at a sudden sound on the metal treads behind her. The engineer appeared and, climbing down from the engine compartment, silently motioned for the group to follow him. They walked a short distance, across a paddock skirting a wooded lot to where a dirt lane led to the engineer's farmhouse. The farmhouse was dimly lit. Water, dried fruit, and bread had been set out on the kitchen table for them.

The refugees hadn't long to wait for the next leg of their journey. Everyone waited, silently and anxiously, not knowing what to expect. Everyone was surprised and shocked when a uniformed border guard appeared at the door. The guard, sympathetic to the revolution and his fellow Hungarians, moonlighted as a guide.

In the crowded kitchen of the farmhouse, the guide stood silently before them. He raised his hand to his mouth and somewhat ominously uttered one word, "Quiet." Without another word he turned, opened the door, and lead the Fürths and their fellow refugees out into the night.

A luminous full moon lit their way through the village and across the fields. At one juncture, a Border Patrol unit passed close by. There was nothing for the refugees to hide behind, so they laid upon the frozen ground at the edge of the ditch parallel to the road. The guards pretended not to notice the little group and drove on. Nearing the border, the guide pointed in the direction they were to cross the Austrian fields before them. It was a distance soon crossed. Stepping from the fields onto a street, they all stood marveling and uncertain of their accomplishment. Nervous laughter tittered from several women. Klári turned to her daughter.

"Mira, quick, pinch me. Yes, pinch me! Am I dreaming?"

The refugees walked together towards a village illuminated by the lights of a Red Cross refugee station. Mira asked her mother what it was she had placed in her purse as they were leaving their home earlier that same day. Klári slipped her hand from Mira's and opened her purse, revealing its contents. Klári looked up to watch her daughter as Mira peeked in. There was her mother's nail polish, a package of playing cards, and Mira's doll. In the years to come, the remembrance of those few possessions to take to their new life would serve as a reminder of all they had braved and of all they had accomplished.

Elek Fülöp had found transport to the border with some of his co-workers from the Ministry of Agriculture. In the aftermath of the revolution, many vehicles were missing. Although they had been sent in search of the Ministry's missing vehicles, Elek's co-workers had instead seized the opportunity to transport friends and family to the Austrian border.

The Fülöp family left carrying a single briefcase. Zsófia had packed the case with kolbász sausage, bread, and the few bits and pieces left in their cupboards to sustain them through whatever lay ahead. Elek walked with his family to the center of Pest to meet his co-workers. Seven people filled the cab. Three men rode in the back.

Each person was given a job or reason for being in the truck. Zsófia and Ágnes were being taken to visit relatives. The men were designated as either truck drivers or mechanics for the vehicles they had been sent to find. Elek and his co-workers knew other trucks from the office had preceded their arrival. The men who drove those trucks had plied the Hungarian border guards with bacon, money, and vodka. Elek had reason to hope any truck with their government emblem would pass without restraint or interruption into Austria.

Approaching the border station each passenger made a pretense at normality. They engaged in conversation or assumed a nothing-out-of the-ordinary posture as the driver slowed the truck. No sooner did the driver downshift than the guard impatiently waved him through. The guard turned his back on the truck and its passengers resuming his place in the gatehouse.

Unbelieving, and yet not daring to look back, they all stared ahead. No one realized they were holding their breath until the driver cautiously glanced at his sideview mirror. Another look then, speaking quietly, as though he might be overheard by the guards, "We're free." Those whispered words triggered a collective exhalation and broad smiles. Looking at each other in turn, they were unaccountably cautious to utter a single word until the driver pulled up to the Red Cross station.

Arriving at the station, they felt incredulous, unbelieving. Elek jumped from his seat in the front to help his wife and daughter. Zsófia took his hand as she stepped down, while Ágnes, brimming with excitement and the release of stress and anxiety, jumped down and hugged her mother and father.

"We're here, Apa! Anya! We made it!"

Many refugees suffered a longer, more arduous escape. The journey between Hungary's capital of Budapest and the city of

Linz in Austria, a four-hour drive by car, was instead a three day journey by train, cart, and on foot for the refugees.[11]

Walking the streets of Budapest, Márkó had found his friend Lázslo. Together, they had walked to the Kelenföld train station and boarded an overcrowded train. An old man stood forlorn at the side of the train tracks. His arm was raised in supplication, calling out to any who would listen, "Don't go, good people, this is your country."[12]

They had found a seat in front of two cloaked women Márkó found vaguely familiar. As if in response to his questioning gaze, the dark haired woman momentarily raised her chin. The woman met his glance before lowering her eyes to whisper to her companion. Marko, recognizing Éva and Lilly behind the fringe of their cloaks, sat, fighting for composure. The women's faces were drawn and bruised. Lilly's one hand was twisted and bandaged. Éva's long hair was now apparently shorn, a long line of stitches revealed along the edge of her scalp before she adjusted her scarf.

As the train pitched and rumbled from one station to the next, officers repeatedly checked each passenger's identification and destination. Most were "traveling" either for a family visit or a harvest celebration. Near the end of the third day, the train stopped at the small peasant border town of Kapuvár, 16 miles from the Austrian border. Éva and Lilly disembarked with many of their fellow refugee travelers at the rear of the train. Márkó and Lázslo exited at the front.

As the travelers gathered and regrouped on the station platform, Márkó could not help but notice the tall, handsome woman circulating in the crowd. The woman scanned the crowd, ostensibly searching for a particular passenger, perhaps a friend or relative she was to meet. Márkó was surprised to see this stranger pass so closely by Éva and Lilly as to rudely bump into them. The woman paused to apologize, or so he assumed, until moments later when she stood just behind him and whispered, "We are leaving tonight for Austria. Meet at midnight at the park. It will be cold."

Markó and Lázslo had met at the designated time, along with many of the other refugees that had traveled north on the train. The refugees were separated into smaller groups by two of the guides. Except for Katalin, the guides were men. All of the guides were gaunt, all earnest, and all brave. In the months ahead, many of the guides would be brought to trial by the Soviets and executed for their part in aiding the refugees. The handsome stranger from the station, Katalin, led her group of twelve including Márkó, Lázslo, Éva, and Lilly, toward freedom. For Katalin, this crossing was different than the many others she had made in the last few days. She did not plan on returning. On this trip she would join the refugees and cross into Austria with them.

Through the long night they passed over a frozen landscape of marshes, farmland, and crude bridges. At times, they crossed small streams. The unlucky few who broke through the ice were allowed only a brief stop on the opposite bank to remove wet socks before they froze to their feet. There was no recourse for their wet shoes.

Everyone was wary, alert, and watchful. On a signal from the guide, the group would lay prostate upon the ground as a patrol passed. On occasion, the refugees would tunnel into haystacks to escape detection as rockets and flares lit the night sky. When the night seemed to wear endlessly on, Katalin whispered words of hope; the bonfires set as beacons by the Austrians would soon be in sight. Everyone looked to the northwest horizon hoping to be the first to sight the bonfires.

The stony field, deeply furrowed, made walking difficult. The ice made it treacherous. Two of their group had either twisted or broken an ankle. Each, aided by a pair of men, hobbled along. People no longer looked for the lights, they watched their every footstep. It was Lilly who suddenly stopped, a sob escaping her throat, pointing where the first glimmer of the bonfires could be seen.

Like the Gergö family, the Schotts were traveling under the pretense of attending the fall pig slaughtering ceremony. Anikó and her family, each wearing two layers of clothing, had boarded a later train and found seats in the last car, what had been a cattle wagon transport. Their destination was the elegant, old, walled border town of Sopron. Anikó sat with her brother, Sebestyén, and another boy of about 8 years who was traveling alone. Anikó's father and mother, Bálint and Anna Schott, sat together behind their children. Bálint carried the family's one suitcase that Anna had packed with a few clothes, salt, paprika, and spices.

The train was nearing the end of the line, there were two stations before they would reach Sopron. Stopping at the first, the train was boarded by the ÁVO, the Secret Police, to check documents. Anikó and her family carefully slipped away. A young boy stayed close beside Bálint, a shadow to his every movement. Safely away from the station, the family stopped. The family looked down at the small boy, who lowered his eyes to the ground and spoke.

"I'm all alone. My parents were taken, and my father was killed. My older brother, killed. Shot by a sniper. I have no one. Please, I won't be of any trouble. Let me travel with you to Austria."

Bálint gripped the boy's shoulder with a nod, "Do not worry. You will travel with us. But you must do as I say. Agreed?"

"Yes, sir. Where will we go now?"

"Just stay with us. Be quiet when everyone else is quiet. Stay still when we are. Do as we do and we will all be fine. What is your name?"

"Dániel. Lászlo Dániel."

"That is a good name. Dániel," Bálint smiled down at the boy, "we will do this together."

Through night and following day the family walked. They would pause to rest well-hidden within a small stand of trees or under cover of darkness. When they reached the small town of Kapuvár they found lodging and dinner at a small inn. The children applied themselves in earnest to their dinner of cabbage stew and noodles, yeast rolls, and plum dumplings.

Bálint was distracted by the urgent need to find a guide to lead them to the border. Even so, he couldn't help to notice the children. Their faces, pinched and lean, had been transformed. The warmth of the inn and warm meal had brought the color back into their cheeks. They smiled and laughed as they ate. Bálint silently gave thanks as he leaned forward to savor the aroma of the first hot meal he'd had in weeks.

As Bálint began to eat he heard a man's voice, "These glasses are cheaper in the West." Without pausing, Bálint enjoyed the first bite of his meal, touched his napkin to his lips, and responded in kind, "Yes, these glasses are cheaper in the West." Bálint turned in his chair to face the man. The two men negotiated terms. The Schotts would be guided to the border in exchange for the bit of jewelry they had secreted under their clothes and money. All of their money. The price they paid was equivalent to half a year's professional salary. And it was all they had.

After dinner, the guide led the Schott family to his home. Other refugees had already congregated there and settled onto chairs and into corners as they could find. The Schotts stood together in the front room watching as more refugees continued to assemble. Before long, the house was a refuge for 96 men, women, and children.

Anna spoke with a young woman near her own age who, along with her son, had also been forced to forgo the train and walk a great distance. A kind farmer had transported them the last several miles concealed in his hay wagon. Anna was horrified to hear the woman tell of the farmer's warning to sit close to the surface. Soldiers were known to thrust their swords into the bottom of the stack checking for fleeing residents.

At ten o'clock the guide beckoned to the refugees. They were to silently follow him from his home. They walked through the night at a steady pace and strictly in single file. To a person, they were terrified. They crossed frozen fields amidst gently falling snow. The exertion, compounded with the layers of clothing, was offset by the cold night air and snowflakes brushing their faces. As the night wore on, the snow changed to sleet. The freezing rain puddled in the ditches into which they scrambled when an occasional, oncoming Soviet tank, searching for escapees, ominously clattered past.

Anikó had been separated from her family when the line was formed. There had been no time to correct the situation. They were unable to speak or call out to each other. Midway down the line, alone, terrified, and fearing capture, Anikó fainted. The line continued. Her father and brother, near the end of the line, found her and carried her.

Excitement and hope merged into a nervous, high strung energy as the group neared the heavily guarded border. A glimmer of light in the distance intimated their goal was close at hand. A sudden bird call riveted everyone's attention. Fear wrenched and tormented them. Were they discovered? So close to freedom, were they to be turned away?

They refugees couldn't have known, for everyone's safety, that the guide had bribed the Hungarian guards. The whistle had alerted the guards to their approach. Now the guide was pointing in the direction of the glimmer of light, confirming their suspicions, whispering, "Austria." A series of whistles denoting whether to advance, be still, or take cover led the group across the field. Unexpectedly, the guide held up his hand. Everyone stopped, their hearts raced, the biting cold freezing their fingertips. Pointing the way ahead the guide turned back and disappeared into the night. The refugees were left to make their way, alone, across the last hundred yards. Ahead, the bonfires beckoned and the Red Cross awaited, ready to transport all to safety.

Following the clandestine visit from Márkó, Péter had left Budapest with his cousin, Erik Hilbert. Erik had arrived at the Türea apartment bereft. Erik's girlfriend had been killed, burned alive in a Red Cross van. The Soviets had targeted the van just as they had also targeted hospitals, schools, and ambulances.

Péter and Erik had decided to travel together and now found themselves traveling by train in a car filled with Soviet soldiers. The two friends sat in silence. Péter considered the senselessness and destruction of war, the feeling of broken hopes, betrayal, and the lack of justice in the world, the pointlessness of politics, of doing or attempting anything. The words of Endre Ady, his favorite poet, came unbidden.

We are the men who are always late
We are the men who come from far away
Our walk is always weary and sad
We are the men who are always late.
We do not even know how to die in peace
When the face of the distant death appears
Ours souls splash into a tam tam of flame
We do not even know how to die in peace.
We are the men who are always late
We are never on time with our success,
Our dreams, our heaven, or our embrace
We are the men who are always late.

Oppressed by the east, abandoned by the west, Péter felt an uncharacteristic, oppressive lack of direction. The rail agent requesting his identification abruptly brought him back to the present task at hand.

Disembarking two stations prior to the end of the line, Péter and Erik waited for nightfall before starting for the border. Too late they noticed the Hungarian soldiers.

"Your papers, please. Your destination?"

Péter and Erik were arrested. The guards walked them to a nearby town where they were ordered to stand by the door of an unlikely building. The three soldiers improbably entered the building without a backwards glance. Many Hungarian soldiers were supportive of the revolution and the plight of their fellow Hungarians. These soldiers were giving Péter and Erik a pass. As soon as the door closed, Péter and Erik ran.

Crossing the short distance over which they had so recently been escorted, Erik blindly led the way. A narrow strip of forest and a double fence row of barbed wire abruptly stopped them. On the fence hung a sign, "Property of the People's Republic of Hungary." A cursory glance revealed a neat opening where the menacing wires had been twisted back upon themselves. Dropping to their knees, the two men cautiously crawled through. The moonlight was mostly obscured by the overstory. They almost blindly groped their way through the forest to where they emerged on an open expanse of frozen, uneven terrain. The landscape before them was swept by a searchlight passing across the field at regular intervals.

"Drop down, quickly!" Erik whispered. Across the field Soviet guards, backlit in the glare, were easily discerned. Hiding in the brush, Péter knelt. Under the trees the ground was not yet frozen. Péter pushed his fingers into the soil, rubbed the small bit of earth between his hands, and raised them to his face, inhaling the damp, musky fragrance. His mind wandered, would he ever again see his home, his friends, his parents, or his country?

The crescent moon offered little light as Erik watched the guards walk towards the sentry house, their backs to the field. Erik saw their opportunity. Pushing Péter's shoulder to get his attention, Erik crawled ahead. Erik and Péter made their way across the field to the darkness beyond the scope of the searchlight. When Russian voices were no longer heard, the men stood and considered the serene, moonlit landscape that stretched before them. Then turning their backs to Hungary, Péter and Erik crossed into Austria.

39

AUSTRIA

JOSEPH NAGYVARY ESCAPED Hungary. Born in Szeged, he was a 22 year old student at Eötvös Lorand University at the time of the revolution. Nagyvary managed to escape, first to Zurich, then Cambridge, and eventually to America in 1964. As a retired professor of biochemistry and biophysics, and a renowned violinist and luthier, he would later write, "Among the people I remember with immense gratitude are the students from the universities of Vienna. Many of them sacrificed an entire semester of study to provide essential services to the refugees." And, as author James Michener wrote: "It would require another book to describe in detail Austria's contribution to freedom. ... If I am ever required to be a refugee, I hope to make it to Austria."

The 1955 Austrian State Treaty established their military neutrality and relatively new freedom from Soviet occupation. As the Austro-Hungary border began to feel the first pangs of political unrest, the Austrian government issued orders to shoot any armed violators of Austrian territory, and they did. The body of a young

Soviet soldier, who had been shot while pursuing a refugee, was returned to the Soviet Union without recrimination.

As the situation in Hungary devolved, Oskar Helmer, the compassionate Austrian Minister of the Interior, took the lead role. In answer to the Hungarian crisis, Helmer issued a declaration to the people of Hungary offering asylum to all political and economic refugees. In what had been a moral and ethical void in the political arena, Helmer appealed to the world to respond to the developing humanitarian crisis. Of primary importance was the request that governments accept all refugees regardless of physical conditions, which had heretofore been reason enough for immigration officials to deny entry.

As Helmer and his government had correctly predicted, the events in Hungary continued to devolve creating a humanitarian crisis. However, they were unprepared for the vast influx of refugees.

Refugees fled Hungary to the nearby Austrian border crossing frozen fields, forests, and canals while eluding border guards. The Austro-Hungarian border was minimally patrolled. Many of the border guards, whether Hungarian or Soviet, were either sympathetic to the plight of the refugees or were exploitive and opportunistic. The guards either looked the other way or willingly took whatever coin, jewelry, or other items of value as could be exacted from the refugees.

Crossing the border, refugees were met by students, farmers, and urban volunteers who had flocked to the border towns answering the appeal Austrian Minister Helmer had broadcast over the radio. The Austrian Federal Army offered their assistance as did numerous charitable organizations. The cooperative efforts of the many agencies, governments, and the United Nations were able to meet the need of the refugees, most of whom had arrived literally with only the clothes on their backs. Some arrived with less than nothing as children were handed across the border, a note pinned to their clothes, "This is my child. Care for him. We return to fight for freedom."

At the center of the Austrian resettlement of refugees was the Intergovernmental Committee for European Migration, ICEM, headquartered in Geneva. There was no international playbook for a refugee crisis of this magnitude. Standards and operations evolved as situations presented themselves. Initially, an estimated 5,000 to 10,000 refugees entered without registration. The Hungarian refugees were distributed to 257 camps throughout Austria.

Volunteers sorted the refugees into groups. Families with and without children and single people were sent to different camps. The camps were clean. Straw beds, some but not all encased in ticking, were provided in school rooms, recreation halls, and available buildings. In Eisenstadt, a large castle had been converted into a camp and staging area for Hungarian refugee families. Children quickly found camaraderie among the other refugee children. The camps provided food, shelter, and first aid. Refugees were directed to registration offices and offered assistance in contacting embassies and family members. Refugees sometimes spent days in the long queues applying for a visa. Staging areas with buses for transport to various countries awaited the "Cold War refugees."

The approximately 18,000 Hungarian Jewish refugees were provided with two kosher kitchens. At some reception centers, refugees were asked to recite the Ma Nishtanah, the Four Questions, from the Passover Seder service, to prove that they were Jewish.[13] Additional support from the international Jewish community provided housing and relief for the refugees as they awaited acceptance, visas, and transport to the countries of their choosing. The International Rescue Committee and the Jewish Joint Distribution Committee, known as the JDC, were of primary support in the sponsorship and resettlement of Hungarian Jewish refugees.

Refugees began to cross the Austrian border following the 23 October revolution. In the aftermath of Operation Whirlwind, thousands of refugees were flooding across the border. Although the Suez Crisis had apparently been of the only importance to the UN council during the later part of 1956, many countries were heeding the plight of Hungary's citizens.

The day following the Russian invasion of 5 November, Sweden announced its intention to accept refugees that were amassing in Austria. In total, 8,000 Hungarian refugees would find safe harbor among the Swedes. As early as 7 November, the French Red Cross airlifted medical supplies and blankets on two flights to Vienna, on which they boarded refugees for the return flights. Belgium, Switzerland, and the Netherlands quickly responded with offers of asylum in their countries.

On 8 November, the first of many trains transported more than 400 refugees to Switzerland. The following day, additional trains transported refugees to Belgium and the Netherlands. Canada and Venezuela were the only countries to accept Hungarian refugees without quotas and waved health condition limitations. More than 35,000 refugees would make Canada their home. Approximately 5,000 refugees chose to make Venezuela their new home. By 28 November, a total of nine European countries had already resettled 21,669 refugees. In total, just under 113,000 refugees were transported from the temporary camps in Austria and Yugoslavia to 37 countries across Europe, North and South America, Canada, Australia, New Zealand, and Israel in less than two months. In the following months that total would swell to 180,000.

In the aftermath of the failure of United States foreign policy and diplomacy during the Hungarian uprising, Secretary of State John F. Dulles was intent to create any sort of a win involving the Hungarian refugees. The State Department had failed Hungary. Members of the CIA were heartbroken, embarrassed by the lack of

US resolve. To this day, as a retired senior agent of the CIA recently revealed, the role the US played in the Hungarian Revolution of 1956 is considered a "...blot on the CIA escutcheon."

By December of 1956, United States President Dwight D. Eisenhower managed to both fast track the admittance of 38,000 refugees and avoid a constitutional crisis when he stretched the use of executive power in his interpretation of the McCarran-Walter Act of 1952. In a special meeting with the President on 26 December 1956, members of Congress and the executive branch convened to discuss the crisis. All parties agreed that the United States was going to have to accept the burden as the primary source of financial support in the transport, aid, and relocation of the refugees. That figure would ultimately amount to $71,075,000. Of that amount, $20 million was donated from American private sources including religious, nationality, and other volunteer agencies.[14]

The United States State Department requested US Air Forces in Europe (USAFE) to airlift Red Cross supplies.[15] Those supplies amounted to 190 tons of food, medical supplies, cots, and blankets from locations in the United Kingdom, Switzerland, France, and West Germany to centers in Austria and Switzerland. The 322nd Air Division provided 25 C-119 Flying Boxcars from the 60th Troop Carrier Wing (TCW) and the 465th TCW at the Dreux and Evreux Air Force Bases in France, and from the 317th TCW at Neubiberg Air Base, West Germany. The world was mobilizing to help the Hungarian refugees as the unprecedented flood of humanity poured into Austria and Yugoslavia. Ultimately, the Austrian ministry assisted 174,704 Hungarian refugees over a period of five months. Austria's neighbor to the south, Yugoslavia, assisted 19,181.

40

REGISTRATION

CROSSING THE BORDER into Austria, Péter and Erik felt a surreal state of being. They walked the streets in the shadows of night under a moonlit sky. It was difficult to comprehend they were in altogether different circumstances. The streets were empty, this late at night, and although they knocked on windows and doors to no effect they eventually found refuge at a church near the center of town. Inside, they were given a straw bed to sleep on and the promise that the next morning they would be taken to Vienna. Relief and exhaustion were a counterbalance to apprehension and unease. The cousins were soon asleep.

The next morning, the promised buses were waiting immediately outside the church vestibule. Péter and Erik stood in line behind a small, quiet, wide-eyed girl traveling alone. Around her slender neck was a string attached to a rectangular placard that lay lopsided on her chest. Scrawled across the placard was written the word, "diabetic," below that, her departure date from Budapest. Within fifteen minutes, the buses opened their doors to be boarded. Children traveling alone sat in the first rows behind the bus driver. Péter and Erik, who had been near the front of the line, sat just behind the little diabetic girl. The girl was soon asleep once the bus was moving at an uninterrupted pace.

Conversation ebbed and flowed as they crossed the unfamiliar landscape during the hour long bus ride from Eisenstadt to Vienna. With the possible exception of the driver, no one on the bus had ever traveled beyond Hungary's borders. Conversation varied little from their immediate, anxious concerns of survival. Many had given all their money to guides, or as payoffs to the border guards, just to escape.

Arriving in Vienna, the bus pulled to a stop in front of a large, imposing building under the jurisdiction of the International Red Cross. Eugene 'Gene" Girard, the Red Cross Director, was there to welcome each of the passengers. A nearby assistant directed the refugees to the registration area. Péter and Erik found themselves in a cavernous room where they waited long hours before the initial registration process.

Completing their registration and receiving their initial documents labeling them as "stateless," the cousins were directed to another area where they would be given meals, services, hygienic supplies, and a place to sleep. The hot soup, bread, and cheese were welcomed. The bedding varied. Metal beds had straw-filled ticking as mattresses. In other places, straw mattresses were laid upon the floor, in others there were simply piles of fresh straw. Single men and single women slept in different areas, families in another with unaccompanied children and babies.

From the center they were directed to several locations around the city to register requests for visas and permits to the countries of their choice. This task was made more complex when Péter learned from a German-speaking Red Cross agent that it was advisable to register for more than one country. Many of the refugees had not known that all countries had annual refugee limits. An officer, overhearing Péter's conversation, gave Péter a German-English pocket dictionary. The dictionary would prove especially helpful in the days and weeks ahead.

In the following days, Péter and Erik went in search of their destinies. Erik determined to find his in Switzerland, Péter had decided on America. The morning following his arrival in Vienna, Péter had registered at the American Embassy. Every day he returned.

On the morning of the fourth day, as Péter was walking towards the American Embassy, he approached a man who intrigued him. The stranger resembled a Hungarian railroad or streetcar worker. The man was as tall as Péter but twice his size. Péter stopped, catching the man's attention, and the two struck up a conversation.

"Have you registered already?" Péter asked.

"No. I walked with some of my family. You understand. I am returning to my village."

"So, you will be staying?"

"Yes, and you? You will be leaving?"

"Yes."

The stranger glanced up and to both sides of Péter.

"And your family? They will stay?"

"Some will stay. Some have already gone. I am here with a cousin, but I leave behind my parents and grandparents."

The stranger paused before responding. He and Péter frankly regarded one another.

"In Budapest? I will be passing through Budapest. Is there anything I can do for you, perhaps to deliver a message to anyone there?"

Péter gladly accepted the hoped-for offer pulling from his pocket a small piece of paper on which he'd written his parent's address on Rósza Hill.

"Please tell my parents of my safe passage, that I am healthy," Péter paused. It occurred to him to inquire whether this stranger would be willing to act as a courier. It was a risk, certainly, but how else could he return to his parents what they undoubtedly needed, would need, and was theirs? "Would it be an imposition to ask if you would consider returning to my parents the money they gave me? I have not needed it, I do not need it, and they, of course, as you understand, will."

"It is not too much. It is an honor. I will see it done."

Péter handed the man a small paper envelope.

"Thank you. They will be relieved. It is a relief also for me."

The two men parted company in opposite directions, one towards hope, the other to certain adversity. Péter stopped and turned watching the kind stranger, strong and resilient, walk away and wondered after him. Péter thought it curious he hadn't even asked his name, although, he admitted, the man could have devised any name. Nonetheless, he seemed to Péter to be an honest person. As the stranger turned a corner disappearing from sight, Péter wondered if he would ever see him again. A sudden chill reminded Péter of his task and, turning his coat collar to the wind, he continued on to the American Embassy. As he walked ahead he thought, "*Perhaps today. If not today, tomorrow.*"

Péter waited at the Embassy as he had almost everyday, conversing with any and everyone he met, learning everything he could about any opportunity available. Every day, all day, he made his presence known with the intended purpose to be remembered. He spoke in German, English, and Hungarian to anyone who would listen on a variety of subjects. He was deep in conversation with an officer regarding recent news; President Eisenhower had increased the total number of refugees the United States would welcome to a place named Camp Kilmer. Suddenly, Péter heard his name announced.

"Peter Turea."

Péter found it curious he was growing accustomed to hearing

his name announced backwards. As he approached the desk, the woman seated there shuffled a tremendous stack of papers, rearranging them into groups and settling a small stack directly in front of her. A cursory glance revealed his own name written across the topmost sheet and an accompanying poor photograph that bore little likeness, or so it seemed, to him.

"Peter Turea?"

"Yes, that is my name."

The woman repeatedly glanced from the photograph to Pèter and back again, finally giving up with a subtle shrug. She was quite obviously overwhelmed with long queues and crowds of earnest, anxious, and hopeful immigrants awaiting their name to be called.

"Peter Turea?" she again asked.

"Yes, that is my name. From Buda."

"Budapest?"

"Yes. There are two cities…" he began but noticed her confusion and corrected himself, "Yes, Budapest."

"Congratulations, Mr. Turea. Please assemble your personal belongings and be at the front of this building tomorrow morning at 7:30 a.m. for transport by train to Bremerhaven. Please don't be late." Shuffling more papers, she withdrew a short stack and offered them to Péter.

"Bring these papers with you. Do you have any questions?"

"*Well, yes, as a matter of fact, perhaps a thousand,*" Péter thought to himself before answering, "What is your name, please?"

"Mrs. Post," she responded as she looked curiously at him then added, "Janine Post."

"Thank you, Mrs. Post. You are from England perhaps?"

Mrs. Post looked at Péter, seeing him for the first time. A hint of a smile dimpled her cheeks. "You're very welcome, Mr. Turea. Yes, just outside of London. I am here with the International Red Cross. Safe travels, Mr. Turea. Next."

41

OPERATION SAFE HAVEN—OPERATION MERCY

ON 8 NOVEMBER 1956, the executive branch of the United States government not so subtly assumed the role of the legislative branch in the oversight of the resettlement process of the Hungarian refugees. The problem to be surmounted was the established immigration quotas, which fell far short of the emergency at hand.

The Hungarian revolution had been the first televised event of its kind in the United States and had an enormous impact on its citizens prompting an outpouring of sympathy and support. Eisenhower would appeal to these sentiments in establishing US strategy, response, and policy regarding the Hungarian refugee crisis.

In the weeks to come, Time Magazine would award their annual "Man of the Year" to the Hungarian Freedom Fighter. Nonetheless, a segment of the population had to be convinced and it fell to the

US government to shape a positive image of the incoming refugees. Of particular note, was what was touted as "Freedom's $30 Million Bonus." This "bonus" alluded to the approximate $30 million in the educational value of approximately 54% of the refugees. These refugees were highly skilled in areas needed in American industry including 18% who were either doctors, engineers, scientists, or other professionals.

On 1 December 1956, Eisenhower released a statement, "...the United States will offer asylum to 21,500 refugees from Hungary. Of these, about 6,500 will receive Refugee Relief Act visas under the emergency program initiated three weeks ago. The remaining 15,000 will be admitted to the United States under the provisions of Section 212 (d) (5) of the Immigration and Nationality Act. When these numbers have been exhausted, the situation will be re-examined." This announcement was followed by another on 6 December; travel arrangements had been completed. The refugees would be provided transport by plane and by ship.

President Dwight D. Eisenhower ordered the conveyance of the Hungarian refugees. Air transportation, code-named "Operation Safe Haven," and ship transportation, "Operation Mercy," were overseen by the Department of Defense. Secretary of Defense, Charles E. Wilson, (head of General Motors until his presidential appointment in 1953), was charged with the transport of refugees and their reception.

The Pentagon ordered the Military Air Transportation Service, MATS (a now inactive branch of the Department of Defense) to prepare the airlift in two phases. The joint military operations, Operation Safe Haven (I and II) and Operation Mercy, would provide Hungarian refugee resettlement to the United States.

Under Major General George B. Dany, military transports were provided from the 1608th Air Transport Wing in Charleston, South Carolina, under the command of Major Fred F. May, and from the 1611th Air Transport wing at McGuire Air Force Base, under the command of Captain Charles F. Vickers.

The planes involved in this operation included 5 Military Sea Transit Service (MSTS) planes and 133 chartered planes. The aircraft included the old faithful World War II twin-engine C-47, the military adaptation of the DC-3, the C-46 Curtis Commando, and the four-jet C-135, the military version of the Boeing 707. The C-118A, the military adaptation of the Douglas DC-6, also known as the "Liftmaster," had a key role in Operation Safe Haven. Other planes put into service included the R6D Constitution, a double decker, prop aircraft from the 1611th Air Transport Wing at McGuire AFB, New Jersey, and the C-121 Lockheed Super Constellation from Charleston AFB, South Carolina, a prop with an 80 passenger capacity. Two pilots and a navigator were assigned to each MATS mission.

The inaugural flight of Operation Safe Haven departed Munich Airport landing at McGuire Air Force Base. Safe Haven I operated continually during the weeks from 11 December 1956 until 3 January 1957, during which time 1,107 flights (missions) transported 6,393 passengers. These flights included special missions that transported late term pregnant women and infants, the ill, and the infirm. In this initial period, MATS transported refugees over a 22 day period at a rate of up to 20 flights per day.

Safe Haven II, in operation from 6 January 1957 until 30 June 1957, transported 3,791 refugees on 66 flights from Neubiberg AFB in Munich to New Jersey's McGuire AFB. Under the dual missions of Safe Haven I and II, the Hungarian refugee airlift was the largest humanitarian airlift since the Berlin Airlift. With the support of commercial contract aircraft transporting a total of 4,170 refugees on 58 flights, and Eisenhower's presidential plane, the Columbine III, a total of 10,184 refugees were transported.

Operation Mercy engaged the Military Sea Transportation Service (MSTS), renamed the Military Sealift Command in 1970. Four World War II United States Naval Service (USNS) Transport Armed Forces Pacific vessels, otherwise known as troop carriers, were put into service: the General Leroy Eltinge (TAP-154), under the command of LCDR. T. F. Crane, USN, the General W. G. Haan (TAP-158), under Master Edward F. Murphy, the Marine Carp (TAP-199), under Master Wilfred Patnaude, and the General Nelson M. Walker (TAP-125), under Master Olaf Anderson. These four ships, affectionately known as "gray ladies" by their officers and crew, sailed in five day intervals. Over a period of two months, Operation Mercy transported 8,944 refugees between Bremerhaven, Germany and Brooklyn, New York in five two-week sailings.

The USNS Eltinge would be the first to sail. Officials checked every refugee's background then made their selection for the first transport of 1,747 Hungarian refugees. The group was composed of children, including 88 children under the age of ten, approximately 200 adult women, and a preponderance of adult males. The refugees were assembled at the American Embassy in Munich, then transported by bus to the port city of Bremerhaven, where they boarded the Eltinge on 19 December 1956. The USNS Eltinge weighed anchor the following day. For most of the refugees this was their first open ocean voyage. The USNS Eltinge arrived 2 January 1957, followed by the USNS Haan on 6 January (whose passengers included András István Gróf, now known as Andrew Grove, the head of Intel), the USNS Marine Carp on 16 January, and the USNS Walker on 14 February. Later, when the administration extended the program, the USNS Gen George Randall transported refugees.

42

RITES OF PASSAGE

PÉTER HAD NO idea why he was selected as one of the 1,747 refugees for the first sailing of Operation Mercy. He puzzled over the question as he stood in the queue, papers in hand, waiting to board. He held a small valise containing a few clothes, the German-English dictionary, and toiletries he'd been given in Vienna. The queue moved quickly, the covered gangway alternately creaking and resonating under the shifting footsteps and weight of the assembled multitude.

Péter had arrived early and stood behind a small group of Red Cross personnel, which stood behind a small group of sailors, each waiting their turn to board at the back of the ship. Without preamble or introduction, one of the women, a Red Cross insignia adorning her left pocket, turned and spoke to him.

"Hello, sir. Do you speak any English?"

"Yes," Péter responded, adjusting the valise in his hand and standing squarely to meet her gaze. "Yes, I have been a student at the University of Szeged. I speak some English, some German, a little French, and, of course, Hungarian."

Péter's pulse quickened. Above all, Péter wanted to stand out, to be of assistance, to garner any acknowledgment that might be of benefit as he navigated this unknown adventure ahead of him.

The woman smiled. "Goodness. Well, you'll do well at university in America. My name is Phoebe Steffy. As you have undoubtedly discerned, I'm with the Red Cross. We will be boarding the ship a little ahead of you, my apologies. I am certain everyone is anxious to board. However, there are a few stations to ready that we had to wait for. I assure you, we will hurry. If you have any questions, please ask, Mr. ?"

"Türea. Türea Péter. Rather, as in your country, soon my country, Péter Türea. And yes, it is my intention to attend American university. Thank you."

"Yes, sir. Thank you, sir."

Péter watched intently as the American sailors were boarded, each turning to salute the United States flag that flew at the stern. The sailors then turned to what Péter assumed must be an officer and saluted again. The sailor briefly spoke to the officer before he stepped onboard the ship and continued to other areas on the main deck or disappeared behind a plethora of doors. Péter had grown used to the, what almost seemed, perfunctory routine when he was shocked to see the officer take a sailor's bag and empty its contents onto the deck. Péter regarded his valise with concern, wondering if any item within might be cause for his removal from the ship.

The Red Cross representative, Steffy, noticed his concern.

"Protocol, sir. No cause for alarm. You will be boarding this ship."

As the last of the Red Cross personnel were ushered onboard, a chain was draped across the gangplank. Time passed quickly for those waiting in the queue as they interestedly watched the processes and people as the various Red Cross stations were outfitted and staffed. Finally, Péter stepped from the gangway to the deck and stood, momentarily closing his eyes, feeling the universe shift in its course, a great undertaking ahead of him.

"Welcome to America, sir."

Péter opened his eyes to find a uniformed officer's hand held forward in his direction. Reaching out in response, Péter involuntarily gave to the almost crushing handshake, subtly dropping his shoulder. Thankfully, the officer eased his grip.

"Excuse me, sir. This way, sir." The officer indicated a small group of Navy personnel assembled at a table somehow spirited there without Péter having noticed. Seated at the center front was a sailor whose name tag read, Perisyi, FA. Péter was interested to hear the man address him in Hungarian although Péter, wisely, chose to respond in English.

"Név, uram?" (*Name, sir?*)

"Péter Türea. From Buda....Budapest. Student."

"Beszélsz angolul, Mr. Türea?" (*You speak English, Mr. Türea?*)

"And you speak Hungarian, Mr. Perisyi."

Perisyi only slightly smiled as he quickly continued, fully aware that the first mate standing nearby was keeping a close eye on the boarding process. Perisyi began in a quick, monotone speaking in Hungarian.

"Perisyi Nicholai. Fireman. That's my assignment onboard. I am one of only two men on board who can speak Hungarian." Perisyi continued without pause, changing to English, "As you can imagine, we would greatly appreciate your help as a translator, if you would be willing. Are you single or married?"

"Yes, I would be willing. I am single."

"Are you traveling with anyone?"

"No."

As the two men spoke, another sailor stepped to Péter's side holding a white armband. Asking Péter to hold his arm up, the sailor wrapped the band around his upper arm, securing it with safety pins, while addressing him.

"Thank you for your assistance, Mr. Turea. This armband will signify you as an interpreter. You will report to the bridge and the radio room. All of the officers and crew will know that they can address you and ask you to act as an interpreter. This armband will also allow you access to most of the ship where you will, undoubtedly, be needed. Report to the bridge tomorrow, 0600. Straight ahead Mr. Turea, to your left. Bachelors will be taken to their quarters in groups."

The American sailors divided the refugees into groups designated to specified areas on board. The ships' 250 cabin spaces were allotted to families. Single men and women were assigned to separate quarters. Péter stood on deck with the other 1,746 refugees who had received their quarters and listened to messages of welcome read over the public address system in Hungarian and English. The commanding officer, LCDR. T. F. Crane, formally welcomed them followed by a recording of the Himnuz. For the refugees, hearing their national anthem was a bittersweet moment. They would spend the night on the ship at berth in Bremerhaven and weigh anchor early the next morning.

Péter was exhausted but excited. Péter turned to follow directions to the single men's bunk area where he had been assigned. Suddenly, he was surprised to find his arm in the grip of a sailor who looked desperate.

"Help me, please. These women over here are talking a mile a minute and I haven't got a clue what they're saying. They won't stop. Be a pal, help me outta this, would ya'?"

In attending to that request, Péter found himself uncomfortably surrounded by an increasingly larger circle of women and then men. Péter was asked, and repeated, the English terms for simple phrases and directional terms such as *bathroom*, *dining room*, *help*, *right*, *left*, *up*, *down*, *stairs*, and *deck*. As he answered questions, with the help of the sailor, he noticed there were other, similar groups about the ship's deck and imagined the same scenario was being repeated. Finally, he was able to move away from the diminishing crowd as they, and he, sought their quarters.

Péter had had little time to apply himself to his own interests and curiosity. Many of his queries were answered as he endlessly acted as an interpreter from the very moment the passengers had been directed to find their quarters. That night, in his berth, Péter tossed and turned, unable to quiet his mind. Morning, and the Eltinge would weigh anchor. Soon he would be in America. The possibilities were limitless. Images of his father and mother, his sister and grandparents, bore silent witness to his meditations.

As a single man assigned to one of the 1500 bunks, narrow cots stacked in three layers, Péter soon found out the men's quarters were located in the least desirable locations on the ship. Overall, the conditions were unpleasant. During the coming two weeks, the ship would heavily pitch and roll as the crew of the Eltinge navigated the Atlantic. Péter's berth was close to the bow at the water line. He had seen and heard of conditions in the other men's quarters. He was glad not to have been quartered in the area near the propeller, the "screw," where the incessant noise ceaselessly and loudly resonated. He was as thankful not to be near the bowels of the ship where the hot, oily smells of petrol from the engine room hung heavily in the air and clung to hair and clothes. However, quartered at the bow was going to have its own unique hardships.

Péter awoke to find the ship already at sea although the hour was just after dawn. The ocean was calm. Péter dressed and reported to the bridge where he was introduced to Lt. Donald C. Chase, the officer of the deck.

"Mr. Turea. Glad to meet you, sir. Is here anything we can do for you?"

"Thank you, I'm fine. Everyone has been quite helpful."

"Well, sir, I'm told you've made yourself useful. Where are you berthed?"

"I believe it is called forward, at the front of the ship."

"A suggestion, Mr. Turea. When the seas are turbulent, and they will be, try not to move about the ship. If you have to, stay close to the bulkhead.

"The quartermaster here, Officer Davies, is the ship's on-duty navigator and meteorologist on the bridge. He checks to see if the barometer is rising or falling. That's important information as it relates to the weather ahead, indicating whether we'll have calm or storm conditions. Assuming most of our passengers have never been aboard a ship on the open seas, this information is put to good use when planning activities. Especially for the passengers, planning what they may, or may not, eat for the day. Please spread the word. I'll request the quartermaster's report to be included in the daily announcements.

"As the officer of the watch, part of the bridge watch crew, this is my boatswain's mate, Carmichael, who will repeat the OW's verbal announcement following Naval tradition. When you're ready, Carmichael."

At that, Chase called out, "All passengers: designated groups will be called in order to breakfast beginning at 0630 hours." The shrill pipe of the bosun's mate caught Péter unaware and was immediately followed by Carmichael repeating the OW's announcement into the ship's main circuit (MC).

"If you would please step forward and interpret for us, Mr. Turea."

Péter did as asked, then returned to where he had stood, expectantly but patiently, awaiting what else might be asked of him.

"Thank you, sir. Please report to the bridge at 0630, 1130, and

1730 for mess call."

"Yes, sir."

"Then I suggest you next meet with the senior medical officer, Van Peenan. Mr. Turea, I appreciate your continued help in acting as an interpreter. Thank you, sir. Seaman Beste, if you would please."

With a nod, Lt. Chase returned his focus to the instruments and ocean before him. The sailor that had stood by during the conversation motioned Péter to the hatch. As the pair made their way in silence down the ladder and through a maze of corridors and ladders, the sailor suddenly looked back before speaking, then, quietly, as if sharing a secret.

"Chase is a good man. He'll take care of you if you need anything. He was just sizing you up."

"Sizing me up?"

"Finding out what kind of man you are, you know, if you're a regular Joe," and seeing not a glimmer of understanding added, "You know, if he can count on you. The name's Ralph J. Beste, Seaman Ralph Beste, Minnesota. You?"

"Péter Türea. Student. Budapest. Very nice to meet you, Mr. Beste."

"You'll be fine. You need anything, just ask. Here we are. The Infirmary."

Seaman Beste rapped sharply on the hatch and was answered with a crisp command.

"Enter."

Beste briefly raised his eyebrows and smiled at Péter, then opened the hatch as he stood aside snapping a sharp salute.

"Passenger and interpreter Peter Turea, sir, courtesy of OOD Lt. Chase."

"Thank you, Seaman Beste, that will be all."

Van Peenan invited Péter to sit opposite him in the only

other chair occupying the cramped compartment, every inch of space having been put to functional use. Péter wedged his long legs into the cramped space between chair and desk. They discussed matters onboard. Van Peenan questioned Péter's opinions regarding the general constitution of the refugees and the various concerns for the voyage ahead in regards to the health of the passengers.

"I wonder if I could prevail upon you to regularly visit the infirmary, especially during times of heavy seas and foul weather. I anticipate quite a lot of seasickness. Music can be quite calming. What do you think, Mr. Turea? What would your fellow countrymen find comforting?'

"Yes, I agree. I believe most people would find comfort in music."

"Hungary is a country with a proud heritage. Bartók, Kodaly, Liszt. I'm sure we will find a way.

"And you? Are you fit?"

"Yes, thank you. I am well. I do not require anything at this moment. If I can be of service, you need only ask."

Their conversation ended, the doctor took Péter on a brief tour of the infirmary, its location at midships, where he was introduced to the few patients already assembled.

"Mr. Harry and Gabriela Matusek, Mr. Peter Turea. Peter," the doctor indicated with a sweep of his hand. The doctor looked expectantly at Péter, who quickly understood to enjoin the couple in conversation determining and discussing the reason for their presence in the infirmary, which was quite obvious, or so it seemed to Péter. Mrs. Matusek was heavily pregnant.

The next patient was a boy. Van Peenan checked the records and spoke with a firm kindness, "Peter, meet Daniel Laszlo. He's 13 years old. His father was killed in Budapest, his mother captured." Péter gazed at the slight boy who stood when Péter addressed him. They spoke together in Hungarian, quietly and privately, the boy casting furtive glances in the doctor's direction. When Dániel had finished, Péter took the boys' shoulders in his hands and they kissed on either cheek. Péter turned to the doctor.

"He will be fine. He has had a terrible experience but he says there is a group of men who are attending the boys at meal times, helping and advising them. He is uncertain about his hair, but is concerned about what you might think of him."

"What I might think of him?"

"Yes," Péter searched for the right words, not looking at the boy, "how to explain? That you might think he's ...dirty."

"I see, does he suspect he has head lice?"

"Possibly."

"Let's have a look." As Péter spoke to the boy, Van Peenan took a wooden tongue depressor in one hand, a flashlight in the other, then gently and carefully lifted locks of the boys thick, brown curls, inspecting the hair and scalp, before snapping off the light.

"There are no signs of lice. However, the boy does have a rash. Here's a note," the doctor wrote as he spoke. "Ask him when he is at dinner to find a deckhand in the mess, a helper in the kitchen. Have the boy give them this slip of paper. They'll give him apple cider vinegar. Do you know it? Yes? Good. Well, ask him if he does, would you?" Van Peenan turned to the boy as Péter spoke briefly to Dániel receiving a vigorous nod from the boy. The doctor continued.

"Yes? Good. Tell the boy to wash his hair, rinse it with clear water, then pour the vinegar onto his scalp and let it sit for a few minutes before rinsing with clear water. He'll be fine."

Péter finished the conversation with the boy who, visibly relieved, rose from his chair, bowed to the doctor, and left. Their time together concluded, Péter held his hand out to the doctor and promised he'd check in throughout the day.

Walking back towards the bow, Péter emerged at an intersection of passageways to find a group of men and a few older boys huddled in serious conversation. Péter was surprised to see the boy, Dániel, among them. As he approached, Péter could see the focus of their interest, a Coca Cola dispenser. The conversation was heated.

"I have been watching them. The American sailors often stop here, dropping coins in a slot. Out comes a paper cup containing the drink. You, András, you tell them!"

"It's true. I help in the main dining area. There is another of these machines close to the mens' quarters below, near the engine room. It is foul smelling down there, and hot. I have watched many sailors at the machine. They drink it like my father drinks pálinka, down his throat in one shot!" The men laughed knowingly, this common experience easing the strain as they found camaraderie in shared laughter.

Again they closed in around the machine, hunkering down and examining it, perplexed and hesitant. Scattered comments rose from the group.

"I read in the newspaper it was poisonous."

"Yes," several voices responded in union, "poisonous."

"It's supposed to be a drug."

"What if that's propaganda?"

"I've been told it tastes like Odol. Mouthwash."

"10 cents, hmmm."

"10 cents!"

Most were discouraged by the 10 cent price the machine demanded. At the time, in their situation, 10 cents was a great deal of money. The conversation continued in regard to the pros and cons of daring to taste the poisonous liquid.

"Would the U.S. Navy make this drink available to its sailors if it were really as dangerous as we imagine? I think not. Therefore," Péter announced and continued, "I will not only invest 10 cents, and get a cup of Coca Cola, but will actually take a sip of the drink, and find out how it tastes. Furthermore, anyone who would like to can also take a sip and decide for himself."

And so it happened. Péter invested the 10 cents, slipping the coin into the designated slot. No one spoke, not one word, as every man watched the silver coin, pinched between Péter's thumb and forefinger, disappear into the designated slot and, with a rattle, fall into the machine.

Someone among the group spoke up, concerned, "Is it broken?"

As if in answer, the machine made a series of spinning, clicking, and on and off noises as the inner workings were actuated.

"Quiet, everyone!"

As they watched, a paper cup dropped from above, haphazardly caught askew by a metal sleeve above the perforated grate, and was soon followed by a forceful stream of bubbly brown liquid aimed into the cup. As the cup filled, it corrected its stance within the metal sleeve then seemed to begin to give to the weight of the liquid as the volume increased ushering an occasional gasp from the crowd.

Filled and finished to the last drip, Péter reached into the opening to extract the cup and took a sip. Everyone watched and waited in silent apprehension.

"It tastes terrible," Péter said, grimacing.

Indeed, Péter found it repulsive and searched his mind for the closest bubbler where he could rinse the offensive taste from his mouth. Meanwhile, the cup was making the rounds as others took a cautious sip. Finally, they came to the unanimous conclusion, it tasted horrible. How could these Americans like it?

Just then, a watch change approached including Seaman Beste. The hearty men, relieved of duty, were in a good mood. Several approached the machine, each exchanging a silver coin for a cup of the offensive liquid. The Hungarians silently looked on, mystified, and exchanged questioning looks. A few of the sailors slipped additional coins into the slot and offered the drinks to the men with a nod of their head, not having the language skills to otherwise offer their good will. Those closest to the proffered cups unwillingly took the cups in hand and returned the smile and laugh as they carefully sipped, then laughed, with the sailors.

"Coca cola! You like it?"

No. But what could they do? Thankfully, the sailors moved on towards the mess hall. The cups were emptied onto the perforated grate within the dispensing machine.

Day followed day in an enjoyable routine for Péter as he reported to the bridge and then the mess where he ate with the first seating. From the mess he reported to the infirmary, then returned to the bridge. Péter repeated this process twice during the course of each day.

One morning, with Péter acting as interpreter, a passenger sought out the sailor who blew reveille asking if they could play the instrument. Their conversation resulted in the sailor getting permission to make the other musical instruments onboard available to the passengers in a corner of one of the mess halls that had been specifically designated as a daytime gathering space. By the fourth day at sea, Péter found a quartet in the infirmary, the music quite obviously of comfort and being enjoyed by everyone.

The fifth day, Christmas Eve, dawned spectacularly. Hues of yellow, orange, and red colored the morning sky. As Péter made his way up through the ship, he firmly held onto the ladder handrails and taffrail at the weatherdeck to the bridge. At the bridge, the quartermaster indicated the barometer. Péter noted the difference from what had been standard during the previous days, it was lower in the glass. Péter proceeded to his place next to the bosun's mate and took up the MC awaiting the announcements for the morning, which came forthwith:

"24 December 1956. There will be special services today at 1900 hours, Navy Chaplain LTJG Otto Schneider will give Catholic mass in honor of Christmas Eve. Refreshments will follow in each of the dining halls. Everyone is invited and welcome to attend.

"We are on storm watch. Expect rough conditions. If the ship begins to pitch, please limit your activities, stay close to bulkhead walls, and keep a tight grip on the handrails."

Péter then outlined the order and menu for breakfast. Today, breakfast for the passengers would be a simple meal of tea and biscuits. However, many of the men requested, and even insisted, on the hearty meal they saw the sailors enjoying. By midday, to a man, they would regret that choice.

That night, following dinner and despite rough seas, many of the passengers slowly and cautiously navigated the passageways to attend mass. Afterwards, a Christmas Eve celebration was attended by all but the very ill. A welcome sight greeted the refugees as LCDR Crane, dressed as St. Nicholas, distributed stockings filled with toys, noisemakers, and candy. Volunteers with the American Red Cross handed out toys and toiletries. WAVE Dorothy Flannery distributed Christmas presents while the Navy band played a variety of Christmas songs. Afterwards, several of the Hungarian musicians took up the instruments and treated their American hosts, and the assembly, to a beautiful arrangement of Hungarian Christmas melodies. The evening was joyous.

The storm had waited for Christmas then blew in making up for lost time. Ultimately, the Eltinge would be 3 days behind schedule. Most of the passengers spent their days below decks, self-confined to their berths. In Péter's berth, the bow caught the brunt of the force as the ship pitched on the mountainous seas, alternately rising steeply then crashing with a resulting, thunderous bang. Most of the men in Péter's berth were seasick. It didn't help morale on the ship when Péter stated, during the morning announcements, all passengers would be participating during morning drills in case of sinking. Péter kept to the bridge and infirmary, avoiding his berth, thankful he was not suffering as were his fellow passengers. Before the crossing was over, seasickness would prove to be the most prevalent illness. Dr. Van Peenan treated 90 severe cases and dispensed 12,000 Dramamine pills.

The crew of the USNS Eltinge worked harder than ever through the storm. The transatlantic journey was always perilous with the ever-present possibility of storm conditions. Down in the belly of the ship, the engineering room was sweltering. Engineers, mechanics, technicians, engine men, and electrician's mates labored continuously monitoring the pressure gauges, valves, tachometer, while oiling and fueling the engines. These sailors rarely saw the light of day as they kept the engines and generators running providing the propulsion, electricity, and freshwater for the ship.

Finally, the storm blew out. Crew and passengers prepared for arrival. During the day, an increasing number of passengers were found on deck at the ship's rails awaiting their first glimpse of America. On the evening of 29 December, the refugees presented a farewell program of traditional Hungarian music, dancing, and the recitation of Hungarian poems. As it neared its conclusion, the refugees stood to sing the Hungarian National anthem. When everyone was again seated, Olive Keve stood and read a letter of appreciation and thanks to the officers, crew, and volunteers aboard the USNS Eltinge.

Although the seas had calmed, Péter slept fitfully those last nights as he mentally planned and reviewed dozens of theoretical possibilities for what might await him in this new country, America, the "land of opportunity." While he desired to be master of his own destiny, he pragmatically acknowledged there were many unknown variables which, with every decision, presented a myriad of possible outcomes. His bright mind wrestled with the complex challenge until he firmly set it aside with a whispered prayer of hope and request for guidance.

43

A DISTANT SHORE

THE MORNING OF 31 December was calm and bright. Péter quickened his pace to the bridge on what he hoped to be their last day at sea. Lt. Chase greeted Péter as he as stepped onto the bridge.

"Look ahead, Mr. Turea."

Péter turned and took a short, faltering step laying his hand on the window ledge to his left as he squared his shoulders and gazed ahead. America. As yet a thin brown line on the horizon, but still, America. Impossible but true. Two months ago it wasn't even a distant thought and now, here he was, standing on the bridge of an American military ship. Having crossed the Atlantic ocean, to stand and gaze upon another continent, another country. America. Péter stood transfixed as the country to which he was entrusting his hopes and dreams materialized before him.

"Mr. Turea."

Péter turned. Lt. Chase stood before him.

"Mr. Turea. On behalf of LCDR. T. F. Crane and the American government, I want to thank you for all you have done on behalf of myself and the crew of the USNS Eltinge, for the safety and well-being of all aboard. I want to personally thank you for your assistance. Mr. Turea," Lt. Chase extended his hand which Péter took in his own, "your courage and bravery, at home and aboard ship, and that of your fellow passengers, are humbling. Thank you, sir."

Péter nodded in modest acknowledgement. "Thank you, Lt. Chase. It is I who owe you a debt of gratitude."

Both men stood a brief moment before breaking the handshake and returning to the business at hand.

"Carmichael."

"Yes, sir!" Carmichael switched on the MC and piped the introduction to the mornings' announcements. Péter found the now familiar task bittersweet realizing how fortunate he had been to have had this experience. Soon, very soon, he would be leaving the ship. The announcements for the day concluded, breakfast group assignments made, Péter shook hands with Carmichael and turned to leave as a call rang through to the bridge.

"Mr. Turea. You're wanted in the infirmary ASAP."

It was Péter's custom to attend the infirmary after the morning announcements. He wondered, as he hurried along, holding firmly on the handrails, what might have happened to a fellow refugee or crewman.

Péter entered the infirmary and found the doctor standing beside a bed, taking the pulse of Gabriela Matusek. Gabriela's obviously distressed husband, Harry, stood at the foot of the bed alongside a young woman.

"Mr. Turea. Thank you for joining us. Please, assure Mr. and Mrs. Matusek that the baby is fine, labor has only just begun. A first baby can take their time coming into the world. Mrs. Matusek should relax and rest. She has brought a friend, Mrs. Vizi, whom we all agree would be helpful. Mrs. Vizi, Mr. Turea."

Péter bowed his head towards Mrs. Vizi, who slightly curtsied in acknowledgment.

Gabriella looked up to Péter, her eyes bright and hopeful, "Péter, I met Mrs. Vizi, Enikő, and her family the first day on the ship. She has two children and has been a great help. She is a good friend. When she offered to sit with me, I was so thankful."

Dr. Van Peenan called for two sailors to set up and anchor screens around Mrs. Matusek's bed to give her some privacy. There were only a few other patients, he would attend to them and send them back to their berths. Van Peenan hoped no one else would need his ministrations that day. Two stitches, a second-degree burn cleaned then rinsed with cool water for half an hour, and an ankle wrap later, the infirmary was now a maternity ward.

Enikő sat with Mr. Matusek while the nurses helped Gabriela get changed, cleaned, and put back to bed. When the nurses emerged from the behind the screens they motioned to Harry and Péter.

"You may go to your wife now, Mr. Matusek. She is ready for you," Péter said, unmoving. He was glad to be of assistance but found he was a little uncomfortable with close proximity to an impending birth. Translating from a distance suited him.

"Please, call me Harry."

"Harry. May you be blessed with a healthy child."

Harry had already turned and gone to his wife, disappearing around the privacy screen. Péter turned to go when Dr. Van Peenan reappeared.

"Péter, this birth will undoubtedly take some time. Nonetheless, if you could check in frequently, you will undoubtedly be a great help."

Péter walked the corridors on his daily routine first encountering Seaman Beste in the company of the boy, Dániel Lászlo.

"Peter! I'm going to miss this boy! Smart boy! Laszlo. I told him when he's old enough, he should join the Navy. Do you two know each other?"

All three stood with kind regard for one another and shook hands. The excitement in the air was infectious as everyone onboard, crew and passengers, anticipated their arrival at port. Péter made his usual rounds, exchanging greetings and good wishes as everyone he had any degree of familiarity with approached him. As the hour neared 1030, Péter attended the infirmary and found it empty.

"They've gone on a walk, Mr. Turea."

Péter turned. It was Dr. Van Peenan.

"A little exercise is helpful for the baby and mother, and a good distraction. There's no one else here, Mr. Turea. It seems the excitement of our arrival has proved a tonic."

"Perhaps, if you wouldn't mind, doctor. I'll return again after lunch."

"Thank you, Mr. Turea."

Péter walked with a quickened step to the bridge. He was anxious for the view it afforded of the horizon and wondered how marked the change would be since that morning. He wasn't let down. Standing on the bridge, what had been a narrow band of color now had substance and form. Péter took a deep breath before he turned to Lt. Chase.

"The eastern seaboard, Mr. Turea. Home to the original thirteen colonies that became what is now the United States. Home to most of us on this ship. Home to you and your countrymen during the coming weeks.

"I can't promise we'll make our berth at the Brooklyn Army Terminal by 1700. In fact, its marginal. Vessels arriving after 1700 hours anchor for the night in the harbor and disembark at their berth the following morning, after the medical inspectors and inspection. Ships are boarded in the quarantine area between 0700 hours and

1700 hours. Vessels such as ours, under a special dispensation granted under the powers of Operation Mercy, will be given preference.

"I've already received orders for this ship. We will be boarded promptly at 0700 hours and disembark immediately after inspection. The passengers will be transferred by bus to Camp Kilmer where roughly 1500 refugees have already been welcomed and are in the process of being transferred to their new homes across America.

"Breakfast will be served at 0530 hours tomorrow morning."

At the sound of the watch pipes, Péter's attention was turned to Carmichael. Péter took his place at the MC, translating the order of the lunch group seating, followed by the much anticipated arrival, mooring, and landing information that Lt. Chase had just privately related to him. The announcements ended with the encouragement to pack and ready themselves for disembarking the following morning. As he opened the door to leave, Péter paused for a last glance at the horizon.

Following lunch, the passengers returned to their berths to wash, pack, and otherwise ready themselves for their first experience in America. Anticipation and excitement were palpable. Everyone wanted to look their best. Péter briefly returned to his berth and packed his few belongings in the small valise from Vienna. Returning to the infirmary, he found Gabriella once again laying on her bed, her hands caressing her belly. Harry was no where in sight. Gabriella looked up.

"Hello, Mr. Türea."

"Péter, if you don't mind."

"Thank you, Péter. Exciting, isn't it, coming into port? After all we've been through, it seems a dream, doesn't it? The doctor says the baby isn't yet ready, it will be tonight, but," Gabriella paused and, grimacing, drew a deep breath and began to pant as she brought her knees up. Péter, uncomfortable, turned to leave but

Gabriella continued. "Just like that, it's over. You're not married, Péter?"

"No, I'm a student. I have a great deal of work ahead of me. One day, perhaps."

Gabriella laughed, "Yes, Péter, one day."

Péter turned and went to the doctor's office where he found the doctor sorting through medical records.

"The ship will be boarded by a medical officer tomorrow for inspection. I am making certain all of the records are in order. You've seen Mrs. Matusek?

"Yes."

"Thank you. I sent her husband to the dining room to have a meal and with instructions to get some rest. It's going to be a long night for him and his wife. Could you check on him, please? Mr. Matusek should still be in the dining room."

Péter easily found Harry, the area was virtually deserted as everyone prepared for the morning. Harry was appreciative of the additional information from Péter. They agreed to meet early that evening at the infirmary, just before his group was called to the dining room for dinner.

Péter hurried to the deck, where passengers had begun to assemble and already crowded as near the rail as possible as the ship approached the harbor. The crew was busy attending to the many and varied instructions, heard over the MC and shouted orders, as they crawled over the ship like ants. The afternoon hours slipped away as the refugees watched the shoreline swell. Gradually, as shapes began to form, everyone looked for the famed Statue of Liberty. All too soon, night began to close in on the spectacle before them. In the distance, the shoreline of Massachusetts was already decorated with lights twinkling in the evening marine layer. Before them, the lights of the harbor began to flicker on. The passengers were beguiled.

Péter slipped away to meet with Harry and Gabriella Matusek. After speaking with them, Mrs. Vizi, and Dr. Van Peenan, Péter hastily made his way up to the bridge. His breath caught in his chest at the view presented there. He had seen Budapest from the vantage point of the Rózsa Hill at night, its beauty illuminated by the many lights. He had never imagined such an expanse of lights extending to such a distance. America was enormous. Such a duality presented itself in the vastness of the country; the unlimited possibilities before him, yet how inconsequential one man seemed in comparison. On the other hand, what couldn't he do?

"Mr. Turea. I trust you've had a busy day. Is there anything I can do for you?" Lt. Donald Chase was in the bridge.

"Thank you, sir. I am prepared to leave the ship. There is an impending birth. I am aiding the doctor as a translator. Otherwise, everything seems to be in order."

"We will be anchoring in the harbor at approximately 1830. We will proceed to the berthing area at 0430 tomorrow morning. Breakfast will begin being served at 0530. I do not require your services until that hour, but if you would like to join me on the bridge at 0430 you would be welcome."

"Thank you, sir. I'll be here, dependent on the birth of course."

"Yes, Mr. Turea. Dependent on the birth."

Péter joined Carmichael at the MC and related the dining group assignments. In a departure from procedure, and unfamiliar to Péter, Lt. Chase was at his side extending his hand for the MC. Lt. Chase held it forward, between Péter and himself, and began to speak alternating with Péter's translation.

"To the passengers and volunteers of Operation Mercy, this is commanding officer Lt. Donald Chase, USN. I want to personally thank you for your good work and exemplary conduct on this voyage.

"We will be anchoring in the harbor tonight. Docking at the Brooklyn Pier will be at 0700 hours tomorrow morning. Passengers will disembark to Immigration and from there will be driven to Camp Kilmer. There, many organizations await your arrival to aid you in every way possible.

"You have each undertaken a great endeavor, fueled by courage, bravery, and desire. Such is the American dream which has brought many before you for all the same reasons. It is my fervent hope, and that of the crew of the USNS General Leroy Eltinge, which has served you, that you will live your dream. Welcome to America. Godspeed."

That night, many of the passengers found it difficult to sleep. Péter was called to the infirmary shortly after dinner where he uncomfortably stood by, translating for the doctor, as Gabriella labored to deliver her child, a son, born shortly after midnight on 1 January 1957. Washing before retiring to his bunk, Péter soon fell fast asleep. What seemed like moments later, he was awakened in the dark of early morning by Seaman Beste, who stood next to his berth, whispering in his ear.

"Mr. Turea. CO sent me after you. Said you wanted to be on the bridge when we enter the harbor."

"Thank you, Mr. Beste. He is correct, of course." Péter was up in a moment. Dressed and, with his valise, made his way to the bridge.

"Good morning, Mr. Turea."

"Good morning, sir."

"Stand to the side there if you would, please. It's going to be a busy morning."

The bridge was a flurry of activity as orders were sent, communications received, and sailors came and went. Péter was not easily distracted as he turned to watch the glow of sunrise light the eastern horizon, a shimmering array of golden and soft yellow light brightening the clouds, sky, and harbor as the sun rose into the sky. Alternately, Péter fixated on the harbor as the darkness of night receded like the tide, exposing all of the remarkable, previously unseen, unimagined, and unfathomable characteristics of this new land.

The ship awakened. For the last time on this voyage, Carmichael blew the pipes into the MC before handing it off to Péter to translate the imminent dining group assignments for breakfast, followed by special instructions and announcements. On this occasion there was only one.

"Following breakfast, passengers are encouraged to gather with their belongings on the port side of the main deck as we pass Liberty Island."

As Péter translated, he looked up to the gradually expanding view ahead as the first rays of sunlight swathed the Statue of Liberty in the crisp, wintry, golden hues of morning. It was an uncommon sight.

During the voyage, the passengers had been surprised to be served three large meals a day. Nonetheless, they cleaned their plates, some requested seconds. Meals had been slowly consumed as discussion intermingled with the enjoyment of the meal. Breakfast this morning was unlike any other. With their first view of America, the harbor, the Statue of Liberty and their imminent landing at hand, everyone was overexcited and anxious to get on deck. Péter ate sparingly of the breakfast Lt. Chase had ordered to the bridge. As they passed the Statue of Liberty, Péter turned to Lt. Chase.

"It is time for me to go to the deck as we end this journey and begin another. Thank you, Lt. Chase."

"It has been an honor, Mr. Turea. Godspeed," Lt. Chase said in earnest as he grasped Péter's hand. "Mr. Carmichael."

Carmichael stepped forward at the lieutenant's invitation. "Thank you, Mr. Turea. Best of luck to you." Carmichael extended his hand and Péter took it.

Péter slowly made his way away from the bridge keeping a watchful eye on the approaching shoreline. On deck, he strode past a group of sailors called to assembly, smartly dressed in brilliant, white uniforms, and snapped to attention. Crossing the deck, Péter joined the assemblage gathered along the bulwark who were fixated on the Americans assembled along the shoreline. Even at this early hour, many had gathered. Some were waving small American flags, others were waving their hands in greeting, while still others did both. Cheers and shouts of joy were returned in kind and multiplied.

The ship continued to navigate towards its berth when suddenly, there came into view a group of musicians who, ceremoniously and with great pomp, began to play a wild tune. A group of young men had been standing next to Péter watching and occasionally waving at the crowds along the docks. One of the young men turned to Péter.

"Such gay music, isn't it? Do you suppose it's dance music?"

Behind them, the assembled sailors seemed to be singing along with the music, although most found it rather difficult, the range of their voices insufficient to the melody. This music, America's national anthem, would become very dear to Péter in the years to come.

Unbelievable to many of the refugees, in what seemed a surreal landscape, the ship was at berth. Passengers were anxious, emotions were raw. Sailors scurried to secure lines around the dock cleats. Gangplanks were extended from the pier and secured. The medical officer boarded exactly at 0700. The passengers had formed a queue along the bulwark rails and watched as LCDR. T. F. Crane, who stood above the deck, addressed the crew assembled there.

"Crew of the USNS General Leroy Eltinge, thank you for your good work and exemplary conduct on this historic voyage. The passengers have looked to you as models of the American military. You have served your country well. Together, we have brought the

USNS Eltinge safely across the Atlantic. Together, we have brought these courageous people safely to their new home. You will forever be a part of their story, the American experience. It has been an honor to serve as your Commanding Officer."

The USNS Eltinge disembarked at the Brooklyn Pier on 1 January 1957. As the passengers disembarked, a card was pinned to their clothes that included their name and manifest number. The first passenger piped ashore, America's first American born son of the Hungarian Revolution, was a 6.5 pound boy named Heinrich Tibor Matusek.

Under usual conditions, immigrants are processed at the point of disembarkation. Their assorted baggage is taken to the baggage room and processed by customs men. Interpreters, who spoke an average of 6 languages, would lead groups of 30 to a registration room where doctors would watch for signs of illness or conditions requiring immediate attention. Each passenger had their hair, face, neck, and hands inspected. White chalk was used to mark an "x" on the right shoulder to signify mental deficiency, a "B" signified back problems, "PG" indicated pregnant, and "SC" indicated scalp infection. Optometrists would check for symptoms of trachoma. And last, the primary line inspector, seated on a high stool with the ship's manifest on a desk in front of him and an interpreter at his side, made the final decision if an immigrant could pass.[16]

The Hungarian refugees would instead be transferred directly from Brooklyn Pier to Camp Kilmer. There, a team including the Army, Customs, Immigration and Public Health agencies, worked jointly to process each individual according to the laws of the United States. As the long queue of immigrants stepped ashore, the walkway to the waiting buses, lined on either side with American citizens, military personnel in dress uniform, and dignitaries, erupted in cheers. Everyone extended hands of friendship and words of welcome. A brass band played festive music. A nod of approval, a smile, and "Welcome to America" brought many to tears before boarding the waiting buses for the next step in their journey, the one hour drive to Camp Kilmer.

44

CAMP KILMER

THE FEDERAL GOVERNMENT insisted on a central processing center for the Hungarian refugees. Ellis Island, what might seem the obvious choice, had been closed in 1954. The question of where to accommodate and register the incoming refugees was decided: Camp Kilmer, located in Middlesex County, New Jersey.

Camp Kilmer had its beginnings just prior to World War II, when military officials determined the need for troop staging areas as part of a national security plan. The site, chosen for its close proximity to both railway and highway access, and the New York Port of Embarkation (NYPE), consisted of a 1,573 acre parcel comprised of 792 tracts of land purchased from 47 owners. The bombing of Pearl Harbor provoked America's entry into World War II and accelerated what had been a prescient decision on the part of the US Army command.

Although construction on the camp is said to have begun in "relative secrecy" on 19 January 1942, the fact that the camp employed over 11,000 union workers from the nearby area challenges that claim. The following month, the military announced the name, Camp Kilmer, in honor of the American poet, Joyce Kilmer.

Joyce Kilmer was born on 6 December 1886, in New Brunswick, New Jersey, and educated at Rutgers College Grammar School, Rutgers College, and Columbia University, from which he graduated in 1908. Following graduation, Kilmer married poet and fellow Columbia graduate, Aline Murray, on 9 June 1908. The couple had five children: Kenton, Michael, Christopher, Rose and Deborah. With the outbreak of World War I in 1914, patriotism and a desire to help the war effort was a strong undercurrent in the United States. As a family man, Kilmer was not required to join the services, yet he enlisted in 1917.

Soon after, Kilmer requested and received a transfer to New York City's "Fighting 69th" infantry under the leadership of Major "Wild Bill" Donovan. Deployed to Europe, where he rose to the rank of Sergeant, Kilmer served mostly as an intelligence officer undertaking dangerous reconnaissance missions to the enemy's front line. While overseas, one of his daughters, Rose, died from complications of polio.

On 30 July 1918, during the Second Battle of the Marne while on a reconnaissance mission, Kilmer joined in the battle of Ourcq where he was killed by a German sniper's bullet. Interred in the Oise-Aisne American Cemetery in Seringes-et-Nesles, France, Kilmer was posthumously awarded the prestigious French Croix de Guerre (War Cross) for his bravery. His family mourned his loss while his nation mourned the loss of a beloved poet. Kilmer remains best known for his poem, "Trees," published in 1913 in *Poetry Magazine* and again in 1914 within the volume *Trees and Other Poems*.

I think that I shall never see
A poem lovely as a tree.

A tree whose hungry mouth is prest
Against the earth's sweet flowing breast;

A tree that looks at God all day,
And lifts her leafy arms to pray;

A tree that may in Summer wear
A nest of robins in her hair;

Upon whose bosom snow has lain;
Who intimately lives with rain.

Poems are made by fools like me,
But only God can make a tree.

Camp Kilmer was designed in three sections: the 1,182 acre Original Tract, the 51.35 acre Camp Kilmer Extension, and a 311 acre area to facilitate access to the three area railways: the Pennsylvania, the Lehigh Valley, and the Reading. The camp layout and design were unique and intentional. The plan incorporated design elements such as curving roads and clusters of colorful, vertically striped buildings and roofs. These buildings were painted to resemble clusters of small buildings to meet the Army's expectation that the camp "resemble a country village from the air" for the purpose of misleading enemy intelligence.

Each of the three sections of the camp was comprised of 21 distinct areas of which almost half were Regimental Areas. Each area functioned as a self-contained camp of between 61-65 buildings which provided all services and which included barracks and separate housing for African-American troops, women, and prisoners-of-war.

Later that year, in June of 1942, commanding officer Colonel C.W. Baird took over command of the facility from the contractors. The majority of the construction was completed by August of that year and finalized in February of 1943 when the completion of barracks for the newly formed Women's Army Corps (WAC) were completed. During 1944, responding to a request for additional recreational facilities, the Kilmer Bowl amphitheater (eventually seating 8,000), a boxing and wrestling arena, swimming pools, basketball courts, and baseball diamonds were built. The New Jersey Bell Telephone Company built four telephone centers located throughout the camp.

At completion, the 1,573 acres included 1,230 buildings, wooden barracks, 7 chapels, 5 theaters, 3 libraries, a 1,000 bed Station Hospital, a dental clinic, four fire stations, ten mess halls, 29.9 miles of hard surface roads, 11 railheads, 20 softball diamonds, 30 volleyball courts, 160 horseshoe courts, press headquarters in building 1542, recreation building 1443, and a message board to post notices. Camp Kilmer was, in effect, a small city.

Built to accommodate 37,550 people, the camp would process contingencies of up to 21,500 as incoming troops were processed for Reassignment. A record 52,000 troops were received and processed during May of 1946. The first troops arrived in Camp Kilmer during July of 1942.

Postwar, Camp Kilmer was reassigned as the Army's only Overseas Replacement Depot (ORD) on the east coast. By 1948, Camp Kilmer was to be converted to a permanent Army installation. Instead, during November 1949, Defense Secretary Louis A. Johnson ordered the closure of several World War II camps including Camp Kilmer. The closing proved premature as, with the advent of the Korean War, the camp was reopened in 1950. Camp Kilmer was closed again during March of 1955 and used sporadically until November 1956, when it was commissioned as a refugee center as part of Operation Mercy for the resettlement of Hungarian refugees.

Processing points in Austria were established to handle US bound refugees. United States President Dwight D. Eisenhower appointed Mr. Tracy S. Voorhees as his personal representative at Camp Kilmer. Then on 12 December, Voorhees was selected as chairman for the President's Hungarian Refugee Relief Committee to process the initially expected 5,000 refugees "as expeditiously as possible." Voorhees was tasked to facilitate and expedite finding housing and jobs for the refugees in coordinating contact between the twenty-two governmental and volunteer agencies helping the refugees.

Camp Kilmer, a military installation in Piscataway, New Jersey, was the obvious choice to receive, house, and facilitate the refugees and coordinating agencies. The camp's many attributes included nearby railway lines, existing structures, proximity to the New York Port of embarkation, and a large Hungarian community nearby in New Brunswick, New Jersey. As a mothballed Army base, the Army was charged with the responsibility of coordinating the resettlement effort and all housekeeping services. The rehabilitation and reopening of Camp Kilmer was placed under the command of Army Brigadier General Sidney C. Wooten, a 49 year old West Point graduate. Wooten had served with the 71st Infantry Division in Austria during World War II during which time he was awarded the Distinguished Service Cross for extraordinary heroism. The first item of business was to rename the camp the Joyce Kilmer Reception Center, although it would uncommonly be referred to by that name.

Soldiers from all over the US arrived and worked around the clock to receive, clean, and place furniture, metal bed frames, mattresses, tables and chairs. The soldiers made repairs and restored electricity, water, and heating to the camp. Signs were painted in Hungarian to direct the refugees to needed services. The Red Cross provided comfort bags. Busloads of contributed clothing arrived and were sorted by type and size. Across the country, after initial fears were quelled, there was great support and enthusiasm for the refugees.

On 21 November 1956, Camp Kilmer received its first 60 refugees, flown into McGuire via Operation Safe Haven I and transferred by Army bus. Over the next six months, Camp Kilmer would process almost 32,000 Hungarian refugees before permanent closure on 9 May 1957.

The Hungarian refugees who came to the United States via Camp Kilmer were registered, received instruction, education, and indoctrination to American culture as they either awaited their sponsors, or transportation to their sponsors. For most of the refugees, the average length of stay was twelve days. Relief agencies, and various charitable and religious organizations, arranged most of the resettlements. Of the 38,000 refugees to the US, most would settle in New York, Cleveland, Detroit, Chicago, Toledo, and nearby within the Hungarian community of New Brunswick, NJ. In time, many of the refugees would move to jobs in the west where a sort of competition developed with the east coast in their attempts to lure the highly educated refugees.

45

PROCESSING AND RESETTLEMENT

PÉTER'S SEAT BY the window afforded him an uninterrupted view as the convoy of US Army buses transferred the refugees from Brooklyn Pier to Camp Kilmer. He had briefly met his seatmate, András Kalman. Introductions and a brief background were interrupted as the bus driver closed the door and started away. From that moment, both men intently watched the passing landscape as the bus carried them to their temporary home. The men's attention piqued as the bus slowed. Everyone strained for their first glimpse of Camp Kilmer as it came into view. Ahead, Péter noted a small building, a uniformed guard, and a gate over which a large, white sign announced in bold, black letters: ISTEN HOZTA AMERIKÁBAN—WELCOME TO AMERICA. Péter nodded his head. His fellow passengers gasped and repeated the words. Children squealed in response to their parents excitement and, for some, more tears.

The entry guard waved each bus through the gate to a central processing area where the buses came to a stop and opened its doors. A Hungarian speaking American soldier greeted each immigrant as they stepped from the bus, indicating with a simple gesture the building they were to proceed to. Looking ahead to the building indicated, Péter read the sign over the door, "WELCOME—ISTEN HOZOTT."

The process began with a health inspection. Each refugee was given a complete and thorough medical exam including hair, eyes, ears, mouth, joints, fitness, and immunizations. Army soldiers were posted at every station to translate, assist the doctors, and give instructions.

From there, they were transferred by bus to the Department of Agriculture inspection area where the customs officers had it easy, the immigrants had very few possessions in their very small bags. Any fruits or plants would be confiscated. The officers also looked for contraband, including narcotics and firearms. Péter and András stood next to each other in the queue and were processed simultaneously through the double line. The officer opened Péter's valise and lifted the few clothes it held, then picked up the German-English dictionary. Turning the book over and thumbing through it, Fred DiNardo, 2nd Signal Platoon, assigned to Camp Kilmer, looked at Péter's name tag before looking at him and asked, "D'you speak English?"

"Yes, sir," then repeated as before, since it had served him well, "I speak some English, some German, a little French."

The officer smiled, nodded his head as he replaced the book, straightened the contents with care, then closed the valise. "Welcome to America, Mr. Turea. We could sure use your help around here."

Next, Immigration and Naturalization, including an interview with the Department of Labor, where they made note of Péter's position as student. Another interview noted his height, weight, birthdate, birthplace, age, skills, and occupational history followed by his photograph and having his fingerprints taken. Instructed to the next area, Péter waited as his identification card was typed with his personal information.

"Here you are, Mr. Türea. Please sign here," the Red Cross volunteer indicated with a pen that she then handed to him. Her identification badge read, Mrs. D. Patton. "Please carry your identification card with you at all times, Mr. Türea. Information from your personal interview is being entered into our IBM punch card system. We will identify your interests with those agencies that can best benefit you. There is a camp-wide loudspeaker system. Listen for your name. When you are called, report to the main building where your interviews will be conducted. Here are vouchers for use in the post exchange. Please continue ahead to the Red Cross area. They will help you with clothes and your barracks assignment and other information you will find helpful."

"Thank you, Mrs. Patton." Péter couldn't help but notice her accent but couldn't quite identify the region and asked, "Are you from southern Russia?"

Mrs. Patton, a woman of general good humor and liked by everyone, laughed.

"You are not the first refugee, Mr. Türea! Azerbaijan. I met my husband here. So now, here I am!"

The American Red Cross had originally provided 50 staff and 250 volunteers each day under the leadership of director Jack Henry. With the rapid influx of refugees, as MSTS flew into McGuire at the rate of 20 flights per day, the number of staff and volunteers was doubled. Now, with the onset of MATS ship arrivals, beginning with the USNS General Leroy Eltinge, those volunteers and staff were hard at work.

András, a tall, solid young man of about the same age as Péter, caught up with Péter as he was walking across the main floor of the processing area to the Red Cross station.

"Official American identification and papers! I wonder if they will have clothes that will fit me?" András, speaking in Hungarian, was excited and famished. "I'm hoping we'll have something to eat soon."

"I would like something to drink, some water." Péter was determined not to be distracted by the fatigue that had begun as an ache in his joints. "*Yes*, he thought to himself, *some water and a meal would certainly help*."

A gentleman was standing at the front of the Red Cross station greeting each refugee.

"Welcome. My name is Jack Henry. The American Red Cross is here to serve you. If there is anything you require while you are here in Camp Kilmer, please visit us." The soldier standing nearby translated as Péter held out his hand.

"Thank you, Mr. Henry."

"You speak English," and glancing at the card still attached to Péter's coat, "Mr. Turea?"

"Yes, a little. And some French and German."

"Are you a professional, Mr. Turea?"

"No, I'm a student and intend, if possible, to continue my education here in America."

"In what field, Mr. Turea?

"I am as yet undecided. My preferences are Theoretical Mathematics or another field of science."

"You'll need to meet with Gary Filerman. He's a student, like yourself, representing the World University Service. His team is located at the Reception Area. They are here to help people like yourself matriculate to American colleges and universities. He's the one to help you."

"And you, sir?" Mr. Henry turned his attention to András as did Péter, interested in the response András would give.

"András Kalman. My English is not smuch."

"Hungarian then, Mr. Kalman."

"A student also. I was in my third year of structural engineering."

"Well then, you also must schedule an appointment with Mr. Filerman." Mr. Henry motioned the two men forward, "Please step forward, gentlemen."

Péter and András were asked their size, color preferences, and what they needed. The Red Cross volunteers read from a long list, making notations as the men answered. Next, they received their barracks assignments on a slip of paper from a gentleman seated at a desk.

"How do I find this place?" Péter asked.

"You'll be escorted to the main camp on the west side of Plainfield Avenue. It's on the map, here," he indicated an area labeled 'Holding Village.' "The barracks are designated here in Blocks 6, 7, 9, and 10. If you'll proceed to your right; there is about to be a presentation."

Péter and András sat with a group of about forty refugees as a Red Cross representative, Mrs. Walton Van Winkle, stood before them and introduced a soldier, Louis Nemeth, who spoke Hungarian. Nemeth would act as an interpreter to help answer questions following a brief presentation on what to expect during their stay at Camp Kilmer.

Two soldiers brought a microphone and lectern while Van Winkle was introducing Nemeth. The audience and those nearby began to whisper. No Hungarian had ever seen a Negro before. The men noticed the response but kept to their work. Van Winkle accepted the microphone, tapping the head.

"Please. These men are Negros, they have black skin. They are men."

To a person, every refugee was appalled. No one wanted to be rightly accused of having bad manners.

Van Winkle assured the refugees of the Red Cross assistance in helping them contact friends and relatives in the United States at any one of the four telephone centers. Once they had a sponsor or destination, the Red Cross would arrange for their transfer from camp by train, bus, or airplane.

The Red Cross had also arranged for and oversaw the recreation and entertainment while the refugees were in the camp. A library, Building 1229, had Hungarian and American newspapers, periodicals, and books. The theater, Building 1521, and four gymnasiums were available to them. There were several chapels for the variety of faiths represented by their group. An Information and Education Center, Building 1422, with translators in attendance, was available to them. The vouchers they had received could be redeemed at any of the nine Post Exchanges located across the camp.

A bulletin board at the Reception Center and at the Refugee Center Headquarters, located in Area 15, posted a list of names of all the refugees at the center. There were maps of Camp Kilmer posted at the entrance of every main building with a translator in attendance.

Van Winkle ended with an announcement to proceed to the mess hall in the Reception Area for lunch. András was immediately out of his seat urging Péter to accompany him.

"Which building are you in? It's a wonder they are providing housing for the families, keeping the families together."

Péter selected the paper barrracks assignment form from several he held in his right hand.

"The document says Block 7, second floor, number 683. We should speak in English, András."

"Yes. I am Block 10, second floor, number 1037."

Péter and András sat together in the dining hall without speaking at first. Both men were very hungry. Péter was tired and hungry, nonetheless, he had many questions. He wondered if he knew anyone at camp. There hadn't been anyone aboard the Eltinge, but perhaps here there might be. There were so many tasks to accomplish, each vying for first on his mental list. His thoughts were abruptly interrupted when the older man seated across from them, that Péter somehow hadn't noticed before, spoke up.

"Do either of you understand how we are going to get a sponsor?"

Andràs was quick to speak and Péter was glad to let him. Péter could feel the energy and life returning to his body; the water, as much as the food, was invigorating him. He reached for the refilled cup a woman had just set before him and was thankful he looked in, it was Coca-Cola. Casting about the room, he was able to get the attention of another volunteer and, when asked, requested another glass of water. Péter listened as András continued to speak, in Hungarian, answering the old man's questions, wondering if they both had the same understanding of the process.

"The person who interviewed me with the Department of Labor said they receive offers everyday. Jobs, homes, and educational opportunities. Sponsors contact the offices here and make a request or say what they have to offer. The office puts the request into a machine that has all of our cards.

"The information you gave at the interviews—your birthdate, age, education, work history, everything, yes? They put that information by code, a series of hole punches, on a card.

"The machine sorts through those cards and finds all of the people who match the request. That is when you will hear names called over the loud speaker. When you hear your name, you report to the office for an interview. If you're a good match, if you like the offer and they like you, then you have a sponsor. Interesting, isn't it?

"I am András Kalman. This is my new friend, Péter Türea. What is your occupation?"

"Matyas Peko, locksmith. I arrived two days ago on a plane. I don't care to do that again. I hope they will allow me to travel on the ground wherever it is I go next. I was told many people are here and gone within a few days. I know the men sleeping in the bunks near me keep changing. It seems every day I meet someone new!"

"You will have a job soon, Matyas, I am certain of it!"

Watching András, Péter was struck by the constant stream of enthusiasm András seemed to radiate.

"Just you wait for the big surprise, you two young men," Matyas smiled as he admiringly lifted a large forkful of turkey and mashed potatoes to his mouth.

Péter, who had been politely listening, was now very interested.

"What is it?" András looked from Matyas to Péter and back again.

Matyas smiled and laughed as he finished chewing and took his time with a drink from his cup.

"What? What is it?"

"Hot water. It is unbelievable. As much as you want. Showers, baths. Just stand there and it doesn't stop!"

A young family sat nearby. As the woman looked up, Pèter recognized her.

"Mrs. Vizi?"

Enikő quickly turned to face him.

"Mr. Türea! István, this is the man I told you about in the infirmary translating for Mrs. Matusek. These are our children, Henri and Laura."

Suddenly the loudspeaker crackled to life.

"Welcome to our new guests from the USNS General Eltinge. English classes will begin this afternoon at 1600 hours in the Information and Education Building. Classes are held twice a day at 0900 hours and 1600 hours. The movies presented in the theaters tonight are the King and I, starring Yul Brynner and Deborah

Kerr, and Love Me Tender, starring Elvis Presley. If you have any questions, please speak to any of the volunteers, staff, and soldiers."

Following their late lunch, Péter went to the front of the Reception Center to find the promised map. Finding it, Péter familiarized himself with the layout in general. He hadn't known what to expect but this was not what he had imagined. Everything in America seemed, well, large. Overlarge. The camp resembled a city. András had stayed behind for a second serving but happened upon Péter as he walked across the camp to the barracks. Both men wanted to see where they would be sleeping, including the shower, and to deposit the clothes, pajamas, new coats, and shoes they had received.

"Péter, after you left I met another student. He's from Szeged. He learned that Rutgers University is nearby and offering an eight week English immersion class for scholars. I am unfamiliar with what the term 'immersion' implies. Do you know it?"

"I believe it means that most of the information is presented exclusively in English. You would not be able to speak any Hungarian," Péter smiled.

András laughed good naturedly, thrusting his hands deep into his pockets.

"Ah, you mean to make a fool of me! Hmmm. Well, there is another class, a nine week course, at a school named Bard College. The course is for undergraduates and is being sponsored by an automobile company."

"An automobile company?"

"Yes, the 'Ford Foundation.' I find English an incredibly difficult language. Do you?"

"Our parents had my sister and I begin our study at a young age. Perhaps that made it a bit easier, but yes, I do find it difficult. Much of it makes no sense. The language is not a constant. It is a language of inconsistencies. As one minor example, the letter 'c' will sometimes sound like a 'c' but at others like a 'k'. It makes no sense. The letters t,i,o,n are used to spell the last syllable of the word 'intention,' those letters combined produce the same sound as the word 'shun;' however, the word 'shun' is spelled s,h,u,n. It makes no sense.

"My intention is to attend every English class offered here. I am also interested in the introductions to American culture. The classes are being held throughout the day at the Service Club."

The remainder of the afternoon was spent familiarizing themselves with their barracks and the buildings they would most likely be seeking throughout the day: the Information and Education Center, the Library and Chapel, the nearest Telephone Center to their barracks, and the nearest Exchange. Before it seemed possible, it was time for dinner. Afterwards, curiosity driving him, Péter went to find the board listing the names of all the refugees currently being housed at Camp Kilmer. Péter, finding a large crowd assembled there, resolved to rise early the following day. Understandably, Péter had forgotten this day had begun predawn. Returned to his barracks, Péter found his bunk and was fast asleep.

Early the next morning, Péter returned to the name lists then proceeded to the message board. After checking the announcements, news spread through the camp like wildfire: in an effort to encourage the refugees to return, the Hungarian government was offering amnesty. András found Péter in the mess hall at breakfast.

"Did you check the message board?" András asked as he took a seat next to Péter then answered his own question, "Of course you did. What do you think? Of course they realize the catastrophe they have created for Hungary."

"Please speak in English, András."

"Yes, a good reminder, thank you."

"Of course it is a catastrophe, András. The majority of us, about 140,000 people, are between the ages of 16 and 45. Many of us, those who left, are technically skilled or educated. It is a great loss and will most likely put the country into a recession. I have heard these two situations referred to among the WUS students as a "demographic tsunami" and as a "brain drain" for Hungary." Péter paused, reflecting. "Such strange phrases.

"It will be difficult for all those we have left behind. They have enough difficulties. Mr. Filerman had said that the people and administration of this country recognize our potential. We are an economic bonus. This is why we are being offered so many opportunities. This is why we must apply ourselves in earnest."

"The WUS? You have already met with Mr. Filerman? When? What did you learn? I cannot imagine anyone returning."

Péter marveled at the disconnected stream of consciousness András possessed. He liked András, he had a kind and enthusiastic spirit.

"I awoke early to check the camp lists then went to the reception area to arrange a meeting with Mr. Filerman. As it happened, I was the first to arrive, perhaps because of the hour."

"Did you find who you were looking for?"

"No one, yet. Perhaps I will find a neighbor, a friend, someone from the Institute, or perhaps another student. The list is very long. I will look again, but first I meet with the Red Cross. Afterwards, I will attend the English class at the Information and Education Building and then to write. Not necessarily in that order; I don't know how long I will be with the Red Cross."

"What did Mr. Filerman say?"

"Basically, as a result of World War I, the European Student Relief was established in 1920 as part of the World's Student Christian Federation. This organization evolved into the International Student Service based in Geneva. After World War II, the organization became known as the World University Service, a global network of independent, non-governmental organizations[17] whose sole purpose is to aid students such as ourselves.

"Mr. Filerman is a junior at the University of Minnesota. He and his colleagues all belong to the WUS. They are here to place us at any of the 600 participating American colleges and universities. You need to make an appointment, András, there are already hundreds of students here. I did mention you to him, and your intent to finish your engineering degree.

"There is something very unique about this process. We are to write an autobiography as a contribution to our application and assessment. Mr. Filerman noted it is especially important to reveal our personal experience and the hopes we had with the revolution, although that is not how it began, as we both know. We should include our aspirations, if we experienced any persecution based on social class, and, which I don't understand at all, our feelings and motivations. Why do they want to know our "feelings?" It seems strange to me. The library has writing materials and someone to help with translation."

"That is strange, isn't it? Undoubtedly there will be many differences here, don't you agree? Thank you, Péter, I will go and meet with Mr. Filerman.

"Oh, did you hear the loudspeaker this morning? 'Matyas Peko.' Yes, perhaps Mr. Peko is already on his way to his new life in America! And let us hope, for his sake, that he travels by bus.

"Good luck today. Perhaps we will see each other at class or perhaps at lunch or dinner."

Both men left the dining hall seeking the path to their future.

Péter was not kept waiting long at the Red Cross Center. He supplied the volunteer aiding him with his sister's name and contact information in England and a brief note letting her know he had safely arrived. The volunteer assured Péter they would see that his note was delivered. Glancing at the clock, Péter saw he had ample time to get to class but hurried anyway anticipating a shortage of seats or space, and rightfully so.

When Péter arrived at the Information and Education building he found every chair already occupied; however, he found a space to stand just inside the back entry door. Finding the room stuffy and close, Péter turned to open the window behind him. As he did, two young women looked in, one with a long, thick, dark brown braid. Seeing the classroom overfull they turned away, the door closing behind them. Péter turned back from opening the window only in time to see the women's retreat. Yet, something about them caught his attention. Something about them seemed familiar.

46

BEGINNINGS

AFTER CLASS, PÉTER worked on his autobiography in the library. The librarian who provided him with paper and pen offered to help with the translation and editing. Then the librarian offered him one piece of advice.

"Tell your story in a way that pulls at their heartstrings."

Péter had no idea what the young woman meant but politely nodded and smiled, then found a seat in a quiet, remote corner hidden by the stacks. Péter immersed himself in his writing. It was of no use, hiding, the librarian found him despite his efforts.

"Mr. Türea? Correct? You did say your name was Peter Türea?"

"Yes," Péter smiled, patiently, anxious to return to his work.

"Mr. Türea, your name was just announced..."

Péter was already out of his seat.

"Thank you."

"Here, give me your paper. I'll edit it and kept it at the front desk for you. I'm here all day."

"Thank you..."

"Mrs. Marton. My husband's family came here in '46. Report to the Reception Center, Mr. Türea. Good luck!"

These last words barely caught up with Péter as he was backing away, turning to leave, in an attempt not to be rude. Péter suspected, hoped, that Mr. Filerman must have news for him.

At lunch András magically appeared. Péter had been sitting at one of the tables, perplexed, when he saw András walking toward him. He motioned to András to join him moving his tray as he adjusted his seat down the table making room for his friend at an otherwise crowded table.

"András, my friend. How is it you are able to find me? There are thousands of people here."

"We are meant to be together while here, my friend. I have good news! I have sponsor and school!"

"Yes? A sponsor and a school?"

"I had the idea to go to the Visitor Center where sponsors meet. I met a representative of the Tolstoy Foundation, a woman. I had been looking at bulletin boards when I heard my name called at the loudspeaker. Did you hear? I couldn't believe!

"The University of Michigan has a very good engineering program, one of the best in the country. The school is just finish their term. The next term doesn't begin until later this month. There is that problem.

"We cannot leave unless we have sponsor. Did you know there is a large Hungarian population in Michigan?" András, in his excitement, hardly paused for Péter's response. "No? So, I returned to the Visitor Center and found woman from Tolstoy still there. She had been in meeting and had several of the IBM cards in front of her. It turned out, one of them was mine. They are sponsoring me while I await the start of next term. And I didn't have to write the autobiographer!"

"Autobiography. And, yes, you do. I'm very happy for you, András."

"Thank you! I do?"

"It is for a scholarship. How else will you pay for school? Did they already offer you a scholarship?"

"For first term, yes."

"So write the paper and get the scholarship, András. The librarian in the library near our barracks is helping with editing. Her name is Mrs. Marton. When do you leave?"

At this, András' shoulders slumped and a look of concern shadowed his face. It was, perhaps, the first time Péter had ever seen this man unhappy about anything.

"It is alright, András. I, too, have a school. I, too, must wait but I have chosen to stay here."

"This is wonderful news, Péter. I am happy for you!"

Suddenly a voice from nearby interrupted their conversation.

"Excuse me, I've only just arrived. Lászlo Ispanky, from Vienna"

"Welcome. My name is András Kalman, Szeged."

"Péter Türea, Budapest. You said, Vienna?"

"Yes. Hungarian Army. Siberian POW camp; eleven months." He paused for a moment. "I'm also a student, an artist. A sculptor, actually. Where do I go, or who do I speak with, to find a school?"

Péter and András answered simultaneously, "Gary Filerman." Péter continued.

"Filerman is with the World University Service, located in the Reception Center. Go there after lunch." Péter said.

"Thank you."

"Péter, you didn't say, what school? Where will you go?"

"And you didn't say, András. When do you leave?"

András slumped over his tray. "This afternoon sometime. The Tolstoy representative already has families anxious to help Hungarian refugees. There are several families with room for single adult but there was one, both professors, looking for male student.

Can you believe? After lunch I return to the Red Cross. They are arranging transportation. I think perhaps I will take a sandwich with me. And you, Péter?"

"I will be going to Georgetown University in Washington, D.C. They have a very good mathematics program. It is an interesting city if I should have any time to myself, which I don't anticipate. Mr. Henry said I may stay here at Kilmer. I can help with translation while I study English here, although, I hope to join the Rutgers program."

A small boy, accompanied by a young man, squeezed onto the bench next to András. The boy had a disheveled shock of brown hair, huge brown eyes, and an engaging smile.

"Hello!" the boy looked directly at Péter.

"Hello," Péter chuckled, looking at András who smiled in return.

"My name is Johnny S. Wunder. This is my brother, Charles. They took my picture today!"

"And I am Péter Türea." Péter held out his hand to the boy.

"András Kalman, very glad to meet you."

"We're in America!"

Everyone within hearing distance chuckled indirectly or laughed out loud.

"Yes, Johnny, yes we are!" András replied.

Everyone at the lunch table and nearby smiled, softly laughing, as introductions were made. The little boy was very pleased with himself.

Leaving the dining hall, András and Péter faltered as they extended their hands to say goodbye. Instead, each stepped forward and cheek to cheek made their goodbye.

"Look for me. You never know, I might find you again!"

"Best wishes, András. I hope to see you again."

Péter walked toward the library in a cheerful mood. He was happy for his friend embarking on his journey, happy to have secured the beginnings of a future for himself. After the library, after English class, he must find time to visit a telephone center and send this good news to Júlia. His sister would get the news to their parents. Péter hoped such news would be a salve.

After working on the autobiography, Péter again left the draft with Mrs. Marton. Although there was a little more than an hour until the afternoon English class, Péter was determined to at least have standing room, if not a seat. He didn't mind standing. All that was important was to be in attendance. Péter walked briskly; his hat, shoes, and coat were no match for the dipping temperatures and light snow that had covered the ground.

Anticipating a full room, Péter entered from the back of the room. He was almost forty minutes early. Péter found several seats available and chose a seat in the third row behind a rather burly, large man many years his senior. Péter had not noticed the young woman seated in the first chair, directly ahead of him, until the older man ahead stood up to find the restroom.

"I'll return," the man softly spoke in Hungarian as he draped his jacket across the seat back.

"I will watch your seat for you," Péter responded, holding the man's attention as he nodded.

When Péter lowered his gaze he was startled and puzzled to again see a long, thick, dark braid. What was it about ... and in that instant, as he puzzled at its familiarity, the woman turned around.

Recognition was instantaneous as they both sat motionless, momentarily struck dumb. The young woman swallowed hard, Péter stuttered something in the way of a greeting then laughed at his foolishness.

"My apologies. It is Rebeka, isn't it?"

"Mr. Türea!"

"You are here. Well, of course, you are. My apologies for saying something so stupid. Is your family here?"

"Yes, some of my family," Rebeka haltingly answered.

Noting her response, Péter looked around the room then back at Rebeka before asking, "Would you mind? This is an important class for all of us, but would you mind missing this class?"

Rebeka nodded, standing with her book and papers, retrieving her sweater and purse from the back of her chair. People in the room had been watching, those closest stepped forward quickly slipping into the vacated seats barely before Péter and Rebeka had walked away. Rebeka stopped in the hallway and turned to Péter.

"Shall we go to the Social Club? There are tables and chairs there where we could sit and have a cup of coffee or tea?"

Péter nodded as he responded, "That would be fine."

As they walked to the Social Club, Péter questioned his response in seeing Rebeka. Astonished at his awkwardness, he attributed the lapse in composure to his being taken by surprise. For her part, Rebeka wondered at the sense of joy that had filled her at seeing Péter. Such a surprise!

The two sat over cups of tea that grew cold as they talked incessantly, recounting their experiences of the last weeks. They were alternately solemn or animated, incredulous at the impossibility of the short expanse of time which had inexorably changed the course of their lives in every way possible.

"When did you arrive?"

"We were on the first flight. And you?"

"You flew." Péter was impressed. He was certain that he was glad to have traveled by ship. "You were with the group that arrived on 6 December? And your family?"

Rebeka smiled and looked away momentarily before turning back to Péter's watchful gaze as he unconsciously noted everything about her.

"Not everyone. As you know. My Nagypapa, you remember him, don't you?"

"I do, yes. A good man. I remember him well. I will always remember."

Rebeka pressed her lips together, nervously continuing, rushing through the days following their departure from Budapest, returning home only to leave again. Nagypapa leading them to the border. Nagypapa's farewell. Rebeka paused, forcing herself to relax, to let her heart beat again before continuing. "And then we were on a plane to America. It was unbelievable. My nose was pressed to the window with precious little Bella's face there beside my own. We hardly slept a wink until we couldn't see for the lack of light and were forced to, simply by circumstance. We landed in Nova Scotia, to refuel, before arriving in the United States."

"Where is your family?"

"They were jointly sponsored by the American Hungarian Federation and the Church World Service. They left, a week ago, for their new home outside of Cleveland. My father will be employed on a quarter horse farm. Everyone was happy. Placement was very quick. The interview went very well."

"What about you, why are you here?"

"I have been accepted at a school." Rebeka's attempt at modesty amused Péter. It was obvious how pleased and excited she was as a smile tickled at the corners of her mouth revealing little dimples in her softly flushed cheeks. She held her hands in her lap to keep them still.

"Oh, I guess I can't really hide my enthusiasm, I just really can't believe it. I'll be studying literature at Wellesley. Of course, I will yearn for the time when I can visit my family and see the horses. But, I am excited to begin the term in two weeks. I'll be attending the English classes here. I had hoped to attend Bard, but there isn't the time. They have interesting programs and lectures there. Eleanor Roosevelt gave a presentation two days ago. But what about you, you haven't said a thing!"

Péter briefly paused, reflecting on Rebeka's enthusiasm and her sparkling brown eyes, before continuing. Péter looked down at his now cool cup of tea and, taking it in his hands, related the last days with his family in Budapest. He was halfway through the escape across the border when it was time for dinner. The two looked up in surprise. Rebeka laughed.

"We've been talking for two hours!"

They didn't stop talking as they walked to dinner, continued their conversation as they picked at their dinner, then returned to the Social Club to again order tea. Above the growing cacophony, they shared the details of the past weeks and their hopes and dreams for the future until they realized, with sudden, mutual surprise, the club had become quite quiet.

"Oh, Péter, it must be so late!"

"Yes, I'm afraid it is. We should leave. I will walk with you, my barracks are on the other side of the camp."

Rebeka paused, faltered, nervously getting to her feet. Péter could see the worry across her face and understood her concern. In Hungarian custom it was inappropriate to be seen out late at night with a man. Mrs. Marton approached their table to pick up the tea cups.

"Mrs. Marton?"

"Mr. Türea. Did you enjoy the presentation and dance?"

"Mrs. Marton, this is a friend of mine from Hungary, Rebeka András. I'm afraid we have been comparing the events of the last several weeks and sadly missed the entertainment you must have labored over. Please accept my apologies."

"How very nice to meet you, Miss András, or may I call you Rebeka? I'm Evelyn."

"Oh yes, thank you. I'm happy to meet you. 'Rebeka' is just fine."

"Mrs. Marton, would you be able to escort Rebeka to her barracks. I'm afraid I didn't keep track of the time."

"I'd be happy to. Mr. Marton has his hands full finishing up here with the crew. I was just waiting for my friend Vera to join us. She's been here with her daughter for several days; they received their sponsor two days ago. Here she comes now."

Péter and Rebeka agreed to meet the next morning for breakfast. Walking to his barracks, tidying his few belongings before readying himself for sleep, Péter marveled over the coincidence of meeting Rebeka. All the coincidences of meeting Rebeka. Péter fell asleep wondering at the probability and impossibility of their chance encounters.

Rebeka walked home listening to Evelyn and Vera talk about Vera's daughter, Horachia, and the family that was sponsoring them. Occasionally, Rebeka had a question.

"You have a family sponsoring you in California? I hadn't heard of any sponsor so far west."

"Exactly right, Rebeka. This sponsor lives in Los Angeles. Daniel and Dorothy Krieger. They have an aunt who lives in Toledo, Ohio which is where the National Catholic Welfare Council has quite a large membership, which includes the Krieger's aunt. Apparently the Krieger family owns a duplex in Los Angeles, that's a single building but with two apartments side by side. One side of the duplex is vacant. The aunt contacted Daniel and Dorothy Krieger when the council and the Hungarian Relief Agency decided to send a large group of people from here to the Los Angeles basin. Vera and her daughter were one of the families chosen.

Are you ready for your new home in California, Vera?"

"Yes, although is a little frightening. My daughter is very excited to see the movie stars there."

"The wedding day was quite wonderful." Mrs. Marton said, a broad smile on her face.

"Oh, yes, it was!" Vera laughed. Rebeka listened, curious.

"Oh, my dear," Mrs. Marton continued. "Not one but three couples were married."

"Is that unusual?" asked Rebeka.

"Well, yes, dear. They were married at the same time. It was a triple wedding. A Hungarian performed the ceremony. I remember his name as Bartalan, Reverend Bartalan."

"What a story their families will have. They have survived so much."

"Well, here we are, Rebeka. Have a good nights' rest."

"Thank you, Evelyn. Good night, Vera."

The next morning Péter found a place for two and waited for Rebeka. And so he did again the next day. The following day, as Péter awaited Rebeka's arrival, he heard a familiar voice.

"Péter, Péter Türea!"

Péter turned to see Lászlo Ispanky veering toward him, Lászlo's large bushy mustache made him easily identifiable. There was nothing to do but let him sit down across the table as he excitedly told Péter of his plans.

"I've been sponsored for one year by the student union at the Cranbook Academy of Art in Deerfield, Michigan. I will study, and," he added emphatically, "I'll also teach sculpting. I leave later this morning, before lunch. I'm so glad to have found you. To be able to see you before I leave, and to thank you. Have you found a sponsor or a school? Is there anything I can do for you?"

"I am glad for you, Lászlo. Congratulations. Yes, I will be attending Georgetown University in Washington, D.C. You're very kind, but I think at the moment and for the foreseeable future I have what I need. We are both very fortunate."

Péter was surprised and relieved to have Lászlo suddenly stand.

"I must be leaving. I have to pack my valise and wait at the Red Cross station for my ticket. I'm going by airplane! I don't want to embarrass myself. It will be my first time. They say every seat has a bag, just in case, you understand. What do you think? Have you flown?"

"No, not yet, Lászlo. I'm certain you will be fine."

Lászlo rose and came around the table to where Péter stood to meet him. They took each other's hand and stepped together to kiss cheek to cheek. As quickly and surprisingly as he had appeared, Lászlo disappeared into the crowd and was gone.

As Péter watched Lászlo walk away, he saw Rebeka in the queue at the door and held up a hand in salutation. Mistaking who he was waving to, the Vizi family, standing in line several feet ahead of Rebeka, waved back. Noticing Péter's gaze averted, Rebeka turned to look up the queue and let out a stifled cry of joy. Her hands had flown to cover her mouth too late. Everyone looked from Rebeka to the Vizi family, moving aside to allow Rebeka passage to where the Vizi family stood. Everyone standing nearby watched, tearfully smiling, at the joyful reunion.

Over the course of the next two weeks Péter rose early each morning to a structured routine of breakfast with Rebeka, English class with Rebeka, then reading every reference he could find in the library on Georgetown, Washington, D.C., and theoretical mathematics. Rebeka would meet him for lunch, after which they both attended the American culture presentations, the afternoon English class, dinner, and again time in the library. Gary Filerman was able to provide both Péter and Rebeka with information pamphlets for Georgetown and Wellesley.

The days passed quickly, their time in camp punctuated by the comings and goings of thousands more of their fellow Hungarian refugees. One morning, after breakfast, Péter and Rebeka were both surprised to receive their transportation vouchers to their school destinations.

"Péter, is it possible, we leave the day after tomorrow? The time has gone by so quickly, hasn't it?"

"It was inevitable. I knew it, and yet it is surprising."

Rebeka was curious that Péter had slipped into Hungarian.

"Rebeka, I have carefully spent a great deal of time planning the next few years. I plan to finish my education with a doctorate in three years, perhaps four. Then to find a position as a professor."

"Yes, Péter. I'm very excited for you."

"You will get your degree at Wellesley. That is also quite an accomplishment. I admire you, Rebeka. I have great respect for you and for your family. During our time here together I have come to realize that I love you, Rebeka. I want to share the rest of my life with you. Will you marry me, Rebeka?"

Rebeka's hands dropped into her lap. She wordlessly considered the man before her, which caused Péter some degree of discomfort.

"After we complete our studies?"

"I willingly agree to whatever you prefer. Whatever you believe to be wise."

Rebeka again sat and wordlessly considered. Then with a broadening, brilliant smile, "Yes. Yes, Péter, I will. After we complete our studies."

Péter and Rebeka completed their studies. It had taken four years, both earning their degrees summa cum laude. Péter had received a personal phone call from John Kemeny, head of Dartmouth's Math Department, offering him a position. Stanford had also offered Péter a position within their cutting edge math department. They had worked relentlessly, sending no less than recently retired Gábor Szegő, who did his best to recruit Péter. Péter had struggled with the decision. It had boiled down to Kemeny's pioneering use of computers in the classroom, and it's supportive use in solving problems at an unprecedented rate, that weighed in the balance against Pölya's work on probability theory at Stanford.

Rebeka had been supportive, although it was obvious she flourished in the environment of New Hampshire in general compared to San Francisco in particular.

The choice made, the wedding was to be held at Wellesley in St. Paul's Catholic Church. Júlia had flown into Boston on Friday and taken the train to Wellesley. Rebeka's family was due to arrive later that day from Cleveland. Sitting at a table in a local restaurant with Júlia, Rebeka and Péter had laughed and cried together as they recounted their experiences. Júlia paused, reaching out across the draped table to gently squeeze Rebeka's hand, and looked lovingly at her brother.

"Péter, I have something."

Júlia stood up and withdrew a previously unseen package from beneath the unoccupied chair at their table. It was obvious the package was of some weight as she set it in front of the couple.

"This is from your Nagypapa and Nagyanya."

Péter repeatedly, alternately, gazed from Júlia to the package and back again, overcome with emotion. For a moment he simply sat, one elbow upon the table, his hand cupping his chin, staring at the package. Rebeka gently laid her hand upon his sleeve. Finally, adjusting his seat, he leaned forward and began to untie the simply wrapped package.

"It's heavy."

Júlia only smiled and waited patiently.

"Oh, Péter!" Rebeka softly exclaimed as he lifted the top of the beautifully crafted, linden wood box revealing the sterling silverware József had labored over so many years ago. The gift for his bride, then hidden for decades as war and discord repeatedly ravaged Hungary and Hungarians.

"How is this possible?" Péter asked as he lightly traced the engraved initials of his grandmother.

Rebeka's eyes darted from Péter to Júlia. It was easy for anyone to see that Péter was overwhelmed. Júlia was exceptionally pleased.

"Oh, Péter! Isn't it incredible? Isn't it gorgeous! Nagyanya didn't even know that Nagypapa had saved it from the Nazi's, or how he kept it hidden away for so long. When you first wrote of Rebeka," at this Júlia turned to Rebeka and, with a smile so full of love, reached out to grasp her hand, "and your engagement..." Júlia's voice trailed off as she fought tears then continued, "Well, it took some time to contact our family but with the help of friends and over the past three years Nagypapa sent it to Vienna and on to me. The last pieces arrived just two months ago. There's only a teaspoon missing. Nagypapa was disappointed he was never able to find it."

Péter sat, one hand upon the table, the other pensively curled at his mouth and chin, his elbow resting on the table. He looked up to Rebeka and back to the box.

"Long ago, Nagypapa, József Kovács, as I have told you, was a silversmith. He made these for his Gizella, Nagyana, as her wedding present. She never spoke of it, she thought it was gone. It was a great disappointment for her. But our Anya remembered. She would tell us of it when it was just the three of us, Anya, Júlia, and me. Anya wanted us to know."

47

1998

YEARS PASSED. PÉTER and Rebeka created their life with purpose and intent as they had imagined and dreamt of in the weeks following their escape from Hungary, during those bitterly cold and frightening days and nights crossing into Austria, the days of uncertainty spent in the refugee camp, and then in traveling to the unknown, a country demonized all their lives, and, finally, what they came to remember as halcyon days at Camp Kilmer. At his work, Péter had found Dartmouth fertile ground. He was welcomed, supported, and encouraged in his work aided by access to a worldwide computer network allowing him and like-minded mathematicians to work and solve complex problems at an unprecedented rate.

Péter and Rebeka had found a simple but beautiful home in the northern wood reminiscent of Rebeka's earlier life. Her home had satisfied and served to salve her wounds, her loss, in creating a new life. Her mother had sent several tiles to adorn their fireplace. The tiles stood to either side of the centerpiece, the Turul tile Enikő and István had sent as a wedding present. Rebeka had attached the note, written in Enikő's diminutive script, to the back of the tile *"...to protect your family as we were protected with the love from your family."*

Péter and Rebeka's family grew, filling their home with the laughter and happy chaos of four children: Erzsébet, Laura, Henry, and Joseph. Joy was tempered with sorrow. Rebeka occasionally received a letter from György briefly assuring her that he was well, although getting older. Too soon came a note that Sándor had died, then Kriska and Janga. Rebeka was surprised, then worried, when he had given Tomba and János to their neighbor, Dávid Marton. György explained he had retired to work a small vegetable garden for himself and old friends.

Júlia had become a doctor, a pediatrician, married, and had two children of her own. Péter learned that his parents had received both his message and the returned money Péter had entrusted to the kindly stranger on the streets of Vienna during those first days in the refugee camp. This news had come from Júlia with the news of József's death. Within the following year, Péter's grandmother, Gizella, and his parents all passed away within three months of each other. The frustration Péter felt being unable to attend to his parents and grandparents was tempered by the knowledge of certain reprisal. Should Péter attempt to return, he would be "detained" and could expect, at the very least, imprisonment. Hungary had rebuilt the Iron Curtain following those fateful few weeks in 1956.

Then in 1989, the Iron Curtain came down again giving Péter and Rebeka reason to hope. Although Péter had concerns, Rebeka was supportive and encouraging.

"Certainly, you should go. Júlia may not get this chance again until after the children are grown. Her practice, her family. Please go. We all want you to go."

Péter, as the department chair and for his work on the Riemann Hypothesis, had been invited to a two week guest lecture exchange program. The program would begin at the Swiss university, École Polytechnique Fédérale de Lausanne, located near Geneva, followed by the University of Oxford, just west of London, where he would spend the week with Júlia. While there, he and Júlia planned to spend one short weekend in Budapest; Júlia's in-laws would help with the children during her absence.

"Péter!"

Péter looked up from the baggage cart to see Júlia and her family waving. He was glad they'd been able to meet him, glad too for the company. He had enjoyed his week in Lausanne, especially his time with Daniel Ueltschi discussing quantum lattice models. Péter looked forward to meeting with his colleague, Robin Wilson, who he had met through his good friend and collaborator, Paul Erdős. He and Erdős shared a similar fascination with set theory and had a similar past; Erdős was a graduate of the Technical University in Budapest. The week was enlightening and enjoyable although, as the weekend approached, Péter grew more introspective and thoughtful.

The flight was only two and a half hours from Heathrow to Budapest. When the plane landed, Péter wondered at the reluctance he was feeling until he was thoroughly intrigued by the moist imprints left by his hands on the arm rests. He lifted and turned first one palm and then the other to inspect them. Péter had grown to scrutinize "logical" and "illogical" actions to a degree where it had become a personal characteristic that not only his family, but he too viewed with a sense of humor. Now, sitting in a plane on the tarmac of Budapest's International Airport, this scrutiny caused him to laugh. Júlia had stood and was pulling her overnight bag from the bin above their row. She glanced down.

"What is funny?" she asked, glancing in the nearby vicinity for whatever had caught his attention.

"Me."

Júlia smiled and thought it better not to ask. There were demons here, real and imagined. Flying in, as they approached Budapest, Júlia had leaned over her brother's shoulder. They both strained to see their childhood home below. It was a beautiful morning, the city gleamed, but they both knew where there was light there was also darkness. They knew they had to be cautious, watchful, slow, and purposeful. They had carefully planned the early morning flight, the day's schedule, then the late evening return flight. Better to not risk staying overnight. A colleague at the University, András Recski, had asked to meet them and take them to brunch. András was giving them the use of his vehicle for the remainder of the day.

Disembarking, looking out from the top of the mobile stairway, Péter remembered that long ago icy winter night as he hesitated before crossing into Austria, that moment when he had turned to look back on the moonlit landscape wondering if he would ever return. Now he had returned to a landscape devoid of those he would have returned to.

As Júlia approached, Péter muttered under his breath to her, "I feel as if we are being watched."

"Of course!" Júlia smiled broadly as she kissed him on both cheeks and looked into his eyes. "Come, let's go."

András had met them at the front of the terminal. Péter introduced Júlia to András as they placed Júlia's bag on the backseat of his bright green Suzuki Swift sub compact.

"Through customs so quickly? I'll be certain to thank Ueltschi."

Júlia turned to Péter, "Your colleague at the Ecole de Lausanne?"

Péter nodded, "He said he might be able to help."

"It is better now, every day it is better. Still, be careful my friends."

András treated his friends to brunch at the Pesti Vendéglő, near St. Stephen's Basilica, well-known for their traditional Hungarian delicacies. When András heard the bell of St. Stephen's, the largest in the country, at eleven he interrupted the lively conversation by offering his car keys.

"Here, I am going to my office for the remainder of the day. I'll see you there at four to return to the airport. Who's driving?"

"I am."

"She is." Péter answered simultaneously with Júlia. "She prefers it, I do not."

"Here you are," András said as he handed the keys to Júlia with a quick nod to a small key held between his fingers.

"Do you mind if we leave the car here for a little while? We thought we'd walk a bit at first," Júlia asked as she stood, kissing each of András' cheeks.

"Of course. I know I do not need to remind you to be careful. I will see you soon. Perhaps next time you can stay longer."

Júlia and Péter emerged from the restaurant and momentarily stood in silence. They each looked across the city, each experiencing that magical transcendence of time, that curiosity of scientists in measuring an interval of time.

"The distinction between past, present, and future is only a stubbornly persistent illusion," Péter quietly remarked.

"Einstein," Júlia responded. "Never before in my experience as at this very moment. But that's what you meant, isn't it?"

"Yes."

"Unless you've changed your mind, let's begin."

The siblings walked in silence to the square in front of the Parliament Building, then down to the Danube Promenade to Margit Bridge where they crossed midway to the island and sat for a few minutes. Walking back along the Danube, they paused at the shoes. Continuing, they glanced at the balcony where the composer Zoltán Kodály had waved to the crowd. Péter and Júlia continued to the Freedom Bridge, where they again paused. Péter cleared his throat. Júlia waited, then remembered and smiled.

"This is where you first saw Rebeka, isn't it?

Péter nodded slowly, placing his hands behind his back and holding them there. "All that transpired that day. At times, like this, it seems impossible, and then you realize there is more to this life than we can imagine. But I don't want to talk about any of that now. I would like to observe and commit to memory what has become of what we began so long ago."

Júlia walked toward the bridge where she stopped and waited under one of the Turul statues at the portal. Péter eventually joined her and together they crossed the bridge returning to the borrowed car in a comfortable silence.

"What time is it?"

"Two-thirty. We have plenty of time."

Nothing had changed, yet everything had changed. The configuration of the streets were mostly the same, the buildings varied by location. Budapest, located at an international crossroads, was influenced throughout its history by the evolving architecture across Europe. Some areas were restored to the grand façades of that time so long ago when artistic sculpture and flourish were realized in stained glass, ornamental metal work, commemorative statues, high-relief plaster work, and colorful glazed ceramics. In other areas, buildings yet bore the wounds of those few days so long ago. Once elegant façades remained ravaged, pockmarked with bullet holes, weathered with time. Interspersed among the traditional melting pot of elegant, Hungarian architecture were the remnants of the drab, cement, communist apartment buildings that amounted to nothing more or less than rectangular prisms devoid of any architectural interest.

Júlia drove a circuitous route, passing the four story apartment building on Dohány Street that had once been home to their family. As children, their family had found refuge there after fleeing the bomb shelter on Rózsa Hill as the Russians and Nazis razed their home and much of Budapest. Júlia had few memories of that time in her life although she bore the scars of the frostbite she suffered there as a child. As Júlia drove, Péter recounted the story of their mother tucking the two of them under the kitchen table to keep them from the snow as it drifted through the broken walls.

Péter remembered his friend Lászlo Bójtós, who had later lived in the building with his family, then, during the revolution, had found refuge there in the basement.

"I had a letter from Lászlo. He sent a photograph. Barnát and Izsák are both married now. Barnát has a son and daughter. Izsák, two daughters."

"They are all in Switzerland?"

"Yes. Lászlo has retired."

"Will you?"

Péter turned to his sister with a look of serious contemplation. Júlia laughed.

Again they crossed Margit Bridge, this time continuing up Rózsa Hill where Júlia found a parking space. From there they walked to the building that was the object of their quest. On the site of what had once been their family home, burned to the ground by the Nazis, an apartment building had been erected.

"No one will be with us, correct?"

"Yes, Péter. András said I should wait at the top of the stair and flicker the light should anyone approach. Inside the building or out."

"Should a vehicle approach?"

"Yes. Or anyone. Péter," Júlia began as they were about to enter, "what do you hope to find?"

"Dust. We were children. I want to see it as an adult. To see with historical perspective what our great grandfather, grandfather, and father did to save all of us."

Opening the heavy, wooden, unadorned door to the simple, tiled vestibule, the stairway ahead led to the apartments above. Both Péter and Júlia regarded the flight of stairs, searching for anyone, listening for any sound. Nothing. Wordlessly turning to one another, Júlia motioned to the left where a locked set of double doors led to a stairwell, which in turn led to the bunker. To the right of the door was a light switch for the single, bald lightbulb at the top of the bunker's stairwell.

Júlia carefully, quietly lifted the switch turning on the light then unlocked the door with the key András had subtly indicated. The lock responded loudly as the tumbler fell into place. Péter and Júlia's heads snapped up, wide eyed, then back towards the vestibule and stairs. Júlia gave a quick twist of her head and flick of one hand, indicating Péter should go. She again looked apprehensively up the stairs and towards the front door with the forefinger of her other hand pressed to her lips.

Péter held his breath as he opened the door, fearful the hinges would protest or the door itself might catch against its casing or scrape across the floor. Instead, miraculously, silence. Péter cautiously kept to the side of the narrow wooden stairs walking into the soft darkness below.

Péter paused in the shadows at the bottom tread where the weak light from the bare bulb no longer penetrated the darkness of what had been the bomb shelter. From his pocket, Péter withdrew a small flashlight, slipped the wrist band over his hand, and turned it on. In its limited field of illumination he found familiarity and a black and white snapshot of history. The gray cement cylinder and floor, thick with dust, a monochromatic image fading into black. There was nothing, or so it seemed.

Péter's great grandfather, grandfather, and father had fitted the shelter with wooden benches, shelves, and boxes of various shapes and sizes for clothing, cooking utensils, bedding, and food. A slatted wooden floor had provided an expanse to stand on rather than the diminished curve of the cylinder. Over the years, time and an occasional heavy rain had combined to rot everything. The resulting thick layer of dust all but enveloped his shoes, only his laces stood testament to their existence.Viewed from behind, Péter appeared to be balanced on trousered pegs.

Péter purposefully walked to the end and, seeing nothing, turned. With his first step, Péter felt a small bump beneath his shoe. Blindly reaching into the dust, he extricated and held to the light a faded green bit of Bakelite, a remnant of what had been their first aid kit. Encouraged, Péter stooped over his knees with one hand holding the flashlight while the other, with long fingers only slightly spread, sieved the dust. Working across the floor he found a screw, the remnant of what had been a wooden-handled screwdriver, a small metal, hinged enameled toy box, a small knife with a broken blade, and another screw. At the last, one half of a walnut shell which had the appearance, to Péter's amazement, of having been discarded only recently although it had been more than forty years awaiting this moment of discovery. As Péter marveled over the unexpected artifacts that long ago fell through the slatted floor, the bare lightbulb at the top of the stairs began to madly flicker.

Péter turned to bolt up the stairs. Somehow, mistakenly, he turned off his flashlight. In the immediacy of instant blindness, Péter tripped and fell hard on his knees, his arms flung forward to break his fall. All Péter had gathered radiated in diminishing arcs, obscured by dust and darkness. Hitting the floor hard, the stairwell lightbulb continued to flicker madly. Péter scrabbled to find purchase only half acknowledging the unyielding object at his fingertips around which he closed his fingers. Standing, the flashlight on, he quietly and quickly as possible ascended the stairs where he stood, listening.

The door flew open. Júlia grabbed his hand that had been upon the door and hauled him into the vestibule. Pausing only for a moment, Júlia peeked out the front door and up the street before bolting out the door to where she had parked the car. Júlia drove the roads behind Castle Hill then down to Gellert Square crossing Petofi Bridge before she felt her fear and panic subside. Péter, his pulse racing, had tried to maintain the "look" of the average citizen out for a drive while stealing glances in Júlia's direction.

"What happened?"

"I am sorry. I fell."

"Oh, Péter!"

"No, it was stupid of me. When you signaled, I overreacted, somehow turning off the flashlight resulting in my tripping and falling."

"Are you hurt?"

"Thankfully, no. Somehow I didn't tear my trousers."

Júlia had crossed the Freedom Bridge and now pulled up in front of the University where András stood awaiting them, as promised.

"Did you find anything?" András asked as he crouched into the small vehicle.

"I did. Small bits, including a little toy enameled box we once had, do you remember?" Péter asked turning towards Júlia. "However, I lost everything..." Péter's voice abruptly faltered as he looked at his closed right hand. Júlia followed his gaze and gasped.

Péter's still clenched hand had opened to reveal a small, sterling teaspoon with the entwined initials GK beautifully engraved on the handle.

48

CHRISTMAS EVE

IN THE SHARED remembrance and gratefulness of those gathered around the table, in the light of Christmas reflected in the faces of all whom we held dear, we sat together, our attention captivated by our Grandfather.

Looking from one to the next, Grandfather held the small teaspoon aloft for all to see as we awaited his decision. Who would receive the spoon? The candles flickered and the table sparkled as candlelight danced across the colorful assortment of tableware, glasses, and serving dishes. The fire in the fireplace crackled and popped, casting a dance of light and shadows across every wall and into every corner of the room. As Grandfather loving regarded each of us, he suddenly paused.

The spoon was passed around the table, each family member gazing at it for a brief moment before passing it on to the next, until it was handed to me, his youngest grandchild. It was the first time I had been chosen. To this day, I remember the joy I felt at that moment; I thought I would burst.

My family quietly waited, enjoying the experience through me, with me. I savored the moment gazing upon the spoon, this small symbol of a story of endurance, of love.

Then, as was tradition, I arose from my seat and brought the spoon to Grandmother. She held it close and said a prayer of thanks, then placed the spoon back upon the table. We all held hands, we all laughed, and some wiped a tear sparkling upon their cheek.

ENDNOTES

1. Kiss, Tamás. "Tamás Kiss." *Association of Hungarian University and College Students*. Szeged, 2006. Editor Csaba Jancsák. ISBN 9573248.
2. Miller, Jacob. Inspiring Photos of the Hungarian Anti-Communist Revolution. October 28, 2017. https://historycollection.com.
3. American Hungarian Federation. The 1956 Hungarian Revolution: 16 Points. http://www.americanhungarianfederation.org.
4. Gelberger, Judith Kopácsi. Hungarian Free Press. Dr. Sándor Kopácsi–An Unorthodox Hero, Who Wouldn't Fit the Mould. November 12, 2015.
5. American Hungarian Federation. eNews. October 2012.
6. Pastor, Péter. The American Reception and Settlement of Hungarian Refugees in 1956–1957. Hungarian Cultural Studies. e-Journal of the American Hungarian Educators Association, Volume 9 (2016).
7. United States of America, Office of the Historian. Foreign Relations of the United States, 1955–1957, Eastern Europe, Volume XXV Document 218. Notes of a Meeting With the President, White House, Washington, December 26, 1956, 11 a.m..
8. Pastor, Péter. The American Reception and Settlement of Hungarian Refugees in 1956–1957. Hungarian Cultural Studies. e-Journal of the American Hungarian Educators Association, Volume 9 (2016).

9. Luce, Clare Boothe—The Ambassador. May 10, 2018, Staff. *New-York Historical Society*.

10. "The Hungarian Revolution of 1956." October 23, 2016. *The Budapest Beacon*. Staff.

11. Percival, Matthew. Hungarian Revolution, 60 years on: How I fled Soviet Tanks in a Hay Cart, CNN.

12. Ibid.

13. Kolosvary-Stupler, Éva. Traversing a Minefield to Escape Communist Hungary. JDC Archives. March 2015.

14. Bradford, Anita Casavantes. "With the Utmost Practical Speed": Eisenhower, Hungarian Parolees, and the "Hidden Hand" Behind US Immigration and Refugee Policy, 1956-1957. Journal of American Ethnic History. Vol. 39, No. 2 (Winter 2020), pp. 5-35 (31 pages) University of Illinois Press.

15. Air Mobility Command Museum Foundation. Hangar Digest, vol 6 issue 1. Jan 1, 2006. https://amcmuseum.org.

16. VonLanken, Lisa. Did Your Ancestors Come Through Ellis Island? 2014. docplayer.net/24271546.

17. Blinken, Vera and Donald. Assisting 1956 Hungarian Student Refugees: Gary L. Filerman. Open Society Archives. January 21, 2017.

BIBLIOGRAPHY

Abel-Hirsch, Hannah. The Hungarian Revolution. Erich Lessing. Magnum Photos. Aug 20, 2017.

Air Mobility Command Museum Foundation. Hangar Digest, vol 6 issue 1. Jan 1, 2006. https://amcmuseum.org.

American Hungarian Federation. eNews. October 2012.

American Hungarian Federation. The 1956 Hungarian Revolution: 16 Points. http://www.americanhungarianfederation.org.

American Rhapsody. [Film]. Éva Gárdos. Colleen Camp and Bonnie Timmermann. 2001.

AP News May 6, 1989.

Blinken, Vera and Donald. Assisting 1956 Hungarian Student Refugees: Gary L. Filerman. Open Society Archives. January 21, 2017.

Bradford, Anita Casavantes. "With the Utmost Practical Speed": Eisenhower, Hungarian Parolees, and the "Hidden Hand" Behind US Immigration and Refugee Policy, 1956-1957. Journal of American Ethnic History. Vol. 39, No. 2 (Winter 2020), pp. 5-35 (31 pages) University of Illinois Press.

Brown, Patrick. Broadcasting Propaganda: Voice Of America's Role in The Hungarian Revolution of 1956. The University of North Carolina at Asheville. 2010.

Butturini, Paula. Chicago Tribune. Hungary Exhumes Bodies, Truth. April 2, 1989.

Camp Kilmer Buildings 801, 806, 871; Written Historical and Descriptive Data. Jennifer B. Leynes, RGA, Inc., April 2016.

"Camp Kilmer." *National Archives*. April 9, 2018.

"Camp Kilmer." *New Jersey Digital Highway*. (excerpt taken from the Camp Kilmer Information Office Fact Sheet 1958).

Carlin, James,A. Refugee Connection: Lifetime of Running a Lifeline.

Cellini, Amanda. Forced Settlement Review. The Resettlement of Hungarian Refugees in 1956. February 2017.

Colville, Rupert. Refugees. No 144, issue 3. 2006. United Nations High Commissioner for Refugees.

Coulter, Harris L. The Hungarian Peasantry. 1948-1956.

DaSilva, Jonathan. Research Assistant. Statue of Liberty-Ellis Island Foundation. August 2021. Email.

Desetta, Al. Chromogram; Arts, Culture, Spirit. Memories of '56. 08/13/2013.

Doe, Jane. Personal interview. March 2021.

Doe, Jenny. Retired CIA agent. Personal interview. February 2021.

Doe, John. A series of personal interviews. December 2006 through March 2021.

Edwards, Leslie S, Head Archivist. Cranbrook Kitchen Sink; Operation Mercy and an Academy of Art Sculptor. September 15, 2013.

Elzy, Martin Ivan. American Governmental Response to the 1956 Hungarian Revolution. Eastern Illinois University. Masters Theses. October 24,1969.

Fabos, Bettina. 1950 Socialist Utopia.

56 Stories: Personal Recollections of the 1956 Hungarian Revolution. A Hungarian American Perspective. http://www.hacusa.org/userfiles/file/56_Stories_konyv_DIGITAL_WEB.pdf.

Fischer, Tibor. Introducing the Poems of Sándor Márai. Hungarian Review. 28 September 2013. Volume XII., No. 1.

Freedom Fighter 56 Oral History Project. "Péter A. Soltész." https://freedomfighter56.com.

Furth, Mira. The Year My Life Shifted Its Orbit.

Furth, Mira. Personal Interview. June 2020.

Gelberger, Judith Kopácsi. Hungarian Free Press. Dr. Sándor Kopácsi–An Unorthodox Hero, Who Wouldn't Fit the Mould. November 12, 2015.

Géza, Kresz. Cellar Hospital 1956. Ambulance Museum.

Griffith, William E. The Petofi Circle: Forum for Ferment in the Hungarian Thaw.

Handley, Derick. Broadcasting a Revolution: Radio Free Europe and the Hungarian Revolution. June 7, 2007.

Haulman, Daniel L. Safe Haven I and II. Air Mobility Command Museum.

Haulman, Daniel L. Wings of Hope: the U.S. Air Force and Human Airlift Operations. Department fo Defense. Air Force History. 1997.

"Hungary 1956. Jan 20, 2021 to Jan 20, 2009." US Department of State Archive.

"The Hungarian Revolution of 1956." October 23, 2016. *The Budapest Beacon*. Staff.

"Hungarian Revolution of 1956." *New World Encyclopedia*.

The Institute for the History of the 1956 Hungarian Revolution. Nov 27, 2003.

Jancsák Csaba. PhD.The List of AHUCS Members and Organisers in Szeged and Students Taking Part in the Events of the Revolution. http://acta.bibl.u-szeged.hu/67647/1/szemtanu_eng_161-166.pdf. 2006. University of Szeged.

Jancsák Csaba. PhD. The Spark Of Revolution (1956)—The Association Of Hungarian University And College Students (AHUCS). University of Szeged, Department of Applied Social Studies. http://www.coldwar.hu/publications/JancsakCs_Thesparkofrevolution_1956_AHUCS.pdf. University of Szeged.

Jancsák Csaba. PhD. Voices of the Revolution: the History of Scroll No. MR D565. 2017. June 14. University of Szeged.

Jancsák Csaba. PhD. Whose Association Is It? Three MEFESZ in History of Hungary. 2021. Belvedere Meridionale vol. 33 no. 4. 64-92. pp. ISSN 1419-0222 (print) ISSN 2064-5929 (online, pdf).

Jobbágyi, Gábor. Hungarian Review. Bloody Thursday, 1956: The Anatomy of the Kossuth Square Massacre. Jan 15, 2014. Vol 5, No. 1.

Johnson, A. Ross. Setting the Record Straight: Role of Radio Free Europe in the Hungarian Revolution of 1956. December 2006. Senior Scholar, Woodrow Wilson Center and Research Fellow, Hoover Institution.

"Joyce Kilmer, 1886–1918." *Poetry Foundation*. April 2021.

Kaufman, Michael T. Some Hungarians Remember 1956, Some Forget. New York Times. Oct. 24, 1986.

Kay, Alan C. John George Kemeny. IEEE Computer Society.

Kennedy, John F. A Nation of Immigrants. October 16, 2018. Harper Collins.

King, Harrison. Remembering '56: The Hungarian Revolution. https://origins.osu.edu/milestones/october-2016-remembering-56-hungarian-revolution-sixty.

Kiss, Tamás. "Tamás Kiss." *Association of Hungarian University and College Students*. Szeged, 2006. Editor Csaba Jancsák. ISBN 9573248.

Kolosvary-Stupler, Eva. Traversing a Minefield to Escape Communist Hungary. JDC Archives. March 2015.

Koza, Patricia. From 'Counter-Revolution' to National Tragedy. United Press International Nov 2, 1986.

Krieger, Daniel. Personal interview. March, August 2021.

Lauer, Edith K. Eyewitness to the Hungarian Revolution of 1956 and its Aftermath of Freedom. (Opinion) Updated Jan 11, 2019; Posted Oct 21, 2016.

Lauer, Edith. Freedom Fighter '56 Oral History Project. Paul Maléter—Child of the five Year Plans. As told by Paul Maléter.

Laszlo Ispanky Obituary (2010). Trenton, NJ. "The Times, Trenton".

Lister, Tim. Today's Refugees Follow Path of Hungarians who Fled Soviets in 1956. CNN Updated 1428 GMT (2228 HKT) September 7, 2015.

Luce, Clare Boothe—The Ambassador. May 10, 2018, Staff. *New-York Historical Society*.

Marton, Kati. Enemies of the People. Simon and Schuster. 2009.

Medalis, Christopher. Hungarian Refugee Students and United States Colleges and Universities A Report on the Emergency

Program to Aid Hungarian University Students in the U.S., 1956–1958.

Miller, Jacob. Inspiring Photos of the Hungarian Anti-Communist Revolution. October 28, 2017. https://historycollection.com.

Morse, Donald E. Hungarian Review. 25 January 2017. Vol III, No. 1. From the Streets to the States—Hungarian Poets View the '56 Revolution. Institute of International Education.

New Photo Gallery of 1956 Hungarian Refugees in the US Now Available. Central European University. January 31, 2017.

Niessen, James P. Hungarian Refugees of 1956: From the Border to Austria, Camp Kilmer, and Elsewhere.. (2016) e-Journal of the American Hungarian Educators Association (AHEA), 9, 122–136.

"1956 The History of the Soviet Bloc 1945-1991 A Chronology. Part 2. 1953-1968." Edited by Csaba Békés.

Nóvé. Belá. Eurozine. 21 January 2013. The Orphans of '56. Hungarian Child Refugees and Their Stories.

Ornstein, Anna. My Mother's Eyes. April 1st 2004. Clerisy Press, Emmis Books.

Pammer, Martin. Austria and the Hungarian Revolution 1956. New Austrian Information.

Pastor, Péter. The American Reception and Settlement of Hungarian Refugees in 1956–1957. Hungarian Cultural Studies. e-Journal of the American Hungarian Educators Association, Volume 9 (2016).

Pelchat, Thomas. Fostering A Feeling of Betrayal: United States Foreign Policy and the 1956 Hungarian Revolution. University of New Hampshire, Durham. 2018.

Percival, Matthew. Hungarian Revolution, 60 years on: How I fled Soviet Tanks in a Hay Cart, CNN.

Pike, John. Revolt Revisited-A Study Of The Hungarian Revolution Of October, 1956. 1984.

"Policy Considerations for Radio Free Europe. October 25, 1956." Wilson Center. Digital Archive.

Roland, W. Charles Troopships of World War II. The Army Transportation Association Washington, D. C. April 1947.

Sealift Magazine. pg 22. March 1966.

Sheridan, Vera. Disclosing the Self: 1956 Hungarian Student Refugees Creating Autobiographies for University Scholarships in the USA. Life Writing. 25 Jul 2019.

Siegel, Adam B. A Sampling of U.S. Naval Humanitarian Operations. Naval History and Heritage Command. Oct 30 16:54:28 EDT 2017.

Sobocinski, André B, BUMED Historian. In the Shadows of Revolt: Hungarian Relief, the U.S. Navy and Humanitarian Assistance during the Cold War Part I. Navy Medicine Live. Official Blog of the US Navy Bureau of Medicine and Surgery. April 20th, 2021.

"Soviet Tanks Crush Resistance." *The Guardian*. US Edition. Mon 5 Nov 1956.

Stavridis, James G., Adm. USN (Ret). What Was Life Like for Sailors During the Battle of the Atlantic? Series: Beyond the World War II We Know. New York Times Magazine. April 14, 2020.

"Timeline: Hungarian Revolution." I 25 September 2006.

Tonka, M. The Catholic Church In Hungary. Encyclopedia.com.

"Transcript of a Teletype Conversation Between the Legation in Hungary and the Department of State." Department of State. Office of the Historian. Foreign Relations of the United States, 1955–1957, Eastern Europe, Volume xxv. Document 108. October 25, 1956.

Ulannoff, Stanley M. "MATS: The Story of the Military Air Transportation Service".

United States of America, Office of the Historian. Foreign Relations of the United States, 1955–1957, Eastern Europe, Volume XXV Document 218. Notes of a Meeting With the President, White House, Washington, December 26, 1956, 11 a.m..

Ürményházi, Attila J. The Hungarian Revolution-Uprising of 1956. 2005. American Hungarian Federation.

Várallyay, Gyula. Students of the Budapest Technical University in the 1956 Revolution. 25 January 2017.

Virag, Major Zoltan. All World Wars; Factors that Contributed to the Success of the Revolutionary Forces in the Early Phase of the Hungarian Revolution of 1956.

VonLanken, Lisa. Did Your Ancestors Come Through Ellis Island? 2014. docplayer.net/24271546.

White House Statement Concerning the Admission of Additional Hungarian Refugees. December 01, 1956. The American Presidency Project.

White House Statement on the Termination of the Emergency Program for Hungarian Refugees. December 28, 1957. The American Presidency Project.

World University Service (WUS), 1955–2007. Warwick. The Library; Modem Records Center. Last visited, August 9, 2021.

Made in the USA
Las Vegas, NV
07 May 2023

71701062R00249